ABACABAX

Abacabax

mikeNaylor

Cover artwork: Matteo Bocci
Illustrations: Muhamad Fanny and Mike Naylor

Chapter 1: Abacists

Click, click, click ... Saul stared impatiently at the mechanism as it steadily ticked away under his gaze. "Almost there," he muttered under his breath. The row of twenty-four gears danced in their intricate pattern, spelling out the letters of the name one by one. After one month of ceaseless operation, the algorithm was nearly complete and he would once again do what no one else could dream of accomplishing: step into another world.

He admired his workmanship. The machine had lain dormant for years, hidden away from the occupying army in one of the many secret rooms beneath the city. Restoring the device had taken months of meticulous labor, but his work was flawless. He had proven this four weeks ago when he had finally reopened the portal and made a startling discovery. The Abacist Prime was alive!

His excitement grew as he considered the enormity of what he was about to accomplish. Sixteen years ago this device allowed him to discover that fantastic other-world filled with unbelievable and dangerous powers. He was certain he could harness those powers and use them to secure his family's ascension to the highest position on the planet. Instead, those otherworldly powers had driven his people to edge of extinction. This time it would be different. This time he would bring back the one person who could not only erase Saul's past mistakes but also rewrite the future of his entire family line.

He turned his head to glance at the woman hurriedly entering the vault. "I thought I might be leaving without you, Wendi," Saul scolded. He turned his attention back to the machine. "We are minutes from departure."

"I needed to get a few things in order," she said, touching the bag tied around her waist. She adjusted her traveling cloak, pulling it securely over the bag.

Wendi glanced uneasily at the row of gray creatures looming at the back edge of the room. Strange shadows flickered from the candlelight over the place where their faces should be. They swayed slightly back and forth to the clicking of the mechanism.

Wendi looked back at Saul. "Why are *they* here?"

Saul looked up at the ghoulish creatures as if he'd forgotten they were there. "Oh, I like to keep them close. Just in case," he said, trying to sound off-handed.

Wendi frowned. "You've got the new location?"

"Of course I do," Saul said. "Everything is perfect. Look at it go, over eight million operations and not one single error!"

He turned to his sister, a sudden smile on his face. "Do you remember when we were children, when we used to try to say the name? We thought we would be granted a wish if we could say it in its entirety. But no one could ever say the full name, could they?"

"I don't know that anyone has ever tried hard enough," Wendi said, raising her eyebrows.

"Of course they couldn't," he said dismissively. "But with this ... !" He smiled smugly at his invention. "It really is like being granted a wish!"

"Yes, yes, I suppose it is," she agreed.

"Just think, Wendi, we're about to see him," Saul exclaimed. "The Abacist Prime is alive and well, after all these years! This will change everything. Who knows what he could be capable of!"

"Saul, I can't wait to meet the boys either. *Both* of the boys. But you know my daughter won't allow them to come. You heard her on our last visit."

"Rita will come to her senses," Saul said. "She must. Her son is the solution to everything we've fought for. His powers will be beyond imagination! I know she'll come around now that she's had some time to think about it."

"You know I don't like it. They are not born of this world. Bringing them here could elicit another disaster, and there has been so much bloodshed already. We are only –"

"We've been over this a thousand times!" he snapped. "Really, Wendi? With everything I've done so we could find your daughter again? It was *your* idea to put her there in the first place! And now I've not only found her, but we've got our Prime as well! Oh, no, one way or another that boy is coming here. Everything depends on it."

Wendi bit her lip, staring worriedly at the faceless creatures drooling at the back of the room. "We'll see," she said, her voice barely a whisper. "But remember, Brother, today is just a family reunion. A simple meeting, that's it."

-:- | -:-

Max pushed the end of his tie through the knot and pulled it downwards. Lopsided again.

"I can fold a flapping bird in thirty seconds, but I can't tie a tie," he grumbled to himself. "What's wrong with me?"

His younger brother flipped the end of his own tie through the loop, pulling it flat into a perfect knot. "We each have our own special abilities," Samuel said, patting it flat.

Max pulled off his tie and untied the knot. "There's got to be a better way," he muttered. He stretched the tie out, like a rope, thinking of the rope tricks he used to practice a few years ago. There was a fast way to tie a knot with one hand, and another trick to tie several knots at once ... how did that one work?

He looped the tie around his left hand, then made another loop and turned it a half-turn before hanging it on his left hand beside the first. Yes, that's how it goes. He made two more loops, twisting and hanging in the same fashion until the whole tie was wrapped around his hand. Reaching through the loops he took ahold of the other end and tossed the loops forward while he snapped the tie with a smooth motion.

A series of three equally-spaced knots appeared along the length of the tie. Max laughed. It was like magic.

"Aha! Now that's how to tie knots," he said. He swung the tie in an arc around the back of his neck and caught the end with his other hand, admiring the look.

"Maxwell Teller!" He jumped at his mother's voice. "What on *Earth* are you doing?"

Max turned towards the doorway where his mother stood, her slight frame and usually gentle voice taking on a more imposing tone today. Her expression was tense, the lines in her brow knit together. It seemed to Max an unusual way for his mother to act on his birthday, if not for the guests he knew would soon be arriving.

"Come on," she said, "they could be here any minute." Stepping into his room she offered, "Let me fix that for you."

Max stepped back and began untying the knots. "I can do it myself. I'm sixteen years old."

She stopped. "Sixteen," she said slowly to herself, her eyes suddenly far away. "Sixteen, the age of ..." She shook her head, bringing herself back to the present. She looked pensively at her son. "You're right. Today's your big day. But please hurry, I want the two of you dressed properly and looking like proper citizens of *this* society." She smiled weakly at them, then turned on her heels and strode out the door.

Max flattened out the tie, ready to try again. "She's been acting so weird lately, don't you think?" he said. "When have we ever had to wear ties at home?"

"Well, Grandma's coming and they haven't seen each other in forever," Samuel said. "But yeah, I don't know why we have to wear ties."

"Don't you think it's strange that Mom has never talked about her?" Max asked, threading the tie around his neck again. "That we've never even seen a picture or gotten a phone call or a letter ... it's like she didn't even exist. And then she just shows up at Mom's work last month and wants to meet us, and still Mom won't tell us about her. Other than that she's been helping war victims or something in Argentina."

"I thought it was Africa," Samuel said.

"Exactly! Who knows? I think that Mom's kind of in shock. I'm super-curious to meet Grandma."

"Me too."

Suddenly, Max's tie was tied, the knot laying flat. For some reason, it was so much easier to do when he wasn't thinking about it too much.

Knocks sounded on the front door downstairs. Samuel jumped. "They're here!" he said, bounding from the room.

Max and Sam raced to the top of the stairs. Their mother held the front door open as the two visitors stepped inside. Both wore full-length dark red coats with hoods that wrapped up over their heads. The woman lifted back her hood revealing the gentle face of an older woman. Max was delighted to see ribbons and beads woven into in her long gray hair.

"Hello, Rita," the woman said, embracing their mother.

The man bowed. "Rita, you look to be very well. I'm eager to meet the boys," he said.

The woman looked about the foyer and caught sight of the boys on the stairs. Her eyes lit up as she greeted them with a broad smile. "Hello, boys!" she called.

The man beside her also had long gray hair, but his was twisted into untidy spirals and there were no ribbons. His eyes shined sharply as he grinned at them. "There they are! At last!"

The boys came quickly down the steps. Max offered his hand to the woman. "Hi, I'm Max," he said.

She took his hand with both of hers and squeezed. "Max," she said warmly. "How wonderful to meet you. I'm Wendi." She reached to his face, holding his cheeks as she gazed upon his face. "You look like a miracle," she beamed. She leaned forward and pressed her forehead against his.

The man shook hands heartily with Samuel. "Samuel, my younger sister's youngest grandson. Second of all seconds. Oh, how happy I am to meet you!" He smiled. "I am Saul, and I have wanted to find you for a very long time!"

"Saul, let me take your jacket," Rita said, a hint of irritation in her voice. "These are quite the costumes you have, Mother. They're not really appropriate for this occasion."

Unfazed by her daughter's comment, Wendi warmly greeted and hugged her younger grandson Samuel.

Max turned to the long-haired man, whose attention was still affixed on his brother. "Hello Uncle Saul," he said.

Saul didn't take his hand. He quickly looked Max up and down and bowed his head curtly instead. "Maxwell. The first of the seconds. Pleased to meet you."

He turned back to Maxwell's brother, "Look at you, Samuel, you look like a legend! He looks just like me at that age don't you think, Wendi?"

"Well ... maybe," Wendi said.

"Mother, I'll take your coat as well," Rita said. "Come in, let's not crowd the hallway."

Wendi slipped off her overcoat, and Max saw that beads were hung not only in her hair but also along the neckline and sleeves of her long blue dress. A round brass pendant with a pattern of squares and circles hung on a chain around her neck. Around her waist a small cloth pouch on a leather belt held tightly to her side. Max thought she looked like an artist, or maybe an actress.

Saul tugged at the bottom of his red linen shirt to straighten it out. Instead of buttons, his shirt was fastened down the front with two cords that crossed back and forth making a series of x's. A cloth bag also hung from his belt. As they walked down the hall, Max found it easy to think of them as two travelers who had just arrived from a faraway land, which he knew, of course, was exactly what they were.

Max perched on the edge of the lounge chair in the living room. Samuel and Saul settled in on one couch, Wendi and Rita on the other. The coffee table had been set with a tidy arrangement of small plates and forks. Max looked back and forth between his new-found family members.

"Well, boys," Wendi began, "Saul and I were very excited to find your mother a few weeks ago. She has told us much about you. I suppose she's told you about our work and how we couldn't come to see you until now. We are so happy to find you at last."

Max looked at his mother questioningly. She did not look back at him. "Mmm ... we didn't really talk about your work," he said.

"No? Oh, I see," Wendi said, peering at Rita.

"Your grandmother and Saul have been involved in ambassador work," Rita said. "There's been a war and apparently they couldn't get out until now. And I suppose their technology is not advanced enough to get a message out, either?" she added sharply.

Wendi frowned. "You know we couldn't. Our equipment was all destroyed in the war, and the ... border has been closed. It has just now reopened, and we came as soon as we were safely able to do so."

"Where is the war? Is it still dangerous?" Max asked.

Rita spoke before Wendi could answer. "You know these primitive countries, there's always some war going on." She turned to Saul. "Because warlords are greedy for power and don't care how many lives they destroy," she said coldly.

Saul sat up rigidly. "We've been fighting for years to save lives, Rita, to undo the mistakes of the past." He leaned forward, his voice raising. "And now, finally, we have the chance to –"

Rita cut him off. "To relax and get acquainted again with your long-lost relatives and not make excuses. Yes?"

Saul paused, looked at them, and leaned back. "Yes, of course." He took a breath and then turned to Samuel. "Young Samuel here, am I to understand you are clever with calculating?"

"Oh, did Mom tell you?" Samuel asked. "I just got accepted to start math at the university in the fall. It's just calculus, which I know pretty well, but they say I need to start with that, because I'm only fourteen and college moves a lot faster."

"I knew it," Saul said, smiling at Wendi. "You see?"

Wendi turned to Max, "How about you, Maxwell. How are your studies?"

Max shrugged. "School's okay. I like my science class, and I've got a really good art teacher."

"And mathematics?" Wendi asked.

"Um, it's okay I guess. Kind of boring. I'm not very good at remembering all the steps the teachers want us to know, so I kind of just make up my own ways. Like last week on the test –"

"Not everyone needs to be a star, Maxwell," Saul cut in. "But Samuel, you! Years ahead! Did you know, Samuel, that your grandmother and I are great mathematicians in Arf-ica?"

"Africa," Rita corrected him.

"Yes, Africa." Saul waved his hand dismissively. "Wendi and I have pioneered many exciting new techniques, things no one else is doing. I should very much like if you could train with me, Samuel. We have some methods that would amaze you!"

"Saul. Our agreement." Rita said flatly. "All of us are staying here. Africa is too far away and too dangerous," she told the boys.

"But Rita," Saul protested, "there can be no question that –"

"You are correct. There *is* no question," Rita said. "Now, enough about Samuel, this is Maxwell's birthday. Boys, I've made a cake. Will you fetch it from the kitchen? Both of you, please. Bring some glasses and the lemonade next to the fridge. Give us a moment here."

Max followed Samuel into the kitchen. He could hear his mother and Saul quietly arguing, their hushed voices echoing into the hallway. Max set five glasses and the pitcher of lemonade on a tray and picked it up, deliberately slowly. Samuel was already holding the tray with the cake. They stood there a moment, looking at each other and throwing glances in the direction of the living room like unspoken question marks. They waited until the talking stopped, then Max shrugged and headed slowly out of the kitchen, Samuel following close behind.

The living room was silent as they entered and placed the trays on the table.

"Sixteen years old today," Wendi broke the silence. "The fourth phase of life. I'm so glad we can be here. In our land sixteen is the most important birthday!"

Max puzzled over this strange term – "the fourth phase." What could that mean?

"That's right," Saul said. "Today you're considered a grown man."

"On this side," Rita said sternly, "he's considered an adult at *eighteen*."

A tense silence filled the room, broken again by Wendi. "That is a lovely cake, Rita," she said. "Can I serve it?"

"I've got it," Rita answered, reaching for the knife. She began cutting. Max filled glasses from the pitcher and passed them around.

"Speaking of birthdays," Saul said, "it reminds me of a most puzzling situation I saw when I was in the Southlands. You do like puzzles, don't you Samuel?"

Samuel sat upright at attention. "Yes, of course."

Max looked back and forth between the two. He liked puzzles, too. Why was Samuel so much more interesting to Uncle Saul?

"Well, last fall I was at a birthday celebration in the Southlands," Saul began, "and for the chieftain's birthday, he received a gift of one hundred animals. The animals were deer

10

and pheasants, and as I recall there were two hundred twenty-two legs in all. My host asked if I knew how many animals there were of each kind. Can you tell me, even without seeing them for yourselves?"

Samuel reached forward and grabbed a pad of paper from the shelf under the coffee table.

Max sat back and pictured the scene. One hundred animals, birds and deer marching by the chieftain. What a sight that would be. Two hundred twenty-two legs ... well, Max reasoned, if they were all pheasants there would be two hundred legs, so how many deer would he need to make up the difference? Or – better yet, if all of the deer were standing up on their back legs, then with one hundred animals there would be exactly two hundred legs on the ground, which leaves twenty-two legs waving in the air. He pictured the comical scene, pheasants strutting and deer dancing, twenty-two deer legs in the air. How simple the problem was now! Those deer legs would have to belong to exactly eleven –

Samuel piped up. "Eleven pheasants and eighty-nine deer," he announced, the corners of his mouth turning up tightly. He held up the pad of paper he had hastily scribbled some calculations on.

Saul took the pad and stared at it. "Extraordinary! And you've done it all with these symbols. Wendi, did you see that?"

"Actually," Max began, "the answer is –"

"I set up two equations with two unknowns," Samuel announced. "Then I just solved for x and y."

Uncle Saul was thrilled. "I've never seen anyone solve it so quickly!" he exclaimed. "And in such a manner! Well done, nephew!"

Max was taken aback. Samuel didn't even have the right answer. "Actually," Max began again, "it's eleven *deer* and eighty-nine *pheasants*."

"Scribing, Wendi. The answer is scribing!" Saul said, studying the paper. "Rita, Samuel is the Prime, he must –"

"Saul!" Rita snapped.

Saul turned to Wendi, pleading with his eyes. Wendi shook her head, silently warning him to stop.

"We'll talk later," he said. "This is extraordinary," he said, folding the paper and sliding it carefully into his pocket. Turning to Samuel he said, "I have a special gift for the specially-gifted younger Teller."

Now Max found himself especially irritated. Why was Saul giving Samuel a prize for a *wrong* answer, solved in the most boring way?

Saul reached into his pocket and produced a small wooden box with intricate inlaid patterns. "It's a puzzle box," he told Samuel. "I picked it up many years ago in a town called Quothmire where they make exquisite wooden patterns. The puzzle is to figure out how to open the box."

"Thanks, Uncle Saul!" Samuel exclaimed, turning the box over and over his hands.

"Such talent, I'm amazed," Saul said.

"Hey! I've got a different way to solve it," Max protested. "It's kind of cool ..."

"Come now, Maxwell, don't be sore," Uncle Saul told him. "I'm sure you'll get plenty of gifts for your birthday."

Max felt his ears burning. He looked around and met the eyes of his grandmother. Her reaction was a bigger puzzle than deer and pheasants. She gave him a wink, and then touched her finger to her lips indicating that Max should keep quiet. Max shook his head slightly – he didn't understand. What did she mean?

Wendi's eyes twinkled at him from across the table, and suddenly, Max didn't care anymore if Uncle Saul or Samuel or his mother or anyone knew he had a better solution. His grandmother somehow knew – and that was all he needed to know. He looked back at Uncle Saul to see if he'd noticed the silent exchange between grandmother and grandson. He hadn't.

"I have a birthday present for you, Maxwell," Wendi said. She removed a small wrapped package from her pocket and offered it to Max. The paper was a deep purplish-pink color and crumpled like it had journeyed across the sea in Grandma's pocket. He carefully unwrapped it. It was a wristband made of intricately knotted cords.

"Wow, it's neat," Max said. "Thank you. What is it?"

"It's called a 'quipu.' A special one from ... my travels. It will protect you from many evils." She smiled. "And in any case, I think you will like the pattern."

Max examined the knots. Every other knot was a small single knot, between these were larger knots in the patterns of squares and cubes. In the very center was an ornately woven pattern forming a large single ball.

"Let me see that, Maxwell," said Uncle Saul, removing it from Max's fingers.

"Saul!" Wendi snapped. "Your manners. Give that back to Maxwell."

Saul slowly handed it back to Max. Turning his gaze to Wendi, his eyes narrowed and he said, "Now what would you be doing giving *that particular* quipu to the *elder* Teller boy?"

"It's mine to gift as I will within the family, as per tradition," she said. "And the family includes Maxwell, thank you very much."

They locked eyes for a tense moment. Saul shook his head and turned back to the boys, forcing a laugh. "Yes of course, what does it matter? And there is another family tradition to attend to." He grinned and turned to the boys, "Would you like another puzzle, Samuel? And Maxwell?"

"Yes!" said Samuel. Max shrugged.

Rita stood and dusted crumbs from her lap. "Mother, will you help me in the kitchen?" she asked.

"I'll help too," Max offered.

"No, you boys stay here. My mother and I can handle it – *alone*," Rita said. "Saul, puzzles only, no stories of 'your travels,' thank you very much."

Max looked one more time at the quipu, and then tucked it deep into his pocket. He would look at it later. What a strange series of events were unfolding this evening. He wished he understood what was going on.

Rita and Wendi left the room as Saul drew a set of dots on a piece of paper, three rows of three, arranged in a three-by-three square pattern. "The puzzle is to connect all the dots by drawing a continuous chain of straight line segments, without lifting the pencil off the paper. Here's how you can do it with five ..." Saul drew a square with four line segments passing through the dots around the outside of the arrangement and then connected the center dot with a fifth line. "The puzzle is to do it with fewer than five line segments."

Max thought it looked fun, he supposed he'd try to show Saul that Samuel wasn't the only one good at puzzles. He and Samuel both drew dots on paper and began scribbling. "I can do it with three," announced Max right away.

"Three?" said Uncle Saul, surprised. "You've surely done it wrong."

"Nope! See, your dots have thickness. That means I can draw the first line through the top three but at a downwards slope like this ... see, it still touches all three dots. Then if I go out far enough I can go backwards and slope down again through the middle three ... and then forwards again and slope through the bottom three."

"Sorry, Maxwell, you can't slope that like. Your lines have to be *straight*."

"They are straight," he grinned. He knew the problem probably called for going through the *center* of the dots, but he loved looking for loopholes in the rules. "Okay then, can I use a wide paintbrush? I can do it with one line, then."

"No you can't. A pencil only. Your segments must be infinitely narrow."

Too bad, Max thought. It would be nice if it could be done with just one line. If he tore up the paper he could line them all up in one row, but surely Saul wouldn't like that either. And paper doesn't really stretch, but ... suddenly, it came to him in a flash.

"I know!" said Max. He picked up his paper and rolled in into a tube. "You can roll the paper into a cylinder, and if you get the angle just right ..."

Holding the tube together awkwardly in one hand, he traced a winding path around the outside of the tube with the pencil. "... then you can use one continuous straight line that wraps around three times and goes through them all!" He held the tube aloft triumphantly. The perfect solution – it stayed on the paper, it worked with infinitely thin lines and dots, and it used the absolute minimum number of line segments. To top it off, it was beautiful and surprising. Surely, this was the best solution. Finally he had shown up his brother!

Uncle Saul, however, was not as impressed. "No, you can't roll the paper," he said, annoyed. "Come along, Maxwell, you aren't taking this seriously."

Max started to protest, but Samuel spoke first.

"Here, I've done it in four!" said Samuel. He slid his paper forwards, and Max saw that Samuel's drawing did indeed work, even if it was not as exciting as Max's cylinder solution.

"Bravo Samuel, I knew you'd get it!" cheered Saul.

"Well, if you hadn't kept changing the rules ..." Max said sourly.

"You're the one who was changing the rules, Maxwell," said his uncle dismissively. "Okay, I have another one, boys."

Max felt the heat rising to his face. "Excuse me, I need to ... go to the bathroom," he said, standing quickly. Uncle Saul had done it again. Saul didn't want answers, he wanted his *own* answer. Fine, let him sit there and be amazed by Samuel's brilliant mind. Max would rather be with his grandmother, anyway.

Max stomped through the living room and down the hall towards the kitchen. He froze. From within the kitchen came angry hushed voices.

"Saul is not taking Samuel," his mother was saying. "We are not Abacists anymore, which means he is not the Prime anymore. *You* made sure of that. None of my boys are going there, I promise you, Mother."

Max stepped aside into the entrance hallway, pressed against the wall where he could still hear them talking and not be seen if they left the kitchen. He knew he shouldn't be listening in, but he couldn't help himself. This could explain everything. The Prime? Saul had said something about that. Abacists?

"Of course it's your choice if you want to keep Samuel here, Rita. He's only in his third phase. But Maxwell is of age. He needs to know, and he needs to know *today*. It's important."

Max's heart skipped a beat. Know what?

"Maxwell?" his mother said. "Why Maxwell, by all the moons? Samuel is the one you and Saul are after. You've seen his reckoning. Saul is after his scribing! Well I won't have it. I will not have that life for either of my boys."

Max couldn't breathe. How strangely his mother was talking! 'Reckoning?' 'Scribing?' *'By all the moons'?!*

"This is not something you can protect them from. You've been safe this long, but if events continue the way they've been going, the boys will be in danger no matter how far away we hide them."

Max jumped at the sound of a loud dull slap – his mother slapping the table perhaps. "Then you keep *it* away from *us*! And keep yourself away, as well! You should not have come back!"

This was the most incredible conversation Max had ever heard. Danger? They were in danger? Footsteps stomped his way. Max froze, afraid of being caught listening in but at the same time angry that his mother was keeping a huge family secret from them. He held his breath as his mother stormed down the hallway. She didn't see him around the corner as she passed, stomping towards the living room. Max's indignation fed his courage – he would walk back in and demand to know what was going on. After all, he was sixteen now. In the fourth phase of life, whatever that was.

Max never made the first step. He got a funny feeling in his legs. They grew rubbery, like what happened in his nightmares sometimes when he'd be trying to run away from something and could hardly move. The air grew still. Saul and Samuel's voices in the family room seemed to fade, and the cuckoo clock ticked slower and slower as the air around Max drew tighter and tighter. It squeezed him with a pressure like the water on the bottom of the deep end of a swimming pool.

Like a ghost, his grandmother floated into the hallway and around the corner, a trance-like look on her face. She didn't seem at all surprised to see Max standing there. She had something in her hand, which she slid into the bag around her waist as she motioned for him to follow and sit on the bench by the front door. The air was charged with electricity, Max could feel it lifting the hair on the back of his arms.

Wendi spoke, her voice soft and clear, cutting through the stillness of the world around. Her eyes sparkled like marbles, patterns swirling deep within the glass.

"Maxwell, I have one more gift for you. There are things you need to know, and we haven't much time. You and I share a bond, a power, that you must know of and understand.

"I do not really come from Africa. That is only a name your mother asked me to use. I come from a world called Abacabax. It is not on any map, nor in any country. It is beyond the bounds of this world and time. It is a place of great and profound beauty and meaning."

Max sat at rapt attention, hanging on every word. Abaca ... what? Beyond the bounds of this world and time?

She continued, "Right now we stand in a moment between time, so that I may grant you your inheritance." Max held his breath as she reached into her bag and brought forth a brown leather packet. She handed it to Max. He felt its weight – it was heavier than he expected, an oblong shape. "Open it now," she instructed him.

Max carefully opened the cover, and there, stretching across both of his palms, was a magnificently carved wooden frame ringed with symbols he did recognize. The frame held rows of white beads on vertical rods. It looked very old and well used, yet the beads shone as if years of use had polished them rather than worn them down.

"An abacus?" Max asked.

"Yes. A very special abacus. I have had this a very long time. It was given to me by my grandmother on my sixteenth birthday. Now I give it to you. Someday, you will give it to your child or grandchild."

Max tipped the abacus forward and back, watching the beads slide up and down. "It's beautiful," he said. "What ... ?"

Wendi handed him a small booklet of bound papers. "This will get you started. Once you start you must become your own teacher. Learn to use it well and it will open many great frontiers."

Max looked at the book. The cover read "The Thinking Beads." The binding had been split and repaired with cloth. Max flipped it open and turned a few pages. The book was filled with text and lists and pictures of abacuses, and the margins were full of handwritten notes in a small and tidy cursive.

"Listen Maxwell, this is very important – the most important thing in the whole world. This abacus, Maxwell, is the key to great power. Protect it well and use it wisely. Abacabax is your home and your inheritance. More than that, I believe you will bring what has long been missing."

"Grandma, what should –"

Max jumped as the clock suddenly began ticking again, loudly, slowly and deliberately. "I'm sorry Maxwell, we're out of time. Remember – protect it with your all. We will meet again on the next moon. Put it away and speak to no one of this."

Wendi stood up and the room seemed to grow brighter. Max heard the sound of laughter in the family room again and the rumble of a car in the street. The contrast made him realize how silent it had been during this remarkable encounter.

She watched as he tucked the abacus into his pocket. With a nod, she turned and headed towards the family room. He stood there a moment longer, then followed in a daze.

Max's mother stood in the middle of the living room, her hands on her hips. "Well, everyone, it's getting late, isn't it?" she said with no trace of joy. Saul and Samuel exchanged disappointed looks.

"Late?" Samuel asked. "They just got here. We're just getting started!"

"I'm afraid they need to leave now," Rita said. "It's time for us to settle in for the evening."

"Very well," said Uncle Saul with a frown. "Our transport will be closing soon anyway. Boys, we will meet again,

I'm certain. Samuel, take care of that puzzle box. There's a surprise inside."

They said hasty goodbyes, and within minutes they were out the door.

"I really like Uncle Saul," Samuel said. "Can I study with him sometime?"

"I don't think so," Rita said flatly. "You boys get to bed."

-:- | -:-

Wendi and Saul stood in the trees behind the Teller house.

"I've done it, Wendi!" said Saul. "We found him! Samuel is the key. We need him with us, as soon as we can."

"Saul, we can't risk it. Reckoning from this world is too powerful, too unpredictable. You know full well what can happen."

"No, this time it will be different. You saw what he was using. This is not like those 'electric' devices we tried before. We have paper, we have scribing sticks. There is nothing foreign, except maybe for our reckoner, and he is the second of all seconds – he is our Prime! He can not only turn the tide, he will be the New Origin! The Great Divide is only two months away and he has so much to learn, but I can do it. *We* can do it."

"Samuel should not yet be in our world," Wendi said. "I believe there is another way."

"What, you can't mean *Rita*? She is a fine reckoner but no New Origin. What new would she bring? And she will never return. She has lost too much."

"I don't mean Rita. There is something about Maxwell that is ... different."

"Maxwell?" Saul snorted. "Maxwell is useless, Wendi. First of the seconds, yes, but slow of mind. His reckoning will be substandard. Samuel is the Prime, by every measure, and we've found him just in time. Yes, Sister, this is a great day."

Wendi frowned. "The moons will be low now, we must return," Wendi said.

"It's senseless that we don't just take him now," Saul said. "But we can wait one more cycle and then – the Abacists will have their Prime! This is not for Rita to decide."

Chapter 2: By the Clicking of my Beads

Sleep was the last thing on Max's mind. Sitting in bed, he turned the abacus over and over in his hands. Hundreds of questions swam through his head. What had happened in there? Had time somehow stopped? What does his mother know? What kind of danger threatens them? What is this "other world?" It was all so crazy and unbelievable, but there was no doubt in his mind that it was all true. Everything seemed jumbled together in his head. He forced himself to focus, squinting at the object in his hands.

The frame was some kind of old, dense wood, white and well-worn. The carvings were deep, though, and he could still clearly see the pattern of triangles inside of squares wrapping around the edges. The beads were of a white stone, they slid freely on rods made of ... ivory perhaps? He had expected for something mechanical to happen when he slid the beads – some hidden connection between the rods and beads, but nothing special happened when he moved the stones on the ivory rods. He knew abacuses – or was it *abaci*? – didn't use batteries, so what was the trick? Just a bunch of beads on rods? He tipped it back and forth, watching as they slid up and down. No, this was something special, something important. *Guard it with your all*, Grandma had said.

Max turned his attention to the book. Carefully opening the soft cover, he leafed past the introduction and studied the picture at the start of the second chapter. The abacus in the book had ten rods, Max's had fourteen. There were seven beads on each rod, split with a crossbeam so that two were in the top and five were in the bottom. The book had labeled the upper part "heaven" and the lower part "earth." The caption on the picture read "Abacus in ready position." Max made his abacus look like that. On each rod, he moved the two beads in heaven to the very top and the five beads in earth to the very bottom.

"Numbers are placed on the abacus by sliding beads towards the crossbeam," the text read. "The numbers are thus created where heaven meets earth, as numbers live partly within the knowable, and party clouded within the divine; they are constructs of our own physical action, yet they reach beyond our experience into higher existence."

Higher existence? What had Grandma said – *beyond the bounds of this world and time*? Is that what she meant, that somehow numbers could travel to other worlds? Normally, such an idea would be easy to shrug off, but after tonight anything seemed possible.

He turned the page and studied the next picture. It was labeled with values for the beads. Five beads on the bottom, each is worth one. Two beads on the top, each is worth five. The rod on the far right is the ones place, it holds ones in earth and the fives in heaven. The next rod is tens place, holding tens and fifties, the next rod holds hundreds and five hundreds, and so on. It was organized just like numbers are usually written but with beads instead of symbols. Easy enough.

The margins were sprinkled with handwritten notes that Max couldn't make sense of. They didn't seem to have anything to do with calculating at all. They said things like

"Simple push," "Back and forth to keep warm," "To reduce weight in case of a fall," "Lock in place – how to extend?" and other mysterious fragments that seemed entirely out of place. He turned his attention instead to the lessons which were far more meaningful.

The book suggested starting by just setting up numbers and clearing the abacus, over and over. *Click, click, click.* Max started, fascinated by the arrangements. Well into the night he finally fell asleep, the abacus tucked down the side of his mattress.

The next day he awakened wondering if the evening before had been a dream. He placed his hand between the wall and mattress and slid out the abacus. No, no dream, he thought. He lifted the frame up over his face.

He was puzzled and troubled over what Grandma had told him, and wished he could talk to her. *The key to great power,* she had said. Something about *inheritance.* What did it all mean?

He decided to confront his mother that next afternoon. He told her he had heard them in the kitchen talking about something dangerous. She had become furious with him and swore the only danger was from Wendi and Saul and that those two would never return. The family would never speak of this again, she commanded. Max was "absolutely forbidden" to say anything to Samuel, leaving Max feeling very alone. He did not dare to mention the abacus at all.

Remembering his grandmother's warning, he carefully guarded the abacus, hiding it behind the books on his shelf and pulling it out whenever possible. At least the tension in the house made it easy for him to keep to himself the following days, allowing him plenty of time to read the book and run through the exercises with no one else around. With practice, Max found he could quickly set a number on any rod with a single, quick motion. Addition turned out to be a snap. It was no more than doing the same motion on a rod, whether or not it had a number on it already, and then trading two fives for a ten if necessary. Max practiced adding by twos, by threes, by fours, and so on, and this exercise was all he needed to be able to sum numbers quickly. Each number seemed to have a different personality – that is, a different set of moves associated with it depending on how many beads were already on the rod. So to add seven to a rod, he would either do a pinching move to bring a five and two ones into play, or a twisting move between two rods to subtract three ones and add a ten. Each number was like its own creature in a miniature zoo.

Within a week, Max was getting comfortable with basic arithmetic. Subtraction was a new set of moves, but they were all related to the moves in addition. Multiplication worked like pencil and paper multiplication, too, but all in one line. Once he got into the rhythm of which columns to multiply it became almost automatic. Furthermore, because the addition part of the algorithm seemed to happen by itself, multiplication turned out to be easier and faster on the abacus than using pencil and paper. Learning division took a little longer, Max could see the connection to the pencil and paper algorithm, but it was tricky to keep track of all of the moves.

Max generally didn't care much for arithmetic exercises at school, but this was different. Even though he knew there was nothing magical about beads sliding up and down, he couldn't help but feel something extraordinary had happened each time he set up numbers and *click-click-click*, a *real* answer to a *real* problem appeared on the beads. He even came up with some of his own methods and shortcuts – was that allowed? Grandma said he should become his own teacher, and so he did. Max felt he would have liked to master this tool even without the mysterious promise of great things. Of course the mystery was an added incentive!

As he became comfortable with the operations, Max worked on speed. Day after day, his mistakes grew fewer and the moves took less effort. Max felt he had gotten very good, very quickly.

It had been nearly one month since Max's birthday party. Grandma said she'd be coming *on the next moon* ... did that mean one month, or about one month? Four weeks, or thirty-one days? Or something else? He had grown more and more anxious with each passing day.

He and Samuel got off the school bus and began walking home. The air was mild and the snow had melted, but they were due for an early "nor'easter" this year, when the wind would change direction bringing strong frigid weather in from the North.

"Pretty warm for a February, huh?" Max said. "We should enjoy it while we can. There's a storm coming any day now." In more way than one, he mused to himself.

"Mmm," Samuel said. He seemed far away.

"Something on your mind?" Max asked.

"Oh, uh, just some stuff," he said. He said no more, staring at the ground as they walked. Max shrugged. He had enough on his own mind, he was in no mood to force a conversation with his brother.

When they got home, Max went straight to his room to practice. He had just sat down on his bed with the abacus when a knock came at the door. He quickly slid the abacus under his pillow. "Come in," he said.

It was Samuel. "Hi Max," he said. He stood in the doorway, looking past Max at the wall.

Max waited. "What is it, Sam?" he prompted.

Samuel paused. His mouth opened slightly and closed again. Finally he spoke. "Listen, I know we're not supposed to talk about this, but what would you do if they came back?"

"Grandma and Saul?" Max said. "I'd ask about a million questions."

"Uncle Saul said he wanted to teach me, and I think it's really unfair of Mom to send them away. Why do you think she doesn't want us to see them?"

Max sat silently a moment. "I don't know, Sam, but ... there's something you should know. Grandma and Uncle Saul aren't from Africa. They're from ... another place. I think Mom's from there, too. We're in some kind of hiding. Mom thinks it's dangerous."

"Is it like witness protection?"

Max hadn't thought of that. "It could be something like that. I don't think she wanted for them to find us. She thinks they want to take us there."

"I know," Samuel said quickly. "Uncle Saul said I would be some kind of a king!"

"Did he tell you that?" Max was alarmed.

"Uh ... yeah. While we were doing puzzles. I think it might be really important that we, you know, find out." Samuel paused. "I think we're some kind of royal family."

Max smiled. "He did call you 'The Prime.' Maybe we *are* a royal family, and Mom's a princess?"

"I don't think they can really be mathematicians, I mean, why was Uncle Saul so excited that I could do simple things like algebra? And he calls it 'scribing,' isn't that weird?"

"Yeah," Max said. "They said a lot of weird things."

"Max, he told me I could be one of the greatest ever, and that I should keep practicing for when he comes back, that I could be really powerful. What do you think that means?"

Max considered this. He had also been told to practice but with a different kind of calculating. "I think I need to show you something," he said. Max slid the abacus out from under his pillow. "Grandma gave me this."

"Whoa ... an abacus?" Samuel asked.

"Yes, but you can't tell Mom. Grandma said I had to keep it secret."

"You got a secret, too?" he whispered. "Why would you need to keep an abacus secret?"

"I'm not sure. It's a family relic. It's really valuable."

Samuel picked up the abacus, tipped it back and forth watching the beads slide up and down. "It's nice. Why'd she give it to you?"

"It's a tradition, for a sixteenth birthday, I guess. She told me to practice, just like Uncle Saul told you to practice. So I've been learning how to use it. Do you want to see?"

"Yeah, sure."

Max took the abacus from Samuel and cleared the columns. He showed Samuel how to set up a number and how to add another number to it.

"Pretty cool, huh?" Max said.

"It's all right," Samuel said. "Looks kind of awkward. I'm faster with paper and pencil."

"You think so?" Max said. "That sounds like a challenge."

Samuel grinned, hopping up to grab some paper and a pencil from Max's desk.

"Three digit by three digit multiplication," Max proposed.

"Multiplication? You're on," Samuel said. "How about *one hundred thirty-six times* ... oh, *eight hundred ninety-two*?"

"Alright," Max said. "Go!"

Samuel began scribbling furiously. Max's hand danced across the beads, flicking them up and down. He completed one column, two, three, four, five and six. Done! It took only a few seconds. He set the abacus down and quickly announced the result.

Samuel kept working, summing up the three rows of numbers he'd scribbled on the paper. "Yeah, that's what I got too. How'd you do that so fast?"

"Ha ha! Pretty good, huh? Faster than you!"

"You got lucky," Samuel said. "Try again! *Four hundred seven times nine hundred twenty-two*. Go!"

They ran the contest several more times, each time Max won by several seconds. He explained that after Samuel multiplied the first number by each of the digits in the second number he still had to add up all his columns of figures. On the abacus the addition part takes care of itself, saving a lot of extra steps.

"Well," said Samuel, "It might be good for simple things, but it's just some beads on sticks. People used those hundreds of years ago, but this," he said holding aloft his pencil, "is so much better. This is true power. I will be the King of the Pencils!"

Max laughed and Samuel quickly joined in. It felt good to laugh, a break in the tension Max had felt all month.

Samuel took a deep breath and sat thinking. "Don't you want to go, Max?" he asked. "Find out what all this is? Even if Mom says 'no?'"

"I definitely want to know, but what can we do? Mom says they're not coming back."

"But ... what if they do come back?" Samuel asked. "Would you go?"

"Samuel, we don't do *anything* until we find out more. Agreed?"

Samuel looked hard at Max. "Yeah, um ... okay. I'll tell you if I find out anything. I will."

"Okay, thanks," Max said as Samuel slipped out of his room. Max sat a moment wondering why Samuel thought he might be able to find out more.

-:- | -:-

Back in his room, Samuel closed the door and picked up the puzzle box Uncle Saul had given him. Pieces on the ends of the box could slide a tiny distance in each direction, allowing him to move the lid slightly open or closed. By going back and forth between sliding the ends and moving the top, the box could eventually be opened completely. He had mastered the sequence in a couple of days, and now he confidently slid the parts in the right combination. In fourteen moves, the lid slid off the box.

Samuel removed the paper from inside and unfolded it. It was a letter from Saul, a fantastic letter only for him. He had read it a hundred times already but read it one last time anyway.

"Samuel, you are the most important member of our family, the Prime of all Primes, the final link in a chain of generations and the heir to riches and powers you cannot imagine. It is our destiny to save countless lives and become the greatest rulers the lands have ever known. There are those who wish that you never learn of your greatness and our lands be driven to ruin, so it is of utmost importance that you keep this the tightest of all secrets — especially from your mother and your brother. I will explain all to you in <u>exactly</u> four weeks time. Meet with me on the twenty-eighth day at sunset in the forest behind your house and all will be revealed. Do not fail in this task! Everything depends on you! — Saul."

Samuel felt dizzy with excitement. Twenty-eight days was *today,* and the winter sun was getting low. He looked out the window at the trees across the yard. Would he be there?

Oh, how much he wanted to tell Max, but Max was on his mother's side and Saul was very clear in his instructions.

There was no way Samuel was going to ruin this chance. He could be a king? He could be a king!

It was still a little early, but he couldn't wait any more. He moved silently down the stairs, slipped on his jacket and went out the back door, closing it quietly behind him. The trees stood tall and foreboding, still bare from winter. Samuel walked towards them with a sense of great purpose. After one month of anticipation he would soon know everything.

The ground crunched beneath his feet, leaves and twigs crackling as he stepped between the trees. It was still light enough to see fairly well. He followed the path, beaten down from all of the times he and Max had chased each other through the trees, pretending to be Robin Hood and Little John. The path took him along a creek bed, empty this time of year, until he came near the end where the next neighborhood began. Maybe Saul wouldn't come, maybe it was all a mistake.

He turned and walked back. Partway along the trail, he saw a flicker of light in the trees towards his house. He inhaled and held his breath a moment, listening. Hearing nothing, he sprung quickly and quietly along the path. Ahead, a lone figure in a long red coat stood near the tree that had fallen in last winter's storm.

"Uncle Saul!" Samuel called.

"Samuel!" Saul said turning towards him. He stepped forward with his hand extended, a big smile on his face. Saul shook Samuel's hand strongly and repeatedly.

"I found your note," Samuel said.

"I knew you would," he said. "And you made it here, of course you would! Oh, I have been waiting for this day since before you were born. You, Samuel, are the second child of the second child of all of the second children in our family line, and you will be the greatest reckoner our lands have ever known.

There is so much for you to know! Are you ready to join me? We go right away!"

"We're going now?" he asked. He shook his head. "I can't just go without telling Mom."

"Your mother knows who you are and wishes to deny you of your power. She is no ally of yours, Samuel. She would let her anger betray all of our people. We need you Samuel, you are the Abacist Prime!"

"I don't ..." Samuel began, "... understand any of this."

"It will be easier to understand if I show you something first," Saul said. He reached into his pouch and removed a rectangular shape wrapped in a fold of leather. He flipped his hand and the packet flipped open, revealing a long black abacus with red beads.

He began clicking the beads. "Have you ever seen one of these before?" he asked.

"Only Max's."

"Max has one?" Saul raised his eyebrows but continued moving beads on the abacus. "Did his mother give him one?"

"No, Grandma did. It's got those symbols like yours, but his has white beads ... whoooaaah!"

The air around them was shimmering, as if they were surrounded by a curved wall of very clear water that rippled and bent the fading light. The strange effect got stronger and stronger, then the ripples suddenly slowed, the wall faded away, and it grew still. The effect was gone and all was as it was before. Wide-eyed, Samuel looked over at Saul. Saul was staring back at Samuel, his hand frozen over the abacus and his brow tensed in a frown.

"How'd you do that?" Samuel asked.

"Wendi gave him an abacus?" Saul said sternly, ignoring Samuel's question. "With white beads and symbols like these?" he asked glancing down at the black frame in his hand.

32

"Yes," said Samuel.

Saul's eyes darted back and forth. "That is not for him! That is to be yours, Samuel!" he said, his voice rising. "Has my sister lost her mind? The only one to whom that can be given is the second of seconds. If not, then only to ... no! She cannot possibly ... ?"

Saul turned suddenly to look at Samuel. "Where is Maxwell now?" he asked angrily.

"Um, he's in his room?" said Samuel.

"Take me to him," Saul commanded.

Samuel was suddenly very uneasy. He did not like this abrupt change in Saul, but he led the way out of the woods towards the house anyway. As the house came into view, Samuel could see two women hurrying up the driveway beside the house and turning towards the front door. One of them wore a long red cloak.

"It's Grandma!" Samuel said. He looked at Saul briefly, then stepped quickly towards the house.

Saul grabbed Samuel's shoulder and pulled him to a halt. He kept a tight grip as he studied the house. Lights came on the lower level. "She's here. She's followed me," he said incredulously. "I told her the portal would not be open until tomorrow, how did she know?"

Saul pulled Samuel back beyond the trees. "We have a short delay, Samuel. Don't be alarmed, I'm going to need some help. Step back. Whatever you do, don't move and *don't go anywhere.*"

Saul began clicking the beads on his abacus again, swiftly with great concentration. "Where are you?" he said under his breath.

Samuel stood frozen, frightened but fascinated. Saul kept clicking beads, "Where are you ... ?" he muttered. "Where are you ... ? Ah! Found you."

Shimmerings appeared between the trees, and in the growing darkness Samuel saw pair after pair of pale glowing amber eyes appear. He felt a rising terror as dozens of not quite human-like shapes stumbled from the shadows towards them.

-:- | -:-

Max sat on his bed clicking beads, still puzzled over the conversation with his brother. Samuel knows a lot more than I realized, he thought. The waiting was driving them both crazy.

Max turned his attention to the chapter in the small book titled "Extracting roots." The enigmatic note in the margin on this page read, "*Use to disassemble light, into components or entirely?*" He didn't have this method down yet and was ready to try again. It involved using three different places on the abacus, and the technique involved some guesswork, an element which Max found intriguing.

The door burst open downstairs and Max sat up suddenly.

"Samuel!" His mother's voice called out. "Sam!" Footsteps were coming up the stairs quickly.

Max shoved his abacus under his pillow and opened the door. His mother appeared at the top of the stairs, her face grave.

"Where is Samuel?" she asked.

"Um, I thought he was in his room. He was here half an hour ago."

She put her head in Samuel's room. "He's not here. Where did he go?" she asked again.

"I don't know! What's going on?"

"Go downstairs," Rita said. "Your grandmother's here. I'll be right down." She went towards her bedroom at the end of the hall.

"Grandma?" Max said. He went to the top of the stairs and saw a figure with long gray hair and a dark red coat standing by the door. He bounded down the steps.

"Maxwell," she said, taking his hands. She was not smiling. "We think Saul is here, and Samuel may be with him. Have you seen either of them?"

"I saw Samuel just a little while ago but not Saul." Max suddenly thought of how excited Samuel was while they were talking a short while ago. Did he know Saul was coming?

He followed his grandmother into the kitchen. She pulled out a chair and sat at the kitchen table. His mother came downstairs, walked by the kitchen briskly, looking in the living room and back hall before coming back to the kitchen. She leaned hard against the kitchen counter. In her hand she held an abacus, light gray with black beads.

"You were to keep him away!" she said sharply to Wendi.

"No one can stop Saul," Wendi said. "He is more terrifying than you would believe. There is much you do not understand, Rita, much that has happened," Wendi said. "Please sit, both of you."

Max sat down next to her, facing his mother. He noticed another abacus had appeared in front of Wendi. The frame was a dark golden color and the beads were black and a different shape than his, with a ridge around their middles. The frame was covered with chips and scratches, and Max could easily imagine that this abacus had traveled around the world for a hundred years or more.

"Rita, join us," Wendi said calmly.

"We need to find Samuel!" she said.

"Samuel is not here," Wendi pointed out. "We must assume they are on their way to Tangram, and we need to be calm and make a level decision."

Rita breathed out in a huff. "You need to get him. No, I need to go, too. No, what about Maxwell? You need to …"

"Rita," Wendi said. "We can all go."

"Max is not going," Rita said.

"Mom," Max said. "Mom, please. You need to tell me."

Rita sighed. "Go ahead and tell him, Mother. I can't, I just can't."

"Max," Wendi said softly, "our family are some of the last of the Abacists. We were once the most powerful reckoners on Abacabax, tens of thousands strong." Wendi looked past Max, a sad look in her eyes. "We built great cities, governed justly and protected the beauty and happiness of all beings. We made advances never before seen in the lands.

"My brother, your great-uncle Saul, was a wickedly talented reckoner." She shook her head, a slight smile on her lips. "He discovered many things, including a way to shift to new worlds. He found this world, with even more powerful reckoning than we could imagine."

"And then like a fool he brought it back with him!" Rita spat. "He broke the ancient code, and that was the end of everything! And now he's going to do it *again*!"

"Okay, Rita. We don't know that will happen," Wendi said. She turned back to Max. "Yes, Saul brought back … a plague. It consumed us and brought war upon our people. The world turned against us, burning our cities and killing those who tried to reason with them. Those that weren't taken by the sickness fell beneath the crush of Calculist stones. The Calculists were the second-most powerful family with very well-organized armies, and they took the opportunity to become the most powerful family again.

"Your mother, the second born in our entire line of second-borns, was heavy with child, with *you*, Max, and I could not risk keeping her in Abacabax. So I took her here, to this world, to be safe until such time that she could return."

"But you didn't come back!" Rita's eyes were wet with tears. "I wanted to stay, and fight, and instead you put me here, and now they're all gone. Father and Melani and Carfin and everyone I ever knew and loved! Except for you, Mother, and you never came back!"

"I have cried for you every day, my daughter. I have never given up on finding you. We have all lost so much. But we have not lost all, and what is left is worth fighting for. Rita, you can come home. Abacabax needs you. *I* need you." Rita and Wendi stared at each other, both with damp eyes. Max looked at his hands.

Speaking to them both Wendi continued, "It is nearly the time of the Great Divide. This happens once every fourteen generations. A new line of reckoning will open on Abacabax, and the heir-apparent is a Calculist. He is cruel man. The Calculists have grown even harder and their Prime has a terrible new form of reckoning that may allow them to take all of the faces of the lands. Should this happen, it will mean the end of all Abacists and perhaps the end of all of the other families. All of them."

"Your brother, Samuel," Wendi said to Max, "is the Abacist Prime, second of all seconds, and he too is a candidate to be the New Origin and begin a new family of reckoners. Saul would bring his scribing into Abacabax to both start a new line of reckoning and to heal those harmed in the last plague, but I fear neither of those things will come to pass. Saul will use it instead to unleash a vengeance on his enemies that would result in countless innocent deaths. Neither the Calculists nor Saul can prevail."

"Then what, Mother?" Rita asked. "How do we stop it? Fight both armies at once?"

Wendi took a deep breath. "We *break* the pattern."

Rita looked questioningly at her mother. Wendi tapped her fingers on her abacus. "Max, will you go fetch yours, please?

Max looked down at her fingers tapping her abacus and understood. He raced up to his room, took the abacus from under his pillow and returned. He stood in the doorway, holding the abacus in both hands. His mother's eyes moved from Max's face, to his hands, and then to his grandmother.

"*The Hands of Kael?*" Rita said incredulously. "What is he doing with the Hands of Kael, Mother? Why?"

"I granted it to him on the start of his fourth phase," she said.

"You can't!" she yelled, eyes wide. "He is not the second!"

"I did," she said. "It's done."

"But that would mean ..." Rita began, " ... of course."

"We are going to turn the whole world on its head to save your son."

Rita stared for a moment, her mouth open. Then she straightened her shoulders and her jaw drew tight. "Then let's do it. Let's take the whole thing down."

Wendi smiled thinly and nodded. "Now that's the daughter I know."

"Frames on the table," Wendi announced. "The portal holds open only a few hours and it will take an entire moon to reopen. Max, you've been practicing, I trust?" Wendi tipped her head towards Max's abacus.

"Every minute," he said.

Rita gaped at Max, her face a mix of disbelief and bemusement.

"Good," Wendi said. "Follow closely, this is difficult for your first reckoning. Clear your boards. Enter a *one* on the first rod. Increase the count to *two* on the second, and then repeat all that has come before – that is just another *one* this time, but the pattern grows quickly. Good, you've got *one, two, one*. Now increase the count to *three* and place it on the next rod, and repeat everything that's gone before, *one, two, one*."

Max set the beads, following the directions and also trying to understand the pattern. The right-most rods now showed *one, two, one, three, one, two, one*.

"We continue the tally, increase to *four* and repeat all that came before: *one, two, one, three, one, two ... one*."

Max ran out of rods before he could place the final "*one*" on his abacus.

"When you reach the final rod, continue to the right again, lay the count on top," Wendi instructed. Max saw that she meant if there were already a bead in place on a column, he should add the new number on top of the number already showing. Easy enough.

"Keep the pattern growing," Wendi said.

Click, click, click, Wendi called the numbers, Max caught on to the pattern right away. After each block of numbers, a new number went on the next rod, the pattern was repeated, and this became the new block that would be repeated again with another new number. It had a nice feel to it, but each step was more than twice as long as the previous.

The air began to grow tight. It was the same sensation Max had felt on his birthday when his grandmother had done something strange with time and given him this abacus. He began to feel a lightness, like wind blowing upwards from the center of his chest through the top of his head.

"We're almost there ..." Wendi said. "I'm setting our destination, *zero, zero, one, five, one, one ...*"

Bang! Max jumped. Something had slapped hard against the kitchen window, breaking their flow. All three of them jerked their heads to the sound.

Bang! Bang! Bang! Faces slapped against the glass. Max stared horrified. They were not human. Their skin was gray and leathery, their eyes were too large and there were slits where a nose should be. Small flat teeth dripping with saliva poked out from within a lipless mouth. Hands with long pointed fingers slapped the window with a *bang! bang! bang!* Four, five, six – a dozen faces appeared!

"The Changed!" Rita shrieked as they all jumped to their feet. "What are they doing here?"

"It's Saul! By the moons, he's after Max as well! How does he know?" Wendi said. "Max! Keep reckoning! Find the line, follow the line! Keep going!"

Wendi and Rita were on their feet, sweeping their abacuses off the table. "Keep going," Wendi told him.

Max could barely hear over the thumping in his chest and ears. His eyes were locked on the monsters at the window, their flat eyes burning a dull yellow color.

"Max!" Wendi yelled.

The back door cracked open and the doorway filled with gray, writhing flesh. Wendi and Rita stood side by side, legs bent deep in stances, fingers darting across beads. The beasts were flung sideways, cracking their heads against the walls and slumping motionless to the floor.

Max got ahold of himself. The pattern, the count, what was it? What had he just done? A seven? Yes, it was a seven. *One, two, one, three* he continued, his hands shaking. He would never make it.

But then the feeling returned. The wind blew upwards through his mind, its gentle sound dulling the thrashing and smashing noises on the other side of the room. *One, two, one, four, one, two, one, three* ... somehow Max felt himself relaxing and settling back into the pattern.

The wind stretched upwards, spiraling like a helix and then stretching into a tight line. He could almost see it, it felt like it wanted him to wrap himself around it. He was now only vaguely aware of the two women striking down monster after monster, or the kitchen window shattering in front of him, or the figure springing directly towards him.

He slid the final "*one*" in place on the abacus and looked up just in time to see a monstrous mouth of wet teeth flying through the air towards him. Max had no time at all to react.

The thing struck him like a cannonball in the center of his chest, throwing him backwards. His hand gripped the abacus tightly as it smashed into the cupboard with a hard *crack*! A horrible scream burst forth above the din. Max had barely enough time to realize the scream he was hearing was his own.

The world had come to an end.

Chapter 3: Abacabax

Max fell … and kept falling. His stomach lurched and his head pressed inwards from all directions with such force that he was certain it would be crushed. The world went white and silent and he could not breathe. An eternity passed.

And then he hit the floor … hard! Pain shot from his back through his chest, and his ears were suddenly filled with sound – a huge noise crashing from all directions. He sucked in air with a gasp.

He lay still, eyes screwed shut, as the ground shook and glass broke and pieces of the world fell upon him. The rumbling slowed, and quieted, and then stopped. Carefully he opened his eyes. The creature was gone, but he could still feel its damp breath on his cheek, he could still hear it hissing in his face.

He lay there for a moment, his heart beating loudly in his throat. He sat up partway on his elbows, feeling the weight of pieces of wood on his legs and abdomen. Dust hung in the air, but the creature was gone. So was the darkness. So was everything else that should have been there.

He was no longer in his kitchen. He was in a world of pink and amber stone and broken wood. Chunks of bricks and splintered wooden furniture and broken glass surrounded him. No one else was with him – the pieces of the house were silent. Where were his mother and grandmother? Where was he?

His leg was pinned under a heavy beam of wood. With a grunt, he pulled his leg out from underneath, the edge of the beam scraping sharply against his shin. He squeezed his calf. It hurt, but it was not broken. A single massive beam hung over him at a fearsome angle. It had fallen and stopped just above his head where it had kept the roof from crushing him. Light streamed through the broken roof in thick parallel columns of sparkling dust. Max rolled carefully to his feet, crouching in the cramped space, clutching his abacus.

"Mom? Grandma?" he called. He peered beneath the larger pieces of debris. No one. No leathery creatures, either. He looked around, unsure of what to do, waiting for something to happen. Nothing did.

He picked his way across the floor to a gaping jagged tear in the house – a house not his own, a house that Max had not been in moments before. Through the dust he squinted into the greenery outside, the light stinging his eyes. It had been late evening in a cold February, but now it was midday in a warmer month or climate. He was in some kind of huge terraced garden, layers of rock stacked up behind the house that seemed to go up and up, forming all kinds of triangles made from square blocks. The elaborately engineered garden was now strewn with broken rock and pieces of house.

A cobblestone path led towards an incredibly tall wall. He took a few unsteady steps along the path, marveling at the shapes around him.

Click, click, click. Max stopped and looked to his hand. He still held his abacus. *Click, click, click.* The beads were sliding, on their own, up and down, moving in patterns Max did not recognize. He lifted it carefully, holding it vertically. The beads defied gravity, moving up and down as if by an unseen hand. "I'm dreaming," he thought.

Gingerly, he touched a bead with his finger. *Clunk.* All the beads fell down to their lowest positions on the rods and the abacus was still. He turned it over, shook it gently. The beads rattled freely on the rods – there was nothing to indicate it was any different than it was before.

Except – on the far left column, one of the beads was missing.

He touched the rod on the spot where the bead should be. An image shot painfully through his head, an image of the abacus striking the cupboard in the kitchen. He jerked his finger back, staring at the empty place on the rod.

Max felt a sinking feeling. This was an important abacus – the Hands of ... *Kael* was it? This abacus could make things happen, and now it was damaged. Did it still work? Could it be fixed?

He turned and stepped back through the broken wall and surveyed the floor. He dusted away the splinters and pebbles, but could find no trace of the missing bead.

Fortunately, Max thought, the missing bead was from the far left column, one he rarely used. It would be easy to work around. He reached into his pocket hoping to find the booklet, but his pocket was empty. The book was in his room, and his room was ... nowhere.

The ground rumbled again slightly and Max clambered quickly out of the house, ready for the earth to shift again, but nothing further happened. It was some kind of aftershock, he decided. He wrapped up the abacus tightly within its leather case and slid it deep into his pocket.

Taking a deep breath, he followed the cobblestone path from the broken house towards the wall, eyeing the arrangements of steps in the terrace. Much was cracked and collapsed, but Max could see the overall pattern: multiple sets of steps rose at angles through the trees, meeting other sets of steps to make triangular arrangements of blocks. Some of the blocks were *huge*. In the other direction the ground was flat and came to an edge of a cliff that dropped precipitously down to where the garden continued below. Ahead loomed a wall, a very tall wall.

Nearing the wall, he looked up. It was as tall as a ten-story building, the top edge a perfectly straight line bathed in sunlight. Stairs ran along the wall, upwards to the left and downwards to the right to the garden below, branching off in two directions again and again to make more triangular patterns. The steps ended below in a sunlit gate where Max could see an open street beyond. He would have believed he were in a movie studio, except everything looked too real.

He walked down towards the gate, stepping around fallen rocks and over a broken tree trunk. He steadied himself with his hand on the mossy wall beside him. Voices from the street, loud and tense, shouted, "Where are they?" ... "Looks like some damage on that shelf!" ... "Look at that!" ... "That's not safe, don't go near that!" ... "Did everyone get out?" ... "Thank goodness you're okay!"

He stepped cautiously through the gate, out of the trees and onto the sunlit street. The damage looked even more dramatic out here where fewer trees afforded a more expansive view of broken cubes of stone, fallen trees and a massive fissure across the roadway to the right. Max could see about two dozen people, some standing, some sitting, most of them looking up into the terraces from which Max had come. A woman stood with a cloth pressed to the side of her head, staring absently. A man nearby held a crying baby.

He was too close to the trees to see what they were pointing at, so he crossed the street to find a better vantage point. Like the pathway, the street was cobblestone. There was no sidewalk, and no cars. The people were dressed in a strange collection of styles, some in long-sleeved shirts tied with cords, some in heavy dresses. Some wore tunics, some wore robes adorned with patterns embroidered with golden thread on their collars and sleeves.

He reached the group and turned to see what they were looking at. He could not believe what he saw could be true.

The patterns of stone in the terrace behind the broken house were not just confined to that garden. The pattern went up and up and up. And up. Larger and larger triangles of stone jutting out from the forested slope filled the mountainside in a regular pattern, smaller triangles between larger triangles, with even smaller triangles still between. The largest of the blocks he could see was impossibly big, taller than a skyscraper, filling the sky. Max felt like an ant at the bottom of a stack of building blocks which rose into the heavens until it disappeared into the clouds above.

The triangles, he noticed, were the corners of cubes, stacked together in different sizes so that the faces were divided on the diagonals. He gazed upon the regular pattern, his eyes moving to the place the others around him were looking. A huge block was missing, the side of the mountain gouged where a block the size of a city had scraped away both forest and stone. Clouds of dust hung in the surrounding treetops.

"Never seen anything like it," a large boy beside Max muttered.

"Good thing the western corner didn't drop," another boy beside him said. "Can you imagine *that* falling on Quothmire?"

"That's no natural thing," the first boy said. "This is some mighty crafty reck'ning!"

"You cadets best get yourselves to town."

Max turned his attention towards the voice. It belonged to a man in a gray uniform who had paused in front of them and was eyeing Max sternly. He pointed at Max's head. "And you best get that looked at." He looked Max up and down, frowned, and then continued on his way.

Max reached his hand up to his head where the man had indicated. His fingers came back red with blood. He didn't even remember getting struck in the head, it sure didn't hurt.

Max noticed the large boy beside him was also looking him up and down. He suddenly thought how strange he must appear in his blue jeans and hooded sweatshirt, when everyone else was wearing costumes as if in a play. Max opened his mouth to speak, hunting for words. Awkwardly he asked, "Is this Abacabax?"

He knew it was a mistake the moment he said it. Of course this was Abacabax, there was no place on Earth like this. Since he didn't know a soul in this world and his mother and grandmother were nowhere to be seen, the best thing for him to do would be to stay as inconspicuous as possible. Instead he was standing in the middle of the street in strange clothing asking strangers if this was Abacabax. Foolish!

"Krumm's thumb," the boy next to him said, "That must've been quite a knock on your top-rock, chum. You'd best get yourself to the barber."

The thinner boy beside him pushed forward. "What's that? Take *him* to the barber?" His eyes narrowed above his hooked nose. "He's a filthy finger-biter, he is. What was that you said, chum?"

Max shook his head, taking a step back.

"Abaca-*BAX*,' huh?" the hook-nosed boy sneered. "You's from Quincunx, isn't you?"

"No, umm ... Washington," Max replied, almost as a question.

"Wazzington? Never heard of it. What's your tribe?"

"My tribe?" Max said. Grandma had said something about tribes ... what were they?

"He's a grub-hand, he is," the boy said.

The large boy put his hand on hook-nose's shoulder. "Hey, ease off, now, Wooley. The kid's got a bit of a scrambled egg, hear? Look at his threads, he's no finger-reck'ner."

"Yeah, we'll find out, see. Watch this, Fishhagger," he said to the larger boy.

Wooley opened his hand flat. A dozen small stones spread across his palm and fingers. Underneath three tattooed lines stretched across his palm. "How's about an *eleven times thirteen*, fingerling?" he said to Max.

Max blinked. "What?"

The boy began arranging the stones on his outstretched palm and Max felt a pressure again, building around his head. Maybe he did have a concussion from his injury, this felt strange. He tried to focus on what this boy was doing. "*Eleven times thirteen?*" Max asked. "You mean, *one hundred forty-three?*"

The larger boy suddenly grabbed the stones from the hook-nosed boy's hand. The pressure around Max's head vanished.

"Why'd you do that?" The boy snapped angrily to his large friend.

His friend's eyes were wide. "I think he's right," he said.

The smaller boy took back the stones and slid them around on his palm. He slowly looked up. "Krumm ..." he said. "What in the Corners?"

"Did you see that, Wooley?" the large boy said. "He didn't even move his fingers!"

Wooley looked up to Max's empty hands, then to his face. "What kind of tricksing was that?" he said.

"Tricksing?" asked Max. "It's *one hundred thirty, plus thirteen*." What was this they were playing?

"No fingers, no stones," the smaller boy said, stepping away from Max.

"Wooley, Wooley," Fishhagger said, tugged his friend back. "He's popped the mental game!"

"He's too young for that!" Wooley said, eyes wide.

"You's one of those foreign recruits, ain't you?" Fishhagger said.

Wooley stared at Max, open mouthed. "That it, chum?"

Max's mind raced. This boy just did some kind of calculation – some kind of *reckoning*, with stones. The pressure he felt around his head was not from a concussion – it was from the reckoning! Grandma had talked about stones and the people who used them. "Calculists" she had called them, and they were dangerous. Max would need to be very careful with his next words.

"Yes, that's right," Max said. "I just got here."

"Look, chum, no harm, right?" Wooley said. "We didn't know. We's on high alert now, you know? Meant you no knockin', chum! We'll square this up."

Max let out a breath. He thought he was about to get mugged. Now this kid was apologizing and even seemed a little afraid of Max, all because he knew a simple math fact? Max decided he needed to get them to stop asking questions before they realized just how much he really *didn't* belong here.

"Look," Max said. "I hit my head and I can't really think straight." He rubbed the back of his head for effect. "No harm. I'll be going." He turned and began walking in the direction the man had gone.

The two boys ran up beside him. Wooley produced a small handkerchief from his pocket. "Here's for your egg, mate. Don't worry, we'll get you patched up. My name's Woolsherkle Linesplitter, this is Fishhagger Stoneslide."

Max didn't like these two following him, but maybe he could learn something. If he didn't say something stupid again, that is.

"Thanks. My name's Max," he said. He thought he shouldn't use the Teller name, they might know the Teller family name. He raced to think up an alias. "Max Seattle," he said confidently.

"We's in the academy, same as you," Wooley said. "That's quite a mental game you got, how's your reck'ning? What class is you?"

"Oh ... I'm just a beginner," Max said.

Wooley slapped Fishhagger on the shoulder. "See that, Fish. He's just a pebbler."

"Lucky you found us, then," he said to Max. "I can show you a few tricks. I'm third class. I'd be class four if they'd let me test, but you know how stiff they are. Come along, we's gonna meet up in the square, see what the elders got to say about ... this." He gestured to the mountain and its vast scar.

"You from the North Face?" Fishhagger asked.

Max nodded. "Yeah, North Face."

Wooley's face lit up. "I knew it! What I tell you, eh, Fish? Threads like that, gotta be North Face."

"Well, this must be a fine welcome, huh?" Fishhagger said. "A shelfquake. Nothin' like it."

"We lost an O'sie," Wooley said. "Onyxstead it was. There's not many folk up there, but you never know, do you?"

"Ay, but how's it cobble?" Fishhagger asked. "A shelf-quake, Wooley. My father used to say that three quakes marks the end of the world."

"Them stories is for kids, hard-egg," Wooley said. "I'm thinkin' it's the Darklanders, in which case we may be getting to do some knockin' on some *real* ghoulies! You'd like that, wouldn't you Max?"

Max gave a noncommittal nod. Darklanders? Ghoulies? He had a feeling he knew what they were.

"Yeah, I guess you'd like that," Wooley said.

They were nearing a cluster of buildings, stone and wood constructions with stacks of stone blocks at the corners. Thatched roofs sloped upwards from all four walls, meeting in a line at the center. More people were on the streets now, talking tensely about the afternoon's event.

"Quothmire," Wooley continued, "has the best academy on the South Face. You're supposed to be fourth phase to start, but with the Darklander trouble they're letting some folks train early like me and Fish – if you's good enough, that is. Which we are."

Max knew his grandmother was planning to train him, maybe she was bringing him here to study? She might have friends here. Max knew she was an ambassador and a senior member of the Abacists. There must be people she knows, but weren't Calculists the enemy? How would he find out?

At least with the excitement people would be distracted and maybe not notice *Max Seattle, lowly pebbler from the North Face*. For now, Max let Wooley babble on about how good he is, how good the academy is, and how he and Fish are going to drive out some kind of people with dirty fingers and send them all the way to the land of the ghoulies, who were even worse than the dirty-fingered people.

The road was getting crowded. "Krumm," Wooley said, "let's pop down Sloanestone Alley and cut the crowd." He led them down a path behind a row of buildings. The alley came to an end at a narrow road and Wooley brought them abruptly to a stop. He pointed down the street, away from the city center. A group of four people in green clothing were hitching horses to a post.

"Finger-biters!" Wooley elbowed Fishhagger. "For sure, this time! Now we can do some knockin'. Watch this, Max," he said.

"Wooley, this ain't no time for knockin'," Fish warned.

"No, Fish? Max here's a fresh pebbler, and's entitled to a show of Calculist skillery. Besides, I bet our chum probably don't believe he's in the company of the youngest class four Calculist in Quothmire."

"Class three," Fish muttered.

Wooley crouched at the end of the alley. Fish stepped to the side, stretching his neck out nervously like an ostrich as he looked up and down the street in both directions. Wooley reached to the ground and raked four parallel lines in the sand, then drew a crossbar through the middle. More of the small stones appeared in Wooley's hands. He placed them on the lines and began moving them deftly from line to line. "This is the one I've been telling you about, Fish," Wooley said. "Finger-biters can't crack a hundred, watch this."

Max watched intently. More reckoning – and in a different way! If they could do this with stones, Max should be able to do it with his abacus. But how? He watched closely, hunting for clues. The air tightened the way it did earlier, and Max braced himself. The people by the horses seemed to sense something was going to happen, too. They looked around, alarmed.

The air pressure released and two of the four people spun around. One of them stumbled and the other lost his footing and fell to the ground. The horses reared up in alarm.

Fish let out a long low whistle. "You got two! Two at once! Good one, Wooley! Oops – we've been made." A woman spun towards them. Her green hood fell backwards to spill out long brown hair onto her shoulders. She swung her arms in loops as she stepped forward and stretched out her hands.

Wooley scooped up his stones. "What's she doin', dancin'?" he asked.

Max felt a pressure in his ears. Then suddenly the three were thrown backwards, sliding roughly along the bumpy surface of the alley.

"Ooof, scramble!" Wooley yelled. He and Fish were on their feet, running down the alley and between two buildings. Max hopped to his feet and ran after them, his palms stinging from where they'd slid on the hard dirt. They zigged and zagged down another ally, past barrels and stacks of furniture to the edge of a busy square. Wooley ducked down and sat on the ground at the foot of a planter box next to tables full of people busy talking. The other two boys joined him. Wooley's mouth stretched into a wide smile as he craned his head over the plants looking back the way they came.

"What was that?" Fish asked Wooley. "That wasn't no Dijin finger tricks. She wasn't no Dijin, Wooley! There must've been a Calculist in that band!"

"Relax, Fish. They're Dijins all right and they knows what's a-comin' when they're in *our* town. Besideways, they can't do no fingertricks in the city, it's the Code. We could turn 'em in, you figure?"

"They's allowed to knock back if you knock 'em first," Fish mumbled.

"I guess so," Wooley conceded. "That just ain't right. I hate them stinkin' grub-hands."

Max sat tensely. He should have said or done something to stop them, but he had wanted so badly to see what it was they were going to do. His silence made him a participant, a member of the guilty party. His new "chums" were hoodlums, and Max was stuck with them for now.

A bell rang out from across the plaza. The boys stood to see across the crowd. Three men in embroidered tunics stood on a stage in the center of the square.

"Citizens!" the one in the center called out. "We have been attacked. Onyxstead shelf has fallen. We will find those responsible and punishment will be swift!" The people in the square grumbled assent.

"Military code is hereby invoked," he continued. "Citizen commanders are to report to their posts, and citizens are to report to your C.C.'s at next bell. Stay vigilant!"

Murmurs spread through the crowd. People began moving in all directions. Wooley took a seat at a vacated table, motioning for Max and Fishhagger to join him. He picked up a half-filled glass of amber liquid that had been left behind. "Free ale!" he announced with a grin, taking a sip and pretending to like it.

"So what did you think of that quotient constriction back there – I got two of 'em!" Wooley said, slapping down the glass. "Ha! Two with one casting!"

"That was tops!" Fish said. "What was it? Constrictives?"

"Divisives," Wooley said. "That's top-shelf class four material, there. You reckon like that on the North Face, Max?"

"Well, you got *two* of them," Max said, "but then she got all *three* of us ..." he taunted.

Wooley frowned and leaned across the table. "She was lucky. There was more of them we couldn't see, that's the only way. Didn't play fair, they didn't."

He leaned back and crossed his arms. "Suppose you don't got too many Dijins in the North, hey?" Wooley asked.

"No," Max said.

"No, they's too scared, they needs to hide in the trees, goin' on about how they got the 'purest and true way' whiles they can't reckon past the second digit. They's just burned that they wasn't plucked to be Calculists like us. Pretty much, they stays away from our lands which is just fine. And when they don't, it's a good lark to get some practice!"

Fishhagger shrugged. "For all the dust you stirs, Wooley, it's sumthin' of a miracle you ain't been caught! Oooh, lookee here."

Max followed his gaze to the edge of the square. The group of people Wooley had tripped a few minutes ago had entered the square. They were talking to one of the men who had been on the stage. A member of the group was speaking animatedly, waving his arms.

"You think they're reporting us?" Fishhagger asked.

"Naaa," said Wooley. "Elder Robbins would just tells 'em to keeps on walking."

The man in the tunic directed them to a table near a smoldering grill, gave some instructions to his assistant and hurried off. Max and the boys watched as the assistant took sausages from the grill onto a plate and brought it to the table.

"Is he getting them somethin' to eat?!" Wooley asked incredulously. "Pfff ... what's with Robbins?

"I think that woman," Fishhagger said, "might be that ambassador, the clever one!"

"There's no clever ones of them, Fish," Wooley said. "Nothing beats this." He reached into his bag and pulled out a flat stone rectangle, dropping it onto the table.

Max leaned forward. It was a hard black tablet, slightly glossy, about the size of a large notebook. Perfectly straight etched lines divided the surface into rectangles, like the design Wooley had scratched into the sand earlier.

"You like that, Max? That's how we make 'em in Quarry. Top-shelf, this is, hey? My father made this abax for me."

"That ... is the best 'abax' I've ever seen," Max said, truthfully.

Wooley grinned at Fishhagger.

"And check out my abac!" He reached into a large pocket sewn into his shirt and withdrew a small handful of round red stones that he set on the tablet. "The abac and the abax. The whole world is named for our reck'ning! We's gonna rule all of Abac-Abax!"

Max noticed the different pronunciation. His grandmother had said "Abacabax" in one flowing word, stressing the syllables at the beginning and end, while these boys were saying the name like two different words that matched the names of their reckoning devices, alternating the stress on the syllables. By saying it the wrong way earlier, Max had nearly given himself away.

He wondered if he could get them to teach him something. The abax was clearly a version of an abacus, surely they had some of the same principles. "You said you could teach me some tricks?" he asked.

"Sure," Wooley said. "We've gots some time. I'll shows you some two-lining."

Max leaned forward, excited. Fishhagger interrupted them. "Uh-oh, we've been made, again!"

The Dijin woman was walking directly towards them, her hands clenched. The boys stood up, and Wooley whisked his abax tight into his abdomen, holding it flat on his forearm, fingers on the stones. "She can't do nothin'," he said defiantly, but Max could hear nervousness in his voice.

"You!" she said, stopping closely in front of them. She glared at Wooley, unblinking. "You are young, this feud between the families is not yours. It costs you *nothing* to be civil!"

Wooley snorted and looked her up and down. "I guess all I'm wondering is, what's it *you* cost?" he said. He turned his head to Fishhagger and Max, a smirk on his lips.

Wooley's eyes flew open in surprise as the woman shoved him backwards with both hands. He crashed into Max and Fishhagger, his stones tumbling to the ground.

"Stinkin' finger-biter!" he yelled. He lifted his abax and stepped towards her, ready to swing.

The woman raised her fists as an older man from her group raced forward. "Stop it!" he said, reaching for her.

Max grabbed Wooley's arm, pulling it backwards, keeping Wooley from swinging it at the woman. Wooley tugged twice, trying to yank free from Max's grip. Suddenly, Wooley stepped back into Max and spun quickly, striking Max with his elbow. Max lost his balance from the unexpected shift in weight and fell on his behind, catching himself with outstretched palms.

Wooley turned back to the woman, his abax aloft. The two stood there frozen, glaring at each other.

Slowly, the woman shook her head in disgust, looking in turn at Wooley, Fishhagger and then Max, still sitting in the dust. She then turned her gaze to something on the ground next to Max. Her eyes grew wide. She looked back to Max, her mouth opening in astonishment.

Fishhagger was pointing at the same spot. Max turned. There in the dust next to him was a leather package lying where it had been thrown from Max's pocket. The cover was flipped open, shiny white beads stood proudly in neat rows in their white frame.

"Abacus!" Fishhagger shouted.

Wooley turned, stumbled backwards, suddenly forgetting the woman. "Abacist! It's an Abacist!" he shouted.

A voice from a nearby bench called out, "Oh, by the Corners! Abacist!"

More voices rang out from the crowd. Eyes turned to Max. Suddenly, everyone was staring, shouting. The lady at the next table was pointing saying, "They've come for us!" A man in a white apron yelled, "They're here! It's them!" Someone shrieked, "The Stonebreaker! It's the Stonebreaker!" Wooley and Fish tumbled backwards into the crowd, Wooley yelling, "I knew it! I knew it! Cast him off! Cast him off!"

Max grabbed the abacus, rolling to a crouch on one knee ready to spring. He scanned the edge of the square for an exit. Guards in gray uniforms pushed through the crowd towards him.

A great pressure built around his head, an unwanted feeling he recognized at once. His ears began ringing. He was about to be hit again, much harder than before. He pushed himself forwards, springing to his feet to escape, knowing he would never make it.

Suddenly, an ear-splitting explosion shook the ground. A column of fire erupted from the grill near the tables. The pressure in Max's head broke free as the confusion flared into an uproar. People screamed and fell back as smoke rolled rapidly outwards from the flames.

A hand gripped Max's upper arm and he was jerked forwards to an opening between the restaurant and a pastry shop. A voice in his ear yelled, "Run!"

He half-stumbled and was half-dragged into the alley. He found his footing and began running on his own. Max was shocked to see that the figure pulling him away from the angry crowd was the young woman in green who had just confronted them. He jammed his abacus into his pocket, pounding his feet on the cobblestones as he chased after this unlikely savior.

With voices yelling close behind, they ran past scaffolding, two stories high and loaded with boxes. The woman spun around, touched her shoulder and leg and threw out her hands. The scaffolding tore free from the wall, filling the alleyway with a pile of debris as shouts from the other side rang out in frustration. She kept running. Max's legs, now working independently of his mind, did the same. They kept running, down alleys, around corners, across a street and into another alley. Finally, they stepped through a doorway into a dusty room. The woman quickly closed the door and slid a bolt in place, locking it. She leaned against it breathing heavily.

Max caught his breath. "Who –"

"Quiet!" she snapped. She held her ear to the door, listening keenly. Max noticed a row of earrings through the top of her ear, squares and triangles. He followed the line of earrings down, across the curve of her jaw. Full lips, small nose, green eyes beneath a hard brow. She was younger than he first thought, but she looked just as angry as before.

Max glanced around. They were in a workshop, a wooden workbench with various tools was up against the side wall, the front wall lined with shelves loaded with books and small wooden curios, puzzles perhaps. The room smelled of sawdust.

The woman, satisfied in hearing nothing, dropped her shoulders and turned to him. "Have you slipped off the face? What under all of the moons were you doing?"

Max shook his head, "I, uh, don't know. You mean, the abacus?"

She stared at him. "Yes, I mean the abacus."

"It fell out of my pocket," he said weakly.

She said nothing.

"Look ... I really don't know," Max said. Seeing that she was waiting for more he added, "I just got here."

"Just in time to knock over a few Dijins and start a riot in the town square, huh?"

Max shook his head. "I didn't mean to! And I don't know them. I'm sorry!"

The woman slumped against the door, her face sour.

"Thank you," Max said. "Thanks for getting me out of there."

The woman drew herself upright. "Yeah, well I've had a bad day, too. I am Mindre, daughter of Roggolo."

"Mindre," Max repeated. "I'm Max ... son of Rita?" He extended his hand.

Mindre stepped to the side, away from his outstretched hand, her own hands snapping up in front of her abdomen with her fingers into some kind of arrangement like sign language. She stood there frozen for a moment, eyeing him warily.

Max looked down at his hand, then took it away. Mindre peered at him through slitted eyes. "And where's your partner?"

"Listen, that guy back there – I told you I'm not with him. I'm sorry he was so rude to you, I –"

She cut him off with a shake of her head. "No, not that idiot. Where's Lady Teller?"

Max melted. "Oh! My grandmother? You know my grandmother!"

"Your *grandmother*?!" Mindre took a step backwards, bumping into the door. "That's not possible!"

They were interrupted by a knock on the door. "It's me," a man's voice called through.

Mindre reached for the door handle, keeping her face turned towards Max as she fumbled with the latch. The door opened and a man quickly stepped inside. He pulled down his hood as he shut and locked the door. He was the older man from Mindre's group. He turned expectantly to Max.

"I thought I'd find you here. That was a spot of excitement, hey?" He looked at Max, his brow furrowed yet a trace of a smile on his lips. "Greetings, Abacist. I am Roggolo." He placed his fingertips together and bowed his head to Max. The man's curly gray hair bobbed on his head like wires, but what caught Max's attention was the sparkle in his eyes. They held a power and a kindness that Max immediately trusted.

Max nearly reached his hand out again but caught himself. Instead he carefully returned Roggolo's gesture, placing his fingertips together and bowing his head. "Maxwell Teller," he said.

"Teller ... ?" Roggolo asked, tipping his head.

"Father, he claims to be Lady Teller's grandson," Mindre said sharply.

Roggolo's eyes widened briefly as he turned to look at Mindre, then returned his gaze to Max. "Does he, now?" he asked slowly. "Well, well. I suppose you are the 'thing of great importance' Lady Teller was bringing us?"

"No, he's not," Mindre said. "The Teller line is dead!"

"Is it, now?" Roggolo looked Max up and down, marveling at his unusual clothing. "And where is this *grandmother* of yours, Maxwell?"

"I don't know, we got separated," Max said. "We were attacked, by ..." he held up his hands like claws. "These *things*."

"Darklings?" Roggolo asked. "They are no match for Lady Teller."

"We were in the middle of ... coming here, and I arrived but she and my mother didn't."

"Your mother? Rita Teller?" he asked, his voice raising.

"Yes," Max said. "You know her, too?"

"I know of her ..." Roggolo said. "And where is she now? Have you sent word?"

"I don't know how to find her," Max said.

"Are you not an Abacist?" Roggolo asked.

Max unconsciously reached to his pocket, feeling the abacus within. "Um, yeah, I mean, maybe," he answered. "I really don't know how to do anything other than calculating."

Roggolo and Mindre exchanged glances. Roggolo's expression was one of puzzlement, Mindre's of impatience. Roggolo turned to Max, "I'm not sure I understand."

Max reached into his pocket and withdrew the abacus. After what had just happened, he felt a little uneasy about bringing it out. "I just got it last month. I don't know how to use it yet, at least not to, you know, reckon with it." He opened the cover and held it before them.

Their eyes opened wide as saucers. Roggolo leaned forward as if teetering on a ledge, holding his breath. Max felt as if he had just shown them a diamond the size of his fist.

"By the steps of Nadir," Roggolo finally whispered. "It's beautiful. It is one of the Four Tablets. Only a Teller could possess such a marvel."

He reached out a finger to touch it.

"Father!" Mindre exclaimed sternly.

"Your forgiveness," he said, withdrawing his hand. "I have only caught glimpses of Lady Teller's golden abacus. To see another of the Four Tablets, well ..."

Max thought he should be careful and not let the abacus leave his hands, but when he glanced at Mindre and saw her returning his gaze with contempt, he couldn't help himself. "Here," Max said, setting it in Roggolo's hands, smiling to himself. Mindre glared at them in disbelief.

Roggolo was oblivious to her reaction. He held the wooden frame as if it may explode. "Five beads down here, on each of the hands, like Dijin fingers. Two beads up here, like the Bone-Thrower duality. Arranged in lines, like a Calculist abax. Wood and bone and stone. Oh, it is the synthesis of all reckoning in lower Abacabax! Marvelous! Hmmm ... four beads here, why is that?"

"One got broken on my way here, during the earthquake, I think."

"Broken? Is it dangerous?" Roggolo carefully and quickly handed it back to Max.

"No, I don't think so ..." Max thought about the beads moving of their own accord, and decided to refrain from telling them about that. Instead, he turned to show it to Mindre.

"Put that away!" she spat. "You're a bigger fool than I thought."

Roggolo laughed. "Oh Mindre, my beloved daughter. Who is more trustworthy than you for our friend to share his secrets with?"

"He doesn't know you or me, and even if he did ..." She threw up her hands. "For the love of Brianna, Father, why don't you just ask him to give you lessons?"

Roggolo turned to Max. "My daughter ... you must forgive her. She is stubborn, but wise. Ahh, and once again she is right. You best keep that from the light. How is it you know so little?" His gaze pierced Max, searching for a clue that would make everything make sense.

Max slid the abacus back into his pocket. Roggolo was right, Max knew very little. He thought hard, trying to remember everything his grandmother had told him before they left. Did she say anything about what they would be doing when they got here? Max could remember nothing useful.

"Only an heir to the Abacist line could have a relic of that nature," Roggolo said. "But Max, the Abacist line supposedly ended in the Great Reckoning sixteen years ago. Wendi Teller's daughters both perished."

"Not my mother, Rita. She was hidden away. Before me and my brother were born."

"You *and* your brother!" Roggolo said. "And you, Max ... are you the Thumb?"

Max shook his head. "The Thumb?"

"The Prime? The second of all seconds?" he asked intently.

"Um, no, I'm the first," Max answered. "Samuel is the second."

"Yes, of course, of course. You're the first of all seconds," Roggolo said, glancing at Mindre. Turning back to Max he asked, "And your brother, is he with Lady Teller?"

"I think he's with my great-uncle Saul."

"I see." Roggolo's face grew dark. "Saul is making a play for the New Origin. I thought it bad enough that Biggens, the presumed Calculist Thumb, has positioned himself for that, but *Saul* ..." He frowned. "No wonder your grandmother brings you to us now. We need to find her. You cannot send word, and we cannot wait here. They will search house to house. They'll be going wild knowing there is an Abacist amongst them.

"And this falling shelf," Roggolo continued, "this is certainly why Lady Teller wanted to meet here. She must have known somehow. All tribes tell a story of a destroyer from another world, who arrives with a great shaking of the shelves."

"The Hand of Death?" Mindre said. "That is just a myth."

"Even so, people will believe the end of the world is upon us," Roggolo said, "I'm afraid they will think the Abacists have called this forth. And, if the stories are true, then there is someone, or some*thing*, out there that we do *not* want to meet."

Max felt his stomach drop. A destroyer from another world, bringing a quake? Could that be him?

"By the moons ..." Mindre whispered. "They'll be tearing this city apart to find him."

"Yes, we need to leave quickly," Roggolo said. "Where did you travel from? It is there we should return."

Max swallowed hard. "We can't go back there, it's ... not safe." Max wondered if anyone was safe with him around. Did he cause the earthquake? And what will they do when they find out that he is "from another world?" Max could see only danger in all directions.

"Well, then, you ride with us," Roggolo said. "Without question," he added, looking hard at Mindre. "I suppose that fiasco in the square was, in a way, a fortunate occurrence, otherwise we may not have found you at all."

Roggolo turned to his daughter. "Bring our horses. Twilight is upon us and the darkness will cover our retreat."

She frowned. "And what of our companions?" she asked.

"They will remain in the house of Robbins as planned. We travel light."

Mindre frowned and slipped out of the door. Roggolo set to work gathering curios from the shelves. He worked quickly, and as he did, he spoke absently to Max. "It won't take long for Lady Teller to discover that you are with us. She is the Longwalker, as you know. She can travel where she will. She will find us quickly, if we place ourselves where we can be found.

"She will first seek out Robbins, our Calculist friend here in Quothmire, then Lady Carpus in Quincunx and then Logar, a friend of mine in Vertex. I must speak to Logar right away, and I dare say we can't smuggle you through Calculist land all the way to Vertex. I will need to go there alone. You'll ride to Quincunx with Mindre. We'll leave word here with Robbins." Roggolo handed Max a white long-sleeve shirt. "Put this on," he said. "We can't have you looking such."

Roggolo dug through a box of clothing and lifted out a pair of brown pants. "I think these will fit," he said.

Max's head was still swimming with all of the strange names and places Roggolo had just listed. He took off his sweatshirt and pulled on the shirt. The cloth was light and soft. It fastened down the front with cords as with the other clothing he'd seen.

Roggolo continued packing. "Mindre is a good woman," he said. "You'll get used to her. She's a fourth, like yourself, but she thinks and acts like a fifth. There's no one safer to be with. She's the Dijin Thumb, first of our firsts and probably the best reckoner on the southern faces. Stay with her, no matter what, until we find Lady Teller. I expect my daughter will protest, but there's no helping current circumstances. You just keep quiet and agree with me, okay Maxwell?"

Max nodded, pleased that Roggolo had a plan but unhappy he would be with this unpleasant woman and not with her father. Still, he finally had direction and native help. He felt hopeful for the first time since that nightmare in his kitchen ages ago.

Roggolo traded Max a pair of low leather boots for his sneakers. He turned Max's sneakers over, marveling at the material. He pressed his thumb against the rubber sole before reluctantly throwing them into a box on the shelf. The sound of horses outside the door was their signal to move. They cautiously stepped out of the shop and into the evening light.

Two small horses with saddles and packs stood outside the door. Mindre perched on one of them, looking nervously down the alley. "Squads are going door to door," she reported.

Roggolo tucked a bag into his pack and deftly mounted the horse. "Mindre, Max rides with you."

Mindre frowned as Max fumbled his way up the side of the saddle and nearly fell. Mindre grabbed him and pulled him up. She was surprisingly strong. "Please don't tell me you've never ridden before, either."

Max said nothing. He actually had ridden a horse once, on a family vacation to a state park. He remembered it wasn't that difficult. Of course, that time it had been with a guide on a trail, and Max had the feeling this coming voyage would not be quite so accommodating.

They rode around a corner to an alley that ended in tall bushes. Roggolo steered his horse between the bushes in a space that looked too narrow. Max and Mindre followed. They sped down a path littered with leaves and were quickly away from the buildings and into the trees. Max was relieved they had escaped so easily without being noticed. They bobbed and weaved through the trees, then turned confidently onto a rough trail. They rode silently towards the fading crimson of the western horizon. The mountain rose dramatically to the right. Dark trees blocked the view to the left, but Max could feel the emptiness behind the trees where the earth slipped downwards and hollow air filled the void. He imagined he could feel the gravity of the mountain pulling him towards it, towards the safety of the walls.

They turned down another trail that led them into the trees and to a clearing. Roggolo brought his horse to a halt and dismounted. Mindre did the same. Max swung his leg over, but Roggolo indicated he should stay on the horse. Max was pleased he did not have to struggle to get off the horse and on again, especially in front of Mindre. He listened intently to the conversation between father and daughter.

"Our danger has multiplied many times in one day," Roggolo began. "It is no longer just a vengeful Calculist Prime vying for New Origin but the Mad Teller himself with an unknown Abacist Thumb. Lady Teller is missing, Darklings are back among the Abacists, Max is in possession of a broken abacus, and he arrives here in the midst of a shelf-fall that will drive the world to madness. And, no matter what you think, this could indeed mean the Hand of Death is upon us.

"It is nearly hopeless," he continued, "but we have a gift! *Three* Abacists of the Teller line have returned, and this alone may be enough to balance all threats. Everything depends on finding Lady Teller, or more likely, the Longwalker finding us. Lady Teller has a plan. That plan is Max, so now he is our plan, too."

Mindre glanced over her shoulder at Max, her mouth a tight line. "So where do we go?" she asked.

"There are two places we need to be right now at the same time. I need to find Logar in Vertex, and you must take Max to Lady Carpus. She ... knows things."

"I'm to take him to Lady Carpus?" she said, raising her voice. "In Quincunx? We can't go back there!"

"*We* can't, that is true, but *you* can. You are not in exile, although your father does appreciate your solidarity. You will be arriving during the Festival of the Fives, so it will be easier to slip in unseen."

"Father, we can't split up, not now!"

"Mindre, I must ride to Vertex. If Logar is right, he will need me, and even if he's wrong, Vertex offers a strong chance of finding Lady Teller. She will certainly look for us in one or both of those places. Stay in Quincunx if you can and find Logar if you cannot. I will leave word with Robbins and we will find each other with or without Lady Teller."

"*Quincunx?*" she said.

"Distance yourself from Quothmire as much as possible tonight and sleep far from the roads. No fires. I'm sorry I won't be with you, my daughter, but you hardly need my help protecting yourself. That, and you travel with an Abacist." There was a touch of respect and envy in his voice as he said this. He bowed to Max, and again Max returned the gesture. In a lower voice he said, "Find out his story, he may be the key."

Roggolo embraced Mindre, then was on his horse again. "May the first moon of the second moon bless your voyage." He nodded to each of them, "Daughter, Abacist, we meet again soon." With that he turned his horse towards the mountain and was gone. Max felt a sudden sense of loss, he had felt safe in the presence of this decisive and amiable man, a man who thought of Max as some kind of powerful wizard. Now he was alone with a woman who thought he was some kind of idiot. Max had the feeling it would be a long trip.

Mindre slid into the saddle in front of Max. As if reading his mind she said, "By the four points, it's going to be a long trip."

Chapter 4: Crossing to Quincunx

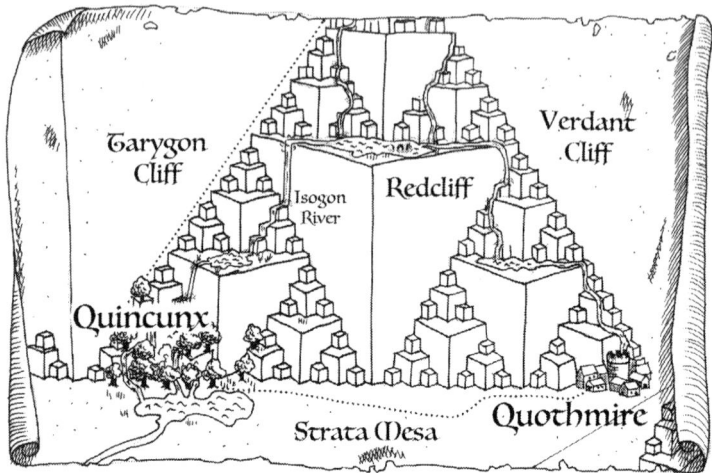

Samuel stood shaking in the trees. Uncle Saul was striding towards him now, limping heavily on one leg. Behind him lumbered the group of monsters, dark silhouettes in the light from the broken windows of the house.

"It's all right, Samuel," he said as he approached. "Looks like your brother got to Abacabax before you, but we'll find him. At least we have these." He held aloft two abacuses, neither of them black like the one Samuel had just seen. One was golden and the other gray. "Those traitors won't be able to stop you now."

Samuel wasn't looking at the confiscated abacuses at all. Wide-eyed, he pointed at the gray flat-faced monsters drawing closer. "Uncle Saul," he croaked, "what are ... those?"

"These, Samuel, are the Changed. They are your soldiers. Oh, don't be alarmed by their appearance, they do only our bidding." Saul stuffed the two abacuses into his pouch and began clicking the beads on his own black abacus.

"Where's Mom? And Grandma? Are they okay?"

Saul glanced at Samuel, flashed him a smile. "They're in the house. They'll be fine," he said curtly.

"I'm going to go see," Samuel said, moving towards the house.

Saul sighed, cleared his abacus and began clicking again. The creatures moved quickly between Samuel and the house, standing shoulder to shoulder, a terrifying wall of flesh and teeth. Samuel retreated quickly back to the trees.

"I've gone through quite a lot of trouble to find you, Samuel," Saul said, not looking up from his clicking abacus. "You are the most important person in the world but not if you sit around here uselessly. You will come with me now. I promise you, great things are waiting for us!"

The air began shimmering in a circle around them, rippling like water, and Samuel felt a wind rise inside his chest.

-:- | -:-

Max and Mindre rode silently beneath a darkening sky. The trip could be long, and Max remembered how sore he was after his first riding lessons. He tried to relax and let his legs hang from his hips, working on matching his movements to the rhythm of the horse's gait to avoid double-bouncing. The night sky awakened and with it the moon, full and bright. The features on the moon were different. Max could clearly see two very bright stars or planets in the sky near the moon, one on each side like eyes beside a round koala bear nose. Millions of stars came into view, the absolute black background filling with countless points of white light in a milky swirl. Max hunted for familiar constellations – there were none.

Max was so tired. He'd escaped the jaws of a demon, had a house drop on him, been hounded by bullies and faced the wrath of an angry mob. Finally all was quiet and peaceful. He gratefully accepted the reward of the steady rhythm beneath the stars and freedom from the endless stream of troubled thoughts.

Eventually, Mindre slowed and reined the horse off the trail into the trees, into cool wet shadows and the soothing sound of a quiet brook. The forest quietly slipped open again, allowing them to tread lightly into a small leafy glen. The moon cast a soft glow onto a sparkling carpet of pale green grass.

"We'll camp here tonight," Mindre told him as they dismounted. She pulled the pack from the horse and set it on the ground. "I'll water the horse, you'll find bedding tied to the pack." Mindre led the horse towards the sound of the river.

Max stretched his back before untying the rolls of cloth from the pack. There was one large sheet of a tightly woven, almost waxy, material. That was the ground cover, Max decided, spreading it out first. It was large enough for the two thicker quilts he unrolled next to them.

Mindre returned moments later and sat down. "Hungry?" she asked him.

"Starving," said Max, joining her.

She handed him a strip of dried meat and a piece of fruit from the pack. He eyed the familiar-looking shape of the fruit. "You have pears here?"

"They grow all over Strata Mesa," she said.

"Strata Mesa?" he asked.

"Our shelf? That we're sitting on? Do you call it something different on your face?"

"On my face?"

"The Northern Face. That *is* where you're from, isn't it?" she asked, growing more annoyed.

The Northern Face, that sounded familiar. Yes, that was where Wooley and Fish thought he was from. "Yeah, um, well … no," he said. He was having trouble putting thoughts together, unsure of what to tell her. Everything he wanted to say sounded wrong.

She sighed and rolled her eyes at him. "Whatever. It's best we not talk anyway."

Max realized that she thought he came from Abacist country, which must also be to the north. A "face" was a side of this mountain and the "shelves" were the flat regions? One of them had collapsed, and Max had a bad feeling he had something to do with it. He was too tired to think, and she seemed too irritated to want to listen, anyway. He'd try again tomorrow.

He pulled off his boots and jacket and slid under the quilt. Mindre stepped to the side of the bedding, removed her boots and stripped off her dress. Max was momentarily alarmed, but she neither seemed to mind or notice that Max was right in front of her as she undressed. Beneath her dress she wore a pale sleeveless tunic cut above the knee. Max could not help but notice the muscles in her calves were round, hard and well-defined – the legs of someone who has walked up countless steps.

She pulled her arms through the armholes of her tunic and began to lift off the remainder of her clothing. Max quickly rolled over, suddenly uncomfortable. He heard her lie down nearby and pull up the covers.

"Good night," he said.

"Hardly," she replied, humorlessly.

Max grinned. At least they agreed on something. He felt himself sinking, and in moments he was fast asleep.

The next day Mindre was gone when Max awoke. He stretched his legs and rubbed his sore backside, trying to clear his head. The line of mountains stood a good distance off, their riding last night had taken them away from that crazy maze of rocky triangles. In the morning mist, he could not make out any but the largest of the shapes he'd seen up close the day before.

He walked through the trees down to the stream they'd drunk from the night before. The water was clean and clear, bubbling through the woods, and in the daylight it looked like it could be one of many forests back on Earth. Kneeling on a rock, he leaned his face to the water and drank deeply, then splashed water onto his face, wondering if the cold would wake him from this strange dream. It didn't. He sluggishly walked back to camp, packed up the blankets and looked for a place to sit while he waited for Mindre. The grass was still wet from the cool night, so he settled down on a roughly cubical stone and pulled out his abacus.

"What have you gotten me into?" he quietly asked the device. He ran his fingers over the beads, delighting in their feel. He cleared the rods and began entering twos. *Two, four, six, eight, ten* ... he loved the different patterns of multiples. *Two-up, two-up, three-and-five-down, two-up, three-and-five-down* then a trade *two-fives-for-a-ten*. The pattern repeated and Max focused on the rhythm. *Click-click-plunk, click-plunk-clack*, repeating over and over. It was a simple exercise he'd practiced when he started learning, and the different rhythms of different numbers he'd add still fascinated him. It was like each number was its own creature, with different habits and different behaviors.

Max felt his stress melt away to the steady clicking of the beads, and as his stress left he felt a warmth within him that spread up from his fingers into his chest. He focused on the pattern, nothing else seemed to matter but the clicking and the warm relaxing feeling. He imagined the sliding beads rubbing together, generating the warmth he was feeling. He lost himself in the pattern, climbing into the hundreds now, until –

"Max!"

He snapped to attention, and then he *really* felt it. He was warm. Very warm, feverish. He wiped his forehead and turned to look up at the voice.

Mindre glared down at him, waiting to be sure he could see her face before she tossed some kind of a root vegetable at him. "You don't know how to use that thing, huh? Ha ha. Let's go." She turned up her chin, spun around and marched towards the horse.

Max looked down. He wasn't the only thing that felt warm. The grass around him was steaming.

Running to catch up with Mindre, Max's mind reeled. Did he create all that heat from using the abacus? Was that reckoning? Mindre was already on the horse when he caught up with her and words came tumbling from his mouth as he struggled to climb up behind her.

"Did I do that? Did I ... make everything get hot?"

"Max, stop it. I don't know what kind of game you're playing, and I really don't care. I'll get you to Quincunx because I have to, but then you and your grandmother can carry on with your secret plans. Just stop treating me like an idiot."

He didn't know what to say to that. He said nothing. She rolled her eyes as she held out her hand to help him climb behind her. They rode in silence. Max battled with himself about what to tell her, finally deciding that it wasn't worth it. It was only one more day with her, after all.

Throughout the morning all Max could think about was taking out the abacus and experimenting, but he didn't dare take it out on the horse. He had little space to work it and feared dropping it on the bumpy ride. By the afternoon, Max was thinking less about the abacus and more about how sore he was. He stood slightly on the seat to lift himself away from the ceaseless thumping of the animal beneath him, which helped a little bit but was really only shifting the soreness to his legs. By the time evening came and they left the road for the safety of the trees, every part of his body hurt. It took very little time to spread the blankets and even less time for Max to kick off his boots and stretch out under the quilt.

Tomorrow they would be in Quincunx. Tomorrow he would get some answers. Tomorrow he would be free of Mindre. He fell asleep thinking happy thoughts about tomorrow.

Max was shaken awake. He felt hands on his shoulders, Mindre's voice quiet and tense saying, "Get up, quickly and quietly. Grab the blankets."

He was instantly wide awake. Something in her voice terrified Max. Tension ran up his back and across the top of his head, pulling his scalp tight. It was still dark, the air was cool and still. Max slipped on his boots, catching sight of Mindre's bare backside as she pulled on her clothing. He took in every detail of the scene around him, as if his eyes and ears were larger than his head, as if his nose could draw in the scent of every pine cone and drop of cold dew.

The horse rocked back and forth nervously as Max hastily wadded up the quilts. Then he heard it. Something was shuffling in the trees. He scanned the trees and caught sight of it. A shadow moving in the shadows, a creature too long, too thin, and too misshapen to be human. It was one of *them*. It sniffed repeatedly, its head jerking back and forth unnaturally. It wants to smell us, Max thought. It wants to smell us and suck us up into its horrible nostrils. It turned its head towards them. In the darkness Max could see its eyes glowing like flashlights with nearly dead batteries.

A screech rang through the trees. Max winced as the ungodly sound seemed to drill into his back teeth. Misshapen heads with amber eyes popped out from hiding places. Salivating mouths advanced in what seemed like slow motion.

Max ran for the horse. Mindre, remarkably composed, waved her hands in rapid, practiced movements. Wherever she gestured, creatures tumbled, shrieking in pain. One fell to the right, two to the left. She turned and nimbly mounted the horse, holding out her hand for Max. He reached for her hand.

A shriveled figure appeared suddenly from the side of the horse and clawed at Max. It grabbed at his leg as he mounted the saddle, then fell back hissing in pain. Max looked down in horror to see the creature's fingers were twisted and steaming. He felt a burning from his wrist. He reached for his wrist and felt the knots of the bracelet his grandmother had given him. They were hot.

Mindre spun about, her fingers of her right hand touching points along her body while her left made a series of intricate finger movements. The sequence ended as her arms stretched outwards. The creature snapped back, arms and legs flailing as it lost all control and tumbled backwards into the darkness. As Max watched, he felt all his fear ebb. He was with some kind of incredible warrior.

The horse reared and sped through the trees. Max grabbed at Mindre for balance.

In moments they were back on the road, the nightmare creatures behind them. Max still gripped Mindre tightly, his thigh burning from the clawed touch, his mind burning with the incredible images of Mindre's grace and power, and his wrist burning from ... from what?

He rubbed his wrist. The bracelet, a "quipu" his grandmother had called it, was still warm. She said it was to protect him from evils. Had this protected him now?

The stars were no longer out, the moon no longer visible. The night grew darker around them. A wind growled from the forest, softly at first and then growing like a hunger. They rode speedily and silently for several minutes.

Max leaned forward and called over Mindre's shoulder, "That was amazing what you did! I've never seen anything like it!" he said with genuine admiration.

"You could have helped out!" she shot back.

"Me? I can't do that! You were amazing!"

Mindre turned in the saddle to look him in his face. She stared at him for a moment, the way one might stare at an odd part found around the house, wondering where it came from and what it's used for, if it should be kept in a drawer or thrown out. Max hoped she wouldn't throw him out just yet.

Mindre turned her gaze back to the road ahead. "Darklings," she said. "They should not be this far east. There will be more. A lot more. We'll need shelter soon, look."

He looked where she had nodded. The clouds ahead suddenly glowed in a flash of silent lightning, the thunder too far off to yet be heard, Max's stomach twisted in knots with a growing dread. He eyed the dark shapes of the trees with a terrible uneasiness, expecting something to jump out at any time.

The trees gave way to rocky terrain and Mindre reined the horse off the trail towards the mountain as rain began to fall. "I know of a cave near here," she yelled.

A flash of lightning much nearer than before illuminated the rocks before them. Max spotted a vertical gash in the patterned stones. They headed towards it as thunder boomed, echoing from the endless mountain face before them, and rode in through the opening just as rain began to pour.

They dismounted and stood for a moment catching their breath. The cave was just tall enough to stand in, with a dry floor littered with small stones. Mindre pulled off the blankets, shook them flat and collapsed to the ground. Max sat down as well.

With an involuntary shudder, Mindre told Max, "I think we'll be safe here until morning. We leave at first light. It isn't far to Quincunx now."

"Quincunx is your home?" asked Max. It was a strange name and felt awkward to pronounce.

"Quincunx is the stronghold of my people. It's on the center of this mesa. Darklings live on the other side, and yet they are here, on the wrong side of our lands." She shook her head, looking straight through Max's face as if searching for an answer somewhere in the distance. "They must be drawn to the shelf fall ..."

They sat in silence for a moment, watching the storm through the cave's opening.

Finally, Max spoke, "Those were the creatures who attacked me yesterday. What are they?"

Mindre's face grew dark. "They are *your* brethren, Max, why don't *you* tell me?"

Max stared in disbelief. *My brethren?*

Mindre pulled her knees to her chest and again regarded Max carefully. "Do you really not know? Max, if you're playing with me, I swear by Brianna ..."

"I'm not playing!" Max said. How could he tell her where he was from without her thinking he was the Hand of Death? He would need to tell her the truth, of course, at least most of it. "Before I was born, my Grandmother, Lady Teller, hid my mother far away. My mother never told me anything of my family or the rest of the world. She hated my grandmother, well, *resented* her for abandoning us. She kept all this from me, until last month when I met Wendi and Saul for the first time. My grandmother gave me the abacus then. She was supposed to teach me but we never got the chance. A bunch of those ... Darklings showed up and attacked us. They were all over the place, one came through the window and almost got me. My grandmother somehow sent me here. I don't know where they are or if they're even okay." Max fought back tears in his eyes. "I don't know what I'm doing."

Mindre frowned. "But Max, I saw you reckoning."

"I was just playing with the abacus practicing some exercises. It's never done that before!"

"If that was your first time ..." She looked at him strangely for a moment, shaking her head.

"Mindre, it's true. If you and your father hadn't found me, I would be totally lost. Please believe me, you're the only thing I've got."

Mindre sighed. "Your mother must have protected you well, Max. It's almost unbelievable. I'm afraid your quiet life will be the end of us. Things are going to get very bad, very soon."

Again she paused, collecting herself. "All right then," she began, eyes tilted up to her brow. "The Darklings, they were once human. The first ones were *Abacists*. You do not know your own history?" She sighed deeply.

Max shook his head, sitting up straight.

"They lost their reckoning. Something spread through the Abacist lands, some kind of disease. Entire cities fell. Men, women and children turned into Darklings and began wandering the lands. It was a nightmare. The Darkling Plague threatened to destroy the Brightlands. There was a war, a long war, and the Calculists finally drove the Darklings to the nightside. There they have been, isolating themselves from the rest of the world. They are mindless and twisted and hateful of all reckoning."

Mindre paused, her face grim. "The war has never really ended, Max. The Darklings still steal people, Calculists,

Dijins, young, old, it doesn't matter. They steal them and their numbers grow. They say there are more Darklings than humans on Abacabax."

The rain and wind outside of their rocky shelter howled, sending a cold shiver down Max's neck.

Mindre continued. "They live a lifeless existence, never knowing the light of reason or the joy of reckoning. I've seen some horrible things in the hinterlands, parents lining up with their children in their arms, offering them as living sacrifices to a god they do not understand. They walk into the darkness and are lost, twisting into these grotesque things." She shuddered.

"But everyone has these powers, so we can fight them?" Max asked.

"It was a lot easier once, when the Abacists and Calculists and Dijins worked as one. But now of course the Calculists have taken nearly everything, your people have all but vanished, and my people hide like cowards. Meanwhile, the Darklanders seem to have gained strength and purpose.

"The Darklanders have a leader, you see. It is an Abacist." She paused, staring at Max hard.

Max's head reeled. "Saul ..." he said. It must be Saul. Of course it was Saul. His very own great-uncle, a king among monsters. He didn't know what to say. "Why?"

Mindre laughed. "Oh, just because your grandmother is the Protectress of Abacabax and one of the finest people I know, doesn't mean that all Abacists are good. Abacists were once the wisest and most just people on the four faces, respected among the Dijins and others, but who knows anymore? And now the most powerful of your people has allied himself with Darklanders and readies them ... for what I don't know. But their numbers are great and our numbers are few, and should he be able to organize them, then he would control an army larger than the rest of the entire population.

"It was the Abacists who brought all of this upon us and may bring it again, so forgive me if I find your people a little difficult to understand ... or trust."

"That explains what happened in the town this afternoon," Max thought aloud.

Mindre continued. "My father believes that the only way to stem the tide is to reunite and rekindle the joy of shared reckoning. But sharing secrets is a quick way to lose power, so I doubt the tribes will ever do that. The Calculists especially will protect their power to the death. As a whole, they have great strength, but their weakness runs deep. They train armies of Calculists, all of them capable reckoners, but there is no perspective, there is no joy. They minimize my people with their codes and scoff at our ways. Many of us have given up on making peace. My father has been a clever ambassador and he was, in fact, once the right hand of Chief Oolong. Now he has been banished from Quincunx and his allies amongst the Calculists are disappearing.

"My father and I were here to meet with Calculists and your grandmother. She was supposed to bring us something of great importance to both our people. I guess that was you.

"We need to find out what Lady Teller's plans are for you, Max." She sat thoughtful for a moment. "I hope Lady Carpus can read you. Our people never allow outsiders in. Even though I'm the Dijin Thumb, you will not be welcomed, so we will need to move in the shadows."

Max could only shake his head. One day with a stranger who doesn't even like him, and he had learned more about his family than his mother had told him in his entire lifetime.

Mindre sat thoughtfully. "There's something else, too," she said. "The Hand of Death, or 'the Stonebreaker' as the Calculists say. What do your people call it?"

Max shook his head. "I don't know," he said weakly, dreading what she may say next.

"No, I suppose you don't. There are stories of a beast from the offworld that will strike Abacabax three times and bring about the end of the world. Some people think that the quake yesterday was the first."

"A beast from ... another world?"

"It's just a story, but as my father said, if people believe it, there will be dark times ahead. It seems like everything is happening at once, and none of it is good."

Max's head was spinning. What if *he* were the beast? His grandmother said that he would have the power to be a savior or a destroyer. Certainly, he had arrived from another world, an arrival heralded by a great shaking of the earth. With everything that was happening it was easy to believe that this was the beginning of the end of the world.

"Anyway," Mindre said, regarding him quizzically, "here you are, an Abacist in Dijin lands, and you don't even know your power. It's like my father said, 'Almost impossible.' But if you cannot reckon ... what use can you be?"

Max winced. Indeed, what use could he be?

Mindre frowned. "We'll see what tomorrow brings. We'd better try to get some rest. We should be safe here. Our friend will wake us if anything approaches," she said, nodding towards her horse. "Animals are very sensitive to the presence of Darklings."

Max settled down and tried to rest, but it was useless. Could he be the Hand of Death? He wouldn't try to destroy the world, but what if it just happens by itself, or if he makes some kind of mistake? On top of that, he couldn't stop reliving the attacks of the past day over and over. After the attack in his kitchen, Max had thought he would never see anything so horrible again in his life, but tonight was just as bad. Max wasn't sure he would ever be able to clear the images from his mind of the eyes and drooling mouths in the dark trees.

He ran his fingers along the knots of the quipu on his wrist. He hoped he could draw comfort from the idea that it might protect him from the dark creatures, but it was of little help. When he finally drifted into uneasy slumber, his dreams were filled with visions of hideous creatures picking at the brains of children.

During the night, the storm passed, and a cold pale dawn spread its cheerless glow into the morning. They rode straight through the early hours of the day with no signs of the monsters from the night before. The sky slowly warmed, lifting their spirits. Mindre did not seem angry at Max today, to his great relief. Nor did she talk much, which disappointed him. He stared at the passing scenery, trying not to think about anything.

They paused for a meal near the base of a massive cliff wall. Water trickled down the sides, Mindre watched it wistfully. "We have the most amazing waterfalls in Quincunx. The River Isigon flows all the way down through the upper steps. For centuries our people have been directing its flow, shaping the cascades. It's the most beautiful place."

Max looked along the edge of the mountain, the lush green colors divided into right triangles by dramatic cliffs of gray stone, the amazing regularity of the formations was still beyond belief to him. "These patterns in the mountain – they are so beautiful. It is hard to imagine something more beautiful," he said vacantly.

Mindre looked around. "The patterns?"

Max was lost in thought, studying the arrangements. Without thinking, he said, "The triangles, the cubes. It reminds me of something I've seen before."

He marveled at the sight. It did seem familiar. Maybe he was dreaming. He reflected a moment longer, then became aware that Mindre was staring at him. He met her gaze.

"*What on all the faces* are you talking about?"

Max caught himself. Only an offworlder would not know these patterns! He stammered, "I just never get tired of the patterns, do you?"

She regarded him a moment longer then turned her head back to the trail. "Yeah, the patterns. Whee. Let's get going."

They rode throughout the afternoon, meeting a river near sundown.

"This river will take us right to Quincunx," she told him. "We'll be there shortly."

The trees thickened as they followed the river. Max could hear the rumbling of water up ahead. Though he couldn't see it, he knew from the sound coming from higher up that they were getting close to the cliffs. The trail passed beneath a portal of sorts. Two trees arched overhead, their branches twisting together in an intricately woven pattern like a living Celtic knot. A skull hung from the center of the branches over the trail. Five dots were marked in the middle of its forehead, like the spots on a dice.

"What did that guy do?" Max whispered.

"Outsiders are forbidden here. That's just a warning. It works."

"Great ..." Max muttered under his breath.

The trail shortly brought them to the source of the sound. The river opened into a small lake, and at the far side was the cliff face. Max caught his breath at the sight. The cliff was not vertical as he'd imagined it, rather it cut back away from the lake in an irregular step-like fashion. Water cascaded down its faces, pounding itself in a fine mist above the lake. Centuries of human engineering and erosion from the river had carved away the stone, leaving a maze of square and triangular crevices and protuberances, stacked upon each other in an astonishing labyrinth.

Max then noticed small wooden structures tucked into the trees on the stepped plateaus on the other side of the water. A system of boardwalks and bridges mixed with the natural stone steps, blending in with the trees and vines. High above, Max caught sight of a small group of four or five people on a boardwalk; they silently vanished into the trees.

"This is Quincunx. That is my village over there," Mindre told him.

"It's ... wow!" was all Max could say.

"Yeah, that's what we think, too. We'll leave the horse here. We don't want any attention."

Max thought of the skull hanging from the trees and silently agreed.

"The festival should have already begun, which means there will be few people on the trails. I can hear the drums already."

Max strained to listen and heard the faint sound of drumming through the trees. They moved quickly along the pathways in the fading light, the drumming growing louder.

Mindre paused in front of Max. "That's not festival drumming," she whispered. "It's ... oh, by Brianna, it's a collective reckoning. They're planning to close the hand on Quincunx! Let's hurry."

She began running. Max followed quickly. He didn't know what she meant, but the urgency in her voice was enough. The forest was growing dim and Max was having trouble seeing the steps. It was difficult enough dodging branches and roots in the light. He began to worry he would twist his ankle, or worse.

They rounded a bend and Mindre stopped abruptly. Grabbing Max, she pulled him quickly downwards off the path into the ferns. A column of men and women hurried past, poles with curved blades held aloft. Soldiers, about twenty of them going the way Max and Mindre just came from. Max thought about the horse – if they found it, what then?

The group passed and Mindre was back on her feet. "Come on!" she whispered.

They reached a fork and Mindre took the upper path. They darted across a walkway affording a view of an open arena-like area below. Mindre paused in the center, gazing at the scene below. Hundreds of people were gathered in a circle. In the center burned a large fire in a huge stone brazier. Four smaller fires were arranged around it in a square formation. The central brazier was ringed by a dozen or more people, men and women alike moving in a patterned dance to the beating of the drums. They were naked, apart from some necklaces and arm and leg bands made from woven leaves. The people in the crowd were chanting a steady mantra, waving their arms above their heads. The chant, the rhythms, and the movement of skin wet with sweat and oil was mesmerizing and seductive. Max felt he could tumble into the crowd below and lose himself in blissful oblivion.

Mindre, stood misty-eyed, hips swaying to the beat. "I've never participated in this ceremony. They're using their collective powers, kind of like a human abacus. I wish we could stay."

Max heard disappointment in her voice. He felt unwelcome in a strange land, but what must it be like for Mindre to feel unwelcome in her own home? And now she was missing out on a something as rare and wonderful as this.

They left the walkway and cut back on another trail. Higher they climbed, up mossy steps through the forest and alongside a wall like the one in the garden Max had seen when he had first arrived. The sound of the drums faded behind them.

Again Mindre stopped suddenly. Max didn't see or hear anything, but she pulled him behind a thicket of trees and motioned him to be silent.

Soft footsteps sounded from the path. They stopped nearby. "Show yourself," a voice commanded.

Max's heart skipped a beat. He stopped breathing, he mentally shrunk into himself, as if he could will himself to become very small.

The unseen speaker's voice sounded again, calmly commanding, "Strangers, come forth!"

The air around Max grew heavy – reckoning! He felt a grip around his body, as if he were a toy figure being grasped by a hand. Despite himself, he stepped forward out of the trees, compelled by an unseen force. He found himself face-to-face with a tall man in a black robe. About the man's neck hung a silver amulet in the shape of a hand with five dots in the center.

The figure opened his mouth to speak as Mindre leapt from the trees, fingers extended towards him. She stopped, eyebrows raising. "Iagollo," she said.

The man nodded at her. "Hello, Mindre. Lady Carpus is waiting for you."

Mindre spoke to the man in whispers as he led them up the path. They seemed to knew each other well. Max thought that everyone in Quincunx must know Mindre, but it seemed to be more than that. "You're just in time," he said. "Already the hand is closing. By midnight, Quincunx will have disappeared."

They reached another set of steps, overgrown like the terraces outside of Quothmire. These steps must fill the face of the mountain, he realized, even here, deep in the forest.

They ascended several hundred steps, turned off the stairs, crossed a plateau, and descended steps on the other side, bringing them to the back of a small hut. The building was surrounded by twisted vegetation. Glass and metal trinkets hung in the windows and a small light burned inside.

The man led them to the back door then stepped aside. "Please go in, she's expecting you."

Mindre gingerly pushed the door open and stepped through with a nod to the tall man who had guided them here. Max followed.

The inside looked to Max exactly like what he would have expected a fortune teller's house to look like. Lush curtains and pillows, herbs and roots hanging from the ceiling in unexpected places, a strong smell of spices. A gnarled figure sat in a chair by a burning fireplace, a book lay on top of a three-legged table in front of her. Two empty chairs faced hers. Max supposed they were for himself and Mindre.

The woman turned her face to them, and the light from the fire glinted in her eyes. She looked older than Max would have imagined, the lines and wrinkles of her face twisting like the vines outside of her hut. She smiled gently. Max felt that behind those marks of great age lay even greater wisdom and intellect.

"Mindre, prodigal daughter of Quincunx, welcome home," she called out in a low, scratchy voice.

Mindre touched the fingertips of both hands to the center of her chest and then stretched out her hands towards the woman, palms up and fingertips bending downwards. "Thank you, my Lady," she said.

"You have found Maxwell Teller," Lady Carpus said, "first son of the second child of Lady Teller, born not of this world but beneath the sign of Brianna nonetheless, bound to the fate of Abacabax as surely as the daughters of the daughters of Kael are bound to their paths in the night sky."

Mindre turned to look at Max, eyes wide and mouth open. "Not of this world ... ?" she whispered to him. Max didn't answer.

"Come, sit a spell, children," the old woman said. "Destiny grows impatient, but it can wait a moment longer."

Max took his seat hesitantly. The chairs were woven from branches but were surprisingly comfortable. Max eyed the wise woman, unsure of what to expect. How could she know so much about him?

"Well, Child," she said to Max. "You have come a great distance to see me. I am honored. Tell me of what you seek."

"I need to find my grandmother, Lady Teller," Max replied meekly.

"She comes for you, Child, but for now she is out of reach. Others come for you, as well, don't they?"

Max nodded, wondering whether she guessed that or if she really did know that Saul was after him. "Roggolo sent us here. Oh, I guess you know that already. I think I'm supposed to show you this." Max reached into his pocket, removed the leather-wrapped package from within and opened it. He hesitated for only a brief moment before setting the abacus down on the table before them.

Lady Carpus leaned forward, her eyes widening. "No abacus is ordinary, my child, but this one is a treasure. The abacus of your grandmother, I have heard of it." She looked from the abacus to his face, reading something from his expression. "Yet, she has not told you, has she?"

Max shook his head. Could Lady Carpus read minds?

"This my child," she explained, "is the Fourteen hands of Kael, carved at the Dawn of the Abacists from the living soul of Abacabax." She did not move to lift it from the table, instead she stared at it deeply, lost in wonder. "I thought I'd never live to see such a relic. You bless me, Child. You bless an old woman."

The three of them looked intently at the wooden frame on the table, the light from the fire stretching the shadows across the table, a flickering glow playing on their faces. The sound of drums from off in the distance intensified. Max waited for her to ask about the missing bead.

Then, without warning, *click, click, click, click*. The beads began sliding, on their own. Mindre gasped, looking at the device with alarm. "What is it doing?"

In a whisper, Max explained, "It does this when I'm not using it." He looked to Lady Carpus, hoping for some explanation. "Do you know what these patterns mean?"

"Tell me child," she said calmly. "What is it *you* see in the patterns?"

Max considered this. He followed the numbers, *fourteen, ten, eleven, nine, eight, twenty-four, twenty-five, twenty-seven*, ... "Well, the changes are usually small, but sometimes they make big jumps. It seems that overall they get bigger. And I don't think I've even seen them repeat a number. It's like it's counting but not in order."

She nodded thoughtfully, then spoke slowly, "This I cannot know for certain, but I believe this to be the pulse of Abacabax, Maxwell. By your bond they are also the patterns of your life. You are gifted with a window to the patterns beneath the surface of perception.

"The fingers of Kael are beckoning for you, Max. The hands of Kael are reckoning for you, Max. And what of this?" She pointed to the place on the leftmost rod where the bead was missing.

"It broke. I think it broke because of the earthquake."

Her eyes flickered. "*Be*-cause of the quake, or *the* cause of the quake? The hands of Kael are wounded, Maxwell. This wound of the hand is the wound of the land."

She leaned forward, looking deeply into his eyes. Max suddenly felt terribly uncomfortable. In a whisper she croaked, "And tell me Max, what do you think will happen when the patterns count to the fourteenth hand?" She tapped the sharp point of her bony finger on the rod where the missing bead should be.

Max could only shake his head, but he felt he already knew the answer.

"The patterns of the *hand* are the patterns of the *land* are the patterns of *your hands*, Maxwell."

Max gulped. "Can I change the patterns?" he asked.

"Everything you do changes the patterns, Child. Everything. Tuck that away now, guard it with your whole, guard it with your soul."

Max wrapped the abacus and slid it into his pocket.

"Your hands, Child," she said. "Show me your hands."

Max glanced at Mindre. She nodded her approval. He stretched his hands across the table, palms upwards.

Lady Carpus reached around and carefully took ahold of his wrists. She leaned forward and studied his fingers intently. "A surprise, yet another surprise for a woman who thought she was beyond revelation. Hmmm ... yet, it must be true. Of course it is true." She turned her eyes to his and squinted ever so slightly to bring him into better focus. "Yours is the Hand of Death, Maxwell."

Max drew his breath in. He heard a small noise escape Mindre It was just as he had feared. He moved to withdraw his hands, but Lady Carpus held on tightly to his wrists.

She turned her gaze to his left hand. "Maxwell," she continued, "yours also is the Hand of Life. Your path branches like the arms of the biforna vines, one side into darkness, one side into light.

She lifted her gaze to look deeply into his eye. "Listen closely, Maxwell. The world hangs in the balance. You will have a choice to make." She turned and looked at Mindre, held her gaze steady for a moment, then returned her gaze to Max. "A choice between lives. A choice between what you know and what you fear. When you can no longer understand the pattern, listen to the rhythm within, Child. Choose what you *know*, not what you *fear*. It is our only salvation."

They sat in silence, eyes locked. Max thought he could see powerful and terrible thoughts behind the cloudy wet surface of those eyes. Lady Carpus released his wrists and turned to Mindre. "And as for you, child of Quincunx, know this: as Maxwell assumes the fate of Abacabax, you must assume the fate of Maxwell. Bring him safely to the Temple of Abacabax. Maxwell's awakening is at hand, only you can guide him. The journey will be longer than you can imagine, yet shorter than you think possible."

Mindre stared, her mouth opened and closed again, her face gaunt in the flickering of the fire. She shook her head, "He is ... what?"

Lady Carpus cocked her head, listening to the sound of the drums floating faintly through the open window. "The power of the collective grows. Soon, the hand will close. No one comes, and no one goes. There is no shelter for you here tonight, you must climb from here and there is little time left to tally."

"Lady Carpus," Mindre gasped, "That will take us to Red Cliff. It will be much safer to take the western rise. And my horse ... she cannot climb beyond Red Cliff."

"The Dark Ones wait below. An unknown path is better than the peril that is known. Iagollo has readied what you will need. Quincunx shall reopen its fist on the fifth moon, we shall learn of your success then. May Brianna be merciful."

She bowed her head, dismissing them. They thanked her and left her abode. Max felt lightheaded and off-balance, stumbling into the doorway on the way out. Mindre looked at him, her face a mix of emotions Max could only imagine. Outside, the drumming was louder and the evening had grown dark, but the cool clean air cut an edge of clarity in Max's thoughts. Iagollo eased a backpack heavy with supplies onto his shoulders while Mindre strapped on her own pack. He walked them to the base of the stairs, and with one final look behind them, they began their ascent towards the upper steps of Quincunx and beyond.

-:- | -:-

Samuel lay in the grass wrapped in a ball, his eyes screwed shut.

"Samuel, it's okay." Saul's voice drifted into his ears. "We're here, Samuel, take a look."

Samuel opened his eyes and looked around. Everything felt wrong. A moment ago he was in his backyard in the dark, and now he lay in a quiet field on a sunny morning.

His uncle stood over him, a broad smile on his face. "Welcome to Abacabax. You're here. You're finally here, I can almost not believe it."

Saul stretched out his arms, tipped back his head, and announced to a non-existent audience, "I've returned The Abacist Prime to Abacabax ... we shall rise again!"

Saul smiled down at Samuel again and held out his hand. "Come, we made it. It's just a short way now. I'll explain everything."

Samuel took his hand and was pulled to his feet. Above him stretched hills filled with patterned terraces that seemed to go up and up and up. At the foot of the hills stood the walls of a city with a palace rising from within. Samuel looked over his shoulder. In two directions stood another gray stone wall, low and long, a ninety degree corner in the middle that edged off the flat grassy field. Gray faceless creatures wandered aimlessly along the wall. Samuel hurried after Saul.

They met a trail along the bottom of the terrace that led to the side of the city and passed through an opening in the wall. They walked in a short tunnel through the thickness of the wall and emerged in a courtyard. Gray square tiles overgrown with weeds created a grid pattern beneath their feet. They headed straight across the courtyard, towards another wall with a tower atop.

Saul stopped in the middle of the courtyard. Several more of the creatures had gathered, emerged from doorways and from behind some of the small buildings on the edge of the courtyard. Saul held his abacus in his hand and began clicking the red beads inside the black frame. The creatures lay down on the grass, no longer interested in them.

Saul looked at Samuel and smiled. "You see? I can control them." He paused. "You can too. I will teach you everything!"

Samuel wondered at Saul's strange powers. Saul could make these monsters do whatever he wanted, and without a word make them lie down.

"Where are we? Why are you taking me here?" Samuel asked.

"This is Tangram, your castle. We have a castle, Samuel! This is where your mother comes from. It is my home, and your grandmother's home, and home to all of your family since the Third Divide.

"This world is in danger, and you, Samuel, are going to save it. You are the only one who can."

Samuel shook his head, feeling very unsure of himself. Saul turned and continued crossing the courtyard toward the stairs that climbed the wall ahead of them.

"There's so much to tell you," Saul said. "I don't know where to begin. These people are victims of a plague, a plague that started sixteen years ago. Your mother was hidden on Earth to escape and to protect her children, you and your brother. Because you, Samuel, are the second child of the second child of the second child and so onwards to Bella, the second daughter of Kael. You, Samuel, are the Abacist Prime, and the heir to the entire world!"

Saul's words didn't make sense to Samuel. He was focused on the creature lying on the stairs they climbed. Samuel slid past with his back pressed to the wall. It turned its gray, noseless face towards him, opened its mouth and hissed.

Samuel jumped after Saul, terrified. "These are ... people?" Samuel asked.

"Well, they cannot think very well anymore. But yes, they are people, Samuel, and we can help them. We can cure them, but I need your help. And we need to do it quickly, because an army is coming to kill us all."

They reached the top of the stairs and stepped out onto the balcony overlooking another courtyard. Below them were hundreds of the creatures on benches, on the ground, on the edge of the fountain. Samuel tried to imagine them as *people* and found it difficult. What kind of plague could do this?

One began howling and others followed. One by one they lifted their blank faces towards the balcony, mouths open like hungry holes. The haunted, soulless howling made Samuel's blood run cold.

Saul turned to Samuel with wet eyes. "These," he said, extending his hand towards the hoard of horrible creatures, "are your people."

Chapter 5: Ascension

Max stumbled upwards, Mindre gliding effortlessly in front of him. "Offworlder? You're an offworlder?!" Mindre said. "Did you not think to tell me?"

"Of course I did," he answered, "but I thought you might try to kill me."

She turned and glared at him, then her face relaxed. "Oh, by the moons. What have you gotten me into?" She shook her head. Max was surprised to see her smile. "An offworlder …"

She continued prancing up the steps. Max could not keep pace. He wondered how she could move so easily. At the next large shelf, she waited, watching him with puzzlement as he puffed up the steps, straining under the weight of his pack.

"Where's your abacus?" she asked. "Oh, you can't even step-count?"

She shook her head and studied his face. "For someone who is assuming the fate of Abacabax, you have much to learn," she said. "I guess you are my student, now. Take out your reckoning device."

Max removed his abacus, opened the leather cover and cleared the rods.

"You need to count on each step. Count *one* on each aya, those are the small blocks. The next largest, the bayas, are *twos. Three* for the cayas, *four* for the dayas, and *five* for the eayas."

Max paused as he considered the strange names. Aya, baya, caya… the names were the same except for their first letters, which moved through the alphabet. He could think of them like A-blocks, B-blocks, C-blocks, and so on. Curious.

As Mindre pointed out the blocks, Max also noticed how lovely it was that the steps were made from different sized blocks, but all were stacked in such a way that the height from one step to the next was exactly the same. The blocks were arranged in a perfect pattern that repeated, yet changed regularly as the steps ascended.

Mindre stepped on the stairway and demonstrated, "One, two, one, three, one, two, one, four." The count was immediately familiar – it was the same pattern he had entered on his abacus under his grandmother's instructions just before he left his world for this one. Clearly this was something of significance.

He focused on the task at hand, watching Mindre closely. Max noticed that as she moved, her hand rested against her thigh and she moved a different finger each step. Of course, she would step-count with her fingers, he thought.

"Get it?" she asked.

Max smiled. "Yes, I know that pattern! Do I put them on different rods?"

"I don't know, you're the Abacist. I use just one hand to step-count."

He would try only using the first rod, then he could hold the frame with both hands and work the beads on the first rod with his right thumb. He entered a one as he took the first step, slid up a bead to make two with his next step and slid the same bead down to make one again with the next. He slid up two more beads to make a three stepping on the next size block.

The beads kept sliding out of position when he took steps, but he found that by pressing the leather case against the bottom of the abacus, the contact kept the beads from sliding unless he moved them himself. It was a good design choice. Abacists need to be able to reckon while moving, he realized. The leather case was not just for protection, it was so the entire calculation doesn't get erased with one jostle.

The algorithm was confusing at first, he had to concentrate and step at the same time. He tried to slide his thumb up or down far enough at the end of each move to catch the proper number of beads to slide on the next step, so that picking up the right number of beads could happen smoothly with one move. He made mistake after mistake and had to stop and restart several times.

"Mistakes will cost you," she said, "and it costs a little on the six, but you can just change legs as one side gets tired."

"I don't even know what that means," he said evenly, not looking up from his beads.

"Do you feel it?" she asked.

"No, the only thing I feel is my pride getting destroyed." He looked up at her standing many steps above him, his face screwed tight in concentration, and she laughed. He smiled. "I'm glad one of us is having fun."

"Oh! All right, I forgot, there's a thinking component, too. Each count is a block. Try to ... hmm, I haven't thought about how to do this since I was a child! Try to see it. Try to make some kind of picture to help you connect with it. It's a kind of feeling ... oh, I'm not describing this very well."

He reset the rod and started over. *One, two, one, three, one, two, one, four* ... small, big, small, bigger, small, big, small, even bigger ... He tried to relax and feel the pattern in his fingers. That was strange, he thought. He was not having to push himself upwards from one step to the next, it felt more like walking on a flat surface! He continued, past the block matching *five* in his count, repeating, coming to six...

Max had only five beads on the lower rods, not six. He stumbled on the *six* count. He lost concentration and almost lost his footing as well. He stopped on the steps. "I can feel it! It's like the steps aren't even there! I think I'm gonna have some trouble with six, though." He thought working numbers greater than five would be awkward if he were going to keep the count going smoothly and quickly.

"Yes, like I said, six costs you," Mindre called back. "You can just skip the count for a beat and start over, but you need to anticipate the extra effort on that step or you'll trip."

He would need to try it in order to understand exactly what she was talking about. He was now on a size six block, an F-block or a "faya" as he supposed Mindre would call it. The edge stretched out from the wall about eight paces to the right. His first step upwards would of course be one of the small "one" blocks. He reset the rod and began the step-count again.

It went easier this time. Each mistake cost him the "boost," if he missed a number he had to make an upwards step as normal. Each time he reached six in his pattern he slid all of the beads down to zero out the rod. This gave no boost to his step, but it made the pattern easier, which in turn made it easy for him to keep the rhythm.

He continued step after step, quickly getting used to the sequence of moves and how it felt in his thumb. He stumbled less and less frequently and found he could easily anticipate when he would come to the end of the sequence and have to put the effort into stepping.

After ten minutes he asked to stop. "My legs aren't tired, and that's amazing, but my brain is tired trying to keep these two things going at the same time."

Mindre peered down towards Quincunx as Max shook out his hand and did a mental calculation. "It's like walking on a flat surface, with only one step upwards every thirty-two steps!"

Mindre turned back reluctantly from the edge, a longing in her eyes that Max knew was connected to the distant sound of the drums below them. She smiled faintly. "You're getting it now. You're a fast learner. But we've only gone a few hundred steps and we've got a few thousand more to go before the hand closes. You ready?"

Max tried to keep up with her. "What is this about 'the hand closing?'" he asked, trying to not lose his place in the pattern as he spoke.

"Quincunx will go into hiding. They will disappear within the safety of the fist." She held out her hand, palm up and closed it slowly into a fist, as if that explained everything. "They are frightened. We should be, too."

Upwards they went, the way becoming more challenging as it grew darker. Max still made mistakes, but they grew fewer. His thoughts grew emptier as he settled into the rhythm.

It grew darker and darker, making the steps harder to see. The steps were not as empty as they had been before, either. Max needed to dodge more and more stones and roots, and his thumb was getting very tired, the joint aching from the repetitive movements. Many times he stumbled as he stepped on a stone or brushed against a root. He was relieved when Mindre exited the steps.

"This is far enough," she said. "I'd hoped to reach Orion Mesa, but we'll be all right here."

Max followed her from the stairs. They were on the corner of a flat triangular "shelf," the width grew as they walked as if the triangle of land was expanding and inviting them in to safety from the edges. The sides of the triangle were marked by the edge of a cliff to the right and the start of countless stairways to the left, zigging and zagging and splitting apart and joining together again. The grass here was thick, the ground softer than the places they had previously camped. They made camp far from the edge.

"That was absolutely fascinating," he said when they settled down. "I think I'm starting to get it. Thank you."

Mindre smiled. "It's the first dihon – the first of the basic moves that everyone learns. At least in Quincunx."

"I don't know anything. I know I'm more than you bargained for, Mindre," Max said. He found it hard to believe that Mindre could have such a swift change of mood. Yesterday, she could barely tolerate him, and now she seemed almost giddy about embarking on this voyage.

Mindre smiled gently. "Yes, you are indeed. Max, this day has turned out quite different from what I expected. An offworlder? And I am to guide you? Oh, I wouldn't turn down this bargain for the world."

It might be "for the world," he thought to himself. He mentally ran through the events of the past two days – the accident, the earthquake, the prophecy, the crowd of people who were terrified of him.

"Mindre," he said, "I *am* the Hand of Death. Am I going to break the world?"

"You're also the Hand of Life, remember? Max, I don't believe in prophecies. You shouldn't either. We reckon on our living flesh, not on the bones of our ancestors."

102

"Bones?"

"We write our own stories, Max. We decide how they will end."

Max smiled. "I like that. Thanks."

"Let's get to sleep, we have a *very* long trip ahead of us, longer than you can imagine."

"But *shorter than you think possible*," Max added, repeating Lady Carpus' words. "Where is this temple we're going to?"

Mindre chuckled. "It's at the top. It's all the way at the top." She chuckled again. "This will be the most ridiculous thing I've ever done."

In the morning, they examined the packs they'd been given. Aside from the wooden puzzles from Quothmire that Mindre had added, there were some socks and hats, and then quite a bit of food: grain and vegetables rolled in soft leaves, fruit, strips of dried meat, some kind of roots. There were small bags of herbs which Mindre explained were medicines. When Max wondered aloud about the lack of any fire-starting supplies, Mindre merely smiled and wiggled her fingers at him. So that's it – she could reckon fire.

Max found himself in surprisingly good spirits, the best he'd been in since he arrived. He had eaten a good breakfast and the sun was warm. The Darklings were far behind them and adventure lay ahead. They had a plan, or at least half of a plan. He had learned to reckon, at least a little bit, and Mindre even seemed to be willing to tolerate him.

From this distance, Max could see more of the wall they had walked beside all evening, but he was having trouble comprehending how it could exist. A vast, flat wall going straight up and disappearing into the haze of distance. He imagined that this wall, too, was just the side of a giant block, placed in accordance with the pattern governing the position of all of these blocks, from the smallest of the steps on upwards, each size of block doubling and doubling and doubling again.

They took a secondary set of stairs back to the main staircase they followed the night before. Max's fingers seemed to understand step-counting better today, as if his brain had gone on learning while he was asleep. He didn't need to look at his thumb anymore and could take in the beautiful features of the strange landscape.

To the east he could make out another wall and its top edge high, high up, almost invisible in the distance. He imagined that Quothmire could lay at the foot of that block. "So that big cliff, which is that?" he asked as he walked close behind Mindre.

"That's Redcliff," she said. My father went up the other side, he'll take the second-ascension along Verdant Cliff and go straight up to Vertex. It's a pleasant route, the way he's going. Verdant Cliff is the largest, it supports Verdant Mesa which is the largest habitable mesa, second in size only to Water Mesa at the foot of the world. We'll soon be clear of the shade of Redcliff, then things are going to heat up. It will be a hot and uncomfortable walk when we get to the top, I'm afraid."

Max shook his head. There were so many words he didn't understand. "What are 'ascensions'?" he asked.

"The longer routes. There are four main ascensions on Abacabax, each one splitting the points in the center. There are eight second-ascensions, they run up the cliffs of the middle mesas. Verdant Mesa is our middle mesa."

"Do you call them 'descensions' if you're going down?"

She laughed, glancing over her shoulder. "*Descensions?* Max, any fool can *descend* – you don't need a special name for that. The stairs are ascensions, ascending is the hard part."

Max caught the gist of what she was saying. He wondered how many people had unexpectedly taken "the easy way down." He swatted at a fly buzzing by his head, and the thought occurred to him that a distraction as simple as a fly could easily be the catalyst for a quick trip down.

They had been drawing ever closer to the top of the large wall and Mindre kept her pace, eager to reach this milestone. The fly continued to buzz Max, finally settling down on his sleeve. It was a beautiful iridescent blue. "Ooh, pretty little critter – Ouch!" It bit him through his shirt. Max smacked at it. He was too slow. It buzzed away, no longer interested in Max.

Mindre, however, was suddenly interested. Her eyes followed the insect's meandering retreat upwards. "That's a bluefly," she told him. "Where there's blueflies, there's trilliberry trees!"

Mindre jogged up the last few flights to the larger mesa. Max lowered his abacus and ran after her. The sight of soft grass and low trees stretching out forever greeted Max's eyes. Far, far in the distance was a wall at least twice as big as the impossibly tall wall they had been following since yesterday. The ground was moist and spongy with fine grass and some other low leafy foliage Max hadn't seen before. They soon reached a small meadow dotted with trees bearing dark red fruit the size of cherries. The fruit hung in triangular clusters, most in threes, but some larger clumps had six or as many as ten.

"Do you have these where you come from?" she asked. "You're going to love these!"

She offered him a cluster of ten berries. The fruit crunched in his mouth spilling out sweet juice, as if watermelon had been wrapped inside of a cherry. Several delicious moments later they were stretched out on the grass, their fingers and lips stained red.

Max squeezed his calves. They were warm but not tired. Step-counting was amazing. He felt like he could keep going and going. "So we're really going to the top?" he asked.

"Somehow. I don't know how, even if we get horses, it would take months," she told him. "But we should be able to make it to Vertex in a week or two. Maybe my father has found your grandmother, and she can transport us like she did with you. "

"A few *weeks*?" Max thought of walking up and up, day after day, and was very glad for his new step-counting technique. "Just how far is it to the top?"

"Well, this mesa is about a two- to three-hour walk along an edge, and that makes it the same distance to the next larger mesa. That would be Redcliff. From there it's exactly sixteen times as far to Vertex. A long way, plus we'll need to make a pretty big detour to avoid most of the Calculist territory. Vertex is at the midpoint of the faces, and from there it's four times as long to Apex on the very top as it is from here to Vertex."

Max struggled to understand the distance, but his mental calculations didn't make much sense. It had to be a hundred times taller than anything on Earth. How would they be able to breathe as they neared the top? "That's so high! What about the air?" he asked.

"Well, the air does get cold. It gets really cold near the top, but a few people make the pilgrimage every year. It's many weeks of hard travel, maybe months depending on the weather. There's rumors of some strange things up there, up in the clouds."

Max shook his head in wonder. Mindre hadn't understood his question about air getting thinner at higher altitudes. Perhaps it didn't. He supposed that physics must work in a different way here on Abacabax, so perhaps he shouldn't be surprised if there's air at altitudes one hundred times higher than Mt. Everest. On Earth, outer space begins at less than one hundred kilometers. The top of this planet must be five times higher. This was clearly not Earth.

"I've done a lot of traveling but nothing nearly as far as Apex," Mindre mused, her excitement growing. "I wonder ..."

She began counting on her fingers again, perhaps figuring out how long it would take them. If only she could move those fingers and float them to the top, Max wished.

As he watched her move her fingers, he felt the faint movements of the relic in his pocket. It reminded Max of something that had been nagging at him ever since he first learned that people use calculations to do seemingly impossible things. This seemed like a perfect time to ask. "So Mindre," he asked carefully, "you reckon on your fingers, why don't you learn to use stones, also?"

"Not just anyone can use any method, Max. Most folks can only use the method of their bloodline."

He wondered about this. "*Most* folks?" he asked.

"A few people can borrow techniques and expand what we can do, beyond our in-born abilities."

"And you've done that, yes?"

"I've borrowed some techniques."

"So you can reckon with stones, or ... ?"

"No, not *stones*," she said with a trace of indignation. "Better than that. Most Dijins can use only their fingers. That's okay for small things, but there are so many more lines we can use." She placed her thumb at her temple and traced a line down her neck, over her breast and hip and down to her thigh. "I use my whole body."

"So, you're, like, a body reckoner?" he asked.

"Exactly. It's an idea I borrowed from the Calculists. I spent a lot of time with the Calculists once, back when our people were a lot more friendly. I had a ... good friend." Mindre looked towards the open sky beyond the cliff edge, her mouth pulling into a tight smile as her eyes spoke of something lost.

"Your father said you were the best reckoner in these parts," Max said.

"Did he say that? Well, you know how parents are."

Max reached into his pocket and removed the leather-wrapped abacus. He traced his finger down a rod, thinking of the lines Mindre spoke of. "So, if you reckon on these lines on your body, and the lines are like the rods on my abacus, I bet you could teach me how to use this thing."

"I can help you with the dihon, the basic strengths, like step-counting. But I cannot teach you full reckoning, body to body, mind to mind. Among my people we do not share the inner thought-paths, except with ... well, it is a very intimate thing." Her face reddened slightly. "It's not something you and I can share. I don't think you'd understand."

Mindre's eyes dropped from his face to his chest, thoughts flickering beneath the reflections on the surface of her eyes. Looking up she said, "Besides, it will takes years of experience until you can reckon well."

"Okay," he said slowly, wondering about this 'intimate thing.' "Maybe you could just give me some tips? We don't need to kiss or anything," he prompted.

Her eyes sprang open in surprise, then she laughed. "Okay, yes, we can start with the dihon. But this doesn't mean that you and I are bound to one another, okay?"

"Yeah, of course not, sure," Max said. He cleared his abacus. "What can I try first?"

Mindre gently motioned for him to lower his abacus. "Let's talk about the energy of reckoning first," she said.

"Performing a calculation gathers energy. You can use that energy to apply a force, and that force can take many forms. You just shape it in your mind with the proper image, like creating artwork. You can push, you can strike, you can squeeze, you can lift. You can cool things or heat things – which you've already learned. Did your grandmother show you that, by the way?"

"Oh, that," Max said, remembering when was playing with his abacus by the river and created a circle of heat around himself. "No, no one showed me, I did that by accident!"

"By accident ... ?" she shook her head. "Warmth is one of the basic reckonings, but I've never heard of anyone learning it 'by accident.' And the amount of warmth you created – few can bring forth that much energy with a dihon. I don't know, Max, maybe you got very lucky. But if you can remember the feeling, that can be helpful.

"Some people can do other things, too, but you will need to find your own talents. The best reckoning happens when your picture-thought matches your calculating. I say 'picture' but it doesn't have to be to a picture, it can be a sensation or an emotion or, well, you'll find what works for you. The more complicated your calculation is and the more confident you are in the result, the stronger the effect. But you won't get any effect if you miscalculate, and it can even turn back on you if you doubt your calculation, so it's better to keep it simple, okay?"

"I think I understand," Max said. He thought of step-counting, how he pictured the blocks matching with the numbers by size. And the morning by the river, when he had been imagining the friction of the beads making warmth. And his first reckoning back in the kitchen where he could see a tunnel of wind carrying him upwards. He knew he could make "thought-pictures." He had, after all, spent most of his days in school visualizing, though his teachers had called it "daydreaming."

Mindre glanced around and reached into the grass to retrieve a small stone. She gently flattened a small patch of grass between them and set the stone on top. "Addittrix," she said. "or ... 'summaries' I think you say?"

"Just 'sums,' or 'addition,' but yeah," Max said.

"These can be used to push. Like this." She held out both hands and they took on shapes, her left thumb lightly touching the pad of her middle finger, her right thumb touching her pinky. The fingers on both her hands moved to different positions as she swept her hands toward the stone. Her wrists bent slightly upwards in a graceful sweeping motion as if she were lightly brushing away dust.

The stone rolled over away from her, turning over two or three times and rocking to a stop. Max grinned. It looked so effortless. "That's amazing!" he said. "Okay, what numbers should I try?"

Mindre cocked her head, tightlipped, and shrugged her shoulders.

Okay, he thought. It's a small stone, he'd use a small number. He put thirty-two on the first two rods. Then I'll push it with a nice gentle *plus sixteen,* half as much again. He pictured tipping the front of the stone upwards and tossed the idea towards the stone. The air tightened around his head ... and the stone flipped over.

Max turned to Mindre, his mouth open. "It worked! Just like I pictured it! It just ... worked!"

Mindre stared back at him. "You've *never* done this before?"

"My first sum!" He would try again right away. He excitedly cleared his abacus and entered the same numbers again. He thought of the stone flipping again as he performed the simple calculation and tossed out the result. This time the stone only wiggled slightly.

"It didn't work that time," he said. He cleared and redid the sum. No movement at all. "It stopped working."

"Are you doing the same thing?"

"Yes, exactly the same."

"That's why it's not working. Your image is spent. You have to use different numbers *and* use a different image."

"Okay." Max set up a bigger number and doubled it, picturing himself giving the stone a hard whack. The stone merely flipped over this time.

"Well, that sort of worked. But I pictured it a lot harder. I used a seventy-four and then I added ..."

"Max! Please don't do that that. Don't ... share that with me, I mean." Mindre looked flustered. "Your thoughts, those parts ... they're private."

She stood up awkwardly. "You keep practicing," she said. "I'm going to, uh, fill our flasks." She spun around and walked off quickly.

Did I say something wrong? he wondered. Was explaining your thinking some kind of cultural taboo? Something you can only do if you are on an "intimate" basis with someone? So, thoughts were the "private parts," and yet Mindre had no problem stripping off her clothing in front of him as she did on their first night. Dijins were a different kind of people, that was for sure.

Max practiced more. He found that since he had first connected the idea that the stone was small, he needed to start with a small number and he could give it a bigger kick by adding a bigger number. He pictured different ways to push a stone and got it to move every single time. He was giddy with the exercise – it was like playing with a remote control, except he could use the controller on anything, not just a toy racecar.

What about subtracting? He tried the operation while picturing pulling the stone instead and yes! He could draw the stone towards him. He ran through several different ways he could think about moving the stone physically – a backwards push, decreasing the distance, sucking it towards him – and attached these images to his numbers. Each time it worked beautifully.

From the corner of his eye he saw Mindre approach and stop a short distance off. He pretended not to notice her as he started a demonstration of what he had learned. Clicking through a series of four calculations, he sent the stone rolling around in a square, forwards, to the left, backwards, and to the right. He hesitated on his final calculation, distracted by the thought of landing the stone exactly in its starting place, and missed by a little.

He smiled to her. "I can do it! This is really fun! You're a great teacher!"

She didn't return the smile. She stared at him. "What are you?" she whispered slowly.

Max furrowed his brow. "What?"

She shook her head. "Let's go, you can practice more when we reach Sier Mesa."

They walked the entire afternoon, not talking much. Mindre seemed annoyed with him and Max wasn't sure why. At least his step-counting algorithm had become automatic, he didn't even need to think about it anymore. Within an hour, however, his thumb had gotten very sore and he decided he needed to switch hands. The leftmost rod on his abacus was missing a bead, and he didn't want to do anything on that rod, which meant he had to rotate his abacus one-hundred eighty degrees and relearn the movements upside-down and with his left thumb. It was frustrating to learn it all over again. Max was slow and Mindre did not wait for him. She got far ahead and disappeared into the distance.

Max trudged upwards, the impossible wall growing closer. The mesas were getting smaller, and he wondered what he would see at the top of the cliff they had been following.

As he passed the edge of a mesa, the air grow tight about his head and his heart jumped. Reckoning! He looked around quickly, and felt a shove. It was Mindre, standing in the distance near her pack in the scrub. He walked back down a few steps to the mesa and headed across flat ground towards her.

"Did you get lost?" she said.

"My thumb got worn out working the beads," he explained, watching her expression carefully. "I guess I don't have it *all figured out*, yet."

She smiled slightly. "We've climbed enough for today," she said.

They ate wet vegetables rolled in leaves with earthy spices for dinner. Max liked these very much.

"I want to try something, Max. You've mastered the dihon in one day, which is unprecedented, but I still don't feel any awareness from you when I reach out. Maybe it's because you are an offworlder and things are different with you. Shall we try sparring? I'd like to see if you can do it."

"Yeah, definitely!" he said taking out his abacus.

"Okay, show me what you've got." She stood with her hands hanging by her sides, right hip tilted upward, pointing at him with her chin.

"Hmm ..." Max thought. What did he have? A push and a pull, of course.

He set up a number on the rods, *fifty-five*, he entered guessing her weight in kilograms. He added *thirty-six*, made an exchange on the rods, and imagined pushing her backwards.

Nothing happened.

"Have you started?" Mindre asked.

He tried bigger numbers in the hundreds, felt the air tighten, sent out an image, and ... nothing. Mindre cocked her head.

"It's not working," he said. He cleared the rods and tried a sum in the thousands. Nothing. Ten thousands. Nothing again.

"You're not reaching me at all," Mindre said. "Can you feel this?" she began moving her fingers.

Max waited to feel something.

She stopped moving her fingers. "No?"

"What am I supposed to feel?"

She didn't answer. She made patterns on her fingers instead, Max watching with interest. She stopped and raised her eyebrows.

"No, nothing."

"Hmm. That's what I was afraid of," she said. "No connection."

Max felt a pang of disappointment. He was beginning to think he was something special.

"But you can feel this?" This time she moved the fingers on both hands at the same time. Max felt the air tighten, shapes flashing before his eyes. He was shoved backwards.

"I felt that!" he said.

"If you haven't awakened, you can't reckon on a living creature and you can't defend yourself either. It may just take some time. Reckoning body to body, mind to mind, requires that you are awake to the energies of life and thought. Lady Carpus told me your awakening is at hand, so let's just wait and see what happens."

The rest of the evening Max honed his skill with pushing and pulling and experimented with multiplication and division. Multiplication could be used as a strike, which he could use to knock branches off of a tree. Division could pull things apart, like to pluck leaves from a branch for example. He found that by alternating between multiplication and division with the same numbers and visualizing a sawing motion, he could cut through wood. It seemed like anything was possible!

Instead of being excited about all of his advances, Mindre seemed more and more worried. She found other tasks to busy herself with.

After dark, they lay near each other beneath their own blankets staring up at the milky night sky.

"You have so many more stars than we do," Max said. "I guess it's just that we have a lot of lights on at night. You put a million people in one place and it kind of ruins things."

"You have that many people on your world?" Mindre asked in awe. "They must burn many fires at night, huh?"

Max didn't bother to explain that they have way more than a million people on his world. "We mostly use artificial fires called 'electricity,'" he said. "It's like lightning, so we can make lights without fire. There's a lot of them. You have to go far away from the cities to see stars like this."

"Such an amazing world. I should like to see it sometime."

"Maybe you can. My grandmother knows how." Max ran his fingers along the knots on his bracelet as he thought about his grandmother. Where could she be? If she was here, and as powerful as Roggolo seems to think, shouldn't she be able to find him with some kind of radar? Or didn't things work that way? Max had no idea. Lady Carpus did say his grandmother was coming but was out of reach right now. That, at least, gave him hope.

"Brianna is born tonight. A good omen," Mindre said dreamily.

Max waited for her to say more.

She raised her hand and pointed to the moon. "The two moons are the daughters of Kael. The first moon is called 'Annia,' but she is not out tonight. This moon is called 'Bella,' she is the second daughter of Kael. Bella has two daughters herself, Brianna and Bellabara. You can see Bellabara just to the right, well, your left, and on the other side, right next to it is Brianna. She's just coming into view. We say she is being birthed this evening.

"When Brianna was born, Kael was so pleased he created Abacabax in her honor. Arianna, the first daughter of Annia, was so envious that she convinced Za, the sun goddess, to never shine on one side of Abacabax so that the gift would be imperfect. That's why we have the Darklands.

"To this day, people claim that the moon you were born under determines your fate. I was born under Brianna, the first of the second, which is supposed to mean I'm both a leader and a rebel."

"I can see that. It fits with you well! I was born under the star sign Capricorn. That's a goat."

"What does that mean?"

"It means I was born in January."

Mindre thought about this. "Where is 'January?'"

Max realized jokes were going to be very difficult. "Okay, I think it's supposed to mean I'm stubborn, but that doesn't really match my personality."

"If it's a goat, maybe it means you're going to climb a mountain soon."

Max smiled. Maybe jokes were going to be okay.

On the following day's trek Mindre told Max they were getting near the top of the cliff wall they had been following. The steps grew wet and slippery. They passed ponds and bogs. Moss hung over the edges of the blocks like botanical waterfalls that had given up flowing and succumbed to sloth.

"There's a freshwater lake up there on the edge of Parchensis desert we should reach this afternoon," Mindre said. "Pickaxe is on the intersection of all of these ascensions, a short distance away. That's a Calculist waypoint we want to avoid. It's not easy to avoid places on the intersections, but I know an alternate route. We're getting close."

The steps weren't just wetter, they were covered with stones and shards of stones, making climbing treacherous. Max's step-counting was useless now, he needed both hands to clamber over larger stones and cling to the safety of the wall beside them.

"Where did all of these stones come from?" he asked.

"Pieces of Verdant Cliff fall off all the time. They hit pretty hard after falling for an hour or more."

Max nervously eyed the wall rising into the sky just east of them. Rocks falling for an hour, or more? At least death would be quick.

"Here it is!" To the left stood a long narrow opening in the rock. Mindre peered inside. "Do you know what this is?"

"A cave?"

"No. I thought you might know, being the Stonebreaker and all," she smiled wryly. "They say this is from the first time the Hand of Death struck the faces and tried to break Abacabax in two." She shrugged. "Or maybe it was just a shelf-quake."

She climbed inside, Max followed. The crack in the wall extended long above them. After a few steps, the floor sloped sharply upwards and it grew dark in the deep shadows.

When it was almost too dark, Mindre paused. A few seconds later, the walls around her began to glow, a soft white light that seemed to come from nowhere. "That's better," she said. "Reckoning forth light is not a dihon, you'll need to find that one yourself."

In the glow they could see a series of rungs, wooden poles set into both sides of the walls. "This is an old Bone-Thrower passage. They used to live all over this area and dug all kinds of tunnels. The Bone-Throwers are gone now, but you can still find some of their artifacts."

The rungs were largely intact, mossy to the touch but easy to grip. In places a rung or two was missing, and Max had to sometimes hold a higher rung and push off the slick wall with his feet to get up. The glowing light followed Mindre but offered enough luminosity for him to see.

"My father took me up this once years ago," Mindre said. "It was in better shape back then, but it was still a long climb for a little girl."

"It's a long climb for anyone," Max said. "I think I need to rest."

"There's a cave we can stop in. It's not much further."

They went up and up, what had once been easy climbing, now was one grueling effort after another. Finally he heard Mindre above him say, "Here it is!"

They climbed into an opening to the side. The shape of the cave appeared natural, but blocks had been carved into the stone to create benches on both sides. They sat down heavily. Max marveled at the sight of Mindre, glowing a soft white in the darkness like a ghost.

"Where does that go?" Max asked, nodding towards a passage at the back of the cave.

"Dead end," Mindre said. "There's probably some bats in there if you want to go look."

"That's okay." Max stretched back his shoulders, not interested in exploring more than necessary. He had never climbed a ladder so high, and there was more to come. "Who are these Bone-Throwers?"

"The second family," she said. "First were the Dijins, then the Bone-Throwers, then Calculists, then Abacists. Bone-Throwers, as you might guess, reckon on bones."

"Weird," Max said. "What kind of bones?"

"Human bones."

"Oh. You mean, like ..."

"They're cannibals," she said.

"Seriously? And we're in their tunnel?"

"No one sees them anymore. My father tried for years to find them in Parchensis, which is where we're heading now. Never found a single one. Maybe they all ate each other."

Max leaned back and stretched out his legs, bumping something on the floor with his foot. He bent over to see what it was. "Well," he said, kicking a small skull towards Mindre. "They left some of their bones behind."

"That's a young jackal skull," Mindre said. "Jackals can't climb ladders." Shadows grew long on Mindre's face in the soft glow of her reckoning. "Listen ..."

Something was shuffling in the passage at the back of the cave. Several somethings.

Mindre and Max quickly and quietly got to their feet. She swung her hands in small loops, touching her body in different places and tossed her hands forward. The faint glow from around her brightened and flowed down the walls, riding the bumps of the rough surface. At the entrance to the passage, two black hairy forms crouched. They hissed at being discovered. Sharp teeth in the open maws of angry cat-like faces glinted in the light. Before Max could register what they were, they pounced.

They sprung forward so quickly, Mindre barely had time to reckon. Max stumbled backwards towards the crevice, claws upon him. Pain burned through his belly as the black beast ripped at his gut. Suddenly the beast was pulled away from him, thrown to the wall where it struck with a cracking noise. It fell to the floor with a thud, lying still. Mindre stood deep in a stance, her back leg bent so her knee nearly touched the floor, hands held forward. The other cat lay motionless at her feet.

"Max, let me see." She was kneeling beside him, unfastening his shirt.

He helped her pull open his shirt, two long vertical gashes bled freely. She took ahold of his hand and forced it onto the cuts. Max winced.

"Press. Keep pressing." Mindre went to her pack and returned with a flask and small bag.

She poured water on the cuts to wash them, then pulled out dried weeds from the bag and rubbed them briskly together between her palms. Flakes of the plant matter fell freely onto his skin where they clumped together with his blood. She packed the rest around the cuts, then slid backwards and began moving her fingers rapidly. "This might hurt," she warned.

The wound felt very warm and the shooting pain from his torn skin rapidly changed to burning. Max clenched his fists together and dared the burn to get worse. Regrettably, it did. Whiffs of smoke rose from the weeds.

Mindre stopped. The intense burning sensation died down to a dull throb. She poured more water on him, carefully brushing away the weeds. "Looks all right," she said. "Good thing they didn't get your tubes. How's it feel?"

Max breathed in, feeling the skin stretch. "It hurts."

"Yes, it will for a while, but you'll be okay."

He carefully touched it. The skin was closed together in two long ridges, and there was no feeling in these lines. The skin around them was an angry red. All the bleeding had stopped. Max had never seen a wound closed so quickly. "Thank you," he said. "You were really fast."

"Not fast enough," she said frowning. She stood and surveyed the dead animals. "Shelf cats. I've run into these before but not this close." She dragged the bodies next to each other, turning them so their heads were together. She then placed her hands on top of their heads and sat silent a moment.

"I don't like to kill," Mindre said sadly.

"You had to."

"No, I didn't. I lost myself."

They sat for several minutes in silence until Mindre asked him if he thought he could continue climbing. His wound stung, but he felt brave enough to tough it out.

They climbed for another half hour, his side aching with every rung, before light began shining from above.

Max pulled himself from the crevice, his eyes stinging in the bright light. After following along the side of the cliff for days, they now stood on the top in the sun. Max marveled at the wonders in every direction.

Ahead of them a sparkling lake of clear water stretched in both directions. The edge of Verdant Cliff to the right was swirled in mist from a river pouring from the mouth of a massive cavern, feeding the lake. The lake in turn tumbled over the edge down the steps by the cliff. It became a fractured river bouncing and cascading through gorges filled with claws of jagged rock as it divided into rivulets and ponds on the triangles of land beneath them. These small rivers again joined together to make wider rivers and falls.

"That's the head of the Isigon River," Mindre explained. "It's carved away at this ascension and goes straight down to Quincunx. Don't fall in or you'll be right back where we started."

Max winced at the thought. If someone were to fall in there, they'd be rushed downstream so quickly they'd have little chance of getting out. With all the sharp points and edges along the way ... it would surely be another quick way to die.

She pointed to a spot above the lake up from the cavern. Max could make out terraces of tiny buildings. "That's Pickaxe. We won't be going there."

Max pointed at the cavern where the water fell from the cliff wall. "Where does all this water come from?"

"All the way from the Verdant Mesa," she said pointing up.

Max's eyes followed Verdant Cliff straight upward to where it disappeared from view. Standing so close to the cliff like this made it appear all the more impossible.

"It pours into the crevices on the distal plains of that mesa and comes out at several points. Some of the water flows out on the other side of Verdant Cliff, so high that the waterfalls turn into clouds before they reach the bottom. That's why the eastern face of Verdant Cliff is so green. On this side, this is one of the few places it comes out."

"It's beautiful, like the Grand Canyon and Niagara Falls put together," Max said. As an afterthought he added, "Those are places on Earth."

Mindre pointed back towards the desert. "We'll be heading into one of the driest stretches on these faces. We'll camp on the end of the lake tonight over there. Let me see your wound."

Max lifted his shirt. The skin was raised along the pink swollen lines. Mindre stepped forward and placed her palm gently over the lines, warm against his skin, a warmth spreading unexpectedly to other places in his body.

Mindre squinted into his eyes. "I failed you, Max."

"Mindre, you saved me from –"

She cut him off. "No, I failed you. I am tasked with assuming your fate. We will surely be facing greater dangers. I will try to not fail you again. You will find your connection that you may awaken, before we meet real trouble, I hope."

-:- | -:-

Samuel stood in the courtyard with his pad. It was like a home-made clipboard, a stack of thick paper fastened with a string through two holes to a thin wooden backing. His pencil, too, was home-made, a stick of charcoal covered with hard wax. Saul called it a "scribing stick," a name Sam found rather funny. Though the paper was a little bit too rough and the scribing stick a little bit too thin and waxy, the set-up worked just fine for scratching out numbers. Saul sat on a bench nearby, leaning back against the courtyard wall and watching impatiently as Samuel tried to reckon.

Two-hundred seventeen plus eighty-five, Samuel wrote. He added up each column as he thought about what he wanted the creature in the courtyard to do. "C'mon, spin in a circle," he whispered to himself. The creature began to turn. "Yes, that's it!" Samuel said. It turned only far enough to look at him, then reached up and scratched the back of its head.

"Feel a connection, Samuel," Saul prompted. "You should be able to just ... reach in and make it move how you like."

"I don't know what I'm supposed to be feeling," Samuel complained. "Can't we go back to levitating stones? That is so much more fun."

Saul squeezed his temples together. "Let's take a break, Samuel. Come on, I need to show you something."

Samuel tossed his pad down on a table and began following him. Saul stopped. "Take that with you. Always have your weapons at the ready."

Samuel sighed and picked up the materials, trudging after Saul.

"We haven't a lot of time, Samuel. The Calculists could come any day, but that's not the most important thing. I need your power for something else."

They reached the top of the stairway, turned a corner and headed to Saul's quarters. Samuel had never been invited in before. They entered an airy room. One wall was full of shelves filled with books, wooden geometric shapes, cups with bundles of sticks poking from the top, folded paper forms and a miscellany of odd artifacts. A table held a stack of small cubical blocks, a saw and hand drill. From the ceiling hung sculptures of wooden sticks and string that hung together in a way that seemed to defy gravity.

"Some of my inventions," Saul said. "I'll teach you sometime. Come in here."

Samuel followed him through a door. This was Saul's bedroom. Saul's bed was twice the size as the one in his bedroom down the hall, the blanket pulled up in an untidy bunch. What caught Samuel's attention right away, though, was the large cage in the corner of the room. One of the creatures was inside.

Saul walked to the cage, motioning Samuel to follow. Saul sat in a chair beside the cage. The creature pressed its face against the bars, turning its head up to Saul and hissing quietly.

Samuel watched in sick fascination as Saul reached through the bars and stroked its cheek. "There, there, I'm back," he said. "This is Lydala."

"Is he your ... pet?" Samuel asked.

"No, no. It's a *she*. This is my wife."

Saul looked up at Samuel as he continued to stroke the burnt skin of the creature in the cage. Samuel pulled back his jaw in disgust. Saul, noticing his discomfort, spoke quickly.

"She was once beautiful, the love of my life. And she will be again, Samuel, together we can – ouch!" He jerked his hand away, the creature snapping at his fingers. Its mouth hinged open and it began howling, banging its head against the bars. Saul quickly pulled out his abacus and slid a few beads. The creature calmed down right away and Saul went back to stroking its face. "Shhh ... shhh ..." he whispered.

"I've tried everything to bring her back," Saul said. "I've learned to reach their minds and control them. I can even control some humans as well, which has proven to be very useful at times I assure you! But the reckoning that created her is countless times more powerful than the abacus. That's why I need you, Samuel. Your scribing can be as powerful as these calculating devices you use on Earth. With it we may be able to bring her back. We may be able to bring them all back!"

He withdrew his hand and turned in the chair to face Samuel. "But you need to master reckoning. You've got the most powerful reckoning tool in the world and you're the only one who can use it. I need you to work harder!"

Chapter 6: Bone-Throwers

It was a relief to be on flat land and be able to move without having to slide beads or climb mossy rungs. Max took this as a small consolation, given Mindre's present mood. She was angry once again. He was supposed to be some kind of great reckoner, but he could not defend himself, leaving her with the responsibility. Perhaps also she blamed herself for not being able to help him get this connection he needed in order to fully reckon. It didn't seem to matter to her that she had taught him so much already and then saved him not only from the cats but also from bleeding to death afterwards. In fact, her quick first aid had sealed his skin more securely than any stitches. Adding to her troubles, he assumed, was the fact that they were now heading into a desert that she said was once inhabited by cannibals. Even though she claimed it was now devoid of life, he knew she wasn't so sure. What could he say?

Max decided he should try to get her thinking about something else. "What was it like growing up in Quincunx?" he asked.

Mindre shrugged. "I lived with my aunt until I was seven and then I went traveling with my father."

"What about you mother?" he asked.

"I don't know too much about her. She was ... well, she was a Calculist," Mindre said, "and that, I'm afraid, is something that just isn't acceptable to anyone. Except for my parents, perhaps. She couldn't keep me, of course, so my father took me to Quincunx to be with my aunt."

"Quincunx closed the fist during the Abacist Plague. I was three at the time. When it opened again I was seven and that's when I started traveling with my father. He tried to find her again, but she was dead. So that's the story. I don't know much about her at all and it doesn't really matter."

"I'm sorry to hear that," Max said.

"If I had a mother I wouldn't have gotten to travel. Father and I saw some amazing things and some pretty horrible things too, I guess. We saw a lot of different kinds of reckoning and that inspired us to learn even more."

She smiled. "My father is very social. He made a lot of friends and became an ambassador of sorts. He thought he could make peace between the tribes. We met your grandmother several times. I like her. All of the other Abacists were far up above Tangram, but she can move like the wind. 'Wendi Longwalker,' they call her. They said she could travel the length of Abacabax from Water Mesa to Apex in a single day. I'd believe it. She carried messages and would find rare medicines from places no one else could go. The Council of the Whole named her as Protectress after the war, which was pretty significant, given how unpopular Abacists were and all."

"But you haven't been back to Quincunx? Your father was exiled?" Max asked.

"My father has never felt bound by tradition. I guess you could say he broke one too many rules. We lived in Vertex after that and made a lot of trips down to Quothmire, until the troubles began last winter."

"What troubles?"

"That Tangram massacre, of course. Vertex went into lockdown, afraid that Saul could infect minds. Luckily, my father and I are ambassadors and could still travel in and out."

"Massacre?" Max asked. "What happened?"

"Oh, by the Corners, you don't know of that, either? I guess you wouldn't. Saul entered Tangram, slipped inside in the middle of the night and killed every single person over the course of two days. Over five hundred people."

"What?!"

"Yes. He used to be one of the most respected reckoners on all the faces, but the man has become a monster. Vertex is going to war with him, they've only been waiting for the winter winds to subside to begin the march. Their general has a new kind of reckoning that is probably going to raze Tangram to the ground."

Max thought of Samuel. What was worse, being under the power of Saul the murderer, or being in Tangram when it was about to be leveled with a military strike?

"My brother's with Saul," Max said. "They're probably in Tangram right now. We've got to try to get him out."

"First, we get to Vertex and find Lady Teller. We have allies there who can help. If your brother's with Saul, there's nothing we can do about that. Tangram is surrounded by Darklings and Saul is more powerful than anyone ever imagined. This war will not end well for anyone."

They walked in silence for a while. His plan to cheer her up by getting her to talk about something else didn't work as he hoped. Now he was nervous, too. He felt his side where his wound was. It was sore but remarkably good. He thought better of complimenting her healing abilities again.

"All these travels you've made," Max said, "do you ever get lost?"

"Lost? How could you get lost?" she said. "Over there is a P-mesa, so the next larger ones are the Q-mesas, the smaller ones on each side of the P-mesa are O's, those between are the N's and so on. The letter in the name is just the size, in the same pattern as these smaller ayas and bayas we step on so often. So, you just have to make a quick count and you know exactly where you are.

Max eyed the colossal sizes of these cliffs. The A-blocks, or *ayas*, were small enough to step on comfortably. The B-blocks, or *bayas*, twice the size, and so on ... was it really possible that in so few doublings they could be so large that by the time you reached a *paya*, the sixteenth largest block, the size was as tall as the tallest mountains on Earth?

"What about your world?" Mindre asked. "Is it easy to find your way?"

"Oh, not at all. Not like this, at least. We have to put up a lot of signs and if you're going far you need a map. It's really easy to get lost."

"A landscape without form. That must be so amazing."

"It is beautiful, in places. We have huge flat areas with green grass or yellow grains, and hilly areas with rivers and ponds, and deserts and forests like you do. We have a lot of mountains in my part of the world, but they're nothing like this." Max indicated the endless mountain of steps rising like a jagged wall in the distance. "Ours are at different angles and are different sizes, and they stand alone or in groups and don't go *nearly* as high as yours. They're also worn down by the weather, I don't understand how all of these steps haven't washed away, or how these cliffs can be so tall without collapsing."

Max shook his head, wondering what kind of forces could hold this planet in such an ordered shape. "My world is so random," he said. "I never thought about how chaotic it is until I saw this. These rocks, these shelves, these mesas, all the patterns! Fantastic!"

"Are you kidding?" Mindre countered. "It's the same everywhere. If it weren't for the landscape, it would be entirely repetitive. Even the smallest steps could just as easily be a model for a village or for Quincunx or for the entire face. Your world sounds much more interesting."

They had walked to the western end of the lake and turned to follow the shore towards the mountain. Sprouts of grass and weeds poked through the dry earth as they neared the lake. They came to the top of a rise that sloped down to a sandy beach and the lake's edge. The late afternoon sun sparkled on the hints of ripples on its surface.

"We'll camp here tonight. Water will be harder to come by tomorrow." She grinned at him. "Last chance to go swimming before the desert. I'll race you!"

"Swimming? That water's got to be really cold ..."

He suddenly noticed Mindre already had her boots off and was unlacing her dress as she darted toward the lake.

"Oh, all right!" he yelled. He kicked off his boots and pulled off his shirt as he bounded after her, catching a glimpse of her bare white back as she dove into the sparkling water and disappeared beneath the surface.

She came up shrieking from the cold as Max was tripping over his pants. So much for modesty, he thought, as he clumsily stumbled towards the edge. Mindre laughed as he tumbled in on his side.

The cold bit into him painfully. He tried to stand and fell in again. Giving up on standing, he jumped towards deeper water so he could paddle his arms and kick his legs in a desperate attempt to generate body heat. "Oh! Oh! Oh! It's cold!"

"It's wonderful!" Mindre called. "You'll get used to it!"

"You don't get used to this temperature," he gasped, "you just hope you get numb fast enough that you can't tell the difference! Oh! This is what ice feels like just before it melts!"

Max swam out, keeping his head above water and moving his arms furiously to try to keep warm. It was exhilarating and it felt good to be clean again. The cold also felt good on the skin where Mindre had burned him back together.

He swam in her direction, out into deeper water. Mindre dove down and swam underwater towards him, farther than Max thought possible. He watched her swim beneath him and surface close by on the other side.

"Getting used to it yet?" she asked.

"N-No," Max stammered. If anything, it was feeling colder.

"Need some warming up?" she offered with a grin.

"What?" Max said, suddenly nervous about what she was offering.

She laughed and began reckoning with her fingers. Max felt a tingling, then a warmth all around his body. The water was still cool, but the cold had lost its edge. "Oh, that's great," Max said, "It must be nice to always have your abacus in your fingers."

"Yeah, it's too bad for you that you're not a Dijin!" she dove under the water and swam away. Max felt the cold again immediately.

They swam for a few more minutes, then Max walked ashore, skimming water off his body with his hands. He didn't worry this time about being naked in front of Mindre. After all, she thought it was only natural. If she liked going around naked, Max didn't think he'd mind so much. Still, when she walked out a couple of minutes later smiling broadly at him, he tried to avoid looking at her. A little bit, at least.

They set up camp on the sparse grass at the top of the rise over the beach, where a few low trees gave them a feeling of security. Max had not put his boots back on when he dressed, enjoying the feel of sand beneath his toes. He filled their jugs from the lake while Mindre gathered driftwood for a fire. The water from the lake was the freshest and coldest Max had ever tasted. Filtered through unimaginably many layers of rock and sand, it must have been cleaner than anything on Earth.

Mindre sparked the fire into life with a long pattern of finger movements. Her dress hung from a tree branch. She seemed content to wear only her light tunic in the warm evening air. Max sank down contentedly next to her on the blanket. "This has been quite a day," he said.

"Tomorrow will be hot. Our goal is the corner of Tapper Cliff, halfway across this mesa. We should leave at dawn so we can stop in the hottest part of the day and continue in the evening. It will be about nine hours walking, much longer than I want but necessary. I hope you're up for it."

"It's a nice change, not having to reckon every step of the way," Max said.

Max picked up his abacus and entered a number. Eyeing the stack of driftwood Mindre had gathered for the fire, he clicked up a sum and sent a piece of wood rolling from the pile into the campfire. He smiled at Mindre.

"Keep practicing," she encouraged him. "And keep ... searching for a connection."

Max cued up another number and did a quick series of calculations. Another stick stood on end, the top wobbling in an ellipse like a top trying to fall over. "I don't know how you can resist not doing this all day long!" he said.

"Most people use their reckoning sparingly," she explained. "It can be difficult to come up with new images all the time."

"Really? I can think of about fifty ways to make this stick spin ... and probably another fifty when that's used up."

"You have a powerful imagination, Maxwell. That is a great strength, awakening or no awakening."

"I wish I could feel the things you do."

"I've been thinking about it, Max. Maybe it's your abacus. Reckoners have a strong connection to their tools and yours is broken. Maybe you'll awaken when we get it repaired and then you can experience full reckoning."

"I hope so. But I've been thinking of what I could do in the meantime. Watch this." Max stood, took three sticks from the firewood pile and arranged them standing up in a tripod. He walked away ten paces, found a fist-sized stone and picked it up and showed it to Mindre. He tossed it on the ground at his feet and then turned to face the tripod.

Pointing at the tripod, he said, "Hungry shelf cat. *Scissors.*" Pointing at himself, he said, "Me. *Paper.*" Pointing at his feet he said, "*Rock.*"

Mindre regarded him quizzically, trying to make sense of his words. Max just smiled. Pulling up his abacus he flicked and pinched numbers. Like lightning, he flipped through a three-digit by two-digit multiplication and flung the result with the sharpest image he could imagine.

The stone launched from his feet and whizzed through the air, striking the tripod with a crack. The sticks scattered in three directions.

"Stone beats scissors," Max announced.

"Max, that was ... you can use that!" she said enthusiastically. "The speed of that rock ... impressive!"

"Maybe I don't need *full* reckoning to be of some use."

"You continue to surprise me," she said.

They settled down early and rose just before dawn, packing quickly. Max was reluctant to leave this place he had enjoyed so much, but Mindre was eager to start while it was still cool.

The scenery changed dramatically from that which he saw during their days ascending. Now they walked below the steps instead of on the steps, over hard-packed reddish-brown sand. The sand was littered with cubical boulders both large and small, as if a fleet of giant cargo planes had dropped their payloads haphazardly in the desert. Clinging near the shady side of the stones grew spiny leafed plants with thick gnarled stems. The sun shimmered off the stones up the face of the mountain. Though it looked mostly dry and lifeless, the dusty faces were dotted with patches of green and blue vegetation.

"What are the green spots?" Max asked Mindre.

"My father and I wondered about that too," Mindre explained. "There's underground rivers in different places, as if the water decided to just skip this part of Abacabax and go right underneath it. Some of it makes it to the surface, though, and it's easy to tell where it is. My father spent most of his time searching those areas, thinking the Bone-Throwers would be nearby. We didn't find them but we'd best to steer clear of those now, just in case."

Throughout the morning's walk, Max felt a pricking on the back of his neck, a feeling like someone was watching. Was it just his "powerful imagination" as Mindre had said earlier, spooking him in this hostile terrain, or was he picking up on some kind of subliminal clues from the environment? Mindre was not relaxed like she was the evening before, either. Her tenseness made Max even more uncomfortable.

As they skirted the edge of a cluster of boulders as tall as Max, Mindre spun suddenly on her heel, calling forth strange energy from her fingers, searching for a target in the rocks. Whatever she had thought she'd seen was gone. She lowered her hands slowly and walked on, quietly asking Max to ready his abacus.

He slid it out of his pocket and opened the case. His stomach felt tight, it was the kind of feeling he had years ago when his family was in the basement waiting for a tornado. It was a feeling of both dreading and hoping that nothing would happen but also secretly dreading and hoping that something would.

He rehearsed moves in his head, keeping his eyes on stones he could fling. Would he be able to call forth the energy in an actual confrontation? Practicing with sticks was one thing, but could he remain as calm as Mindre does in a fight? He mentally mapped and remapped escape routes as he walked, in case fight turned into flight. He wondered if he could operate the abacus while walking or running. The leather on the back of his abacus kept the beads from sliding out of position, but how well would it hold if he were running? He cursed himself for not thinking of practicing while running.

"Max," Mindre whispered, as they kept walking. "I think we're being watched."

Max scanned the steps up in the hills, uneasy about being so close to the shelves. The ledges and shelves above them were filled with low trees, evidence of water as Mindre had explained earlier, and with it who knows what kind of life?

Seeing no signs of life, they gradually relaxed. "Let's go up here and find a place to rest," Mindre said, indicating a block of steps that was largely collapsed. "This one looks protected, we can keep a lookout just in case." She began picking her way up the pile of stones. The route was more stable than it looked, the smaller pieces of stone had long ago either tumbled away or settled into the spaces between the larger pieces of rock.

At the top, the triangular platform of rock held a surprise: the remains of a wall. Blocks had been stacked here once, the foundation of the wall still visible as a straight line of stones. Most of the stones were scattered and mixed with the shattered blocks that had tumbled from the steps over many years, but the wall was still knee-high in places. Mindre walked the length of the ruins. "This was a door," she said indicating a space in the row of blocks.

Max picked up a curved piece of dusty red pottery. "Bone-Throwers?" he asked.

"I think so. There's plenty of bones here, at least."

"I wonder if there's any treasure?" Max said hopefully, though there seemed to be very little of anything left.

Near the back corner, Max found his treasure. "Carvings!" Max said, noticing markings on the steps along the wall. "Bone-Thrower hieroglyphics, or something?" He walked to the steps, brushing dust away. Straight lines, each about a hand-width long, were neatly cut into the top faces of each step, groups of four lines in a row on each. Some lines were horizontal and some vertical. Mindre approached, curious.

"What do you think they are?" he asked.

"I don't know," Mindre said. "Decorations of some sort, I suppose."

Max looked from step to step to step. "There's a pattern," he observed. "At the base here, there's four horizontal lines. On the first step, the last one is vertical, and look, the last one on each step alternates horizontal and vertical."

"Uh huh," Mindre mumbled through a mouth full of fruit. Max hadn't seen her take a pear out of her pack.

"And, the second ones alternates by twos. *Horizontal-horizontal* and then *vertical-vertical*, then back to horizontals. Oh, this is binary! These steps are all numbered in binary!"

"Binary? What's that?"

"It's a number system, based on twos. I did a project on it in school. These horizontal lines are like zeros, and the vertical lines are like ones. These four different positions are worth *one*, *two*, *four* and *eight*.

"So, this one here for example," Max said, pointing at the step at waist level. "This has two vertical lines at the four and two positions, so it's worth six. *Four plus two*. The next one has ones at the four, two and one positions, so it's a seven – *four plus two plus one*."

Max pointed to the next design which started with one vertical line and then three horizontal lines. "After seven comes eight. This has a *one* in the eight position and the rest are zeros, so that's just *eight*. Then it goes *eight and one, eight and two, eight and two and one, eight and four* ... and keeps going, counting up by one on every step."

Mindre looked up and down the steps. "So, this is all *zeros* at the bottom, and then *one*, then *two*, then *two and one* which is *three*, I see ..."

"I wonder if this was the way they used to make numbers, or if it's just a design like you said," Max said.

"My father said Bone-Throwers used a primitive number system that relied on twos ... I think these might be their numbers."

"Cool! I wouldn't say it's 'primitive,' though. All of our computers, that is, our calculating machines, use this system. It's actually pretty important on Earth, even though we mostly use a system with tens, just like you."

"It's so strange," Mindre said.

"You think so? You use it, too," Max teased.

"Me?" Mindre said. "I have never used a system anything like this."

"You did when you lit the campfire last night. I was watching your fingers, you were going like this ... " Max held out his hands and tapped his fingers against his thumbs, recreating her pattern.

"Max! That is rude," she said angrily. "If I'd known you'd be studying my reckoning I would have given *you* a piece of it, that's for sure!"

"I couldn't help it, it was such a nice pattern," he teased.

"Max!"

"Oh, Mindre, c'mon. We can talk about this stuff! We do it all the time where I come from, it's really okay!"

"Not where I come from, this is very ..."

"*Private*, yeah, you've said that," Max cut in. "And yet, you've learned things from other people. You told me about this Calculist."

"Yes, well with him, we had a ..." She rolled her hand, fishing for a word.

"Okay, I get it," he said. "But I've got an idea, for something that could be really useful. I think we can extend your fire-starting pattern and make it more powerful, if you'll just listen for a minute."

Mindre eyed him suspiciously.

"We're hidden up here in the desert," he said, "behind a tree. No one will see. I won't tell, if you don't tell!"

Mindre stood looking at Max, her mouth open, not sure what to say. Max smiled inwardly, he could see she was embarrassed for some strange Dijin reason, yet she was burning with curiosity. She would listen!

"You started with your thumbs on your first fingers, that's like zero and zero. Right hand is ones, left hand is twos. Right thumb goes to middle finger, now it's zero and one. After that, your left thumb moves to two and your right goes back to zero. Finally, left is on two and right is on one. You've just counted zero, one, two, three ... in binary! Then you repeat it over and over and you make fire."

Mindre said nothing, watching his fingers indignantly.

"These numbers on the steps, they're the same. You were doing the last two digits with your fingers. Maybe you could raise or lower your hands for the other two digits, the way you use your arms with your own system. Lift your right hand up for a four and your left hand up for an eight, maybe? You could count from zero to fifteen – four times as much!"

Mindre looked Max in the eyes, her mouth pulling to a tight line. He wondered if she was going to be mad. She frowned but said, "Show me," determinedly.

Max hopped on the etched lines at the bottom of the stairs and held out his hands, thumbs against forefingers. "Zero!" he sang out. He then went up one step and changed his finger position. "One!"

Step to step he hopped playfully, making the changes in his fingers and raising and lowering his hands as he counted up to fifteen. "C'mon, it's fun!"

She bit her lip, then held out her hands and walked up, making the same motions.

"That wasn't so bad, was it?" Max asked. Mindre's face was flush, her pupils wide even in the bright desert. She looked down and shook her head.

"The numbers keep going. Let's grab our packs and see where they go!" Max said. He hopped down the stairs, counting down.

Mindre followed, making the movements with her hands but with much smaller motions.

"Look, I'm sorry if I embarrassed you," Max said. "I just think we could learn a lot from each other."

She smiled faintly and said nothing.

Max took the lead up the steps, noting that every etching that ended with a vertical line was on one of the smallest steps. The second digit changed on every block of the next size up, and so on. "These digits match the pattern in the steps as well," he called back to Mindre. "Wow, this is pretty cool!"

The steps were broken and cracked near the top where their numbered stairs reached a larger shelf. Max had to hang on to the wall to steady himself for the final steps. The shelf came into view. It was dotted with denser weeds and bushes, greener than the steps below, indicating underground water as Mindre had told him. He froze and crouched down as he caught sight of movement on the shelf. He peered over the edge, Mindre's head popping up beside him.

"Look, lizards!" he whispered.

A group of six or seven spiny green lizards the size of dogs lay on the weeds and stones just a few steps away. One turned its head their way. Its eyes moved independently, rolling around in its head until it fixed on them. It opened its mouth and made a chirping noise that sounded like a clacking tongue. Its upwardly curving jaw gave Max the impression it was smiling.

"Oh, they're really cute," Max said. "Are they dangerous?"

"I don't think so. Look, they're eating plants."

Max climbed up on the shelf and took a few steps forwards, staying low to the ground. The lizards did not seem concerned. The closest one turned its eyes upwards to a branch above its head and stretched, trying to reach the leaves.

"Watch this." Max took out his abacus, set up a number and subtracted, directing the reckoning at the branch. It bowed downwards and the lizard took a mouthful of leaves, chomping contentedly.

Mindre laughed. She held out her hands and made a series of moves. "Don't watch me," she warned lightly. A branch bowed down near another lizard who likewise took a bite.

The other lizards were interested now, gathering around the tree and competing for position. Max and Mindre bent down branches again and again, until the first lizard began moving towards them in a waddling motion.

"Now you've done it, he's on to you," Max said.

Mindre slid off her pack and hunted around inside of it. She brought out a round, red fruit.

"Trilliberries!" Max said. "Do you think they like them?"

"Who doesn't?" Mindre said. She tossed the berry to the lizard who snapped it up. The other lizards waddled up, not wanting to miss out. Mindre threw a berry to each.

One of them chirped up at them, a double chirp like a high-low clack. Max tried to make the sound by sucking his tongue to the top of his mouth and clacking. It was a fairly close match. Interested, the lizard returned the chirp. Another lizard joined with a low-low chirp, which Max repeated.

"You never told me you speak lizard," Mindre said.

Max laughed. "Doesn't everyone?" For fun, he tried to chirp the same pattern as Mindre's fire reckoning sequence. The lizards stared at him curiously.

"I think our shade is returning, Max," Mindre pointed out. "It'll be cool enough to start our trek."

"Yeah, we should get going. No secret Bone-Thrower treasure room, here. Still, kind of a treasure finding these guys!"

They crossed the shelf to descend the stairs on the other end. The lizards followed.

"Looks like they adopted you, Max," Mindre said.

Max made more chirping noises at them. "Goodbye!"

They followed him partway down the stairs. Max heard a clacking noise from up on the steps. It drew the lizards' attention. They stopped suddenly, looked behind them and then turned and began walking up.

"What was that?" Max asked. He chirped again. The lizards stopped, uncertain, and began walking back to him.

"Max, let them be," Mindre said.

Max listened intently. The clicking again. A double click. It was not quite like the lizards call. It was more of a "clack" than a "click." The lizards began walking up the steps. Curious, Max followed them onto the shelf. They continued up the stairs. Max chirped again. The lizards turned to look at him.

Click-clack came the noise again. Max could not tell the direction from the echoes on the stone walls, but the lizards looked up the steps. Max followed their gaze but could not see anything. He chirped again, testily.

The air tightened around his head. Reckoning! He turned to leap down the stairs and felt a shove. Missing his footing, he tumbled down the stairs towards Mindre and the unforgivingly hard edges of the steps.

Mindre swung her arms. Max's fall changed direction in response to Mindre's unseen power, and instead of tumbling down the stairs Max rolled onto a small shelf. Mindre sprang upwards, leaping like a deer.

Max rolled to his feet, pulled out his abacus and ran after her. On the other side of the shelf crouched a person wrapped in sandy brown clothing. Outstretched hands quickly made movements on small objects like sticks in the sand.

Mindre stopped mid-reckoning. Max watched as her face momentarily crunched up in concentration. Was she defending from an attack? She tossed her head as if throwing something out of her hair and opened her eyes again. Her fingers flew in an intricate pattern and her opponent snapped backwards as if kicked. Pouncing back to the small sticks, the sandy reckoner spun them deftly. Mindre's foot jerked out to the side and she sank awkwardly to one knee, her palms in the dust.

Max didn't wait anymore. His fingers danced over his abacus, reckoning a product almost automatically as he eyed a stone. The stone whipped through the air, striking the sand in front on the reckoner, knocking aside some of the instruments the reckoner was manipulating.

The sandy figure swept up the objects and dove to the side, rolled over cleanly and was back in a crouch, the objects instantly spread in a neat row on the sand. Max felt another hit, like he was slapped across the face, hard! Mindre's arms spun as she pulled herself upright.

Why are we doing this? Max thought. "Stop!" he yelled.

Surprisingly, Mindre stopped, her gaze fixed on the figure in the sand. The reckoner's hands stopped moving as well, a face turning slightly towards Max.

"We don't want to hurt you!" Max yelled. "And I don't really want to get hurt, either!"

He waited tensely.

Beneath the hood, Max could see a mouth. The corners pulled wide apart into a toothy grin. "Then why are you trying to steal my lizards?" came a woman's voice.

She withdrew her hands slightly from the objects in the sand. Max saw they were bones.

"You're a Bone-Thrower!" he said.

"And you're an Abacist and a Dijin," the woman said. "Unlikely company."

"These are ... unlikely times," Max said.

Mindre stepped up beside Max, her hands outstretched and ready. Max motioned for her to lower her hands. She did not.

"We like your lizards, but we don't want to steal them. I'm Maxwell, this is Mindre." He waited. The woman crouched motionless, her hood still covering all of her face except for her mouth. Max glanced at Mindre, she stood tensely, not returning his look.

He waited for a reply. The figure remained motionless, face hidden under the hood. After an uncomfortable pause, Max said, "Okay, I think we can just be on our way."

"Be on your way, then," the woman said.

Max and Mindre backed away to the steps and carefully descended.

They walked quickly along the foot of the cliffs.

"A Bone-Thrower, Max! That was a Bone-Thrower! There must be others." Mindre looked nervously towards the mountain.

"They still exist," she said as if trying to convince herself it were true. "My father tried for years to find them, deep in this desert, and here is one, so close to Pickaxe. Did you see the bones?"

"Yes, like little sticks," Max said. "She had them lined up in the sand, horizontally and vertically, just like the numbers we saw on the steps. I wish we could have found out more."

"I think we're lucky to be gone before more of them come. Where do you think they get those bones from, Max? Long ago, they used to cut the hands off of Dijins."

Max glanced up in the stony hills, the grotesque image turning in his mind. Maybe it was good Mindre's father had never found them. "Your father will be excited, at least," he said.

"Yes," Mindre said. "My father is easily excited, and it's gotten us into no end of trouble. *Bone-throwers*, Max. Where have they been hiding?"

They kept their pace up, Mindre eager to put as much distance between them and the sandy figure with the herd of lizards. Max was inclined to agree. They stopped only once briefly to drink from their flasks.

144

Max began to feel the danger was long behind them, but Mindre kept watching the rocks and steps as if feeling invisible eyes upon them. Her intuition turned out to be correct.

"Max, up ahead!" In the distance in front of them stood a lone tall figure, wrapped in cloth the same color as the sand. They came to a halt. The man was facing them, not moving.

"I think he's waiting for us," Max said. Mindre did not reply. After a moment Max prompted, "Why don't we go talk to him?"

Mindre looked around, up in the hills and behind them. She turned to Max and nodded, her mouth in a tight line.

They strode warily forward towards the figure. "Get your abacus ready," Mindre said.

"I think it's okay," Max said. After a few more steps, he took out his abacus anyway.

They stopped a respectful distance away. Mindre flexed her fingers.

The figure lifted back his hood. It was a dark-skinned man. Intense white eyes stared at them beneath a head of black hair, cut very short. Ivory rings hung heavily from his ears.

"Abacist, Dijin," the man said. "Chieftain Tarsa requests your presence."

Max looked at Mindre. She met his eyes and threw a glance towards the hills, returning her eyes to his. Max turned his head to look to where she had indicated. Perched on the shelves along the foot of the mountain were a dozen figures, hands down on the sand on what Max knew would be rows of human bones.

Max sucked in a breath. He didn't think they had much choice. "We would like that, very much," he said more bravely than he felt.

The man stared hard at them, back and forth between the two, reading their faces. Unexpectedly, his mouth curled up into a grin. "Don't worry, Dijin," he said. "We won't be eating you. Not tonight, at least." He laughed a rolling chuckle and led them towards the hills.

As they mounted the steps, Max began clicking his step-count algorithm, the effort of climbing steps instantly reduced to little more than that of walking on the flat desert sands. The others in the hills stayed back until they had passed and then fell in line behind them. The man led them upwards, across a long shelf and up the other side. They reversed direction across a shelf, and then up again. Max wondered why they were changing direction so often when a direct path would be much shorter. Perhaps many of these stairways were missing steps. Perhaps the Bone-Throwers themselves had removed steps to turn the path into a maze.

Max and Mindre did not speak. Mindre's face was dark. She kept glancing back at the group following them and throwing sidelong looks into the shelves as they passed.

They arrived at a large shelf, perhaps large enough to be a mesa, thought Max. A blocky ridge of stones the size of apartment buildings stood away from the steps. They headed towards the opening between the ridge and the steps, entering a kind of gulch. At the foot of the crumbling steps stood a large open canopy gently flapping its canvas roof in the warm wind. A few dozen men and women gathered around the canopy, all eyes turned to Max and Mindre.

Hesitantly, Max and Mindre followed their chaperone into the tent. The men and women were not clad in the loose sandy robes like their escorts wore but rather short brown tunics covered with fanciful arrangements of bones hanging from cords around their waists, chests and necks. Each person had a set of longer bones fastened with leather straps to one forearm.

146

The tent was sparsely furnished, empty except for a few baskets as if all had been hastily put in place. In the back of the tent, a woman in a long white tunic sat on the steps at the base of the stairs, a row of long polished bones hanging across her chest. She would be their leader, Max assumed. In front of them, their guide swept off his cloak and tossed it aside as he strode towards the woman, his bare muscular back shining with sweat. He took a seat beside her and motioned them forward.

Max and Mindre approached.

The woman addressed them, an unreadable expression on her face. "Maxwell the Abacist and Mindre the Dijin, I am Tarsa, Chieftain of Parchensis. This is Zarza, my chief hand. Tell me, young Abacist, what are you doing here in the Drylands?" Her eyes shone clearly, she was perhaps younger than the hard wrinkles on her face suggested.

Max's throat felt very dry. He swallowed. "We are traveling to Vertex, to meet my grandmother."

"Your grandmother?" Tarsa asked. "And what is your family name?"

Max glanced at Mindre. She pulled back one corner of her mouth and raised her eyebrows. She wasn't sure either how much he should say of his family. Would they know of the Teller name? And would it help them or hurt them?

"Teller," Max decided. "My name is Maxwell Teller, grandson of Lady Teller."

Zarza leaned inwards and whispered something to her. She nodded slightly.

"And so, where is it you have come from, grandson of Lady Teller?"

"Quincunx," Max answered simply.

Zarza shook his head and started to speak. Tarsa raised her fingers to silence him.

"I see before me a Dijin and a boy with an abacus. I do not see the Longwalker whom you claim relation to. I will ask this only once more, so please think carefully and speak the words I need to hear. Where is it you have *come from?*" She tipped her head knowingly.

Max paused. She knew of his grandmother. She also did not believe he was her grandson. Why should she? Everyone "knew" his immediate family did not exist. She was also not satisfied with his answer of "Quincunx" ... did she know more? And what could he say to convince her? The only thing he could think of was the truth.

"I am from Earth. I am from offworld."

Zarza sat up, turning to whisper in Tarsa's ear. She smiled at him, then addressed a young man standing nearby. "Bring our guests some seats. And citrus water, if you please."

The room was suddenly in motion. Several pillows were brought forth and set in a ring. Max was shocked at how quickly everything changed with his simple words. A circle of pillows quickly formed and Max and Mindre were seated in a ring with a dozen other people. Bone ornamentations clinked around the ring as their hosts sat down. Clay cups filled with liquid appeared in Max and Mindre's hands. Max took a sip, the water was cool with a strong lemon taste.

Tarsa eyed them curiously. "Wendi told me on her last visit that she had found you and your brother ... offworld," she began. "I found it hard to believe, but there is much about your grandmother that is hard to believe. Why has she sent you two here?"

"She didn't send us," Max said. "We had trouble with Saul, and we got separated. I came to Abacabax alone. I'm afraid I don't know where my grandmother is right now. If Mindre hadn't found me, I don't know what would have happened."

"Mindre of Quincunx," Tarsa smiled to Mindre. "You are his guide? We welcome you here."

"Thank you," Mindre said, glancing left and right wide-eyed at the company of bone-clad cannibals.

"Maxwell, Wendi Teller is a very special friend. I had expected she would be visiting soon given the recent events on the surface. When my daughter," Tarsa paused to nod towards the young woman sitting on a pillow near her feet, "told me of an Abacist in our lands, walking directly towards the Nightsiders, we were, shall we say, curious."

The young woman grinned, her mouth wide and toothy. Max recognized the smile.

"You!" he said. The mouth belonged to the lizard shepherd. Without her hood, Max could see that she was a young woman, perhaps about his age. Her dark skin contrasted sharply with her striking white-blonde hair.

Mindre nodded to the young woman, then turned back to Tarsa. "Nightsiders?" she asked. "You mean Darklings?"

"Yes, the Dark Ones. The settlements near the Western Ascension are overrun. I fear your chosen path would be a difficult one."

Max and Mindre glanced at each other. Max easily understood from the shape of the terrain that all the steps from their mesa converged either to the east in the heart of Calculist land, full of their enemies, or to the west on the Western Ascension, full of Darklings. Both directions led to danger. They were between a rock and "dark" place, so to speak.

"We need to get to Vertex," Max said. "We hope to find my grandmother there, and if not, we need to get to Apex."

"To the top of the spine? What awaits you there?"

"My abacus is damaged. It may have caused the quake and if it is not repaired it could cause more quakes and even more damage. We need to get it to the temple so it can be fixed."

Zarza leaned over to Tarsa and whispered something. They exchanged a few words, then she turned back to Max. "The happenings on the surface often hold little interest to us. However, this quake has shaken Abacabax to its bones. You have our attention. Tell us of these happenings."

They shared the story of their travel and what little Max knew of the coming conflict. They listened carefully, Tarsa not moving her gaze from Max.

When they had finished, Tarsa exchanged a few words with Zarza and turned back to Max.

"I have known your grandmother since I was a young girl. I lay sick with a deadly fever when she first made contact with us. Wendi traveled far to retrieve medicine from the edge of the world and she has been my friend ever since, though we rarely meet. She came to me before winter to warn us of these coming troubles.

"Your grandmother saved my life, Maxwell," Tarsa continued. "We will gladly offer you shelter tonight, and tomorrow perhaps we can grant you guidance on your travels further."

"But first," she called out to all in the tent, "we shall have a feast for the young Teller and his brave companion!"

Max and Mindre sat in the shade while Bone-Throwers came and went quickly, carrying carpets and pillows and baskets of food down thirty-two steps from the shelf above. Max guessed there was an entrance to some caves up above where they lived.

"They are so different from what I would have believed," Mindre said, swirling her cup of citrus water. "Though I'm still not sure we won't be on the menu!"

Max laughed. "I doubt they'd get much meat off of me," he said.

"I think they live underground," Mindre said. "Did you hear how she referred to 'the surface?' That's why no one sees them."

"I think you're right. They're a little bit ... creepy, but I like them!" Max said. "Oh, here comes our friend."

The young woman with the wide grin approached them, her dog-sized lizards following behind. She no longer wore her sandy brown cloak and Max was fascinated by what had laid beneath. A short brown tunic served as a backdrop for her bony ornamentation: a necklace, a bracer on her left arm, and most dramatically a human ribcage wrapping around her chest. Max thought she looked as though she were part skeleton.

She sat down between them, a little too close for Max's comfort. Her necklace of round lumpy bones clacked against the ribcage as she sat. Max recognized her necklace bones as vertebrae. The bracer on her left arm was the same as was on the other Bone-Throwers arms they'd seen in the tent. It was made of three long bones that traveled the length of her forearm, fastened on each end with leather bands.

She cocked her head and looked at Mindre. "I've never seen a Dijin reckon before," she said. "You use living fingers!" The young woman held up her hands and waved her fingers wildly. "That's so interesting!"

Mindre scooted backwards. "And you use bones."

"Yes!" She reached into a pouch around her waist and brought forth a handful of small bones. "I have twelve. These are from my grandfather. He had six fingers on each hand!"

"Those are finger bones?" Max asked.

"No, silly. Finger bones are too small. These are from his hands." She tapped the bones against the back of her own hand before putting them back in her pouch.

"I'm Lunata," she said. "These are my lizards, would you like to pet them?"

Lunata slid a thin bone from the arrangement of bones on her left forearm. Using it as a kind of mallet, she struck each of the other two long bones once each, like striking a bony xylophone. They made two different sounds, the noises which Max had heard from the shelves when they first found the lizards.

Responding to the sound, the reptiles crawled forward. One climbed comfortably onto Lunata's lap. "This is Jasper," she said, scratching him under his chin. Jasper chirped happily. "He's too small yet to eat, so he won't be part of the feast."

Mindre raised her eyebrows. "You eat these?"

"Oh, yes," Lunata said. "Well, maybe not Jasper, he's my favorite. They're quite delicious, but they need plenty of sunlight, so I walk them every day. They're not used to meeting strangers. No one ever comes out here."

She tipped her head, looking at Mindre's hands. "You are very clever with your fingers," Lunata continued. "I did not know Dijins could fight so cleverly."

"Thank you," Mindre said.

"And, you, Maxwell Teller. I did not believe you to be an Abacist at first. You are so weak. You do not fight at all. You only throw stones and try to snap my bones."

"It worked, didn't it?" Max said, taken aback.

"I was more worried about a Dijin than an Abacist, and that is most unlikely."

"You were worried enough to let us go," Max countered. "I thought Bone-Throwers didn't want anyone to know where they were."

"In order to walk, it is not necessary for your bones to do all of the work. It is enough to direct pressure and let natural forces take over. You were walking directly towards the Dark Ones. That was enough."

"So you would have let us keep going?" he asked.

"Zarza insisted on questioning you in case Lady Teller had sent you. My mother is quite fond of Wendi."

"And you are the Chieftain's daughter?"

"Yes. You could be skinned for attacking the future chieftain, you know." Lunata stared at them hard, and then burst into another broad toothy grin.

A series of wooden tones rang out from the canopy. "Feasting!" said Lunata, hopping to her feet. "Come, you sit with me!"

Max was eager to try some new food. The food in their packs was satisfying, but after four days of fruit, leaf rolls and dried meat he was more than ready for something different. He hoped it would not be lizard.

The meal had been set up surprisingly quickly. Max had the feeling that Bone-Throwers could appear and disappear in a blink. Carpets made of a rough woven material the color of their desert cloaks had been rolled out under the canopy. Broad white pillows were laid out in a circle. Round platters woven from plant stems lay in the center, filled with piles of smashed vegetables in different colors.

Lunata sat beside her mother, indicating that Mindre should sit beside her. Max sat next to Mindre. On his other side was a quiet young man. A platter of flat moist bread was passed around. They were shown how to dip pieces of the bread into the vegetable pastes.

The food was delicious, different spices and textures and colors. Max particularly liked the red paste made with small yellow beans that had a spicy-hot zing. Mindre and Lunata chatted away while Max made awkward conversation with the boy beside him. He introduced himself as Hamata, son of the chieftain and younger brother to Lunata. He explained that he was training to be a river engineer.

"Are there enough rivers in the desert?" Max asked.

"Oh, plenty of rivers. We make them flow where we will," he told Max.

"Where are they?" Max asked. He hadn't seen water since they left Pickaxe.

"Wherever we want them to be," Hamata said with a mysterious smile.

As the platters were being taken away, clacking noises outside of the canopy drew Max's attention. Two women stood beside a pile of branches, tapping rapid patterns on the bones on their forearms. The pile of branches burst into flame.

Two men brought forth instruments covered with rows of tubes made from wood and bone, like a cross between xylophones and marimbas, Max thought. The dinner guests rose and clacked bones on the forearms enthusiastically, filling the tent with sound. The two men took their positions, smiled and nodded, and began hammering on the tubes with long white mallets.

A joyful melody sprang forth, tones from the wood blending with clacking rhythms from the bones. Lunata grabbed Mindre's arm and pulled her out towards the fire, bouncing to the rhythm. Others hopped towards the bonfire and began to dance. Max watched for a moment. He was normally shy dancing in front of others, but something in the rhythm spoke to him. A pulsing pattern that felt both novel and familiar, it thrummed in his chest and rolled up to the top of his head. He wasn't sure if it was that he had a belly full of delicious food and was feeling giddy with their good fortune, or if it were some kind of enchantment from the pattern in the rhythm, but the draw was irresistible. He threw himself into the mix with pleasure.

The dancers were clacking rhythms with round tubes over their thumbs and forefingers. Hamata, the chieftain's son, handed Max a set, two pairs of two tubes connected with a piece of leather. Slipping one on each hand, Max could make two different tones, a low "doon" sound with one hand and a higher "din" sound with the other, by simply pinching his thumbs and fingers together.

The rhythm on the marimbas changed, becoming repeated triplets, over and over, made from two different tones. The sequence of tones changed in every triplet, yet it didn't feel random. It moved with a purpose. It was going somewhere, to a place it would never reach but pleased with the journey nonetheless. Max thought it felt good.

He swayed with the rhythm, trying to clink his wooden tubes in time with the tones of the bony triplets: doon doon doon … doon doon *din* … doon *din* doon … doon *din din* … *din* doon doon …

The first note of the triplet was the same for four beats and then it changed for four beats. He began slapping the pattern, feeling the strange rhythm creeping into his bones. He was surprised how quickly he caught on, was it some kind of reckoning? It felt more and more familiar. Max listened to the last two notes of the triplets. They always repeated the same four beat pattern.

It was the pattern he and Mindre had played with earlier! The realization hit Max like a flash of electricity through a circuit board. This was a binary rhythm, with three parts instead of four. It was counting in binary from zero, "*doon doon doon*," to seven, "*din din din*." The pattern was crystal clear now, he found he could follow and anticipate exactly.

His ease with the rhythm did not escape attention. Zarza found his way in front of Max, they matched tones precisely. "Four beats!" Zarza called to the musicians.

The pattern changed and the pace picked up. They were now playing series of four tones. *Zero* to *fifteen*, or more correctly *zero* to *eight-four-two-one*, Max thought. Zarza leaned in towards Max, his hands held close to his face, clacking out the pattern.

Max matched him beat for beat, stumbling a little on the transition from seven to eight, or "doon *din din din*" to "din *doon doon doon,*" but catching it perfectly the next time around.

A thumping grew in his chest, as if a subwoofer nearby was throwing out pulses of low frequency energy. Max became aware that the pulses were matching the throbbing of his heart, blending in with the rhythm of the clacking of the bones in his fingers.

"Five!" Zarza yelled.

The pace accelerated. The five-beat rhythm felt unusual, but Max kept up with the count ... it felt strangely natural. As they neared the end of the thirty-two number cycle Max found himself calling out "Six beats!" Without missing the count, Max and Zarza jumped from a five-tone thirty-one to a six-tone thirty-two and kept going. Max was consumed by the totality of the beating encompassing his entire chest.

Zarza's face split into a disbelieving laugh. The others around the fire cheered, now making a circle around Max and Zarza as they clacked away, matching beat for beat.

"*Din din din din din din!*" Max threw out the final count in the six-beat pattern and threw his hands in the air in victory.

"Seven!" called out Zarza. Max waved his hands, shaking his head and laughing. "No, no, I can't! You win!" he cried. He could not keep up. The strange feeling in his chest flowed down into his arms, aching in his elbows and wrists.

Zarza, laughing, held up both hands towards Max, open-palmed. Max gave him a double high-five, clacking his rhythm tubes against Zarza's. Zarza tipped back his head and howled, then grabbed Max gruffly and hugged him so hard his feet left the ground.

The melody and rhythm changed again and Max found himself dancing, passed from man to woman to woman to man, laughing, cheering, hugging, dancing, until he found himself in the arms of … Mindre.

She beamed at him, herself swept away in the joy of the moment. "How'd you do that?" she asked.

"It's the same pattern we practiced before! I've never done it quite like this, but it feels so … it's … oh, I'll explain later! Let's dance!"

The next morning Max awoke feeling wonderful. They had slept on a pile of pillows, the most comfortable bed Max had laid in since he came to Abacabax. He thought of his bed at his home, how far away it seemed now. He watched Mindre laying nearby breathing slowly. He studied her face, watching her lips as she lay peacefully beside him. She was so beautiful, he thought. He wished they could stay here, with these happy people and good food and music, and forget the long voyage ahead into dangerous territory.

She stirred and he quickly rolled away before she caught him staring at her. Others were awake. Several Bone-Throwers had slept under the canopy with them, including Lunata and Hamata. Max rose quietly and joined Hamata at a large pottery bowl of water that had appeared since last night. Hamata showed Max how to use the bowl to wash his hands and face. The cold water quickly brought Max fully awake.

Mindre woke shortly afterwards. From the corner of his eye, Max could see her watching him as she washed up.

The group shortly gathered again in a ring of pillows. Tarsa and Zarza descended from the steps, joining them. A young girl and boy brought forth oranges and grapes which the group ate with the leftover bread from last night's feast.

Lunata spoke quietly with Tarsa during the meal, repeatedly glancing over at Max and Mindre. They seemed to reach some kind of agreement. Lunata looked over at Max and Mindre with her large grin before running up the steps.

Chieftain Tarsa addressed them after breakfast. "Maxwell Teller," she began, "I understand you can reckon to the beating of the heart of Abacabax."

Max thought of the strange feeling in his chest during the dance with Zarza. So it was some kind of reckoning? Was it a Bone-Thrower enchantment that made it so easy for him to follow the beat?

"There are few who have mastered our structures so easily," Tarsa continued. "You have shown yourself to truly be a child of Kael."

Turning her gaze to Mindre she said, "Mindre of Quincunx. My daughter tells me you are the Dijin Thumb, with reckoner powers beyond those of all your people. Maxwell is fortunate to have you as his protector.

"I have been in council with our historians. It is vital to our interests that you reach your destination and we have decided to aid you. The children have replenished your packs. You will join us now."

They arose, gratefully accepting their heavier packs from two young children decorated in necklaces of bone. Max and Mindre followed Tarsa and Zarza behind the canopy and up the steps. The upper shelf, like the one below, was partially collapsed as well. They picked their way around fallen stones to the back edge where a house-sized block had collapsed and was leaning forwards, propped up by a block half its size beneath it.

Lunata came out from behind the block and stood beside her mother. She was now dressed in her sandy brown cloak, the large hood hanging down from her shoulders.

158

"We offer you a guide," Tarsa said. "My daughter Lunata has chosen to accompany you. She has many skills that will ease your travel."

Lunata grinned, her teeth shining like a row of pebbles on a dry beach. Max smiled back, a little unsure of this strange young woman, but surely another reckoner could only be of help.

"Secondly, we grant you passage to the Uplands." Tarsa raised her hand in the air.

"The Uplands?" Mindre asked.

"Verdant Mesa," she answered. "It is sooner than you think possible."

Max and Mindre exchanged glances. *Sooner than you think possible.* The words of Lady Carpus echoed in their ears.

"We trust few outsiders with our inner knowledge. Wendi Teller has been an exception and she has kept her word. I have faith that you will do the same. You are not to speak of our people or say anything of what we will show you now."

Max nodded. "You have my word."

"You have my word as well," Mindre said.

"Your word is bonded to your marrow," Tarsa said. She turned to Zarza and raised her eyebrows.

"I am satisfied," he said simply.

Tarsa tapped a rhythm on the bones along her left forearm, a sequence of twenty or so tones. Max listened but could not discern the pattern. "A blessing for your voyage, my flower," Tarsa said to Lunata. The mother and daughter touched foreheads. "Take care of them and return to me."

"Thank you, Mother," Lunata said with a big smile.

"Then," said Zarza, "we enter the Mandible of Kael." He walked towards the fallen blocks and stepped behind the largest. No opening could be seen, only a shadow which Zarza disappeared into. They followed, Max admiring the perfect camouflage. With all of the tens of thousands of shelves in the desert, no one would ever find this opening.

Behind the shadow was a straight passageway, the floor, walls and ceiling perfectly level. The hallway was lit with a dark yellow glow from rough glass blocks set in the wall at even intervals. Max wondered if they were lit from behind, somehow reflecting sunlight into the passage, or if there were powered by some kind of reckoning, which probably involved bones. The smooth passage stood in stark contrast to the roughness of the world they had just come from.

The flickering hallway came to an intersection with similar passages branching off in all directions, including up and down. The opening downwards was partially covered with a wooden platform allowing them to travel straight ahead at the intersection. Wooden ladders were fastened into the walls of the vertical passages. Max thought of the long crevice of rungs he and Mindre had climbed two days before and wondered how far these ladders might travel.

At the next intersection, they climbed downward. The air grew cooler quickly as they descended. Max threw off a shiver, inhaling moist air. They were nearing water.

They reached the bottom where passages extended horizontally in four directions. "This is a quiet place, no speaking here," Zarza said. "Only Kael speaks here."

They walked down a hallway in the direction taking them deeper into the mountain. There were few lights on this hallway and their passage grew darker as the walls grew rougher and farther apart. Max felt as if they were entering a temple or some other holy place. He breathed carefully, wondering if he would feel something mystical.

Then he heard a whisper. Was it the voice of Kael? It was a faint hissing at first, growing to a rumble. It was the sound of water. The air dampened noticeably as they neared a river or a waterfall perhaps. Of course, Max thought, it would be one of the underwater rivers, like at the head of the Isigon River where water flowed out from the cliff. Perhaps it even was part of that river. Was it possible that the rivers had carved out passages throughout these cliffs and Lunata would be leading them up one of these underground passages? Max thought of Hamata, training to be a river engineer. Perhaps the Bone-Throwers had carved out these passages themselves!

The rumble grew louder and the passage opened into a much larger area. A mist spattered against his face, the signature of falling water. Zarza stopped ahead of them. "Behold," his voice straining to be heard above the din in the cavernous space. "The radius of Kael."

More light appeared ahead, growing slowly, defining the silhouette of Zarza. The light was coming from a glassy stone he was holding in his hand. Max could see Mindre, then Lunata and then finally the features of the space they were standing in.

Water, and structures within the water, became visible in the growing illumination. Pounding water rushed through the natural cavern in which they stood, splashing on rolling wheels and gears of shiny stone.

They were standing on a short ledge. Rainbows glimmered in the mist, scattering off stalactites and stalagmites hanging and standing in rows. The column of water below them rushed in from a wide tunnel in the roof, swirled madly in a convoluted pool within the chamber in which they stood and disappeared through a smaller tunnel to the right. Harnessing the power of this river was a massive but agile contraption, tall as a house, whose function Max struggled to understand.

"The desert is not so dry, no?" Zarza exclaimed, more as a statement than a question. "This is the Water Reckoner," he said proudly.

Max marveled at the device. Water poured over great stone wheels as tall as he, rushing into cavities within the wheels and turning them with the force of the flow. Max counted ten wheels in a row. The wheel at the near end spun quickly, the second wheel turned slower, the third even slower, and so on. The wheels on the far end appeared not to move at all, but Max understood that these seemingly motionless wheels were probably turning very, very slowly, the rate of change in speed from one wheel to the next a constant. Behind each wheel, black stone columns the size of coffins rose from the tumultuous flow of the river and sank again beneath the current. On each column was carved a relief statue of a bony human figure. The columns were driven by the wheels, as each wheel completed a revolution, the corresponding column would suddenly rise or fall, either bringing the statue into view or hiding it again.

"What does it do?" Max asked, awed.

"You know, I think." Zarza grinned. "Of course you do."

"Max," Mindre whispered. "It is the pattern you showed me last night."

So it was. It was a water-powered counting machine. "This is your pattern," Max announced. "This is the heartbeat of Kael."

"Yes, yes it is. This was built by our ancestors, the Tappers, two hundred years ago. The power of their bones lives within them."

Max eyed the rising and falling columns. Could they contain the remains of the people who built this, like sarcophaguses forever in motion?

Lunata spoke up. "This is a place of great honor for these women and men. Upon our deaths, most of us gift only our hands. The Tappers, they gifted *all* of their bones." Lunata's voice rang with reverence and admiration. Max wanted to know more about "gifting" bones – what did that mean?

"Come," Zarza instructed. He led them to a wooden bridge on the left side of the cavern, they walked above the river to a large wooden basket dangling just above the raging water. "Climb inside."

"May the bones roll well, my brethren." He embraced them each, then clacked a quick rhythm on his forearm.

Zarza pulled out a rod from the side of the basket and it dropped suddenly into the water. Max was momentarily alarmed, envisioning the basket crashing into the great stone wheels. The current, however was now flowing in the opposite direction, as was the water wheel. The basket floated with the current towards the opening where the water previously had flowed in and downwards and was now flowing out and *upwards*. The basket tilted away from the reverse waterfall and rose, floating upwards, up into the darkness of the tunnel above.

"Stay in the basket!" Zarza yelled after them. His laughter rang out after them as they vanished upwards into the darkness.

Chapter 7: Accounts reckoned

Lherzo stood near the edge of the Eastern Wall, dissolving leaves on an unfortunate bush already struggling to find footing in the stony soil. He balanced his abax awkwardly in both hands as fingers moved from hole to hole on the underside. No abac lay on the top of his abax, quite the opposite. Instead of stones on the stone tablet, his abax was covered with the *absence* of stones, rows of holes along the lines where abac would normally sit. He could see through the holes to where his fingers danced on the underside, marking numbers that were "the opposite" of the numbers on the top face of the abax. His was the only "anti-abax" on all the shelves, his own creation that allowed him to visualize numbers that were somehow "less than zero."

He had been certain this was the creation that would allow him to claim his rightful place as Calculist Prime. That was before his father had laughed at the idea, cracking his first anti-abax in two and forbidding him to continue this "unnatural" reckoning. By denying the presence of the abac, his father admonished, his creation was antithetical to everything the Calculists stood for. As further punishment, Lherzo had been put in charge of the Tower Watch. Most hours of his days were now filled with checking on all thirty-three outposts on the entire outer wall of Vertex. It was only at the end of his shift when he could traverse the Eastern Wall to the far corner which often stood empty and unguarded, that Lherzo was momentarily alone and could continue his practice in secret.

He was fascinated with these anti-numbers, and with practice and extreme concentration he could cause matter itself to cease to exist. He had been unable to erase nothing more than porous materials like tree bark, leaves and insects, but he was sure if only he could have had more time to devote to the practice, he could learn to erase stone itself. What a demonstration he could make then!

Lherzo knew it was too late. His father had claimed status as the Prime with his own invention, Tricalculus, and even Lherzo had to grudgingly admit that its power was indeed awesome. Still, Lherzo's advancement represented something dramatically different. All of the New Origins thus far had only brought forth advancements in reckoning that were structurally the same, only more efficient. His father's reckoning based on groupings of three was another such incremental advance. Lherzo's anti-numbers, in comparison, were an entirely *new kind* of number, one that could potentially double the space of numbers upon which to reckon! Surely, this was an idea that could have, and should have positioned Lherzo for his proper place as the next New Origin, but sadly he had not been able to develop it enough for anything more than the weakest of effects. Instead, his father's name would live eternally as the first of a new line of reckoners.

The evening horns sounded from the upper palace, three long blasts, calling all commanders to the council at the close of each day. Lherzo slipped his abax into his inside jacket pocket and headed back to the fortress.

The council room sat stoically in the corner of the upper tiers, a heavy square room where Lherzo had attended council meetings since entering his fourth phase, four years ago. Long windows along both the south and west walls of the chamber gave panoramic views of both the city below and the ascension towers perched in a row like watchful birds along the Western Ascension.

Lherzo took his place at the far end of the table, farthest from his father and two older brothers. In any other family, Lherzo as third-born would have had the seat of honor, but his father had decreed that he himself was the final link in the chain of Calculists. Lherzo was merely an afterthought. On each side of the heavy granite table sat the commanders of each division, a group of hard men varying in age from the geriatric Bacchius, who must be nearing the seventh stage, to Lherzo himself, the youngest member of the council.

General Biggens' monstrous hand placed his abax on the table with a heavy thunk, indicating the start of the meeting. All conversations stopped at once and all eyes turned to him.

"Our situation has changed," he began without introduction. "The Abacist Prime, second of the seconds, lives."

Lherzo sat up straight. Mumbles went out around the table, the commanders glancing at each other.

Biggens continued, "The Abacist sighted in Quothmire last week is believed to be the *first* of the Abacist seconds, grandson of Lady Teller, son of Lady Rita, whom we thought perished in the War of the Plague. This boy spoke of his younger brother, the second of the seconds, who is also very much alive. We now have confirmation that he is in Tangram with the Mad Teller. We advance our timetable and move on Tangram within the week."

"Sir," Commander Basal spoke. "We are on track to march after the Great Divide. When you take your rightful place as the New Origin, no number of Abacists or Darklanders will withstand your force."

Biggens stared at Basal. "Do I need remind you of the threat that the Abacists continue to offer, even with their small numbers? Does anyone here doubt what the emergence of the Abacist Prime could mean to our position on the faces?"

"There are none that can match your might, General," Basal said. "Your position is secure."

Biggens gave Basal a stony look. Without breaking his gaze he called out, "Gordon, your report."

Gordon stood from the center of the table, his face grim. "I have sought council from the Triangulators." He paused, allowing the weight of his sacrifice to sink in. All eyes turned to him. Lherzo fixed his attention on Gordon's mouth, looking for evidence of the price.

"The Abacist Prime is indeed in Tangram," he said.

Lherzo caught sight of Gordon's teeth and the empty spaces in between. He frowned in distaste.

"This of course begs the question of where he has been all these years," Gordon continued. "Care to guess?"

"Gordon, get on with it," Biggens snapped.

"Before he was in Tangram, he was *not anywhere*."

A confused murmur arose from the table. "What do you mean, 'not anywhere,'" a commander asked.

"I mean that this is a person who has never before set foot on the faces, *anywhere* on Abac-Abax."

Lherzo wondered how that could be. By the sound of the voices around the table, many of the men wondered that as well.

Biggens broke their chatter. "He is an offworlder. The Abacist Prime is an offworlder. It is now clear why the Mad Teller took Tangram. It is so he could again open a portal between worlds, and he certainly brings with him unknown powers that are not meant for this world."

The commander beside Lherzo called out, "It could mean another plague!"

Bang! Bang! Bang! Bacchius, the oldest member of the council, beat his abax on the table. The talking stopped, as eyes turned to him.

"The Stonebreaker," the old man said. Groans of disagreement rolled forth from around the table. He banged his abax again and held aloft his hand.

"You are too young for the stories and perhaps too old to pay them mind, but we do so at our own peril," Bacchius said. "The Triad in my day told of a prophecy never fulfilled, of an offworlder who will break the very foundations of Abac-Abax. *First quake, the shelves to shake.* Our first quake has happened, in Quothmire. On that very same day a young Abacist from the highest order is discovered there, and his brother, *an offworlder*, appears in Tangram. This is no coincidence. The Stonebreaker is here. The Stonebreaker is in Tangram."

The table was silent, the men looking at each other uncertainly. Lherzo had a sinking feeling. It all seemed to be too big of a coincidence.

Biggens spoke. "We advance our timetable. Each day is another day the Mad Teller grows in power. I want our troops on the march in seven days. We take Tangram, we crush this threat *before* the Great Divide. Make it happen. All but my sons are dismissed."

The men stood and gathered their abaxes, whispering worriedly as they filed out of the room. Lherzo was nervous but excited, his endless watch duty would now end and he would be on the march to war, to Tangram, to the glory of battle.

Lherzo moved to a newly-empty seat at the head of the table with his father and brothers. His oldest brother, Kalkar, sat leaning back in his chair looking bored, his arm draped over the seat beside him. Gerard, just two years older than Lherzo, spun an abac on the table, watching it spin on its rounded edge. Neither brother seemed surprised by any of the news. It was of course his father's style to wait to tell Lherzo anything, but to make him wait to learn of it until the council meeting seemed particularly cold.

"The coming weeks will secure our glory," he said proudly. "With this young Abacist dead, there will be none other to challenge us for the New Origin. We have a tight timeline and I expect you not to rest until it is met."

"Father?" Lherzo asked. "How much of a threat is this young Abacist? Is the Stonebreaker story real?"

"I will take no risks, none!" Biggens slapped the table with both palms. His hands, twice the size of anyone's, connected with a smack that echoed between the hard walls.

"If any of you foul this up, I'll have you flayed on the Southern Wall. Understand Lherzo?"

"Me?" Lherzo said.

"Kalkar, you are to press the Master of Board to have the provision chariots stocked and distributed appropriately in the line. I want no time wasted setting up the camps. We are moving with all forces, save Homefront."

Lherzo raised his eyebrows. All forces would mean nine thousand soldiers to move on a walled city manned by two humans and a few hundred Darklings.

"Gerard, you are to assist Basal and Gordon ensuring the chariot, cavalry and ascension scouts are in order. We ride on the seventh day. Can you handle that?"

Gerard tipped his head. "Which chariot? Will I get my own?" he asked.

"Which chariot do you think?" Biggens sighed.

"Oh, the big one!" He turned to Lherzo and grinned smugly. Lherzo rolled his eyes. Of course his dim brother would be excited about getting to ride in the big chariot.

"And Lherzo ..." Biggens said, "I am going to trust you with a monumental task."

Lherzo drew in his breath. Would he finally get his own command? "Yes, Father, I'm ready," he said.

"Good. You are to find this other Abacist, the first of the seconds, seen one week ago in Quothmire, before he becomes a threat. Word is that he is weak and hiding with Dijins. That seems like something even you could handle."

"You want me to go south, while you all ride north?" Lherzo protested. "Are these not the weeks of glory? Why do you punish me so?"

Biggens rolled his hands into giant fists, pressed them on the table and leaned in to Lherzo. Lherzo leaned forward, unflinching. "You wish to share in my glory? Find the Abacist and return in seven days, and I'll reevaluate your fitness to join the march."

"I'll ready my squad," Lherzo muttered.

"I require your squad, we cannot afford nannies for you at this time. Have them report to Kalkar."

Biggens pushed down with his mighty fists, lifting himself to his feet. "All dismissed!"

Lherzo shoved another potato sullenly into his mouth. Dirigo, his comrade and first hand, wiped gravy from his bushy black beard and eyed his friend tentatively. "So, are you going to tell me about the meeting, or are we going to sit here in silence all night?" Dirigo asked. It was the second time he'd asked since Lherzo sunk into the seat across from him.

Lherzo swallowed and turned to friend. He breathed out loudly. "You and the squad are to report to Kalkar tomorrow," he said flatly.

"Kalkar? Why, what are you doing?"

"Not riding north," he said. "I'm going on a fishing trip instead. I leave tomorrow."

"What? I heard we're all going on the march? You were to have a command!"

"Nope. I'm going on one of my father's special missions," Lherzo said humorlessly. "To Quothmire."

"No! Why? Quothmire's a mess. The Quothmire division is on their way *here*."

"I'm being sent to look for the Quothmire Abacist. By myself. If I can find him and return within seven days, then I can ride north with the division. *Maybe*."

"The kid? He's sending you to find *that* kid? How can you do that? No offense, but all of Quothmire couldn't find him. And Lherzo … Quothmire and back in seven days?" Dirigo shook his head. "It can't be done. Even if you ride like mad!"

"I know, it's a fool's errand, another of my father's ways of seeing to it that I fail. Again."

"Lherzo," Dirigo said, lowering his voice to a forceful whisper. "You are so much better than that. You should be the Prime, if only you were allowed to show what you can do. It's your birthright, he's stealing it from you."

"Well, it's a little bit of a gray area, isn't it? Besides, he's created Tricalculus and what have I got? Anti-numbers, and they haven't yielded any positive results."

"I still don't get it. I thought your father only cared about the Great Divide. When that happens, the Abacists won't mean a thing. What's so pressing about Tangram all of a sudden?"

Lherzo looked around. Three men at the end of the table were laughing, another sat alone at the next table swirling a mug of ale. "Let's go outside," he said.

They walked along the terrace outside the mess hall, stopping to lean on a rail. The plazas below were lit in irregular points of light from torches and the glowing squares of open windows.

"That kid in Quothmire is the first of the seconds, and his brother is here as well," Lherzo told him. "The Abacist Prime."

Dirigo opened his mouth to say something, then closed it again, his eyes wide.

"They've been *offworld*, if you can believe it. The Mad Teller has reopened the portal and brought them both here," Lherzo continued.

"What!? Oh, that's some very dark reckoning! Last time he did that, I mean, I was just a boy, but I remember!"

"Yeah, me too. Who knows what could happen this time? My father is mostly worried that now the Abacists can make a claim for the New Origin. That's why we're going to retake Tangram now. Or, why the rest of you are going to retake Tangram."

Dirigo let out a long low whistle. He snapped his head to Lherzo. "Your father's got it in for you. When he becomes the New Origin, what then? Are you going to be left behind?"

"I'm just going to have to find this kid," Lherzo said.

"How do you even start? Quothmire's too far. And it's been a week, he could be anywhere."

Lherzo watched through the window as a group of men stood from a table, empty plates in hand. Commander Gordon was among them. Lherzo stared at his mouth, thinking

172

of the empty spaces within. "I think there's a price I will need to pay to find out," he said slowly.

"The witches? Lherzo, no," Dirigo protested.

"Shhh ... you can't call them that," Lherzo whispered. "Listen, what else can I do? If I miss the ride out, I'll never be more than watch supervisor."

"Lherzo, those women ... I don't know. You'll have to leave a *piece* of yourself there. What do you think they want those pieces for? Seriously?"

"Dirigo," Lherzo said, a dark look on his face, "you're not going to change my mind. Meet me at the stable at first bell, I'll have my mission plan by then. Don't tell any of the squad what I've told you. I'll see you in the morning."

Lherzo strode away, a pit in his stomach. It was still a few hours until midnight, but he couldn't think of anything that might change between now and then.

The Triad House lay in the steps up in a corner of the city, a place forgotten or ignored since the days Vertex enjoyed its spectacular growth during the Calculists' golden age. Always there have been three Triangulators in the house, the Crone, the Dame and the Maiden. With the passing of each Crone, the Triad would initiate a new Maiden and the other two women would advance in standing.

The steps to the house were lit with torches, which were only lit when a "seeker" was expected. Lherzo found no comfort in seeing the illuminated steps, it only reminded him that they knew he would be coming.

He stepped onto the entranceway, jumping with surprise to see a hooded figure by the door. The both stood in silence a moment, regarding each other. She then pulled back the hood of her black robe, revealing the face of a young girl of perhaps twelve or thirteen. He took a deep breath and strode forward. The young woman turned her back without greeting him and strode inside. Lherzo took one last look around before following.

The door led directly to an open space, dimly lit with candles. Their light lost most of their power long before touching the features of the stony, columned entrance room. The room was built into the faces themselves, the triangular arrangement of steps now locked in the back of the room away from the light of the sun. The Maiden walked silently up the stairs, her footsteps making no sound. Lherzo's boots clicked on the stone floor, echoing from the haunted walls.

At the top, where the stairs should naturally continue upwards, the steps were gone, carved away with the rest of the stone to create a round room. On the walls hung shapes of tools and instruments, some he recognized as navigating instruments and others whose purpose he did not know and did not wish to know. In the center stood a massive circular table: the Triangulators' abax.

Two figures stood behind the abax. They rounded the table and approached. A middle-aged woman with a sharp angular nose eyed him coldly. The other figure was slightly hunched and hobbled slowly towards him, peering at him with cloudy eyes. The Dame and the Crone, Lherzo understood. The Maiden joined the other two, all three facing him in a line.

"Seeker," the Dame spoke. "The Triad stands at your service. Upon the stones you shall seek, upon the stones we shall turn. The seeker's stone shall be the sacrifice, binding flesh and bone to stone. Do you agree to the price?"

Lherzo straightened his neck and pulled down his shoulders. "I do," he said, as forcefully as he could muster.

"Step forward, seeker," she said, indicating two chairs beside each other with a small table to the right of both.

Lherzo eyed the table as he approached. His stomach turned as he saw a stack of flat stones, a glass jar, and a pair of pliers. The pliers were a dark metal, two S's like snakes that slithered around each other and met in cold, hungry jaws.

They sat him in the seat between the table and the second chair. The Maiden knelt before him and removed his boots. She stacked three flat stones on each foot. The stones were heavy and the pressure was uncomfortable. Beside him the Crone slowly lowered herself into the empty seat. She positioned his hand on the arm of his chair and stacked stones on the back of his hand, straining slightly under the weight of each. On the other side, the Dame did likewise, weighting down his other hand. Lherzo felt pinned in place. It was too late to back out now.

The Dame stood behind him and reached under his chin, rolling back his head. He looked up into her face, the shadow of her sharp nose cutting across her face like a blade. She spoke. "Within your mouth the thirty-two stones guard the entrance to the tunnels within. Knowledge balances strength, you offer now a piece of yourself, an exchange of strength for knowledge. Open."

He opened his mouth. The Dame wrapped her left arm around his head. Lherzo saw the pliers in her hand and closed his eyes. He tried to focus on the weight of the stones at his feet, far away from his head, but his attention was jerked away by the clank of metal against his upper teeth. He braced himself.

Lherzo jumped with the shock of the jolt of pain in his mouth. He clenched his fingers around the arms of the chair as the pain radiated through his head and neck. Opening his eyes, he saw the white tooth with a long red root clenched in the jaws of the pliers. The Dame released his head, lifted the jar and dropped the tooth inside with a clink.

The pain was worse than Lherzo expected. It pulsed through his entire skull, all of his teeth screaming silently, an intense ache driving up through his skull and down through his neck as if someone were driving metal stakes through his head. He squeezed his eyes shut, wet tears pooling at the corners.

The Dame placed the jar on the table as all three women removed the stones from his hands and feet. The Maiden stood and lifted the jar with the tooth inside, bowed her head and took the jar away. She placed it on a shelf on the left of the room, where dozens of other small jars stood in a line.

"The payment is met," said the Dame. "Join us at the abax."

The Crone stood with difficulty and shuffled towards the round table in the middle of the room while Lherzo felt his remaining teeth with his tongue. They had taken the fourth tooth from the center on the right, Lherzo slightly relieved it was not an incisor as they had taken from Gordon earlier this week. He tasted blood. His head felt as if it were in a vise.

He dizzily pulled on his boots, stood unsteadily and joined the women at the table's edge.

The table was built as a series of nested circles. One large circle filled the abax, within this three large circles fit together in a triangular arrangement. Each of these contained three circles in the same pattern and each of these smaller circles held three even smaller circles again. Upon each circle was etched a triangle, each with a symbol that Lherzo did not recognize. Around the entire edge of the table was a ring of triangles, each made with edges that were combinations of single, double or triple lines. Lherzo assumed they would be twenty-seven in number, a sacred number among the Calculists.

"Seeker speak of what you seek," the Dame instructed.

"I seek an Abacist of the Teller line, the first of all seconds, reported seen in Quothmire on the day of the quake."

The Maiden placed her hands on the edge of the table and began to rotate the single large circle that consumed most of the table. It moved heavily but smoothly on some hidden bearing, whispering with a low grating sound as stone slid past stone. As she moved the circle, she spoke, the first time Lherzo had heard her voice. "*Lost and gone unknown, sea and sky and stone, flesh and blood and bone.*"

The Dame placed her hands on the circle and helped to turn the wheel. "*Step and shelf and face, square and block and space, time and phase and space,*" she said.

The Crone joined them as well, a third pair of hands upon the wheel. "*Circles intertwined, hand and wheel and mind, here and now to find.*"

"*Lost and gone unknown,*" the Maiden said.

"*Shelf and step and space,*" said the Dame.

"*Circles intertwined,*" joined the Crone.

They spoke now in snippets, repeating their phrases in different orders. The dame placed her hand on the edge of one of the three larger circles and turned that wheel as it passed. The Crone reached forward and turned a smaller wheel. Lherzo could see that each circle was its own wheel, each could be turned, each bringing with it a change in positions of the circles and triangles within each circle.

The phrases continued, Lherzo lost track of the order, hypnotized by the spinning wheels within wheels. For several minutes the table turned, arrangement after arrangement rolling to create a potential world before spinning into another possibility.

"*Here and now to find,*" the Crone croaked loudly.

"*Here and now to find,*" repeated the Dame.

"*Here and now to find,*" whispered the Maiden.

The wheels on the table slowed and rolled to a stop with a decisive clunk.

177

"Seeker," spoke the Crone. "The one you seek has departed Parchensis desert, two days 'fore."

He's traveled upwards, Lherzo thought, relieved. Teller has come towards Vertex, he might be able to reach him in time.

"Seeker," spoke the Dame. "The one you seek now stands upon Verdant Mesa, south of Lake Varygon."

"That's ... that is unexpected," he said, suddenly unsure. Did the Maiden not just say he was in Parchensis two days ago?

"Seeker," said the Maiden. "Your lines shall meet in two days time, at the foot of Saragis."

Lherzo paused, puzzled. "Is this ... certain?" he asked. "Saragis is far from Parchensis, and Lake Varygon."

"We divine only the who, the where and when," the Dame answered. "Our services are fulfilled, our account is reckoned."

Lherzo looked back and forth between the women, wanting to hear more, wanting to say more. He frowned. "Thank you," was all he said. He turned to leave, then paused to see if one of them would see him out. They did not move. He nodded and departed their company.

Outside the house, Lherzo walked carefully down the steps, his head still throbbing with terrible pain. The Triad now owned a piece of him. Dirigo had asked what they did with these teeth they collected, was it some kind of dark reckoning? Could they now control his fate? It was too late now, he had paid the price.

And what did he get for this unsettling price? A confused report. For the Abacist to get from Parchensis Desert on lower Abacabax to Lake Varygon would take a week on horse, *at least*, not two days as they said. That could not be correct. From there he could not get from Varygon to Saragis in two days, it would take three days on the fastest horse and probably longer. Nothing about their report made sense.

In any case, if their conclusion was correct and he could find the Abacist in two days at Saragis, the information would well be worth the price.

Tomorrow at first bell Lherzo would start his trip. He would find his prey.

Chapter 8: Divided

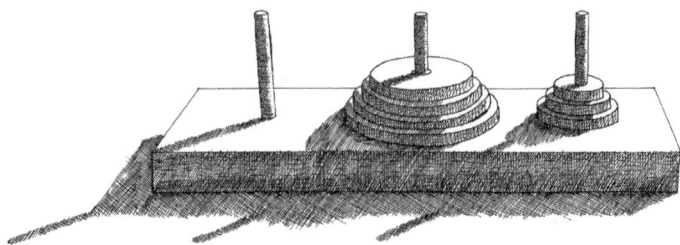

Samuel poked around the shelves in the hall outside of the dining room. The shelves were full of puzzles, which Saul liked very much. Every evening Samuel was to find a new puzzle and bring it to dinner. Saul told him that reckoning was not just about being able to calculate, but also being able to visualize. Puzzles were an important tool to develop strong reckoning.

Samuel picked up a curious object from the collection, a board with a row of three sticks, each pointing straight upwards. On the center stick stood a stack of seven disks of increasing size, each with a hole in the middle that fit around the stick. The smallest disk was on top and each subsequent disk was a little larger so the stack resembled a cone with the largest disk on the bottom. He took it to the dining room, where Saul was placing bowls on the table. Samuel eyed the food with distaste. It was wheat-meal. Again.

"Ah, you found one of my favorites!" Saul said. "The Towers of Abacabax."

Samuel sat down. Ignoring the bowl of white mush, he lifted the disks and moved them around.

"You need to try to move the whole tower to another pin," Saul explained, "but you can only move one disk at a time and you cannot place a larger disk on top of a smaller disk. The solution is closely connected to the name of our world."

Samuel began moving disks.

"At the very top of Abacabax is the Apex Temple," Saul said. "I've been there before, it is a very long trip. The mystics there are fairly talented reckoners. It is said they have such a tower with twenty-four disks made of the finest marble from the upper reaches. For the last one thousand years, they have moved exactly one disk every day. When the entire tower is moved, the world will come to an end!"

Samuel raised his eyebrows. "Really? When will that happen?"

"No," Saul said with a sigh. "Not really. At least, I saw no such tower. It's a story. The puzzle is to figure out how much danger we are in. How many years it will take until the world ends?"

"I have no idea," said Samuel. He kept moving disks. "Maybe we should go there. Maybe they can find out how to help me reckon."

Samuel paused. He looked up at Saul, his face gloomy. "How come I can do it with books and bricks and plates and stuff, but nothing happens when I try it on the Changed? I can't feel this thing you say I'm supposed to feel!"

Saul sat thoughtful a moment. "You can reckon on the inanimate but cannot connect to the living. I've never heard of this in an Abacist, but I believe it can happen with more primitive people. These Finger-Reckoners I mentioned, they are already very weak and only the older ones can reckon on the living. Some of them never learn to reckon at all. I wonder ..."

Saul stood from the table. "I'll be in the library." He left suddenly, his bowl of wheat-meal only half-eaten.

Samuel shrugged and went back to moving disks.

Rita turned off the burner under the kettle. The kitchen now looked as if they were renovating, with a transparent shower curtain she and Wendi had hastily nailed into place over the shattered window. With the shards of glass swept up, the dishes restacked and broken picture frames stacked in the corner, the two women felt a little more in control. Rita poured the boiling water into a yellow teapot and carried it with two cups hanging on one finger into the living room.

Wendi sat on the couch, a dark look on her weathered face.

"So, Samuel is in Tangram with that monster brother of yours," Rita said, setting down the cups and teapot, "and you don't know where Max is. I don't know which is worse."

"Max is probably in Quothmire, at my wayfaring house."

Rita shook her head. "Why were we going to Quothmire, of all places?"

"It's quiet and out of the way. I planned for us to meet with some friends, some strong allies, a Calculist and a Dijin. It's possible they will find Max and he'll be in good hands."

"But he won't be able to reckon, is that right? Neither of them will?"

"No, they won't. By giving the Hands of Kael to Max instead of Samuel, I invoked the Exception. Their power is now divided and neither boy will have the natural ability to reckon. Saul will not be able to use Samuel's abilities."

"And Max? Max knows nothing, Mother!" Rita said. "He knows no one, he's never seen that world and now you're saying he won't even be able to reckon? And Saul and Samuel, what is it that he ... what about when ... oh, this is too much, I can't even ..." Rita slapped her hands against the sides of her head and pressed her temples hard.

"Saul will take care of Samuel," Wendi reassured her. "He is blood. Samuel will be all right, but Saul won't be able to use him and that will give us time to get them both back. Saul cannot be trusted with that kind of power."

"But doesn't Saul want to heal the Changed?" Rita asked. "I thought that's what he has been working on all these years? That's what he wants Samuel for."

"Saul has made no progress. There is little left of the minds of the Changed, and I don't believe anything can be done. They are no longer human. I have already mourned their passing.

"Saul now only seeks revenge. He blames the Calculists, he thinks he could have saved our brethren if they hadn't taken his laboratory. Saul is the greatest reckoner of anyone by far. I am stunned by what he can do. He can even control minds, which gives him a small army of twenty or so Darklings to command. With Samuel's algorithms, Saul could command a thousand times that number and reach into *anyone's* mind. There is no telling what he would use that power for, but he certainly can't use it to bring back the dead. He will use it against the Calculists.

"That's why I invoked the Exception," Wendi concluded. "Saul will be at an impasse."

"And that was your plan?" Rita snapped. "Cut off Samuel's reckoning ability and let Saul take him away, powerless? What kind of plan is that?!"

"I could not stop Saul. And I can't stop him now, either, not alone. But there is something else, there is another way. You know the mental game we play when we reckon? The picture or the idea that is required to draw power and focus the reckoning? This is the part of reckoning that is difficult for most people. It is the reason powers grow stale in the populace, why Calculists don't use reckoning for everyday tasks and why

Dijins won't share their ideas. It's why half of the Abacists were powerless against the plague sixteen years ago! Power is created from new ideas, but what are new ideas created from?"

"Go on," Rita said.

"Down from Quothmire, close to the Water Mesa, is a group of mystics who study this very question. I believe the answer to that question may hold the key to the future of reckoning. There is a different kind of ability, the ability to create new ideas, new images, new connections. It requires imagination and visualization and the ability to shape a new world inside of consciousness, with a structure that mimics the physical world but wherein the rules can be changed.

"I see this trait in Maxwell. I saw it right away. His thinking ... it is wondrous in scale and physics-free. Maxwell doesn't have the algorithmic skill of Samuel, but he has something much deeper and much more important. Since the beginning, Abacabax has moved steadily towards better and better methods of reckoning but at the cost of imagination. As our reckoning grows stronger, the power behind the reckoning grows weaker. The reason for gaining power has become only to gain more power. Abacabax has been slowly sinking into darkness. Maxwell may help restore the balance. He could bring a gift to the world that could transform Abacabax, bring light and peace to all the faces.

"We could end the wars over reckoning and who will be next to invent a more complicated algorithm that only leads to more fighting," Wendi continued. "We could create a new kind of thinking *beyond* reckoning that everyone could benefit from. Invoking the Exception breaks the final link in the final chain and gives us a chance to start anew."

"Is that the best we've got?" Rita said dourly. "We'll just bring back imagination and everyone will hold hands and sing songs and be friends again?"

Wendi sighed. "It's a start. It's the only way I see to bring us back from the edge. Right now, we've got to find both of the boys."

"How can we do that? How on Earth are we going to get them back now? Saul has taken our abacuses. Only the Four Tablets are strong enough for that level of reckoning."

Wendi sighed. "There is a way. It is long and difficult and I hoped I would never have to attempt it. We must invoke the full name of Abacabax."

"Invoke the full name ... how ... ? What are you talking about?"

"Saul's portal uses a mechanical device to spell out the entire name of Abacabax. We have no such device, but we can use the same principal with an incantation. If we *say* the name, we can open the portal from this side."

"*Say* the name? The *entire* name?" Rita stared at Wendi in disbelief. "To the twenty-fourth level? All the way to 'X?' Do you have any idea how long that will take? No one can do that!"

"We can do it together," Wendi said. "We need not do it nonstop, but we need to do it without error."

"It can't be done."

"It must be done."

"Without a mistake?"

"Without a mistake," Wendi said. "If you'll get some paper, we can begin charting the name now, and we can start in the morning."

-:- | -:-

Samuel sat on the wall, watching as the shadows on the steps and shelves made interesting patterns that shifted quickly in the low light of the setting sun. The steps stretched up and up until he could see them no further. Saul said if he walked for a month or two he would find the temple at the very top. Samuel was sure he would not want to try walking there. He doubted he could even get up to the next giant block.

Below him lay the empty city of Tangram. Empty, that is, except for the Changed who wandered aimlessly through the deserted streets. Samuel would have loved to explore the deserted buildings and passages below, but Saul did not offer to take him and Samuel dared not go alone until he knew how to control those frightening creatures. He thought of the monster in Saul's bedroom biting Saul's hand and shuddered.

"Samuel?" He heard Saul calling in the distance. "Samuel!"

"I'm down here!" he yelled back. "I'm coming."

Samuel trudged up the steps. It was no wonder they didn't get any visitors. Who would ever be able to walk up stairs all day?

Saul met him at the door. "Come, come to the study," Saul said eagerly.

Curious, Samuel followed. The study was a quiet room, sound dampened by the carpets hanging on the walls. Samuel had wondered about the patterns on the carpets during his time exploring the castle while Saul was busy with his inventions. He had planned to ask about them but never had.

Saul motioned him to a low table where an open book and a glass jar were carefully placed. Samuel slumped into a padded chair. Saul took a seat opposite him, leaning forward with his elbows on his knees.

"I found this in Wendi's book on Dijin herbology. Your grandmother used to walk all over the faces, gathering plants and flowers from the corners of the world. Here, listen to this:

"The purple flowers of the salvendia bush have mildly hallucinogenic properties. Dijins use these in sacred rituals and in cases

where members fail to develop their reckoning. A patient can sometimes connect to a host and trigger an event they call 'the awakening.'"

"An awakening?" Samuel asked.

"Yes, I believe it allows Dijins to connect to other life forms. I'm not sure, the Dijins are so very little interesting I never paid much mind when Wendi talked about them. She used to love visiting Dijin country, I don't know why, but it looks like her follies may have had some value after all. I found this in her workroom." Saul lifted the labeled jar from the table. Inside were dried flowers, purplish-brown in color.

"It is salvendia. I'd like to try this with you," Saul said, opening the jar. "I have a method of entering minds, and perhaps with some help with these flowers, we can unlock your abilities."

"Hallucinogenic? Is this like L.S.D. or something?" Samuel asked.

Ignoring his question, Saul poured some of the leaves on the table. "We'll take half to start with and more later if need be. Here." Saul placed a pinch of the dried leaves in Samuel's hand. He took the remaining leaves from the table, tipped back his head and swallowed them.

Samuel looked at the leaves. "Okay ..." he said. He hesitantly placed them in his mouth and started chewing.

They sat for a minute. "I don't think it's doing anything," Samuel said.

"Just relax," said Saul. "I'm going to connect with your mind." He took his abacus and began clicking the beads. "Welcome me in."

Samuel felt the air tighten around his head as it did in practice sometimes. He closed his eyes. Suddenly, his stomach felt as if he had just gone down a drop on a rollercoaster. He felt dizzy, sparks appearing before his eyes. "I feel something," he said dreamily.

"Samuel," Saul whispered. "It's working. Don't resist, allow it to happen. I can see the structures of your mind ... hmmm ..."

Saul continued clicking away. Samuel felt his head growing warmer. A tingling sensation crept over his scalp, down his cheeks and into his mouth. He felt as if his brain were floating above his skull.

"It's your symbols ... I see your reckoning ... it is all here ..." Saul whispered.

He kept clicking the beads steadily. "That's it," he murmured. "I can just ... take ... it ... all ..."

Samuel slipped backwards, motionless in the seat. His skin drained of color, his open eyes empty and unblinking.

Chapter 9: Accident

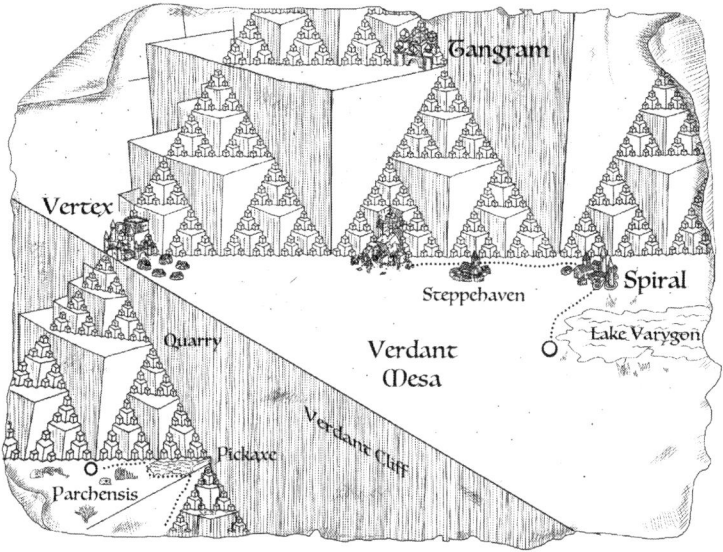

"This thing is moving fast!" Max said.

All three stood clinging to the edge of the basket. Lunata clutched a brightly glowing crystal, the same as Zarza held in the cave and probably the same as were set in the walls of the passages they had traveled through on their way to this upwardly-flowing river. The walls of the tunnel sped by in a blur, the water much quieter than Max would have expected. How smooth the passage must be for the water to rush by so quietly, he thought.

The passage rose at a steep angle, but the basket floated level and stable as it bobbed up and down. The surface of the river curved upwards on both sides where it met the walls, making an aquatic half-pipe with the basket riding in the center. Max tried to gauge the speed. He could not even make a good guess.

"How long until we get to the top?" he asked.

"Three or four hours, I think," Lunata said.

They sat down, the basket was just wide enough for Max to nearly stretch his legs out if he slid back tight against the side. Mindre sat facing the same direction, Lunata across from them in the middle. Here in the bottom of the basket the air was quieter and it felt much safer.

"How many of your people are there?" Mindre asked Lunata.

"Oh, I've never counted," Lunata said. She set down her crystal by her thigh and the light dimmed. "A few thousand, but we live in different systems."

"Do you all live in the tunnels?" she asked.

"It's not *all* tunnels," Lunata said. "There are many caverns and theaters, some we have made ourselves. And not everyone likes the tunnels. I like the surface better myself."

"Where do you get your food?" Mindre asked.

"We grow most of it in our harvest chambers. We're kind of experts with light, and we direct the water where we want it to go. Of course we have fisheries, as well, and I shepherd lizards. It lets me be outside."

"Is that the only meat you eat?" Mindre asked.

Lunata raised her eyes in thought. "Well, do millipedes count as meat? I suppose they do. Oh!" She looked at Mindre and slowly grinned. "You're wondering if we eat Dijins?"

"Do you?"

Lunata laughed. "I don't know why you still think that. Okay, maybe because ... you see, the first of our line was a ... brutal man, shall we say? He was also extremely clever. He made things out of bones, sculptures and the like, and learned to reckon with them. After the first Great Divide he became the New Origin and our civilization flourished. He tamed the water, controlled it and changed the rivers. Unfortunately, the rivers he took were also the rivers that fed the lands of the Old Dijins and there was a war. It did not go well for the Dijins, sorry Mindre."

Mindre huffed. "It was long ago."

"Being the start of the Bone-Thrower line, there was a shortage of metacarpals, the hand bones, you know. So he took the hands of his enemies, which were many. It was all very practical, you understand. I suppose that's where the stories began, but no one ate the meat from the hands. At least ... I don't think so.

"I've never eaten human," Lunata continued, "but I imagine it would taste a lot like lizard." She thought about this for a moment.

"Your bones, the ones you reckon with," Max said, "you said they are your grandfather's?"

"Yes, nowadays we gift our bones when we no longer need them. When you enter your fourth phase, you select bones from your ancestors. Some choose hands from different ancestors, I chose both from my grandfather. Look, he had twelve fingers!" Lunata took out her bones and spread them out like fanning a deck of cards. "We were very close, grandfather and I. He would be very happy to know I chose his."

Mindre rubbed the back of her hands, looking uncomfortable.

"They're very nice," Max said. "Some of them have burn marks on them?"

Yes, I've marked mine, a burn on each side. With these markings, I can double-reckon."

"So, you can ... set up a number both with how you turn the bones and with which marks are showing?" Max asked.

"Aren't you a clever one, Max?" Lunata said. "I think you must be part Bone-Thrower. How did you know our beat count during the dance, by the way?"

"We found some of your numbers on the steps near where we met you. I recognized it as binary."

"Binary?"

"That's what we call a number system based on two. It's connected to the pattern of the steps, so it's something I've been getting a lot of practice with while we've been walking."

"Yes, two-ness. It is sacred to Abacabax. The entire world is built on twos. We were surprised that when the Calculist family was born, they returned to tens, much like Dijins' fives."

Max found it strange that binary developed so early in Abacabax's history, but given the doubling nature of the terrain, it made sense. "I suppose," he said, "that reckoning is a combination of the power of the world with the power of humans, so both twos and fives are important." He took out his abacus and indicated the groupings of five beads on the bottom and two beads on the top. "The Abacists use twos and fives together, so it's a little of Dijin and Bone-Thrower combined."

"But Max, your reckoning is very weak for an Abacist," Lunata said. "And Mindre, you reckon like one hundred Dijins assembled. I don't understand."

Max looked at Mindre. She smiled and answered for them both. "Max has not yet awakened. It is perhaps because he is an offworlder, perhaps because his abacus is broken, but he cannot yet connect to the life energies. However, Max has other talents, as you've seen."

Max smiled at her, pleased that she didn't think he was entirely useless.

"And like you," Mindre said, "I have learned to extend my art, so I reckon not only on my fingers but on my entire body."

"So you are also a Prime?" Lunata asked.

"*Also?* You are the Thumb!" Mindre said with surprise. "Of course!"

Lunata grinned. "That's why my mother allowed me to join you, methinks. A chance to prove myself and perhaps be New Origin. I suppose we can't both be New Origin, now, can we? But let's not be rivals ... let's be sisters!"

Lunata laughed. "I've always wanted a sister. No, we won't be rivals. Anyway, the New Origin is probably going to be the Calculist general, but now that Max's brother, the Abacists' Thumb, is back, it could go either way."

"Imagine that," Lunata said. "Two-and-a-half Primes, all in the same basket. Floating up to who-knows-what? Exciting!"

They talked nearly the entire trip upwards. Lunata was curious about everything ... what Earth was like, what cities were like on the surface, where Mindre learned to reckon, what kind of food Max ate, who made Mindre's boots, what kind of bone was used in the rods on Max's abacus, what kind of lizards they had in Quincunx, and on and on. Max was pleased that Mindre and Lunata seemed to get along so well. By the time they neared the top, Max was no longer worried about having a strange addition to their group but rather enchanted with her eager curiosity and blunt observations.

The sound of the water changed, becoming a broader, more hollow sound as the upwards-flowing river leveled out and entered a large cave. The current flowed in a whirlpool in the round room, exiting through an opening in the rough wall. The basket followed the current, rolling up against a flat ledge where a row of posts had been set into the stone. Lunata tossed a loop of rope over the first post, pulled it tight and the basket stopped.

"Welcome to the Uplands!" Lunata said, climbing out of the basket.

She unfastened the rope when they were all ashore, letting the basket spin into the watery spiral. "That will return when the current reverses," she explained.

Lunata led the way down a narrow passage, up a short ladder and then through a crack barely wide enough to squeeze through.

They stood in the daylight on a rocky hill on the edge of a huge lake. Far away they could see the faint shapes of triangles stacked upon one another and fading into the sky.

"It's Lake Varygon," Mindre marveled. "Your river saved us many days of climbing, and we avoided the Calculist lands altogether!"

"Yes," said Lunata. "There are settlements along the base of the mountain and routes to both Vertex and Tangram from there."

"That's Trigarra cliff," Mindre said, pointing to the middle of the triangles of the mountain. A faintly visible line dividing the faces of the cliff stretched upwards into the clouds. "There's a free city called Spiral there, which is friendly to Dijins. We can all pass as Dijins. We may be able to barter for transport to Vertex from there and with luck we'll find my father and Lady Teller in the big city. Only three or four more days, Max!"

Not long now, Max thought. Had Roggolo found Max's grandmother? If she were on her way as Lady Carpus asserted, why had she not found them yet? Roggolo thought she should have been able to contact Max. Since his grandmother was the Longwalker, able to travel "like the wind," shouldn't she have found them by now? In any case, Vertex seemed to be the center of everything and one way or another they would discover what came next.

They picked their way carefully along the rocky hill, coming to hard grassy plains on the other side. They followed the lake's edge as it curved towards the mountain. Here they found a trail, the ground flat and bare beneath their feet.

They made camp far from the trail in a grove of trees with light green leaves and ashy bark. Max spread out bedding while Mindre gathered firewood and Lunata hunted for herbs and "Upland spices." She returned proudly with a collection of dirty white roots.

"Look, I found radix!" she said proudly. "They're hard to extract because the tendrils make all these right angles. Try one!"

She put one in her mouth and offered the bunch to Max and Mindre. Max wiped most of the dirt off of the root and bit into the root. It was spicy and pungent, like horseradish, and made Max's eyes water slightly.

Lunata pulled from her pack a bowl made of thin, hard, translucent material. She placed it on the fire and created a soup from vegetables and spices in their packs. The meal burned in Max's stomach, but he was pleased to have a warm meal and complimented her skill with cooking.

The evening air was clean and fresh, and Max felt very content as they stretched out beneath their blankets. He fell asleep easily, eager to see what the morning would bring.

They rose early, ate quickly and resumed their trek. By afternoon they neared the mountain. The blocks of Abacabax spread like an endless wall in both directions. The trail joined another trail and widened into a road, taking them past several small farms. A pair of tracks worn into the road indicated traffic with wheels. Max wondered what the vehicles might look like. He didn't wait long for an answer. A horse-drawn cart bumped down the road towards them. The driver held up a hand in salute as he rode past.

"There's the free city," Mindre said as they came over the top of a rise. A cluster of wooden buildings in brown and red and white gathered along a narrow river that wound its way back and forth from the edge of the cliffs. Other buildings sat stacked up on the faces of the mountain like birds watching for bread crumbs.

"What's a free city?" Max asked.

"They're neutral to the feuds of the families," Mindre said. "All kinds of reckoners used to live here. Now it's mostly Calculists but there's still quite a few Dijins. It's one of the few places my people are still welcome. Reckoning is strictly off limits, so keep your devices hidden. It's a friendly place and they have a very good market, but we'll need to get guilds, first."

The free cities, Mindre explained, have a common money system controlled by a group of bankers called "The Guild." On all of Abacabax, money is called "guilds" in general, though different regions have their own means of exchange. In Calculist cities, the guilds are crystals with twelve rhombus-shaped faces. Some Calculists use these in place of the abac stones on their reckoning boards. Abacists used flat beads made of a rare pink stone called "thulite," while Dijins traded rings.

The guilds in the free cities were coins and trading would be easy if they could get ahold of some. Mindre still had several small wooden puzzles in her pack which her father had designed. She explained they should be relatively easy to sell or trade for supplies.

The market was a vibrant scene. Unlike the other groups of people Max had seen, everyone was dressed quite differently from one another in robes, suits, dresses, kilts, hats with feathers and tall boots with silver buckles. People of all kinds hurried about their business.

Lunata pointed at a man arguing with a merchant about a string of onions. "Look at that!" she said. A woman pulled along two children in a wagon. "Look at that!" Lunata said, spinning around.

Mindre turned to her. "We don't need to draw attention to ourselves, Lunata. Max, will you look after her while I try to ..."

Two soldiers shoved them out of their way as they stormed past. They pushed through a knot of people, spilling an older man to the ground. The people nearby scowled at the soldiers but said nothing as the men hurried on their way.

"Soldiers, here?" Mindre whispered. "This is a *free* city. They won't be looking for you here, Max, but be careful. You two watch out for each other."

Mindre approached a man with a thin beard who was selling various knick-knacks from a cart. "Puzzles," she told him. "I have Roggolo puzzles from Quothmire, of the highest quality."

Max stood back watching her bargain. She spoke with confidence. Her steely voice did not waver as she asserted the value of her wares. She knew their worth and what price they would draw, but the man refused. "No one's no gona ha' the thoughts for puzzles," he explained in his strange accent. "Seen ya the soldiers? Vertex is calling in the reserves. But why dona ya try the berry merchant. She's hadda many customers, and she loves the puzzles, she does."

Max and Lunata wandered through the market. Max kept his eye on Mindre as she moved on, talking to various merchants.

"Look," Lunata whispered through her teeth. She stared fascinated at a man who was crouched near the ground talking to an earnest-faced farmer and tapping the ground. They stepped closer to hear the farmer tell the man a series of numbers.

"He's reading his numbers," Lunata whispered.

With his palms down near the ground, the crouching man tapped his fingers inside five circles drawn in the sand. He was a Dijin, Max guessed, but if he were reckoning it was not something he had seen Mindre do. Mindre had said reckoning was not allowed, so maybe this was just for show.

"Dark times are coming," the Dijin said, "but they will not reach your family. Oh, I see a child ... do you have a son or daughter, or know someone who does?"

"Yes!" the farmer said excitedly. "I have a son!"

"I thought so," he said. "Your son will be making a trip to a small or a large city, and when he is there he will meet someone ..."

The Dijin paused. He and the farmer looked up at Max and Lunata. The farmer scowled. "I suppose you're wanting to find out what happens?" he said impatiently.

"Oh, yes, please!" Lunata said eagerly.

Max took her elbow. "Sorry," he muttered with an embarrassed smile, leading her away.

Mindre had moved on to the next merchant. Max and Lunata walked slowly on, taking in all the movement and life around them. A group of children sat around a woman who was drawing in the sand. Max stopped nearby to watch. She had placed a dozen small stones in a grid pattern and was drawing a weaving line traveling diagonally between the stones as she told a story. Max paused to listen.

"The farmer went back to the river and caught a fish, then walked around the river bend towards the healer," the woman was saying. "When the healer saw the fish, he snapped it up!" Her finger wove around the stones as she talked.

"And the farmer saw that the healer was not a man at all but was really his long-lost rooster!" She finished the curve, the looping path in the sand resembling a bird. The children clapped.

Max thought the story was ridiculous, but the pattern was wonderful! He turned to smile at Lunata, but she was gone.

He walked further down the street, looking behind flower carts and vegetable stands. No Lunata. He began to be concerned ... he only had one job to do and that was to watch their easily-excited friend. He caught sight of Mindre again, talking animatedly to a thin man perched in a two-seat buggy hitched to a black horse. The man was shaking his head and showing her his palms as if to say there was nothing he could do to help.

Mindre turned from him with a frown, and seeing Max, she strode towards him, the corners of her mouth down. "Soldiers are requisitioning all of the horses and all of the carts. There is an operation the army is launching at Vertex. They're marching on Tangram in a few days. We need to get there before then, but we won't make it in time walking. We need horses."

Looking about, she asked, "Where's Lunata?"

A man in a plumed hat dashed up and took ahold of the hand of a woman in a ruffled dress nearby. "Mabelli, you've got the see this – there's a bone reckoner casting numbers!"

Mindre looked at Max accusingly. They both sprung after the man and woman into the market.

"You're supposed to be watching her!" Mindre admonished as they sprung across the market.

They found Lunata quickly. It wasn't difficult. She was in the center of a crowd, kneeling on the edge of her cloak which she had spread flat before her. Without her cover, her bone ornamentation and jewelry were on full display as she turned the neatly arranged line of her hand bones. A soldier in a gray uniform was crouched in front of her, listening raptly.

"Ooohhh ... your number is two-hundred fifty-five," Lunata announced in a grand voice, "a great number, that of near-completion. You will do *great* things."

"Yes," the soldier whispered, "but will I die?"

"Oh, indeed you will," she said confidently, "and it will be a glorious death."

The soldier's eyes misted over. "Thank you," he said, a smile on his lips. Reaching into his pocket, he withdrew a coin and dropped it into Lunata's hands. "Thank you so much!"

"Lunata," Mindre said sternly. "It's time to go. Now!" She pulled her fortune-telling friend to her feet. Lunata grabbed her cloak and her pack and the three of them marched down the street.

"Look how many monies I got!" Lunata said enthusiastically, holding out a palmful of coins.

"Get that cloak on! We don't need to draw attention!" Mindre barked.

Lunata fumbled with her cloak as Max glanced over his shoulder. The soldier was talking to two other soldiers and pointing in their direction. They looked alarmed, and Max guessed their interest ran deeper than getting a numerological reading. One of the soldiers' gaze felt straight on Max. "Hey!" he yelled.

"We've drawn attention," Max said quickly.

Mindre threw a glance back. "This way, hurry!"

They sprinted after Mindre, down the side of the street. "Give me those guilds!" she shouted to Lunata as they ducked behind the buggy where Mindre had been unsuccessfully negotiating with the driver moments before. The driver stood on the other side, looping a length of rope. Grabbing the coins from Lunata's hand she commanded Max and Lunata. "Get in!"

The three scrambled into the empty seat, Max hunched over with his full pack still on his back.

The thin man on the other side of the buggy spun around. "What are you doing?" he shouted.

Mindre threw the handful of coins at him. "Sorry, we're 'requisitioning' this!"

With a snap of the reins, the horse jolted forward.

The thin man darted after them, yelling, drawing the attention of another group of soldiers across the street. Max grabbed the rail in front of him, hanging on as the cart bumped and jerked on the stony street.

Mindre swerved the buggy to the middle of the street, narrowly avoiding a group of men in matching flat hats.

"Fruit cart!" yelled Max. The buggy jerked to the side as the back wheel struck the cart. Looking behind him, Max saw melons spilling everywhere into the street. The merchant stepped out from behind the cart, cursing and waving his fist angrily in the air.

Mindre swung the buggy down an alley, onto another street and across a narrow wooden bridge over the river. She snapped the reins again, coaxing the horse as fast as it could run on the road out of town.

"Exciting!" yelled Lunata, her mouth pulling into a wide grin.

Max watched the road behind them. Through the dust, he saw three horses turn from the bridge. The riders wore gray uniforms.

"They're after us," Max said.

"Of course they are!" Mindre said angrily. She handed the reins to Lunata. "Max, help me out."

She turned in her seat to face the riders, fingers moving, hands touching herself in different places. Max pulled out his abacus. What could he do? His mind raced. He couldn't affect the riders or the horses. He could throw stones, where was a large enough stone? There was only tall grass on both sides. Could he slow them down ... or could he make their own buggy go faster?

He glanced forward. The road ran straight, parallel to the stacks of blocks making up the mountain on their right. The blocks were all in a straight line, the pattern of their heights *one-two-one-three-one-two-one-four-* ... the same as the clacking pattern two nights ago, the same binary pattern, the same pattern that gave him a boost when walking. Why not use the same pattern to get a boost now?

He began entering the step-counting pattern, trying to visualize it pushing the cart. There was no effect.

"There's three more!" Lunata called.

"One down!" Mindre shouted. "Max, what are you doing?"

Max focused on his calculating. Step-counting wouldn't work of course, the cart's already going much faster than walking. Max shifted to the next rod on his abacus and tried doubling the pattern. *Two-four-two-eight-* ... Did he feel something that time?

Moving to the next column, he began *four-eight-four-sixteen-* ... That felt like something! He shifted to another rod on his abacus and began another pattern starting on eight. Yes, the buggy was definitely moving faster now.

"What are you doing?" Mindre called.

Max didn't answer, it was hard to concentrate on these numbers. He had practiced step-counting to the point where it had become "finger memory" and those movements were now automatic. He had no such experience with these different numbers. His pacing was erratic and the "push" he was generating was more of an uneven pulsing. He needed more.

He moved to another column and then another. What he lacked in smoothness he would make up for with sheer volume! He pictured the oncoming cliffs like steps he was climbing, but the bigger cliffs were like small steps, like the entire world was scaling down to match his pattern.

"Whatever you're doing, it's working!" Mindre yelled.

Max focused solely on keeping the pattern going and picturing the buggy rolling like normal while the world and its distances shrunk. He was vaguely aware of the cliffs whizzing by, here and gone in a blink. His excitement grew as the largest cliff since Trigarra appeared. He moved to enter one-thousand twenty-four on the eleventh column, his algorithm reaching all the way to the leftmost column on his abacus. He slid a bead on the fourteenth rod.

There was a crack, so loud that it sounded like the planet beneath their feet had been frozen into a thick slab of ice and smacked so hard that it had snapped violently in two. The shudder from the noise wracked Max's body like a jolt of electricity. He was barely aware of smashing into horse and human, tumbling into the air.

He floated, his mind grabbing every detail at once so that it felt as if time had slowed to a crawl. Mindre hung in the air beside him, her arms tapping across her body in slow-motion. She stretched out her arms and drew them in close again. Max's trajectory in the air shifted course as the three airborne bodies drew together in a collision course, the horse and buggy long gone from beneath them. He saw the grassy plain rushing up at him. He had just enough time to realize he would hit the ground at an angle and pulled his arms in to his head. Max's world exploded in pain as he hit the ground and rolled. The sky spun sickeningly all around him.

His ears felt as if they would burst from the rumbling. He lay twisted in a thicket of bushes, his eyes screwed shut as the thunder continued to roar. Max was aware of the earth shaking, stones falling, the ground rending and tearing deep beneath him.

He lay still for a long moment as the rumbling ceased, pain pulsing through his body. With great effort he rolled over out of the bushes and sat up. His arms, wrists and hands burned. He slid his pack from his shoulders and found he could still move his arms. By doing so, they felt both better and worse at the same time. Somehow he was still clutching the abacus in his left hand, the beads hanging dead under the weight of gravity.

He turned around and stood dumbstruck at the sight. Behind him stretched a swath of devastation Max had never seen the likes of. The neatly patterned rows of steps and blocks they had been effortlessly flying by a moment before were now toppled and torn, pieces scattered in piles. Blocks continued to tumble. In the distance a cliff the size of skyscraper hung forward at a precarious angle, threatening to crush the world below.

Were there people back there in the debris? Where was Mindre? Where was Lunata?

He looked at the abacus in his bloody fingers. He had done this. He was the Destroyer. He was the Hand of Death.

Chapter 10: Betrayal

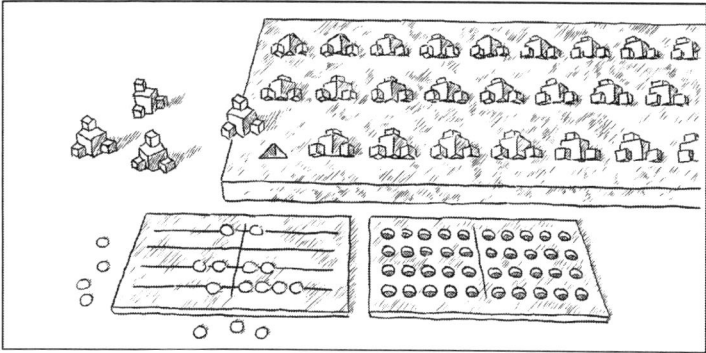

Warm wind blew in Max's face, stinging his skin with sharp bits of dust. He squinted, looking around helplessly. Was he totally alone on the edge of this destruction?

The wind ebbed and he heard a grunt from beyond the bushes. He rushed towards the noise. The ground sloped downwards behind the bush. Two bodies lay on the decline. "Mindre?" he called. "Lunata?"

Mindre and Lunata were both moving. Max wanted to say a prayer of thanks but wasn't sure which moon he should be thanking.

"Max ... you're all right ..." Mindre said, smiling weakly. "It worked ..."

Max slid down the slope to Mindre's side. "Are you all right?"

"I'm okay. Lunata?" Mindre asked.

"All bones intact," Lunata croaked, pushing herself to sit upright. "Oh, you're bleeding," she said.

Max wiped his bloody hands on his pants.

"Don't do that Max, let's get some water on those," Mindre said.

"You caught us, in the air, didn't you?" Max asked as Mindre reached for her pack.

"I tried to slow us down, I think it worked," Mindre said.

"You are the fastest thinker, ever. I don't know how you managed that."

"Max, what you did ..." Mindre said slowly.

"You moved us like the Longwalker!" Lunata said.

Max frowned. "Come see what else I did."

Mindre handed the water flask to Max as she and Lunata carefully stood. They stepped up the incline and stopped, staring in disbelief. Lunata gave out a long, low whistle. Mindre said nothing, her eyes hard.

"I know. I did that," Max said, grimly.

"Max ..." Mindre began.

"It's the second quake," Max said. "You know what they say about the third."

"We're going to get to Apex before that happens, Max," Mindre said. "And you know what I say about prophecies. We reckon on the flesh of the living, not the bones of our ancestors." She looked at Lunata, clad in bones. "Well, most of us, anyway."

"Well, we have our packs, but ..." Max began, not wanting to finish the thought.

"Our horse is probably dead," Lunata said matter-of-factly, finishing the thought for him.

"Are there people back there?" Max asked, dreading the answer.

"We came past Steppehaven," Mindre said. "I'm not sure how far that scar reaches."

"Horse!" shouted Lunata. In the distance, among the scattered blocks at the foot of the mountain lay the body of a horse.

"That's not ours," Max said. "C'mon, someone could be hurt."

They walked back towards the horse. Max's knee hurt, he swung his weight to ease the pressure from it as he walked. There was no sign of their own stolen horse or the buggy. As they drew closer, they could see a flag with a black triangular insignia hanging from the saddle of the lifeless horse.

"Calculist military," Mindre said. "Be careful."

They rounded a corner of a massive block. A soldier in gray lay on the ground, his leg pinned beneath a table-sized cube of stone. They hurried to his side.

Mindre gasped. "Lherzo?!"

Max looked at Lunata, then back to Mindre. "You know him?"

Mindre knelt beside him and held his face between her palms. "Lherzo? Can you hear me?" She patted his cheek sharply.

The young man's eyelids fluttered and opened halfway. "Mindre? What ..." he muttered, eyes falling closed.

"We need to lift this stone!" She set her fingers and hands, ready to reckon, and then stopped. "We'll never move this."

"We can all work together," Max said.

"Let me do it," Lunata said. "Making tunnels is one of our specialties." She crouched, spreading her bones out in a line. Max watched closely as she turned the bones horizontally and vertically, rolling them from burnt side to polished side, sliding them up and down from their line. He could see that not only did the bones have two different orientations and two different sides, but they could also be slid up or down into two different positions. He could not make sense of her operations at all.

"This is called 'muqabala,'" Lunata said. "That means 'taking apart.'" A thin line appeared on the center of the edge of the block, lengthening at an even pace. Lunata continued turning the bones. The narrow crack reached the opposite edge and continued on the adjacent face. The stone split in two with a grinding sound as the halves separated slightly.

"Now we can try," Lunata said.

Beside him, Mindre moved her fingers and touched her body, hands dancing down her chest and thighs. Lunata spun the bones to a new position and continued reckoning. Max dared not touch his abacus.

The two halves of the stone block slid apart a few hand widths. The soldier groaned.

Mindre hopped forward, reaching under his arms and across his chest with both of her arms and pulling him backwards. His leg slid out from between the halves, bent at a grotesque angle. "Max, get the knife from my pack," she said.

Max dug out Mindre's blade and gave it to her quickly. He watched uneasily as Mindre cut up the leg of the soldier's pants and pulled aside the cloth. His leg bent horribly in a wrong angle, the skin red but not from blood. "We've got to try to set this. I've never done this before."

"I have," said Lunata. "Bones are my main specialty." She placed her hands on the soldier's leg, one above the break and the other at his knee. "You should steady him," she said to Mindre.

Mindre wrapped her arm around the soldier's head and nodded to Lunata. With a push and a pull, she straightened his leg. The soldier opened his mouth and howled. One tooth was missing from the top row.

Lunata turned back to her hand bones, organizing them into two groups. She set up numbers on each group and became moving the twelve bones from one group to another. "This is something I developed myself," she said. "I call this 'algebra.'"

"Algebra?" asked Max, surprised by the name.

"It is the complement of muqabala. It means 'putting together,'" Lunata explained, not looking up from her reckoning.

His skin rippled, the leg shifting slightly as it straightened completely.

Lunata turned a few more of her reckoning bones. "The equation is complete, the bone is whole," she said.

The soldier opened his eyes and bent his head upwards, looking at Lunata, at his leg, at Mindre, and back at Lunata. Mindre released his head and sat back next to Max.

"It's going to hurt for a few days," Lunata told the soldier, "but it should hold your weight. You should rest it before you try walking, there is probably muscle damage."

"Thank you," he grunted, then looked up at Mindre. "You, of all people, what are you doing here?"

"We are on our way to Vertex," Mindre said simply. She looked up at the others. "Max, Lunata, this is Lherzo Biggens. He is ... a friend."

Lherzo squinted at Mindre. "Just a friend?" he asked.

Max looked between the two of them, wondering what history they may share and feeling an unexpected pang of jealousy. "Biggens?" Max asked. "As in ..."

"Yes, son of General Biggens," Mindre said. "But a good friend, nonetheless. Lherzo, these are my friends, Lunata from the Bone-Thrower tribe, and Maxwell, from ..."

"Maxwell Teller," Lherzo said.

Mindre's eyes flew open. "How do you know that?"

"You're the one I've come to meet," he said to Max.

Max felt a surge of hope. "Did my grandmother send you?"

"So you really *are* the Abacist," Lherzo replied. "No, we've not seen Lady Teller in several months. This quake ..."

Lherzo looked around at the haphazard stack of blocks around them, "Is it your doing?"

Mindre spoke before Max could answer. "Lherzo, Max is in possession of the Hands of Kael, a powerful Abacist artifact. It is broken and it is causing these quakes." She looked hard at Max as if to remind him that it was the abacus, not Max himself, that was responsible.

"We need to find Lady Teller," Mindre continued, "or at least my father who is in Vertex right now. Then we need to get this abacus to Apex as soon as possible, before this happens again."

Lherzo smiled grimly. *"Third quake, the stone to break,"* he said. "Bacchius was right. This changes everything."

Lherzo sat thinking a moment, a struggle playing out across his brow. "Mindre," he said, "I will help you. I've been sent to find Max before he becomes 'a threat,' but the threat is already here. My father certainly won't help, but I know many who will. I can get you in to meet with the council, or at least with some of the elders. They will understand the importance of this."

"Max is not going near the council!" Mindre objected.

Lherzo frowned thoughtfully. "No, maybe not. I think you're right," he said. "I'll go alone. If the council won't listen, I can at least find out where Lady Teller is. I know three women who can help with that."

"The witches?" Mindre asked.

"It's only a tooth," Lherzo shrugged.

"We need to rest, all of us," Mindre said. "It will be two or three days to walk to Vertex."

"My squadron knows where I am," Lherzo said. "After this ... event, they'll be on their way. Then we can ride to Vertex. I know a good place outside the wall where you can stay hidden while I find out who we can trust."

Mindre thought for a moment. "Max, Lunata, can you set up camp? I'd like to stay with Lherzo."

Max nodded. He and Lunata walked towards the road where they had dropped their packs. "I don't trust him," Max said.

"Oh, he seems nice," Lunata countered. "He's very handsome. Nice cheekbones, a strong jaw ... and did you see his kneecaps?"

"His kneecaps?"

"They're very beautiful!" she said. "I can see why Mindre chose him as a lover."

"A lover? Do you think ... ?" Max looked over his shoulder. Mindre and Lherzo sat closely, talking intensely. He frowned.

"She told me of a powerful Calculist with whom she shared many things, including secrets of reckoning," Lunata explained. "Dijins do not share reckoning with just anyone."

"No, no they don't," said Max glumly. He glanced back one more time. "Let's set up camp."

They spread out blankets and built a fire, even though it was only late afternoon. "Fire is calming," Lunata said. Lherzo and Mindre joined them a short while later, Lherzo stepping gingerly on his wounded leg.

"This is incredible, Lunata," he said, squeezing his leg and sitting beside her. "I have never met a Bone-Thrower before."

Lunata grinned. "You have such nice bones!" She took his hand and ran her fingers along the ridges of bone on the back of his hand. "Your hands are quite large. I would very much like my children to have your bones."

Lherzo stammered, "You mean ... you want ... what?"

"My children to have your bones," she replied, "when you're dead."

"Oh!" he said relieved. "I thought you meant ... never mind." Then, suddenly alarmed again, he said, "When I'm dead?"

"It's a compliment, Lherzo," Mindre said.

"Well, then, thank you," Lherzo said. "I'd ... like my children to have your bones, too. You're a great healer."

Lunata grinned at Mindre. "I like him!" she said. "Let's keep him!"

"Mindre's a great healer, too," Max offered.

"Only the flesh," Mindre said. "Not bone. Not the mind either." She looked at Max, a sadness in her eyes. Max felt a pang of helplessness. If only his mind could be healed and connected to this source of power, then he could do something constructive instead of destructive.

"Lherzo," Lunata said, "your father is to be the New Origin? Why is it not one of his children? Where are you in the succession line?"

Lherzo shifted uncomfortably. "I'm the third of the thirds, actually, but my gift never fully developed." Glancing at Mindre he added, "Through nobody's fault but my own."

"It is always a danger sharing reckoning," Mindre said sadly. "You knew that."

"Not for *some* people," Lherzo replied staring directly at Mindre, an edge in his voice.

"What is this gift, Lherzo?" Lunata asked. "Max's brother reckons with written symbols, Mindre is the only body reckoner and I have created the complement of muqabala. What is your gift, Lherzo? Do tell, please!"

Lherzo hesitated. "Well, Mindre's seen the first attempt, here's what I study."

He reached into his jacket and slid out an abax. It was larger than the ones Max had seen back in Quothmire ages ago, and this was covered with holes cut entirely through the black stone.

212

"This started as an attempt to combine finger reckoning with the abax, but I found it can do more than that," he said.

Lherzo plucked a leaf from the grass, held it aloft and set it down. Touching fingertips through the holes on both sides of the board, his long fingers stretching from hole to hole as he concentrated on the leaf. Suddenly, layer after layer of the leaf vanished, leaving only the veins. He finished his calculation and lifted a delicate ghostly form of intricate fibers, like the skeleton of the leaf. It was beautiful.

"You can remove flesh from the bone!" Lunata said. "How unlikely! You really are the Calculist Prime!"

Lunata grinned at her companions. "Three Primes together in one place, this is most unlikely. Oh, Max, if only you were your brother, imagine how powerful we would be!"

Max sunk a little lower. Three top reckoners, each extending the arts of their families, and Max, the odd man out.

"I call them anti-numbers," Lherzo explained. "They are opposite the actual numbers, and I can use them to remove material."

"It is like something I do with muqabala, the reduction," Lunata said. "You see, I create a complement of a number and then adding becomes like taking away." She spread out her bones and began arranging them. Lherzo leaned in, his attention riveted.

Normally Max would have been burning with curiosity. Anti-numbers? Complements? Reduction? At the moment it all felt like a part of a world in which he did not belong. He stood up. "I need to, uh, you know." He tipped his head towards the bushes.

Mindre nodded to him absently, lost in her own thoughts. Lherzo and Lunata did not look up, absorbed in the arrangements of the bones. Max walked towards the road, weaving between blocks of stone, turning towards the gouge in the side of the mountain. A block twice as tall as Max sat uncomfortably out of place with several smaller blocks nestled against it, making it easy for Max to climb to the top. He sat down on the edge, looking to the broken mountain. The sun was setting behind him, casting strange shadow lines on the new randomness in the hills.

If only he were his brother, Lunata had said. Yes, maybe then he would have something to contribute. What did he have? The basic reckoning of children with no ability to fight or to heal. The only real power he seemed to have was to be able to break apart the world. The next time it could mean the end of everything.

Now they had met another Prime, another mighty reckoner taking on the lowly job of chaperone. Mindre had taken him from Quothmire to the desert, Lunata from the desert to Verdant Mesa, and now Lherzo would take him Vertex. All of these powerful people whose role it was simply to guide him. What could he offer?

"May I join you?"

Max looked to the side. Mindre stood over the edge, her elbows resting on the top of the block.

"Sure," said Max.

She climbed up and sat quietly beside him, her legs swaying back and forth lightly. "They're talking about things I'm not very comfortable with," she said.

Max nodded, staring off at the shifting patterns on the hills.

After a moment, he asked, "So, you and Lherzo? He was your boyfriend?"

Mindre huffed a humorless laugh. "I guess you could say that. When I lived in Vertex. He convinced me we could learn from each other. It inspired me to become who I am now, but it ruined him. When you share reckoning, it can weaken your power. He was never able to develop his craft afterwards, and that was my fault."

"But you got stronger, didn't you? Maybe it's not sharing, maybe it's something else," Max said.

"My father shared reckoning with Chief Oolong in Quincunx and the Chief lost his power. That's why my father was exiled. Now I've been teaching you and you can't reckon either."

"I wouldn't be able to do anything without you, Mindre. You know my lack of ability has nothing to do with you. Look at you, you're smart, you're strong, you're brave and calm and quick and beautiful. You're a great leader. If anyone should be New Origin, it's you."

Mindre looked up, her eyes sad but a smile on her lips.

"And what can I do?" Max asked. "This, this is what I can do." He waved his hand at the panorama of destruction in front of them.

"Max ..." Mindre said, "you have powers like no one else. You can imagine things in ways I never could. You see patterns and just ... take them in like you're breathing air. You have a role in this grand calculation. You heard Lady Carpus."

Max smiled grudgingly. "I thought you didn't believe in prophecy."

"Even if she were only guessing, it doesn't mean that it isn't true."

"Thanks, Mindre," Max said. "You're a good friend."

They sat a while in silence, watching the colors of the setting sun paint the broken landscape in orange and pink.

Lunata and Lherzo were still talking as they returned to camp. They quieted as Max and Mindre reached the fire.

"Learning something?" Mindre asked.

Lherzo and Lunata glanced at each other. "Yes," Lherzo said. "It's surprising what can be learned if one's partner is willing to be open."

The corners of Mindre's mouth pulled upwards in a forced smile. "Good," she said. "Let's eat."

Over dinner Lherzo sketched out the Calculists' plan. An initial force would set out in four days' time with the job of outfitting seven posts, each a half-day's march. The following day, the main force of nine thousand soldiers would launch, marching a demanding distance each day. After three days of ascension, they would cross to Tangram and the siege would begin on the next day. The council had no idea how strong the opposition would be, but a force of this size had never been sent to battle before, and the council, Lherzo included, was confident their numbers could not be withstood.

Lherzo expected his own squad would already be on their way looking for him. It would be a small force, perhaps only his squad of twelve but possibly a larger force to investigate the quake. They would have horses. They should arrive at Vertex with enough time to secure allies and make their case.

The soldiers arrived as anticipated, but the group was smaller than Lherzo had expected: six soldiers on horseback and an enclosed carriage wagon drawn by two horses. A thick-bearded man dismounted and greeted Lherzo.

"Lherzo, you crazy stoneslinger! You could have been buried out here!" he said.

Lherzo and the thick man swung their right arms towards one another. They grasped each other just above the elbow, momentarily locking arms in greeting.

"You don't know the half of it," Lherzo said. "Dirigo, do you remember Mindre?"

"Mindre! Of all the people at this time and place ... good to see you again." Dirigo nodded. Glancing at Max he asked nervously in a hushed tone, "Is that the ... fellow?"

Lherzo nodded. "It is, and nothing is what we think it is. We have a serious situation, more critical than the Tangram Offensive. I need to get to the council, as soon as possible."

"And, is that a ... ?" Dirigo nodded uncertainly towards Lunata.

"Bone-Thrower, yes. I know, quite remarkable," Lherzo said impatiently. "We can talk on the way."

"Lherzo, Darklings swarmed the city last night. Thousands of them. It's like the dead woke up. You know, like, '*Second shake, the dead to wake.*' We've got more troops in Vertex than ever before, so we're wiping the steps with them, but they keep coming. You have no idea how many there are! No one knows what this means for the march."

"All right. Well, I'm happy to see you brought a carriage. Let's load up!"

"Yeah, well, that ..." Dirigo said.

The door of the carriage opened and out climbed four stern-looking characters, men and women identically dressed in black pants and jackets. "Western edge of the quake zone is Saragis, E-one," a stiff looking man barked. "We can begin charting here."

"Surveyors," Dirigo explained. "We were allowed to come look for you if we escorted them." Dirigo explained.

Lherzo was already on his way to the carriage. He reached through the open door and began unloading bags from the cabin.

"Sir, Commander Sir," the stiff man yelled, running over and flapping his arms like a bird.

"Is this all of your gear?" Lherzo asked. "I am requisitioning this vehicle. Continue your work and ride back with the soldiers when completed."

"Sir, we cannot work without our carriage," the man protested.

"Um, Lherzo, that's not really ..." Dirigo began.

"Not up for discussion," Lherzo said. "Blackwell! You're in charge. Dirigo, I want you as coachman. Mindre, Lunata, Max! Climb in! Let's go, Dirigo."

Dirigo shrugged to the stiff man. "Change in the mission. Sorry, good luck!"

The man continued to argue as they quickly entered the cabin. A few seconds later, the carriage was on its way.

Max and Mindre sat on the padded bench seat facing backwards, Lherzo and Lunata facing forwards on the opposite bench. "Luxury travel," Lherzo said with a smile. "The surveyors are going to be plenty sore about this, but it is the end of the world, after all."

He lifted a bottle from a pouch attached to the inside wall. A cloudy liquid sloshed inside. "Spirit wine! Drinks, anyone?"

"What did he say about Darklings?" Mindre asked, ignoring his offer.

"They swarmed Vertex last night, as if the 'dead had awakened.' The Darklands on the other side of the ascension are filled with them, if they're swarming the entire extension upwards towards Tangram, which they probably are, then we're in for a difficult trip up over."

Lunata leaned forward. "Max, you can just do your longwalking again and we'll fly past the Dark Ones and right up to Apex!"

Max felt the abacus in his pocket, its beads clicking quietly. The feeling of the clicking was no longer a comforting

218

curiosity, it now felt like a ticking bomb. "I am never using that abacus again," he said flatly.

The others exchanged glances. Mindre looked worried, "Max, you've used it a lot this past week with no problems. Why do you think it happened this time and not any other time?"

Max bit his lip and reluctantly slid the abacus out from his pocket. The beads fell silent at his touch. Lherzo leaned forward attentively as Max opened the cover.

"It's broken here," he said, pointing at the fourteenth rod. "I almost never use this rod for anything, unless I'm doing a really long division or five-digit by four-digit multiplication, for example."

"Five by four!" Lherzo gasped. "You can do that many?"

Max shrugged. "When we were riding, I kept increasing the power of the algorithm, using rods all the way up the abacus," Max continued. "It was then that I used that last rod. That was the first time I've tried to use that rod since I got here, and that's when the quake started."

"So just don't use that rod!" Lunata said.

"I don't know," Max said. "I still could make a mistake."

Mindre reached up and began untying the thin leather lace on the front of her dress. With a few deliberate motions, she tugged a length of the lace free and held it out towards Max. "Fix it so you can't make a mistake," she said, offering him the strip of leather.

Max took the lace and considered it. "Do you really think this will work?"

Mindre shrugged. "Your abacus has worked perfectly with all the other rods. Why shouldn't it continue to work? Max, we need it to keep working. We need *you*. Remember, you are the Hand of Life."

He looked at the other faces peering at him expectantly. This tool could bring such destruction ... could it also bring an equal amount of good? The others seemed to think so, even if he wasn't so sure himself.

"All right," he said. He fed the string around the fourteenth rod and began looping it around the frame.

Lherzo clapped once in approval. "That's it, you've just got to put your stones on the line again!"

Max finished looping the lace around and around, tied a knot and pulled hard. It looked good and secure, the rod completely laced from top to bottom. He shook his abacus up and down. The fourteenth rod sat silent while the other beads rattled freely.

Mindre nodded. "It looks quake-proof. I think you should keep practicing. We're going to need it soon." She looked out the window. Out there in the distance, Vertex was drawing closer.

Max leaned back, relieved to have a safeguard on his abacus but still apprehensive about their destination. They were now heading to the enemy capital and it was swarming with monsters. It seemed like the wrong choice but also the only choice.

He glumly looked across to Lunata. She was bouncing on the seat, testing the padding, a grin of pure joy on her face.

Farms turned to settlements turned to towns as they rumbled closer to the end of the largest mesa on this side of the planet. Mindre had moved to sit with Dirigo in the coach seat, supposedly for fresh air though Max suspected it had more to do with Lherzo and his interest in talking to Lunata.

Max spent his time watching the edges of the cliffs as they passed, hypnotically getting shorter and taller and shorter and then impossibly tall, always predictable and yet always surprising. Now the tallest cliffs were being replaced by shorter cliffs, their corners far up in the sky in perfect alignment sloping downwards. If Max were to draw a line through all of the corners it would meet the horizon at a point, like the perspective drawings he'd made in art class. Vertex lay on this focus point, in the very center of the unthinkably long stairway known as the Western Ascension. All of the shelves and mesas he'd seen so far ended at the wall of a cliff, but this mesa had no wall at its end, just open sky and drifting clouds. Vertex truly sat on the edge of the world.

They could see the city now, a stack of countless white buildings rising from beyond a long wall. They piled upwards on the steps like a display of boxes in a grocery store. Tall towers along the diagonal horizon reached skyward like needles.

"How many people live there?" Max asked.

"Around thirty thousand," Lherzo said, but there's almost forty thousand right now. All troops have been called in from as far away as Quothmire and Vista."

Dirigo swung the carriage from the main road towards the mountain, then onto a trail alongside a stand of trees. They rolled to a stop near the base of the mountain.

They climbed out from the cabin. Max stretched his legs. It felt good to be standing again.

"This is it," Lherzo said. "There's a brook at the foot of the steps, here. I'll be back as soon as I can, but it might not be until tomorrow morning."

"Thank you, Lherzo," Mindre said. "We're counting on you."

Lherzo nodded grimly and walked back to the carriage.

-:- | -:-

The bells were ringing from the fortress grounds as Lherzo and Dirigo climbed the steps to the inner gate. The streets were nearly empty, citizens staying inside while soldiers fought on the Western Wall at the opposite side of the city.

"Lherzo, you're in time!" the second-commander on watch told them as they entered the upper terrace. "Biggens is demonstrating the Tri-Reckoner on the Northern Outlook."

Lherzo and Dirigo hurried up the stairs to the tower and cut through the gallery to a balcony. "Would you look at that?" Lherzo said. To the left, the Western Ascension rose in a undulating tangle, the perfect straight line of the steps now buried in a sea of gray flesh. Hundreds of Darklings crawled the surface, spilling over the stairs, tumbling down steps, clawing at the stone.

On the terrace below, a small crowd had gathered, lined along the wall to witness the demonstration. In the center stood General Biggens, flanked by a man on each side. Before them was the largest abax ever created, Biggens' Tri-Reckoner. Lherzo had seen an early test and knew something of its power, but now the abax was three times as long. He squinted, trying to determine who the men were standing with his father.

"Hey, aren't those your brothers?" Dirigo asked.

"Yes," said Lherzo bitterly. Not only had his father completed the abax without telling him, he had also been training Kalkar and Gerard in its use.

"Ready!" shouted Biggens below. The crowd quieted at once. The three men began turning stones on the abax. Lherzo guessed each of the three parts of the abax had three rows of blocks. Each block was a cube with three smaller cubes on adjacent faces, like a small set of steps from the terrain of Abac-abax itself. The blocks could be turned to one of three different positions which represented a different digit in his father's system of threes.

Lherzo could barely hear his father giving instructions to his brothers as they turned stone after stone. He felt a prickling. A static charge raised the hairs on his neck and arms.

"This is going to be big ..." Dirigo whispered.

Cracking noises rang out from the hills. The air warped like a mirage, lensing the light to give the illusion of ripples rolling up the ascension through the mob of Darklings. Gray bodies lifted in the air and were cast to the side as if being brushed away by a giant invisible hand. Ten, twenty, fifty Darklings were swept violently off their feet and tumbled over the far side of the steps.

Lherzo sucked in his breath. It was the most powerful and terrifying reckoning he had ever seen, as if an entire well-coordinated platoon were casting at once. The ripple of destruction rolled upwards one hundred steps, two hundred steps, *five* hundred steps, and more before the wave quieted. Dust swirled in the wind, carrying with it the howls of the survivors as they crawled away.

"How is that even possible?" Dirigo said, breathing hard. "There's only three of them! You never told me he could do that!"

"I didn't know," Lherzo said.

"But, they're your brothers ... ?"

Lherzo frowned. "C'mon, let's find Bacchius."

They entered the terrace from the stairway. The crowd was clapping and talking excitedly. They searched the faces in the crowd, hunting for the oldest member of the council.

"Seven-hundred twenty-nine steps," Biggens was announcing. "Unparalleled reckoning force! We will clear the ascension from Vertex to Tangram and grind the Abacists to oblivion!"

The crowd cheered. Lherzo caught sight of Bacchius and the two men worked their way to the elder statesman's side.

"Young Biggens, you made it to the demonstration," Bacchius said. "Impressive, yes?"

"Bacchius, I need to speak to you right away," Lherzo said urgently.

"The High Council will be meeting now, can it wait?"

"No. Please, let's talk over here."

"Well, all right," the old man croaked hesitantly.

Lherzo led him to a covered gangway, near a door behind ivy covered pillars. "I found Maxwell Teller, inland at the site of the quake."

Bacchius' eyes flew open wide. "You found him?"

"Yes, and listen, Teller has an abacus called the 'Fourteen Hands of Kael.' It is damaged and it is this *abacus* that is causing the quakes."

"The Fourteen Hands ... that is one of the ..." Bacchius' brow furrowed. "Fourteen Hands you say? Then the youngest Teller is not the Stonebreaker, the Stonebreaker is the *first* of the seconds! Where is he?" Bacchius looked around, suddenly nervous.

"Outside the city," Lherzo said.

"There are Darklings out there!" Bacchius said.

"Dirigo and I have him in a safe place. Bacchius, we need to help him get to Apex. We need to do it before there is a third quake. The Order of the Whole can fix the abacus and stop this, but we need to hurry."

"I see, I see." Bacchius frowned. "Yes, I suppose if anyone could prevent a third quake, it would be the Order."

"Have you seen Lady Teller?" Lherzo asked. "The Longwalker could get the abacus there right away."

"No, no, I haven't seen the Longwalker in ages. I assume she is in ..." Bacchius' eyes grew wide again. "The Stonebreaker may be planning to join the Tellers in Tangram. Their union could mean a swift end to us all!"

224

"Max has no intention of helping Saul Teller. Getting this abacus to Apex is the only thing that matters, and it must take priority over everything else. I need you to convince the High Council to support this. We must escort Max and the Fourteen Hands past Tangram. We'll need chariots, supplies and men for the whole trip. Can you do that?"

"I'll be meeting the High Council now. They will have to listen. Wait for me here, I will convince them." Bacchius departed.

Lherzo and Dirigo waited for the crowd to clear. A team of soldiers carried sections of the Tri-Reckoner inside. "They're going to need the Grand Chariot for that," Dirigo mused. They crossed to the railing overlooking the northern part of the fortress. Soldiers were on the ascension now, clearing away bodies of the Darklings that had met the brunt of the force of Biggens' reckoning.

Time passed slowly. Lherzo felt like a rock was in his stomach. "What can be taking them so long?" he asked.

"It's only been half an hour," Dirigo said.

"Feels like forever."

A door opened on the fortress wall. Two figures walked briskly towards them. It was Lherzo's oldest brother Kalkar with Commander Gordon, the man who had given a tooth to discover the Abacist Prime was in Tangram.

"Lherzo, father is so pleased," Kalkar said with a smile. "You've done something right for once! Dirigo, you are to accompany Gordon and fetch the Abacist. Lherzo, the High Council will see you right away. It's a hero's welcome for you, Little Brother!"

"So they will help?" Lherzo asked, brightening.

"Of course! No one imagined you'd actually find him."

Lherzo breathed a sigh of relief. "I had better go with Dirigo. I'm not sure they'll trust anyone else. Wait for me, Dirigo, I'll address the High Council first."

"I'll take Dirigo to ready the riders, then," Gordon said, nodding knowingly to Kalkar.

Lherzo walked excitedly beside his brother. He had found the Abacist and gained his father's favor, Bacchius had convinced the council and his friends would have a full military escort to Tangram and beyond.

He entered the High Council chamber proudly and smiled at his father.

"My son has found the Stonebreaker?" said Biggens. "Well accomplished!"

Lherzo looked at the faces around the table. Bacchius was looking down at his hands, a frown on his face. Lherzo understood something was not right.

"Yes, and we will escort him to Apex," Lherzo said.

"We have discussed at length how to deal with this problem. Bacchius did not agree that destroying the Fourteen Hands of Kael could prevent another quake. On the other hand, an abacus without a reckoner is no threat at all."

"I've given my word to help them! This is more important than Tangram or the Great Divide!"

"Son, it's very simple. Eliminating the Abacist defeats the Stonebreaker and weakens the Abacists. You've ensured our victory!"

Lherzo stood speechless. It had all gone horribly wrong. He quickly considered his options. For years he had held his tongue and played along with his father's wishes, knowing that dissention quickly led to harsh consequences. For years he had practiced biding his time waiting for the right opportunities. This was not one of those 'right opportunities,' this was the time of all times to put those years of practice to good use. He clamped down his emotions, sending them deep beneath his stony face. "I'm glad I can be of service. All right, I will join Dirigo and we will bring him here."

"No need," Biggens said. "Gordon is departing now with a hundred men to seize the Abacist. Have a seat. When we have our prize, I will reconsider your position."

"It will be a great honor," he said, feeling suddenly like a traitor.

"Now, Lherzo, tell us everything you know about this Stonebreaker."

-:- | -:-

Max, Mindre and Lunata were pulled from the wagon and forced towards the door. Max's arm tingled painfully from his cramped position in the wagon, wrists bound tight behind his back. In front of him, he saw Mindre's hands. Not only were her wrists tied, but her thumbs were bagged with a piece of canvas and lashed tightly together with a strip of leather, an extra precaution to keep her from reckoning.

The soldier dragging her along shoved her head brutally into the doorframe as they entered the fortress, rapping her skull with a loud crack. "That's for the beating you gave me, grubfinger," he growled. Mindre scowled back at him through clenched teeth.

The skirmish had been short but intense. They were far outmatched, one hundred to three. Mindre and Lunata fought well, even though they knew they had no chance. It ended with the three of them crushed down to the earth under the weight of a huge force of reckoning while soldiers disarmed and immobilized them.

Gordon led them into the High Council chamber. Lherzo jumped to his feet as they entered, staring open-mouthed at the beaten faces of the ones he had pledged to help. Mindre glared back at him, shaking her head.

"Maxwell Teller and accomplices," Gordon announced. "Mindre of Quincunx, whom we've dealt with before, and, interestingly enough, a Bone-Thrower. We have some artifacts of interest, as well." He placed Max's abacus and Lunata's finger bones on the table in front of Biggens.

"Kind of you to join us," Biggens began, eyeing the strange devices suspiciously. "In the interest of expediency, we have already concluded your trial. Maxwell Teller, first of the seconds of the Abacist line. You shall be no Stonebreaker, two quakes is more than enough. Tomorrow at dawn you are to be publicly crushed beneath a pile of stone until dead. It is both a fitting end for you and a fitting start for our campaign to finish the last of the Abacists.

"Bone-Thrower. You are, shall we say, of academic interest to some members of the High Council. You are to be fitted with chains and will be our guest for as long as you prove interesting.

"Mindre of Quincunx. You have sullied the Biggens' name long enough. I heeded my son's plea for mercy once and yet you betray us again. Your ambassador status protects you no longer. You will join the Abacist beneath the stones."

"Lherzo, how could you?!" Mindre snapped.

"Not every day can be a flower field, Finger-Reckoner," he said coldly. "General, may I cast the first stone tomorrow?"

Biggens laughed. "Take them away!"

The three were led down flight after flight of stairs, through a guard room and to a hallway with a row of four barred cells. Each was shoved in a separate cell, Max in a cell between

Lunata and Mindre. The doors locked behind them with a dismal clang.

Max leaned against the bars and slid down to sit on the floor. The cells were narrow with floor-to-ceiling bars. Against the wall in the back of each was a hole in the floor, an unpleasant stench coming from these primitive lavatories.

The soldiers left, leaving a lone guard who sat at the end of the hallway with a dim lantern, as far from the smell as possible.

"Did he plan this all along?" Max whispered.

"I don't think so," Mindre whispered back. "He spoke of a flower field. We sat in such a field once and he told me how tired he was of pretending to be someone different, that it was a mask he was only wearing until the time he could be free."

Max considered this. Perhaps they would be rescued. Was Lherzo still in love with Mindre? He felt a stab of jealousy, a useless feeling in this dark place.

They tried to untie each other through the bars. The ropes and lace were imbued with some kind of tacky material, tree sap perhaps, and the knots would not move in the slightest.

"I don't think this is so exciting anymore," whispered Lunata from the next cell.

They sat in the cells, waiting. Max had no sense of time in the dim space. Had it been minutes or had it been hours?

"Do you think he's coming?" he said at last.

"I don't know," Mindre answered.

"Are you sure you can't reckon?" Max asked. He had asked once already in the wagon and didn't really expect the answer had changed.

"I can't move my thumbs," she said. "No thumbs, no reckoning."

Max considered this a moment. "What about my thumbs?" he asked.

"What?" she answered.

Max shuffled on the floor, turning his back to the bars between their cells. "Move over here, you can use my thumbs."

"Max, that's ..." Mindre sighed, paused a moment, and then turned to press against the bars behind him.

Her fingers found his in the dark. She ran hers over the surface as if to map their location. Her fingers tapped against his thumbs, her pads and nails making brief contact. "Bend your thumbs a little more," she whispered, her breathing growing deeper.

Max began to feel warm from the contact. He want to take ahold of her fingers and hug them in his palms. Instead he held steady, trying to picture her movements.

"I can't ..." Mindre whispered.

"Try something simple. Light a fire," Max suggested.

"Yes ..." She tapped her fingertips against his thumbs. He pictured the pattern he had seen her use at the campfire on the lake. *First-first, first-second, second-first, second-second.*

"I think it's getting warmer," Max whispered.

"It's awkward, it's not nearly strong enough."

"Do you remember the pattern with four beats? When we used our arms? I'll be our arms." He tapped the fingers of his left hand against the back of her fingers. "Zero," he said. He tapped the fingers of his right hand against hers. "One. Got it?"

"Hmm. Okay. You start?" she asked.

"Zero, zero," he whispered, tapping his left hand twice. "Zero, zero," he said as he felt her fingers tap his thumbs.

"Zero, zero," he tapped twice. "Zero, *one*," he said feeling her tap, picturing the slightly different pattern.

"Zero, zero ... *one*, zero," he continued. "Zero, zero ... *one, one.*"

Now he changed his pattern, a tap from the left and then a tap from the right: "Zero, *one* ..." and then as Mindre began her pattern anew he said, "zero, zero." They worked through the entire sequence, starting over after they reached *one, one, one, one.* Max stopped counting aloud the second time through, focusing entirely on the rhythm and the feeling of the tapping. It was easier than he thought at first, he simply tapped identical left hand double-taps four times, with a pause between each for Mindre to tap twice. Then he switched to left-right four times, then right-left four times, and finally right-right four times.

Mindre's breathing grew heavy, he felt her skin moisten with sweat beneath his fingers. Max was feeling warm himself from the touch of her fingers in the dark. If reckoning were so personal and private for her, what kind of effect might this be having on her?

They picked up the pace, the pattern became smooth and natural. Max felt the heat rise dramatically. It was working! Mindre moaned, softly at first, but her cry grew louder quickly as the heat from the reckoning intensified.

She jerked her hands from his. He smelled a whiff of smoke.

"My thumbs are free," she said tensely.

Max glanced over his shoulder. It had worked! The burnt strip of leather lay on the floor on top of the piece of canvas that had bound her thumbs. Her wrists were still tied, but her fingers and thumbs worked together now, fervently, repeating her fire sequence. Fibers in the rope began to glow red and spark. Tendrils of flame appeared and disappeared, then appeared again, licking the surface of her binding.

Max watched in grotesque fascination as the fire danced against her skin. She did not stop or even slow down as the flames grew, burning into her wrists.

"What's that you've got there?" the guard shouted. He moved from his stool, attracted by the glow from the flame.

Mindre's wrists broke free. In the blink of an eye she was on her feet, hands moving out and in from her temples to her hips to her breast and to her thigh, while her fingers performed dances of their own.

The guard was thrown sideways into the wall and then back across the hallway into the bars of Lunata's cell. He fell to the ground, motionless. Mindre made another sequence of movements and his body slid along the floor to the door of her cell. She reached through the bars, snapped the key from his belt and fumbled it in the lock of her cell.

"You're amazing!" Max whispered.

"You're not so bad, either," she smiled back.

Mindre opened each of their cells and drawing a knife from the guard's sheath, she cut loose the ropes from Max's and Lunata's wrists.

Lunata eyed the knife and looked at the guard. "Is he dead? I can take his bones."

"You won't need to," came a voice from the end of the hall. Lherzo stood silhouetted in the doorway, a bag in his hand. "C'mon!" he said quietly.

"Lherzo," Mindre said with a sigh of relief. "I knew you'd come."

"And I should have known you wouldn't wait," he said. "Put these on."

He pulled out three gray uniforms from the bag, including hats. They changed quickly, placing their clothing back into Lherzo's bag.

"I think you'll want these, too." He pulled out Max's abacus and Lunata's bones. "It was some trouble getting these, but Lunata, I used what we talked about and it worked! I'll explain later. Let's go."

He led them through lower passages, a different way than that which they had come. They heard voices echoing nearby from a hallway and they stopped, holding their breath. The voices faded and they moved again quickly and quietly along the passage. Coming to a heavy door, Lherzo produced a key and they stepped outside into a courtyard.

Other soldiers were in the courtyard. "Keep your heads down and walk with purpose," Lherzo told them. They walked by a group of three soldiers who glanced at them but said nothing as they went past.

Out into the street and down steps, they kept moving. They jogged downwards past shops, pubs, houses and alleyways. Max realized the steps were the same pattern as out in the wild. He marveled at how different the steps appeared populated with all these buildings. Although it looked as though this could be a fascinating city under the proper circumstances, all he wanted now was to be far away from this wretched place.

Three or four hundred steps down, they crossed the courtyard near the Eastern Wall and slipped into a stable. Dirigo was waiting with four horses.

"I'm sorry about earlier," Dirigo said. "Glad you're okay."

"You did what you had to, Dirigo," Mindre said. "Thank you for helping now."

"Do you ride?" Lherzo asked Lunata and Max.

"I've ridden a snake," said Lunata. "But I'd love to try a horse!"

"Max?" he asked.

"Sort of," Max answered. *A snake?* he thought.

"We'll only need two then, Dirigo. Mindre, you take Max, Lunata you're with me."

Dirigo had their packs. Lherzo had thought of everything. He loaded the packs onto their horses and the four of them mounted.

"Good luck, Lherzo," Dirigo said.

"Thank you, my friend."

They rode into the courtyard and past the guards who were checking only people entering, not those leaving. They disappeared into the night.

Chapter 11: Awakening

They rode for an hour from the city, back towards where they had been the day before. Was it a wasted trip? Max wondered. They were leaving with a lot of *negatives*. His grandmother had *not* been there. They did *not* find Mindre's father. The Calculists would *not* help. If anything positive had come from the detour, it was this shared reckoning with Mindre. Max knew how private Mindre was about her reckoning and how careful she was with her hands. It must have been difficult for her to reckon using Max's fingers, and for her to have trusted him with a shared reckoning meant something important, he knew.

Then there was Lherzo. He had really come through. Max hadn't trusted him, right up until the moment he showed up in the prison block with their gear and an escape plan. Now it really was a team of four, one from each of the families. *Most unlikely*, as Lunata would say.

Lherzo steered the horses up the steps. They rose quite a distance, passing shelves and mesas. Max wondered how the horses managed to endure the climb. They rode upwards as swiftly and as easily as on the flat roads. Were horses on Abacabax tuned into the patterns as well? Was there some kind of animal version of step-counting that allowed them to navigate the steps as easily as a human reckoner?

They turned from the stairs into a forest and rode several more minutes to an open area in the dark trees. They dismounted. It was late, Max was exhausted.

"Mindre, let me see your hands," Max said.

She held them out and turned them over briefly. Even in the dim light he could see that her thumbs and wrists were heavily blistered.

"We need to get something on that," Max said.

Mindre wasn't listening. She left Max and strode straight to Lherzo, throwing her arms around him.

"You came for us. You defied your father. I always knew you could do it," she told him.

"Well, I've cast my abac with you now," he said grimly. "Let's see this through."

He released Mindre and turned to his horse, unbuckling the packs. Max did the same as Lunata walked into the trees. They made camp quickly, speaking little.

Lunata returned with a stem of fleshy leaves. "This will help with your burns," she said. She squeezed out a gel from the leaves and spread it onto Mindre's thumbs and wrists.

They climbed beneath the blankets and slept late into morning.

Max was the last to awaken. The morning was cool and damp and he was pleased to see that someone had started a fire. Lherzo and Lunata sat on a log near the fire. Mindre was by herself, searching through her pack. He approached her quietly.

"Can I help you with anything?" he asked.

"No, just looking for the herbs ... for these stupid burns." She pulled out a pouch. Inside the pouch were a dozen small cloth bundles tied with string. "Lady Carpus packed medicine for us, there should be something useful here."

Max watched with interest, wondering what kinds of medicines were available on this world. Mindre untied a bundle, green leaves were inside. "Feverfew, that's for fever, no." She opened another filled with spiky brown stems. "Rotbane for fungus? No, thank you." Inside the third were bright purple flowers. "Salvendia? Why would she pack salvendia?"

"What's that for?" Max asked.

Mindre looked at him quizzically. Her brow crinkled making a small 'x' of wrinkles between her eyebrows. She opened her mouth, closed it again, then shook her head and quickly wrapped the bundle back together. "Nothing, I don't know what that's for."

She continued opening bundles, no longer announcing what they were. Max had a strange feeling she'd rather he weren't watching her. At last she found some buds with small yellow flowers. "Hypericum, this will help." She popped them in her mouth and began retying the bundles, not looking up at him.

"Mindre, when we were reckoning together ..." Max began.

"Yeah, um," Mindre said. "Let's not talk about that now, okay?" She stuffed the pouch back in her pack and walked back to the fire.

Okay, Max thought. Then we won't talk about that now. Mindre sat alone on the other side of the fire, not looking at him. Max joined the others, perching on the end of the log next to Lherzo, frustrated with Mindre's frequent mood swings.

"Show Max," Lunata said, leaning forward.

Lherzo smiled. "All right." He picked up a small stone and set it on the ground in front of them. He worked his fingers around the holes on both sides of his abax. Layers of the stone rapidly vanished, the last bit wobbling slightly before it disappeared altogether. Lherzo smiled with satisfaction.

"Lherzo did that to a metal lock on his father's chambers so he could take back my bones and your abacus," Lunata said excitedly. "Stone *and* metal, Max! It works!"

"That's amazing," Max said. "Maybe you can dig us a tunnel to Tangram!"

Lherzo laughed. "That sounds like a plan," he said.

"What *is* the plan?" Mindre called out impatiently.

"All right," Lherzo said. "Here's what I know. My father has a new abax that works with his Tricalculus reckoning. I saw a demonstration when I arrived yesterday. It's strong. Really strong. He can take down dozens of Darklings at a time from the steps, so they're going forward with the march as planned tomorrow."

He took a stick and scratched a triangle in the dirt, connecting the midpoints to create another upside-down triangle on the inside. The triangle was now divided into four equal parts, each a triangle.

Mindre stepped forward, looking down at his sketch. Lherzo placed a stone in the lower left corner. "Okay, here's Vertex ... Apex is way up there somewhere at the top of the world, in our campfire." He waved his hand in that direction.

He placed another stone in the middle of the top triangle in his sketch. "This is Tangram ..." He then dropped a third stone on the bottom edge to the right of the Vertex-stone, halfway towards the middle. "And this is us."

"They leave tomorrow. It will take three days for them to climb the ascension and then one more day of marching for them to get to Tangram. That's a total of five days' time. They'll have nine thousand soldiers, I don't see how Saul can stand a chance."

"My brother is with him," Max said. "We need to get there first."

"We can't go there. We need to avoid Tangram entirely," Lherzo said. "We can bypass Tangram if we head back this way and come up on the other side." He scratched a line with the stick along the bottom of the triangle to the middle and moved it diagonally along the edge of the center triangle. "All of the attention will be towards the ascension, so we should be able to slip past Tangram safely. Then there's nothing in our way except for a long climb to Apex."

"We need to get Samuel," Max interrupted. "If they can make it in five days, we can make it in three."

"Max, Saul killed five hundred people in Tangram, including an entire platoon. He's pledged to kill every last Calculist. He's the most powerful reckoner on the faces and he's not going to give up your brother. There is nothing that the four of us can do."

"But Saul is also my great-uncle, he is an Abacist and he will know the importance of getting this abacus to Apex," Max said, feeling anger rise. "He will help us, unlike your family. In fact, we should have gone to Tangram directly. He may be a horrible man, but he's not an idiot. He will help us stop this."

Lherzo looked at Max hard, then turned to Mindre.

Mindre raised her eyebrows questioningly. "Lady Teller might be with him," she said. "I don't know, Max could be right. I mean, if we try to ride to Apex alone, well, that's not easy. Have you ever been north of Tangram? It's cold. There will be snow and we would need to find food as we go. It will be slow-going, it could take months with the snow melting. Do we have that long before ... you know?" She tipped her head towards Max, and then as afterthought shrugged as if to apologize.

Lherzo frowned and looked at Lunata. "What do you think?" he asked.

"Well," she said. "We have just been to Vertex with hostile Calculists who want to kill Abacists. In Tangram there are hostile Abacists who want to kill Calculists. It all sounds very symmetrical to me. I like symmetry!"

Lherzo threw down his stick. "Fine," he said, defeated. "Tangram, then. Let's get started."

They rode down the steps and to the road. They would ride back nearly to the site of the second quake and then travel upwards and away from Vertex. In two or three days they should arrive at Tangram from the opposite side of the approaching army.

Progress on the steps, however, was slower than Lherzo anticipated. He admitted he had never ridden a horse on the steps with two riders and had underestimated the stress on the animals. They had not traveled as far as he expected when they decided to make camp early, but at least they still had a few days to spare.

At camp, Lunata offered to teach them a game. She set of three rows of small twigs, three twigs in the top row, five in the middle row, and seven in the bottom.

"This is called 'Birds,'" she said. "We normally play this with bird bones, but twigs will do. These are the birds. On your turn, you may take as many birds you like but only from one row. If you take the final bird, you lose."

"Can you take a whole row, then?" Max asked.

"Yes, you can."

"Can you take zero birds on your turn?" he asked.

"No, Max, that could make for a very long game. Birds do not like to wait."

Max gave it a try. They took turns removing twigs, until Lunata left him with only one 'bird' he was forced to take, losing the game.

"You owe me a guild," she teased. "Try again?"

They played several times. Max lost every time, regardless of how he played or whether or not he went first. He knew she must have a system, but he could not figure it out right away. Knowing Lunata, the system probably had something to do with binary numbers.

"Mindre, you will try?" Lunata asked.

"No, I'm going to go stretch my legs," she said standing up.

"Okay, Lherzo, you play with me!"

Max poked at the fire, watching Mindre. She stood at the edge of the camp, an absent look in her eyes. She had been acting strangely since they left Vertex and especially distant since looking through her medicine pouches that morning. He'd give her space, but he hoped she'd come back soon.

Lunata made another hot meal for them with food from the packs and some bulbs she dug from the earth nearby. Mindre added some peppers from one of her cloth bundles of herbs, making for another spicy dinner.

Near the end of the meal, Lherzo and Lunata began to talk about reckoning again. "You've been using numbers and anti-numbers, together," Lunata said. "What if you used two anti-numbers?"

This caught Max's attention. Anti-numbers were like negative numbers and they had some unusual behaviors. "We use anti-numbers where I come from. If you multiply two of them together, you get a positive number, that is, you get a ... *regular* number," he offered.

"Oh!" Lunata said, "it would be like an 'anti-anti' ... maybe you could create matter?"

"What? 'Anti-anti?' Say that again?" Lherzo asked, fascinated.

Mindre leaned in close to Max. "Max," she whispered. "We need to start your training again ... would you mind if we go off by ourselves? There's something I want to try, if you're willing."

"Sure, I'd love that," he said.

She bit her lip, thought for a moment and then nodded. "Okay."

"Lherzo, Lunata," she called out. "I want to take Max up in the hills this evening and work with him on his reckoning. I've thought of something that might help. We might be back late."

Lunata and Lherzo looked back and forth between Max and Mindre.

"Yeah, that's fine," Lherzo said. "Don't go too far."

"It might be morning when we get back," Mindre added, "so don't be worried."

Lunata looked at Lherzo, then back at Mindre. A grin spread slowly across her face. She nodded enthusiastically, then looked back at Lherzo with a smile.

"Let's take our packs," Mindre said, shouldering her bag and stepping to the edge of camp. She glanced back, waiting for Max, an expression in her eyes that he couldn't read.

He jogged to catch up with her as she began walking towards the hills.

"Lunata seems pretty grateful to have some time alone with Lherzo. They seem to be getting along very well," Max said.

"Yes, I think they're good for each other," she said.

"What are we going to work on?" Max asked.

Mindre kept looking down as they walked, a soft smile on her lips. "Something," she said.

They walked up the steps, Max using his abacus to do the step-counting algorithm she had taught him in his first lesson. The leather strip on the left edge made a nice grip. It was reassuring and he felt ready to use it again. He glanced at Mindre in front of him, her fingers tapping the side of her thigh in her own step-counting algorithm. He thought about her fingers, the feel of them when they lightly touched his skin back in Vertex, the electricity of her touch. He was glad to have some time with her alone. He liked Lherzo and Lunata's company, but things hadn't felt right with Mindre since Lherzo had joined them.

A few hundred steps up, they crossed a shelf and found a spot near the back steps sheltered by trees. "Let's make our own fire here," she said.

Max searched beneath the trees, gathering branches. The sun was slipping behind the cliffs and Max knew darkness came quickly on the shelves. He hurried to find more sticks and dragged them back to the camp, breaking them over his knee to proper sizes. Mindre had spread out the blankets and was focused on arranging some small items on it. Max was curious but didn't disturb her. She was lost in a world of her own. He would find out soon enough.

He finished readying the wood for the fire and waited patiently for Mindre to notice so that she could set it ablaze.

"Why don't you try lighting the fire this time?" she asked, looking up from her own preparations.

Max had never tried that before. He thought for a moment. Mindre, he knew, used a fast series of finger taps in a binary pattern. Much earlier, he had accidentally generated heat by counting by twos on his abacus. Maybe the method didn't matter so much, maybe the image was more important.

He cleared his abacus and began adding twos. This was one of the first exercises he learned from the booklet his grandmother had given him. The pattern was familiar and fun to do. He began clicking, thinking of the friction of the beads on the rods, visualizing the heat growing in a spot in the center of the pile of branches. Each two was like a rise in temperature, *adding heat, adding heat, adding heat ... two plus two plus two ...*

The branches began smoking, then flame appeared in the center of the bundle. Max laughed. "I did it! That was easy!" He looked at Mindre.

She was sitting on the blanket, twisting grass around her finger, a faint smile on her lips. "You seem to always know what to do. Okay, we can start."

Max stepped to the blanket, abacus held in front of him. "I'm ready," he said, confidently.

"You won't need that yet. Take off your shoes and jacket," she said, "and maybe your shirt. We should be comfortable."

"Umm, okay," Max removed his jacket, watching nervously as Mindre unlaced her dress. She slipped it off and sat on the blanket wearing only her tunic. He took off his shirt and shoes, dropped them on the grass, and waited for instructions.

"Now, sit across from me," she told him gently but seriously.

He set his abacus beside him on the blanket as he sat cross-legged in front of her. Beside her sat a cup, her flask, a bundle from her herb pouch and a thin piece of wood from which she had stripped the bark. Her face was flush, chest rising and falling beneath her tunic. She turned her gaze to him, pupils large.

"You have come very far these past days, more than I ever expected, and so I find myself now ... in an awkward situation. You have a natural talent the likes of which I have never witnessed, but you are still asleep. As long as you remain so, we are all in danger. I have been charged with assuming with your fate, Maxwell, and I have been unable to protect your fate as must be done. The cats, the quake, the Calculists ..."

"Mindre, you've saved me so many times," he began.

She stopped him with a firm look and an outstretched hand. "Please, just listen now."
Max fell silent.

"I am failing you," she continued, "and we will soon meet challenges a hundred-fold more dangerous: Darklings, soldiers and maybe much worse. I need for you to awaken so that you may learn to reckon, *really* reckon, body to body, mind to mind. I had hoped your awakening may happen on its own as quickly as you mastered the dihon and the Bone-Thrower rhythms and the longwalking, but I was naive. You are new to this world and do not have the connection that is built over a lifetime of dwelling in the patterns of the land. You need to experience this connection, strongly and directly."

Max started to ask how, but he caught himself and remained quiet.

"There is a way, I didn't think of it until today, and even if I had thought of it earlier I would not have ever dared to ask you this." Mindre took a deep breath. "But after yesterday, in that dark cell ... Max, I felt a connection. I know you felt it too."

Max nodded, excited to learn that Mindre had also felt something.

"Our people have a ritual for when two are to become one," she continued. "It is a powerful joining of quintessences. It can have consequences, including stimulating an awakening. I have thought carefully about this and I am ready to share myself with you, if you are also so willing to share yourself with me. I know this is much to ask. I never thought we would be at this place, and yet here we are."

Max nodded, enraptured. Body to body, mind to mind? Share himself with her ... what did she mean? "I trust you," he said simply.

She smiled gently. "That is exactly what is needed. Tonight Max, we will ... connect. This is a serious ritual and you must commit to the experience we will share if it is to work. Are you ready?"

Max drew a breath. "Yes," he said, "I'm ready."

"Then, as we both so will, may we share the Ritual of Quintessence." Mindre set a cup between them and carefully filled it halfway with water from the flask. She seemed concentrated on the task, more than necessary, as if she had never filled a cup with water before and was afraid of spilling a drop. Holding both hands above the cup, Mindre began subtle movements in her fingers, tapping thumbs to first and second fingers. She increased the speed until her fingers were a blur, the soft tapping sounds blending to a tone rising in pitch. The water in the cup began to steam.

Opening the small bundle beside her, she delicately removed the small cluster of flowers she had opened earlier, bright purple petals ringed with a white edge. She lay them carefully on the surface of the water in the cup and pressed them down with the rounded end of the stick. Working the stick up and down, she mashed the flowers in the hot water with firm deliberate motions. She removed the stick and lifted the cup.

"A swallow of pentillium tea, our minds to open," she said. Keeping her eyes locked to his, she brought the cup to her lips and drank a swallow. Bowing her head, she offered the cup to Max. He took a drink, the liquid very warm and slightly sweet. Mindre took the cup and set it aside.

"The ritual has begun. Breathe deep, feel the pulse of Abacabax beneath you," she began.

He closed his eyes and breathed in, feeling the support of all of the blocks stacked beneath him to the center of the planet.

Click, click, click. Beside him, the beads of his abacus had once again begun clicking by themselves.

"Sorry," he whispered, reaching for the frame.

Mindre quickly took his hand before he could touch it. "It is a good sign. Allow it to happen." She held to his hand a moment longer than she needed to, her fingers warm and dry. Max felt a flutter in his stomach. She released his hand and placed both her hands on her thighs. "Feel the pulse of Abacabax beneath you," she repeated.

They sat in stillness, all quiet but for the crackling of the fire and the steady clicking of the abacus beads. Max listened to the rhythm, each click like a heartbeat, pulsing through his body. He imagined the pulse spreading out in a sphere, drawing Mindre inside the shell with him, expanding further into the ground, the trees and the sky. A tingle spread from his neck over his scalp.

"You feel it," Mindre said, not as a question.

"I feel it," he said.

"Do as I do." She reached her right hand out and placed in on his shoulder, then lay her left hand on his thigh. Max did the same, copying her position.

Mindre began speaking in a steady rhythm. "*Our legs are our strength. These are the columns that support us and from which we draw power from the faces. We now stand together, we stand with each other, we stand for each other.*

"*Our legs are our freedom. These carry us to where we will and raise us to heights without limit. We now rise together, rise with each other and rise for each other.*"

Max's legs were tingling. Was the energy real or imagined? It did not matter, something was happening.

After a pause, Mindre lifted her hand from his thigh and placed it low on his belly, thumb downwards with palm against his abdomen.

Max reached forward, laying his hand against her belly. He could feel hard muscle beneath her softness.

"Our belly is our security. It feeds us and gives safe harbor to bear life. We now secure one another, are secure together and are secure for each other.

"Our belly is our courage. It centers us and assures us of life. We now have courage together, courage with each other and are courageous for each other."

The tingling had spread to his abdomen with a growing warmth and feeling of safety. Whatever was happening, Max did not want it to stop.

Mindre raised her hand, placing it on the left side of his chest over his heart. Max raised his hand, hesitating briefly before placing it over her breast. His fingers lay against the soft curve of her flesh, and he felt a flush burning up his neck and into his cheeks. Beneath his hand, he felt the beating of her heart.

"Our heart is our life. Its beat drives us and its blood sustains us. Our hearts now beat together, beat with one another and beat for one another.

"Our heart is our emotion. It grants us compassion for all life and passion for our own. We now feel one another, feel with one another and feel for one another."

Max was burning, his chest throbbing with each heartbeat. The energy of the ritual, the effect of the tea and the excitement of touching Mindre blended together into a sensation he had never felt before.

Mindre removed her hand from his chest and placed her palm against his temple, her fingers laying across the top of his head. Max did the same, finding that her skin was burning as if on fire.

"Our mind is our perception. With it we see the patterns and with it we understand so that we may grow in knowledge. We now understand one another, understand with one another, understand for one another."

"Our mind is our power. With it we shape our reality and change the world. We now think together, think with each other, think for one another."

The energy was now running through Max's body, surging from his feet, up his legs, through his abdomen and chest and out through the top of head. He felt dizzy, thoughts flying loose, until all that existed was Mindre.

He fought for focus as she withdrew both hands and held her palms towards him, fingers spread. He placed his palms against hers and she curled her fingers between his. He closed his fingers on hers, their hands locked together.

"Our hands are our tools. With them we create and shape the world. We now reckon together, reckon with one another, reckon for one another.

"Our hands are our connection. With them we touch those around us, that all may be touched by us. We now touch each other, are touched by one another and are in touch with one another."

Max could no longer feel his own body. They sat, hands locked together. The pattern of the blocks surged through his mind, patterns of Mindre's fingers danced on his thighs, the moons spun around moons spinning within his belly, rivers within the planet flowed through his bones, his body folded into steps and throbbed in rhythmic pulses as light and heat and sound and color and taste and touch blended into one.

Max stirred, opening his eyes slowly. It was the middle of the night. He was lying on the blanket. Mindre lay beside him sleeping, one arm laying carelessly across his chest. He still felt a pulsing in his body. He carefully moved Mindre's arm and stood up quietly, trying not to disturb her. The fire had burned out and the moons hung brightly in the dark sky.

He stepped out from the trees to better see the milky span of stars smeared across the darkness. His legs felt connected to the earth, a power rolling up through his belly, his chest, his head. His hands tingled.

"Max." Mindre stood behind him, her face bathed in soft shadows.

"Mindre," he said smiling. "I have never felt so alive."

"Me neither." She lifted her hand out towards him. "Can you feel this, inside you?" she asked. Her thumb touched her forefinger, flatly, pad to pad, then deliberately withdrew and touched her middle finger, then her ring finger, then her pinky. Her hand rotated slightly as it closed into a fist with a thunk.

With a thunk? Max felt that, inside his chest, as if his throat were in his chest and it had just swallowed hard. He nodded. "I felt that."

Mindre's forefinger curled, her thumb resting on the nail, then on the nail of her middle finger, then ring finger, then pinky. Her right hand opened and relaxed as her other hand now lifted, thumb and forefinger together.

Max swayed backwards as he felt a push, as if she had physically placed a hand on his chest and pushed him gently away. "Ten," he muttered.

Mindre smiled. Her right hand began moving again, the same pattern. Max relaxed, feeling a wave swimming inside of him. It moved in his body, starting near his right temple and flittered down as her thumb moved downwards from fingertip to fingertip. A thunk again in the center of his chest below on the fifth pulse as she closed her fist, then the feeling up by his head again, moving downwards again as she touched the nails of her curved fingers with her thumb.

He could picture it, like numbers on the abacus but in his body. A round feeling moved like beads, a small bead in five different places, the same places she had touched him in the ritual! One, two, three, four ... head, chest, belly, thigh, then like a big bead inside his chest for five. The sensations then repeated but a little bit outside of his body. He understood them as six, seven, eight, nine and ...

Ten! He felt another push into his chest. With this push he felt movement on his left side at the same time, as if the counting were happening on both sides of his body. It was not ten. "Twenty." he said. "You're counting!"

Mindre paused, her eyes widening. Her fingers began to move again.

"I can feel it, moving!" Max said.

Another thunk in his chest at five and he picked up her count. "Twenty-six, twenty-seven, twenty-eight, twenty-nine." He anticipated the coming push on thirty and leaned into it. He felt the touch on his chest, but this time inside of shoving him it washed through him, warm and soft.

The pulses continued, he could almost see them. The pattern on her fingers was playing across his body, he had no need to see her hands now. Her right hand was counting zero to nine, her left picking up the tens. He followed the pattern, anticipating first each five, then not only the ten but *which* ten. Seventy, seventy five ... Max looked at Mindre, her face was flush. Eighty, ninety ... Max wondered what would happen after ninety-nine. He hesitated.

Max was shoved in the chest. He stumbled backwards.

Mindre exhaled as she stood frozen for a moment, her right hand touching her right temple. She then relaxed, her eyes softening. "You felt it. You followed it."

"Yes, like I could feel the pattern of your fingers, I could see what was coming, like counting to ninety-nine."

"I know," she said. "I could feel you, too."

She stood silent for a moment, smiling. She stepped forward, reached out and took his hands. Max smiled. She had never touched his hands before yesterday. She looked into his eyes, rubbing the back of his hands gently with her thumbs. "You have awakened. Tomorrow we can begin your real training. There is much to learn. Come, lie with me."

They returned to the blankets. Mindre slid next to Max resting her head between his shoulder and chest. They spoke no further. It was a long time until Max finally fell asleep.

Max awoke early. Mindre was awake lying next to him, looking at him with her head propped up on one elbow. "Good morning," she smiled. "Shall we go join the others?"

Max wanted to kiss her, but she rolled away and stood, brushing off her tunic and shaking out her dress. They packed up in silence, glancing at each other with fleeting smiles.

"Are we, like, a couple now?" he asked awkwardly as they headed across the shelf.

"We'll see," she said playfully.

They reached the other camp shortly. Lunata and Lherzo were still under the blankets, lying close to each other. Max smiled. Maybe they had "joined quintessences" also.

Mindre started the fire as they stirred, sitting up. "What did you do last night?" Lherzo asked.

"We were up all night!" Lunata gushed. "Oh, show them, Lherzo!"

"Okay, just a minute. Let me wake up," he said, pulling his boots on. He looked up at Mindre questioningly.

Mindre sat down on the log, her hands folded across her knees. "You first," she said.

"Have you been playing dice?" Max asked, picking up a small cubical stone. The ground was littered with small stones, some round, some cubical.

"Show them!" Lunata said again, pulling him towards the fire. They sat on the log next at the fire. Lunata slipped her arm around Lherzo, a big grin on her face. "Do it!" she told him.

"Okay, okay," he smiled. "This is ... well, this is something."

He held his abax on his lap, moving his fingers through the holes. He concentrated as he carried out a calculation. A speck appeared on the ground in front of him, growing quickly layer by layer, making a square form that grew upwards. A rough stone cube took shape.

Lunata plucked it up and held it forth triumphantly. "He can make stones!"

She handed the newly formed block to Mindre. Mindre shook her head and looked at Lherzo in disbelief. "I have never seen anything like it. You can *create* matter? Lherzo ... that's incredible."

Lherzo smiled and shrugged. "It was Lunata's idea," he said, smiling at her. "She's got the wildest imagination."

"We're a good team!" Lunata said. "He can only make small stones right now, but it would not be unlikely if he could make other things, as well. I'm very proud of him!" She stretched over and kissed him on his cheek. Lherzo looked down with an embarrassed smile.

Mindre looked back and forth between Lherzo and Lunata, a questioning smile on her lips.

"So what did you do last night?" Lunata asked.

"Last night," Mindre said, "we performed a ritual my people use that I thought might help Max awaken. It worked. Max can fully reckon."

"Max! You can?" Lunata said, looking at him with a bright expectant smile.

"I ... think so," Max said. "Mindre was something else."

"I thought we could spend some time training before we ride out today," Mindre said. "Maybe you two would like to keep practicing?"

Lherzo looked at Lunata. "Yes. Yes, I'd like that very much," he said.

Max and Mindre stood on the edge of the camp. She ran through a count on her fingers again. Max could feel the movements. He hesitated as she approached one hundred, wondering where the sensation would travel to once she ran out of two-digit numbers. He immediately got his answer: a sharp knock on the side of his head.

"Ouch," he said. "So that's where it is."

"If you don't take ahold of the reckoning, the reckoning will take ahold of you. Follow the reckoning and it can pass through and not even touch you. Okay now, follow this."

She was counting by tens now, Max understood. The hundred came and he anticipated it. No knock, just a feeling like warm water up by his right temple.

"You picked that up quickly, Max," she said. "Okay, try this."

Her fingers flitted, and Max felt a pattern. A number formed in the pulses, changed, and then hit him sharply in his chest. "Ow!"

Mindre smiled. "Follow it. It's a summary, a *sum,* I think you call it. You can do it."

Again the pattern formed ... *thirty-one.* It changed, he followed the addition as it became an *eighty-eight.* This time, instead of a sharp strike, a warmth passed through his chest. "I got it, I ... followed it."

Mindre smiled, a question mark in her eyes. "You did. How about this?"

Fingers moving, pattern building, Max focused on the shapes and the pictures forming in his mind, anticipated the results, and felt another warm wave.

"Again," Mindre snapped.

Again and again Max raced after the patterns. Again and again he anticipated the results and the feeling passed right through him. Mindre's hands moved faster and faster. Max felt the numbers grow. Movements in her arms translated to hundreds and Max instinctively followed. Somehow he understood what these swirls of feeling meant, how the pattern mirrored itself on both sides of his body.

Mindre shook her head. "How are you able to ... ? All right, try this!"

Another pattern formed, but this time it moved differently, the tens and ones jumping wildly. The number grew big – fast! – and slammed into Max. He bounced off of the impact as if he had run into a wall, or more as if the wall had run into him. He curled his arms around his body, his skin burning and ears ringing.

He straightened up and looked at her, feeling a rush of anger. "What was that about?"

Mindre's eyes still burned, and then softened. "Oh ... Max, I'm sorry about that. That was a little fast. I just can't understand how you're following so quickly. That was a multiplix. You'll need to learn to follow those as well.

Max stood up. "Well, now you've got me nervous. You're strong!"

She smiled. "You've just done more in ten minutes than most Dijins ever learn in their lifetimes. Max, we'll have you up to speed in no time.

"Okay," she continued as Max regained his composure. "*Following* is your defense. Follow well and you cannot be touched. You did well, but you will need to learn to follow automatically, while you're thinking of other things. You cannot cast your own reckonings if you are only following. Ready to try some offense?"

"Oh, definitely!" Max said. Max took out the abacus from his jacket pocket and flipped over the leather cover. He ran his fingers over the beads, slid the beads on the top upwards and the beads on the bottom down, clearing the instrument.

"Okay, Max, I'm not sure what to tell you," Mindre said. "Show me what you can do with your abacus, try to connect."

"I'll try counting, like you did." He clicked the beads up one by one, counting to four, then clearing four while bringing down a bead from the top of five. He thought of the "clunk" he felt when Mindre made a five. Could he make a clunk in her with his five?

He tried to make a feeling in his body as each bead moved and imagined the feeling flowing out to her. From her face, to her breast, to her belly, to her hips and to her center with the five. He repeated, imagining a stronger push with the ten, and the twenty and the thirty.

"You're doing it ..." she said.

Max sped through the count to fifty then stopped. Counting by ones was the first exercise he tried with he first got the abacus and it was not as fun as skip counting with other multiples.

"How about this?" He counted by twos. *Click click click*, he made the pattern with the beads as he pictured a current of energy flowing into Mindre, changing places with the changing locations of the beads.

Mindre raised one eyebrow. "Keep going."

Max raced to one hundred and then switched to adding nines. He loved adding nines. A simple twist to remove a one while adding a ten bead, and the rods showed *nine, eighteen, twenty-seven*. It was so simple and beautiful. He fired out the sequence, *plus nine, plus nine, plus nine*, as the sum grew over *two-hundred*, then over *three-hundred*.

Mindre twisted, alarmed. Her face hardened. She stood motionless as a small wind picked up around her, lifting dust swirling into the air, dried leaves, and then small stones lifting as his sum reached towards *one-thousand*.

"Stop!" Mindre called.

Max stopped. *Nine hundred ninety-one*. A final *nine* waiting to send a chain reaction up the rods to exactly *one thousand*. The wind calmed immediately, leaves settled to the earth, dust still hanging motionless near Mindre's feet. He eyed his abacus for a moment longer, and then shook it, scattering the beads to randomness.

"That was strong Max. You can *use* that. You can push even harder and wider."

"I was thinking of pushing those nines at you, like bursts." He paused. She had always stopped him when he described his thinking, but this time she said nothing. Maybe it was finally okay to discuss techniques with her, now that they were "as one?"

"Try some multiplix, but keep the numbers to two digits. You scare me a little," she said. Max thought she might not be joking.

Back and forth they sparred. Max found it difficult to cast and follow at the same time, to simultaneously think about his reckoning while feeling her attack coming in. It didn't take too many times being smacked in the head or in the gut for him to realize it was more important to defend than to attack.

He also quickly discovered how much fun it was to make a calculation, dream up an image and watch it actually work! Joy bubbled inside of him as he reckoned. Mindre picked up on playfulness, too, they laughed as they sent more and more dangerous blows at each other.

"Let's break," Mindre said.

"Okay," Max agreed, setting up one last number. *Click, click, click ...*

"Hey!" Mindre said, stumbling towards him.

Max kept dividing, teasing out more decimals out in his quotient, pulling her in closer and closer. She wobbled unsteadily towards him and into his body. He wrapped his arms around her waist.

"Thanks for the lesson," he smiled mischievously.

She pushed him back with a laugh. "Max, you can do this! You can *really* do this."

Back with the others, Lunata eagerly showed them the shapes Lherzo had made, double-sized cubes and irregular lumpy shapes.

"I'm limited by the number of holes in my abax, I think," Lherzo said. "If I make a new tablet ..."

"You're limited by the number of holes in your head, Lherzo!" Lunata said. "You need wilder images. I know you're not that uptight! We need to work on that, I can think of things we can do to loosen you up." She grinned impishly.

"Max is nearly ready," Mindre said. "Maybe you both can spar with him tonight? He needs to experience some different styles."

"Sure!" Lherzo said. "That would be fun."

"My bones are hungry for you, Abacist," Lunata said, clacking her teeth together.

They loaded up the horses and rode upwards, towards the top of the world. Max felt he was already there.

Chapter 12: Clash of Kings

Saul sat beside the cage in his bedroom, scribbling symbols on a tablet as he focused on the gray creature sitting peacefully within. He reached deep into her mind, flowing effortlessly through passages in a space that expanded hyperbolically as he stretched his perception further and further.

Samuel's scribing gave him access to places in her mind he had never found before. He divided the numbers on the paper, more and more digits than ever possible on his abacus. Finer and finer details opened up, he flowed through tiny corridors in her mind that he filled with his, like water seeping into a sponge.

"It must be here, somewhere. Where are you, Lydala? Where are you?"

The passages were empty. No memories, no images, no thought, only echoes of his own footsteps through the empty space. He searched, on and on, his hand scratching row after row of figures as he pored through her mind in greater and greater detail.

"There *is* something here ... I can feel it! But how do I get in there ... ?" Saul worked the symbols. It was as if a part were missing. His calculations weren't quite adding up. What was wrong? He was certain he had perfect synchronicity with Samuel's reckoning and yet he couldn't go deep enough. Maybe if he tried to ... no. Maybe another way ... no. Over and over he tried, only to find the answer was 'no' and 'no' again.

He scrawled angrily back and forth over his page of figures, screaming in frustration. "It doesn't work! It's not enough!"

He slumped back, running his hands through his hair. "I'm sorry Lydala," he said. "I can't reach you. It's this cursed Exception. Wendi has split Samuel's power, and I don't have enough. It's just not enough."

He stormed to the window. "Wendi!" he screamed at the air. Gray figures in the courtyard below looked up at him. Snatching up his abacus, he began furiously clicking beads. Two of the creatures turned towards each other, mouths biting, claws ripping at each other's flesh. "Die! Die! Die!" he yelled, picturing his sister Wendi and Maxwell viciously ripping each other into pieces. The creatures fell, their bodies forming a bloody heap. They were still feebly trying to claw at one another.

Exhausted, he slumped to his bed, weeping at the injustice of it all.

Saul rose and sulked to the window, leaning hard against the sill. Gray figures in the courtyard milled about, stepping on the bodies he had torn apart. Two soldiers lost, but their lives mattered little. He had many thousands more.

"I must have Maxwell ... that is what is stopping me. He is the final piece, but where is he?"

He took up his pad, circling his charcoal stick idly as he gazed out on the terrain. Maxwell could be anywhere. He scratched some symbols, *one hundred* for himself, *plus one* for the

Changed in the courtyard, *divide by two* to share the mind, reach out and connect. How easily he slipped inside. He imagined looking through its eyes, and then he could. He looked back towards the window and saw himself up above leaning on the window. The Changed had nearly empty minds, they were so simple to take. He walked the creature towards the wall, looking down towards the city where others wandered the streets. If he had to, he would walk the world in this stolen body searching for Maxwell.

"Hmmm," he said out loud. "Samuel can use recursive functions. Like an equation inside of an equation. I wonder ..." Saul scratched another line. Reckoning within reckoning? A strange idea, could he reckon from within the mind of the Changed he now controlled? Make another connection without backing out from this one?

He let the connection linger while he sketched some patterns. Not only was scribing powerful for digit calculations, it was an incredible tool for research. Perhaps he could jump directly from *one hundred one "halves"* to *one hundred two "thirds"*? "Aaaahhh ..." he said, "that is a lovely pattern!" If it worked, he could extend it indefinitely.

Looking through the eyes of the creature he now possessed, he chose one of the figures wandering in the streets below. *Multiply by two-thirds, add one-third.* Suddenly he was down on the streets, seeing from a new perspective.

"I can jump directly from mind to mind!" he said to himself.

He quickly scratched another line. *Multiply by three-fourths, add one-fourth.* Down in the street, he moved his perception to another mind. It worked! *Multiply by four-fifths, add one-fifth.* He was inside another. It was genius! He should be able to link and link and link, right up to the limits of his reckoning, which were vast.

261

Through the creature's eyes, he gazed long down the steps, choosing a lone figure far away. He wrote another calculation and was there.

"Your eyes are mine. All of your eyes!"

Excitement raced through him. He wrote faster and faster. He was looking down the steps. He was crawling on a shelf. He was on the steps. He was standing on the mesa where dozens of the Changed ripped at the trees and grass. Hopping one mind to another he traveled, faster than his sister could longwalk.

The images were fainter now. He concentrated harder. The lines of calculation were getting cumbersome. It was getting more difficult to hold all of these links, to keep track of all of the parts of the reckoning, and yet he could. He found himself standing at the top of the Western Ascension, a day's travel away. He could make out fuzzy figures of the Changed nearby, many of them, stumbling downwards towards Vertex.

"Lydala, this must be what Wendi feels like when she longwalks," he said, "but this is surely better! I see everything! I know everything!"

Could he reach all the way to Vertex? There may be a chain of the Changed reaching far downward. He moved his mind down the steps, hopping long distances at a time. His images drew darker, his vision now a narrow tunnel. His hand ached as the lines of symbols grew longer and longer. Sweat dripped from his forehead, the effort from the nested reckonings draining him physically.

"What is this? Soldiers?" he muttered incredulously. On the ascension stood humans. Many of them. He could make out a chariot, flags, horses. How many? He strained, his hand shaking over his pad.

Suddenly, it all collapsed. Equation after equation came undone, unraveling faster and faster until it cracked like a whip in the center of his forehead. He stumbled back from the window, dropping his pad and clutching at his head as he sank onto his bed.

His temples ached, his forehead burned. "I saw them," he said to Lydala. "An entire army. They are coming for us." He turned and smiled at his wife chewing on the bars of her cage.

"They are far too late, my dear," he said, rising and stretching out his arms. "I am already a god!"

-:- | -:-

General Biggens stood on the bay of the war chariot with Gerard and Kalkar, twisting triangular arrangements of blocks on the abax. Darkling groups had been growing thinner as they ascended and he was hopeful now that they may not need to spend the whole trip sweeping the stairs.

The horses trudged dutifully forwards and upwards, a train of ten horses tugging the massive chariot up the hill. The chariot rolled on four assemblies of wheels, each assembly a set of three wheels in a triangular arrangement, sized perfectly to fit the steps of the Western Ascension. With axles wider than the center step, the triangles turned and made contact with the larger blocks on both sides of the center. As each assembly turned, a new wheel rotated to the next block upwards, found purchase at the back of the step and bit into the stone. This caused the set of wheels to rotate again, bringing the next wheel over to the next step.

The design was brilliant. The chariot rolled evenly upwards or downwards on the right-angled surface of the steps. All of it was made possible by three wheels in a triangle, like the triangular abac on his fearsome new abax or the rotating disks on the Triangulators' table. Three is the true number of Abacabax, Biggens thought, and it would be the number for reckoning in the next family line when he became New Origin.

"Oasis Mesa, four thousand steps," the helmsman called.

A horn sounded. The Forward Team clamored by, split between both sides of the chariot, running up the side steps and converging in the center to spring forward ahead of the chariot. Biggens watched as they moved from shelf to shelf. Their reconnaissance jaunts were far shorter than he liked. The denseness of their enemies required sweeping the ascension every few hundred steps and then sending out the Forward Team again. At the edge of Oasis Mesa, the team again split into two groups as they disappeared from view. A moment later, a white flag swung sharply back and forth from the top.

"Oasis is clear. This is our stop, boys," Biggens said.

"It takes so long to stop and start the march," Kalkar complained.

"Yes, four hours wasted every day," Biggens agreed. "No one's ever marched an army of this size before, but we need the numbers. Let's get on with it."

The chariot stopped just past the vast mesa and the scene filled with action. Cavalry guard moved to unharness the horses as line after line of soldiers fanned out across the mesa in both directions. Over the next two hours a small city appeared on the wind-bare plain. White tents, mess halls and perimeter fences were quickly set in place. A second platoon took position on the shelves above.

Biggens, Kalkar and Gerard gathered for supper with the War Council. The square tent was sparse except for an elaborate table setting.

"The march is proceeding like precision gears," Basal said smugly.

"Except for reconnaissance," Biggens said sourly. "Gordon?"

The nearly toothless commander frowned and shook his head. "The ascension is thick with Darklings. Scout teams are making slow progress."

"Still," another commander added, "these Darklings are not worthy opponents, it's like fighting wild dogs. We've lost fewer than fifty men."

Basal grumbled. "This is a costly excursion. The Mad Teller's guard is only twenty."

"Yes, only twenty," Biggens said, "and yet he slaughtered five hundred of our kind with that tiny army. Now he is joined by the Abacist Prime. If Saul can kill so many by himself, how many can he and the Prime kill together?"

"Sir, they were mostly civilians," Basal pointed out.

"Mostly?" Biggens spat. "There were eighty-one soldiers stationed there! Gentlemen, this is not the War of the Plague, when our enemy was fighting the Darklings at the same time as they were fighting us. Our enemy is now 'King of the Darklings' and has grown exponentially in his power. We strike decisively."

"Nine-thousand soldiers on his doorstep will mean a hasty victory!" Gordon proclaimed. He raised his goblet. "To victory!"

"To victory!" the men cheered.

Biggens smiled. "They are entirely disorganized," he said. "We will take them totally by surprise."

-:- | -:-

Saul stood on the wall, scratching symbols on his tablet. Five hundred Darklings organized themselves into neat rows. He smiled. He could use chain multiplication, *one times two times three*, and so on, to link minds to his control. With the twenty rods on his abacus he could chain no more than twenty-one of the

Changed to his command. With Samuel's scribing, however, he could use exponents and approximations to enslave thousands of minds at once. The control was not perfect, the greater the products the greater the errors, but if he kept the instructions simple he could guide an entire army as one.

By tomorrow, Biggens' army would reach Tangram Mesa. Saul would leave now, gather forces en route, draw back the Changed from the ascension and strike the entire line at once.

"Arm yourselves," he muttered, scratching another line of symbols. Row by row, the Changed ambled to the armory. During their years of illegal occupancy, the Calculists had filled the warehouse with their own armaments. Saul had no use for the stacks of abaxes and crates of abac. His soldiers took up only the simplest of arms, long wooden poles sharpened to a point on one end. The Calculists' military might would be drowned in a sea of simplicity, taken down by a simple algorithm flowing through simple-minded soldiers armed with simple weapons.

He climbed into his palanquin, a tiny room with open windows on a platform resting on two long poles. He leaned back in the padded seat, set the tablet and charcoal stick to the side and took out his abacus. Though his abacus was so much weaker than scribing, he still had a strong fondness for the device and doubted he would ever stop using it. With a few rapid clicks of the beads, four of his minions lifted the poles. The palanquin wobbled as they set the platform on their shoulders, two in front and two in back. A few more clicks and they began to march.

Saul set aside his abacus and scratched on the pad, his army falling in line behind him single file, pole arms pointed to the sky and bobbing up and down as they descended to the mesa.

He smiled at his good fortune. He could pick up hundreds more soldiers from the mesa as they traveled and thousands more from the Darklands on the other side of the ascension. The stretch of steps just below Tangram Mesa was the worst defensible position and the entire Calculist army was marching right into his grip. They were completely unaware that the mindless creatures that wandered the hills randomly for decades were about to display very deadly purpose.

-:- | -:-

Biggens smiled. He had been correct. The final day of their ascent saw almost no Darklings on the ascension. While he enjoyed employing his mighty weaponry, he was relieved to have a break from shouting instructions at his dim sons.

Gerard hung out of the window, looking back at the endless line of soldiers step-counting their way behind the Grand Chariot. Kalkar leaned back in his stool, arms crossed, and yawned.

Biggens sighed and idly rolled tri-abacs in his giant hands. His unusually large palms allowed him to hold a line of five blocks in each hand. He could rotate each block separately, an abax-less method far superior than the traditional Calculist palm reckoning. While others struggled to slide small round stones on the tattooed lines on their left palms, Biggens could securely roll his blocks in both hands and control his reckoning under any physical circumstance without spilling stones. His mighty hands were a genetic gift, bestowed upon him by the long line of third-born Calculists.

He was proud of his hands. When he was young, he was sometimes called "Big-hands" instead of "Biggens," but he was quick to show the other children what his big hands were capable of. He knew his men still called him that behind his back, but Biggens knew it was not said disparagingly but rather with a mix of jealousy and respect.

He rolled patterns in his palms, threes and nines and twenty-sevens and eighty-ones. The system was entirely his own. It seemed difficult to his sons due to its strangeness, but the next generation of reckoners on the faces would all be using his superior system, both in their hands and on abaxes alike.

Gerard moved from the side window to the Tri-Reckoner, leaning his weight on his palms on the black stone as he peered up the ascension. "It's going fast today."

"Don't lean on that," Biggens said.

Gerard rolled his eyes but straightened up. "How much longer?" he asked.

"How much longer?" Biggens repeated, irritated. "I don't know, if only there were a way to tell," he answered sarcastically. Any fool could see the positions of the mesas and know exactly where he was. Even a dimmer fool could see the approaching wall stretching out in both directions farther than the eye could see.

"Oh, is that the cliff we're going to, then?" Gerard said, pointing. "We're so early! Good, I'm so tired of sitting in here."

Ahead of them, the Forward Team waved the white flag, then proceeded upwards. With so few Darklings today, the team could advance farther from the caravan, giving them an extra measure of safety. In about twenty minutes they would be on Tangram Mesa and just one day from their target.

Biggens ran his hand across the abax, admiring the finish, picturing the day when all abaxes would be cut with triangular holes to hold tri-abacs. He thought of Lherzo's idiotic abax with the round holes, cut to fit *fingers*. It was an inspiration from that degenerate girl he had been enamored with. Finger reckoning on an abax? Disgusting. Now that he had run off with her and the Abacist he had been sent to apprehend, it was clear that it was a blessing the line of thirds did not extend to his sons. Especially Lherzo.

A horn sounded, then sounded again. Biggens looked up with concern.

"What does it mean when they do it twice?" Gerard asked.

Biggens didn't answer. He scanned the steps, squinting to focus. The Forward Team was gone. He heard Gordon shouting instructions outside.

The horn sounded again and another team sprinted up the side steps around the war chariot.

"Boys, take position," he said.

"What's going on?" Kalkar asked, hands on the tri-abacs.

"We lost the Forward Team," Biggens said.

The chariot rolled forward steadily. Biggens peered into the trees on either side. The final stretch of steps to Tangram Mesa was dense with trees. Anything could be hiding out there.

"I don't see anything," Gerard said.

"If I were defending this mesa," Biggens said, "it is here I would plan an ambush."

"But Darklings don't know how to plan," Kalkar said.

"Just be ready."

The second team neared the edge. Suddenly, they were running back down. Darklings spilled over the edge, dozen and dozens, down the center and jumping from greater heights to the left and right.

Horns sounded, long blasts, as commanders yelled. Darklings came pouring from the trees. They were under attack!

"Set *zero-zero-one, one-one-one, zero-two-zero!*" Biggens called. All three pairs of hands turned the clusters of stones on the board. "Second line – *one-two-two, zero-one-two, zero-one-one!*" The second rows on the abax were twisted into position. "Calculate!" he shouted.

A ripple spread upwards, scattering Darklings and the unfortunate Forward Team alike to tumble and break on the sharp steps.

"Clear!" Biggens yelled.

"They've got sticks," Gerard shouted, pointing out the window.

"I think those are called 'pikes,'" Kalkar said.

"No, I think they're 'pole arms,'" Gerard responded.

Biggens looked to the forest with disbelief as hundreds of the creatures leapt forward, long pointed weapons in their hands. Soldiers took position out on the shelves, crouching with abaxes on their knees to launch a counterattack.

"They have weapons? That's not possible!" Biggens spat. "Kalkar, Gerard! Set *two-one-two, two-zero-two, zero-two-zero!*"

Outside, soldiers began screaming as the wave of gray flesh washed over them.

-:- | -:-

Saul stood tensely on the edge, directing his troops from a safe distance from the ascension. The Calculist army strung downwards in a straight line along the crest of the ascension, fading into the distance below. Every division of their army must be on that line, he thought.

He wrote another line of symbols, focusing on the simple instructions, "Stab. Bite. Kill." His connections to the Changed spread like a web of lights in his mind. A spider web, Saul thought, wrapping around the caravan like a spider's legs around its prey. He was aware of connections suddenly going dark, strands of his web breaking. It was enough to write another small calculation, reach out with another image and renew his numbers from the thousands of the Changed he had gathered in the forest that morning.

270

The line of soldiers broke in place after place down the line as gray uniforms disappeared over the edges of the steps. A Calculist soldier would have time only to strike down one or two of the Changed before meeting the sharpened end of a pike. He had them outnumbered at least five to one.

His frontal assault, however, was not going as expected. As each wave of his soldiers leapt down the steps from the mesa, they were being swept away en masse. Group after group of creatures bounded over the edge, group after group smashed to the side. He was losing connections at a terrible pace. Worse, if the web were broken here at the start, he could lose the connection all the way down the line. Without instruction, his soldiers would be crushed.

"What kind of reckoning is this?" Saul muttered. "What have you got in that chariot?"

He reached into the mind of a Changed near the chariot but caught only a glimpse before the connection was ripped away, his host smashed against the rocks. He scratched another line, hastily rebuilding lines of his mental web.

He would need to be quick. He wrote his simple equation to jump to another mind near the chariot but only caught sight of bloodied horses before his host's vision went black. The Calculists were more formidable than they had any right to be.

More connections vanished as another group of the Changed were flattened. Saul wrote a line of numbers, and then another, frantically trying to keep up with the losses. He tried to jump to another mind, but the mind went black before he even entered it.

Half of his web of connections suddenly vanished. This could not be happening! He took a deep breath and concentrated. It had taken a long time to build such a web, he could not lose it now. Line after line of calculations appeared on his tablet as he hastily rebuilt the links and then built them again as they continued to vanish in chunks. He couldn't keep this up. He needed to stop whatever it was inside of that chariot.

Saul scanned the carnage near the war machine on the steps. One of his soldiers lay broken on the front wheel assembly but still alive. It may be his best chance. He scratched out the simple equation and entered its mind. The space within was filled with pain and static, but he could see through its eyes, up into the chariot where three men stood before a long black table. In the center was Biggens himself, turning stones on a huge abax.

Could he jump minds from a Changed to a human? Human minds were not easily accessible, not without permission, and chaining the link through a dying Changed would make his contact much weaker. He needed to try. If he were lucky, he might find a mind weak enough to enter.

-:- | -:-

"Calculate!" yelled Biggens. Troops had filled the shelves around the chariot, enough protection that he could continue grinding down Darklings in large numbers. He gritted his teeth in a grin. Nothing would withstand Tricalculus reckoning.

The door opened, Gordon leaned inside. "The lines are falling! There's too many! We need to fall back!"

"Hold the lines! Do your job!" Biggens yelled. "We have the numbers!"

Gordon screamed, his face contorting as a pike buried itself in his side. With a jerk his body was yanked through the doorway.

Biggens stared with alarm at the empty space where Gordon had just been standing. A Darkling stuck its head inside, turning to look at Biggens and his sons with its flat, hollow eyes.

"They're inside! They're inside!" yelled Gerard.

In a sweeping motion, Biggens snatched a handful of tri-abacs from the board and spun them in his fingers. The Darkling's head snapped backwards, its flat eyes suddenly bulging from its skull as Biggens squeezed it to death. With a final turn of his stones he threw the creature through the door, crashing into another Darkling behind it. Both tumbled to the steps below.

He jumped to the door, slamming it shut. Through the window he saw the carnage, piles of bodies in a mash of matte gray uniforms and shiny gray skin. Soldiers worked their abaxes, sending Darklings flying, only to be replaced with rows of others bearing long pointed sticks that they thrust through the bodies of the soldiers. It was an impossible nightmare, the waves of Darklings stretching back into the trees like an ocean.

Determinedly he slapped his tri-abacs back into their spaces on the black stone board.

"Clear!" he called, twisting the bottom row to zeros. Kalkar did the same.

"Gerard, clear!" Biggens yelled again.

"My head feels funny," Gerard said.

Biggens smacked his monstrous hand against the side of Gerard's head. "Get your stone into this, now!"

Gerard turned the tri-abacs to their zero positions.

"Set *zero-one-two, one-two-zero, one-one-zero!* What in the Corners, Gerard?!" Biggens turned, enraged. His dimwit son had stepped back from the calculation.

Biggens barely had time to register the knife in Gerard's hand as it plunged towards his heart.

-:- | -:-

Horns sounded down the mountainside as soldiers fled down and away from the steps. The war chariot stood as a shell, gray creatures throwing themselves against the windows and wheels. The wave of mindless soldiers continued their assault. Tens of thousands of the Changed had fallen but tens of thousands remained. Their ranks had been built up over decades with untold numbers of Abacists and Calculists and Dijins until the faces held more of the Changed than there were humans.

Biggens' army was no match for the sheer numbers. Biggens was no match for Saul.

Saul sank to his haunches, letting his hand go still upon his tablet. The Changed could continue ripping and gouging at any survivors, and at themselves for all that Saul cared, until the connection wound down. His work was finished.

How many bodies lay strewn upon the long stretch of steps below? Saul wondered. Most of the soldiers. All of the leaders. The Calculist army had been absolutely and decisively obliterated. And it was he, one lone reckoner who had single-handedly destroyed the largest military force ever assembled on the faces.

He was dizzy with victory and exhaustion. First, home to rest and celebrate. Next, he would assess his forces and decide on his next moves. He would find Maxwell and take his powers, crush the capital city now laying defenseless below, become immortalized as the next New Origin and perhaps even take the Council of the Whole as his own. Oh, the secrets they possessed ... they could all be his.

Nothing could stop him now. Saul Teller knew for certain that he was the most powerful reckoner that had ever lived, a god upon this world.

Chapter 13: Armageddon

The city of Tangram lay above Tangram Mesa nestled in a cozy woodland of red and orange foliage. Max admired the trees, they reminded him of the Japanese maples his mother had planted in the garden, domed tops with small lobed leaves and multiple trunks joining close to the ground. The steps were dotted with a soft cover of brown leaves.

The farther they ascended, the more trees Max spotted that were freshly scarred and chewed, as if animals had used them to sharpen their claws. Max knew these animals were probably those who had once been human.

Lherzo drew his abax. "Be on the lookout. We're getting close." He had warned them several times that Tangram was a hotspot for Darklings since Saul had taken the city three months ago in the heart of winter. Command at Vertex dared not issue marching orders for a retaliation during the winter months. Storms came suddenly and could be brutal along the Western Ascension, making winter travel difficult at best. In the meantime, Saul had populated the city and the surrounding hills with hundreds of Darklings. They had not yet seen any of the foul creatures, but Max could see the chewed trees were evidence of their recent presence.

Max already had his abacus in hand, watching the trees for movement, listening for sounds other than the steady clicking of horse hooves. They rode upwards beside a mossy cliff wall. Trails left the stairs at irregular intervals onto the larger shelves, the paths lined with white-blossomed trees, pines with black rugged bark and thick-leaved twisted trees in green and gold. It was the loveliest woods Max had seen yet, but his enjoyment was spoiled by the specter of monsters that could be waiting over the next rise.

They turned from the steps onto a broad road lined with pink-blossomed flowering bushes. Ahead rose a line of columns anchored at the top only to the sky, and further beyond lay the arched walls of Tangram itself. Max sucked in his breath. In contrast to Vertex, which was a utilitarian city filled with boxes and industry, this city was like an art museum rising from the center of a botanical garden. It had the natural beauty of Quincunx but blended with architecture finer than any he had seen on either of his worlds.

"This is your ancestral home," Mindre said over her shoulder. "Let's hope it still welcomes you."

They rode into the garden, between flower beds filled with blossoms of every color, competing with weeds and saplings that had invaded their space and flourished through neglect. Fascinating geometric sculptures stood in places, while other flower beds waited expectantly around empty blocks that once held statues. A dry fountain held a beautifully twisted flask whose neck curved around and passed through its side, joining to its surface again on the opposite side like a serpent passing through its own body.

Max pictured the space as it must have been, a serene and gorgeous space meticulously cared for by a culture that valued peace and beauty. He felt a touch of pride knowing this was built by his people, and a touch of sadness that the artisans were now gone. Perhaps one day this could be tended to as it deserved.

"No Darklings," Lherzo commented.

"Maybe Saul has taken Samuel somewhere else," Max offered.

They rode near the wall. Lherzo pointed to a heavy wooden portal set in the back of courtyard. "I can open that door," he said.

"Let's go in the front door. We don't want to surprise anyone," Max said. He did not want to be on the receiving end of any kind of defense of the city by this particular resident.

The city gate was wide open beneath a tall parabolic arch. Colored tiles in mosaic patterns filled the upper portions of the arch. The lower part was stripped bare, missing most of the tiles. Max imagined they were torn loose by the pattern-hating monsters who were once his kin.

The gate led to a central promenade. Arcades on either side stood before lines of doors and broken windows. They rode down the empty streets, past empty alleyways and up the steps towards the fortress. Max thought the fortress was more of a palace, with buttressed walls that held rows of colorful windows lined with frieze patterns.

They dismounted in front of the courtyard gates. All was quiet, not even the songs of birds could be heard, as if they, too, had long fled these neglected grounds.

They walked apprehensively up the final steps. The doors of the palace stood open. Peering inside, Max called "Hello?" not quite as loud as he had intended.

The entrance room featured two stairways that wrapped around to the left and right to join a balcony at the back. Open archways led to spacious rooms on all sides. They stayed together as a group, walking through sitting rooms and galleries, looking through windows to the deserted grounds below.

"There's some Dark Ones," Lunata said, peering through a window. The others moved to join her with alarm. "They appear quite dead," she said calmly.

Two bodies lay in the courtyard below, torn flesh laying in jagged strips on the dry grass.

Max turned away in disgust, catching sight of a book and dishes on a low table. "He's been here recently," he said, picking up the book from beside empty glasses and a bowl caked with dried grain. "This one's about Dijin herbs," he said, showing the cover to Mindre. He opened the book, the pages were filled with handwritten text and inked drawings. "My grandmother wrote this," he said with surprise.

Lunata peered in the next room. "Here's the kitchen. It's well-supplied." The kitchen was stocked with jars and pots of grains and jellies and dried fruit. An open closet was filled with smoked meats and cheeses.

"He's gone to meet the Calculist forces," Lherzo said. "He's taken all his Darklings. Command claimed that he would not know they were coming until they were on his doorstep."

Max frowned. "So Samuel has gone to war?"

"And tomorrow, or soon, either Saul or Biggens will be riding through those gates," Lherzo said. "We need a plan for both contingencies. Let's explore the whole palace and get an idea of the layout. Watch for exits. I understand Tangram has tunnels for emergency escapes. We'd be wise to have an escape plan."

"Shall we eat first?" Lunata asked, chewing on a strip of smoked meat.

"I'm going to keep looking around," Max said.

"I'll go with you," said Mindre.

"Okay," Lherzo said. "I'm starved, I'm going to help Lunata eat some of this food and we'll join you shortly."

Max and Mindre made rounds of the first level. They passed through a large dusty banquet hall, long unused, past small rooms with beds, staff quarters perhaps, and a smaller kitchen. They ascended a narrow back stairway.

The second level was quiet, thick tapestries on the wall blunting the sound of their footsteps.

"Max!" Mindre whispered, alarmed. In a sparsely furnished bedroom a body lay in the center of a bed. They stepped into the room.

"Samuel?" Max rushed to the bed. It was his brother, but something was terribly wrong. His skin was pale, almost gray in color. His black hair looked oily and stuck to his forehead in clumps. Max reached out to touch him, holding his breath.

"Is he … ?" Mindre whispered.

"Sam?" Max whispered, touching Samuel's face. "He's breathing. He's alive." Max shook him slightly, no response. He lifted one eyelid with dread, finding his eye staring blankly ahead, his wide pupil closing slightly in response to the light.

"What's wrong with him?" Mindre asked, touching his chest. "His lips are so dry, get some water."

Max looked about, not certain where to go.

"There," Mindre said, pointing to the nightstand where a half-filled jug of water stood.

"How do we give it to him?" Max asked. "I don't want him to choke."

"Give me that," Mindre took the jug. "And give me that cloth," she said pointing to the decorative mat on the nightstand.

She poured water onto the cloth. "Roll him to his side," she said. Holding underneath his cheek, she squeezed the cloth, letting droplets fall onto his lips and into his mouth. "We can't give him much at once."

She felt his forehead. "He's not very warm, see if you can find some blankets."

Max hopped to his feet, pleased to have a task. He found a woven blanket in the closet and draped it over his brother.

"I don't know what's wrong with him, Max."

Max looked around the room. Samuel's sneakers sat neatly by the door. A desk held waxy pencils and a pad of thick paper covered with numbers in Samuel's handwriting.

"Stay here," Mindre said gently, "I'll get the others."

She returned with Lherzo and Lunata moments later. Neither had seen this condition before. "Seems like dark reckoning," Lherzo said gravely. "Why don't we see what else is upstairs?"

"I'll stay with him," Lunata offered.

"Thank you," said Max.

Down the hall they opened a heavy wooden door. It swung inwards to an airy room. The walls and ceiling were filled with wonders. "Wow," Lherzo said as they entered.

One wall was lined with books, a table filled with tools and wooden blocks stood against the adjacent wall and dozens of shapes hung on strings from the ceiling.

"This must be Saul's workshop," Max said.

"Come see this," Mindre said, standing in the doorway to the next room.

In the bedroom stood a cage with a Darkling curled up on the floor, asleep.

"What is he doing with that?" Lherzo whispered.

"I don't know, experiments?" said Max.

"In his *bedroom*?" Lherzo countered. "What kind of experiments do you do in your bedroom?"

Max didn't want to think of the possibilities. "If he's left Samuel and he's left his ... *pet*, then he's not planning on being gone for long."

The four of them sat in the kitchen, Max sitting on the counter while the others sat at the table eating. Max slowly chewed dried berries. He didn't feel hungry.

"The army is due on Tangram Mesa at the Western Ascension this evening," Lherzo said. "They'll arrive here earliest tomorrow afternoon. There's an armory in the back that is easily secured and a long passage that may be an escape route. We can investigate that in the morning. For tonight, there's some comfortable beds upstairs near Samuel that we can use. We should all sleep together, but we should take turns keeping watch through the night to be safe. Who wants first watch?"

"I will," Max raised his hand. "I don't think I'm going to sleep at all."

"I'll stay up with you," Mindre offered.

"No, you get some rest. I'll wake you later, you can take second shift.

"I'll take third shift, then," Lherzo said, "and you'll take the fourth, Lunata?"

It was agreed. A balcony from the study gave a good view of the courtyard and steps down to the city, this would be their watch point. Max bid the others good night and took a seat on the balcony, dreading what tomorrow might bring.

In the morning, they surveyed the grounds and exit points, avoiding the grotesque corpses in the courtyard and made plans for a quick evacuation. They filled their packs with food and their flasks with water. They led the horses to the far side of the palace and left their packs with the horses. Max insisted they not leave his brother with the Calculists should it be Biggens' army arriving at the gate. The four of them carried his body to a service entry room with a doorway near the horses and made him comfortable on the floor.

The passage Lherzo had found in the armory was a spiderweb-filled hallway that went straight back into the hill, turned a corner and ended at a vertical shaft with a ladder. At the top was an overgrown shelf above the palace with steps leading into the forest, another option for escape.

"Should my father's army appear at the gates below," Lherzo instructed, "we slip away unseen into the hills and find a way to reach Apex alone."

"And if it's Saul?" Mindre asked.

"If it's my great-uncle, I'll face him alone," Max said grimly. "You stay inside and if things go bad, take the tunnel."

"You will not face him alone," Mindre said, peering diligently into his eyes. "*We now stand together, we stand with each other, we stand for each other.*"

Her words, lines from the Quintessence ritual, filled him with a mix of strength and fear, reminding him that he was not alone, for better or for worse. "Oh, Mindre, I don't know what to expect."

Lunata stepped forward. "Then we shall all not know what to expect, together!"

"Together," Lherzo agreed.

The hours dragged by. They took turns keeping lookout and checking on Samuel. His condition had not changed, which was both good news and bad. Max hoped Saul would arrive soon, that he would help them and that he knew how to treat Samuel for whatever sickness had befallen him. Max was most worried for Lherzo, knowing Saul's hatred for Calculists. Surely he would know not all Calculists were bad. Given that Lherzo had abandoned his father to help Max, Saul should at least be appreciative.

If it were Calculists arriving instead, it would mean further hardship ahead, but at least he had his friends.

"They're coming!" Lunata yelled through the house. Max was on his feet racing to the balcony. "It is the Dark Ones," she said as the others arrived.

Down below, at the end of the promenade, two lines of naked creatures walked in formation. Partway back in the line they carried a box, a carriage of sorts.

"It's Saul," Max said.

They looked at each nervously.

"Lherzo, I'm sorry," Mindre said softly.

"We don't know what it means," Lherzo said glumly.

Max hadn't thought of what it might mean to Lherzo if Saul defeated the Calculists. His father, his brothers, his friends, they were all in that army. No matter what his relationship to his father and brothers was, they were still family.

They walked to the front door and stepped outside onto the steps to the courtyard.

"Look at them march," Mindre said. "I've never seen Darklings walk in lines."

"Saul can control minds," Lherzo explained, "though it is supposed to be only small numbers he can command. Look at them all! He has grown in power, considerably. Be very careful."

Lherzo slipped his abax out of his jacket. Lunata drew her bones from her pocket. Mindre flexed her fingers. Max only waited.

The carriage appeared, a cabin on poles being carried on the shoulders of four Darklings. A large black stone table filled with triangular holes rode on top, tied with ropes.

"My father's abax," Lherzo whispered gravely.

Max swallowed hard.

The Darklings set down the carriage and the door opened. A tall figure in black and red with long white hair stepped out, his face smiling in wonder up at them.

"Maxwell!? By the Four Corners, it's you!" Saul cheered. He strode energetically towards them hopping up the steps.

"Day of days! I've been searching for you and here you are!" he exclaimed striding towards them. "It is a victory upon a victory! Arianna smiles upon me!"

"Yes, we found you," Max said, not knowing whether he should be pleased or angry or afraid or relieved. He was a bit of all of that.

"And what is this company you bring?"

"This is Mindre of Quincunx, Lunata of Parchensis, and ... Lherzo."

Saul turned to Lherzo, his face suddenly serious. "You're a Biggens. The third son?" He returned his gaze to Max. "You're with a Biggens?"

"Lherzo left his family to help me, Saul. So that I could find you. General Biggens was going to kill us, and Lherzo rescued us."

Saul looked back and forth between Max and Lherzo. He forced a smile. "Then I should be thanking you, Lherzo, for returning my grand-nephew to me."

"And you!" he said turning to Lunata. "A Bone-Thrower! How rare! One step up from a Dijin, I suppose. You are all welcome here, come, come! Let's go in, there is much to discuss on this triumphant day!"

They followed Saul inside, exchanging dark glances. Max noted that Saul had not acknowledged Mindre at all.

"Welcome to your home, Max. I have dreamed of this day!" Saul beamed. "Come, come, into the study." They entered, taking seats around the low table.

"I have just returned from a confrontation with your father, Lherzo," Saul said, shifting to a serious tone.

Lherzo sat stiffly, looking hard at Saul.

"I am now the general of the greatest army on Abacabax. Every one of the Changed is now under my command. Every single one." Saul smiled tightly. "I believe we can now call you 'General Biggens,' Lherzo. I do hope you will be agreeable to arranging a surrender and we can put an end to this conflict once and for all?"

Lherzo said nothing, his eyes darting back and forth as he considered the meaning of Saul's words.

"Yes, the Calculist army has fallen. The Abacist line is again in control. I could use allies, such as yourself, yes ..." Saul smiled. "We will discuss how you may serve me when you take your rightful place as head of the Calculist line. Can we agree to help each other, or ... ?"

Lherzo nodded, his face a mask. Max hoped he could control that mask, the way he had when they were all in High Council chamber back in Vertex.

"Excellent!" Saul said. "Maxwell, where have you been these weeks?"

"Traveling here from Quothmire, trying to find you and Samuel. What is wrong with Sam?"

"Ah, yes. Samuel," Saul said, thinking. "Samuel has come down with an unfortunate illness. I have been unable to help him, but now that you are here, Maxwell, we can work together. You are the missing piece in all this. Now that we are united, we can heal the Changed! We can bring them all back."

"What about Grandma and my mother," Max said. "What happened to them?"

"Oh, yes," Saul said, remembering. "They're quite safe, I assure you. Max, listen, the night you left ... I'm sorry, I needed to bring both you and your brother here so that we could save the Changed. My sister did not want you to come with me. She wanted you and Samuel for herself, so that she could become New Origin. My sister is not who you think she is. She is a very selfish person who does not care what becomes of the Changed. That's why we quarreled that night. She and your mother are still back on Earth, but if you help me, I can open the portal and you can see them again. How does that sound?"

His grandmother was a selfish person? Saul was lying, flat-out lying. Even though Max had met her only twice, each of his friends had told him stories of his grandmother's generosity and selflessness. Max glanced at his friends. Lunata looked confused, Lherzo's face was a blank. Mindre spoke to Max with her gaze: *be careful!*

"That sounds great. I'd love to help Samuel and if we could bring back the Changed, well, I don't know what I can do, but I'll try."

"I know you can't reckon, Maxwell. Samuel couldn't either. Wendi made sure of that, but I know ways around her tricks. We can begin today!"

Samuel couldn't reckon, Max thought. Max held his tongue, this could be an advantage letting Saul think Max was also powerless. "Saul, there's something important. We need your help, too," Max said.

Max took out his abacus. He noticed Saul instinctively reaching for his own pocket. Saul left his hand over his pocket as he leaned forward to see what Max was doing. Max lifted the cover.

"Yes, *The Fourteen Hands of Kael.* It is the sister abacus to my own," Saul said. He took out his abacus, a long black frame with red beads. "This is *The Inspiration.* Twenty rods with beads of the purest red garnet. It is the most powerful abacus ever crafted."

"Mine is damaged," Max pointed to the final rod wrapped in wound rings of leather lacing.

"So it is," Saul said, reaching forward. Max leaned back, withdrawing the abacus from his reach. He set it on his lap and ran his fingers over the beads. Saul smiled thinly and withdrew his hand.

"It has caused two quakes already," Max said, "and people believe a third quake can mean the end of Abacabax. We need to get it to Apex to have it repaired before that happens."

"The quakes! That was the doing of the Fourteen Hands? Fascinating ..." Saul said. "I will research this and find a solution, don't worry. That abacus was made with beads wrought from the High Stone of Apex. It has a very special connection to the structure of the world. It is no surprise the world is disturbed, but one abacus is not capable of destroying the entire planet. Most people are superstitious savages, Maxwell. Don't worry, we will come to know everything."

"My guests," Saul announced to the group, "please make yourself comfortable. There is food in the kitchen. I have some matters to attend to, but I hope we can get started tonight, Maxwell. Oh, should you want to go outside, stay in the western courtyard. Our friends out there can be rather unpredictable."

"Lherzo, are you okay?" Mindre asked after Saul had left.

"I feel nothing, strangely," Lherzo said. "That sounds horrible, but my father and brothers were not nice people. They abused me for years. I don't know why. They can't hurt me anymore." He frowned.

"Still ..." Mindre said. "It *is* your father."

"I am my own man, now," Lherzo said resolutely.

"You are chieftain?" Lunata said.

"I guess I am," Lherzo said. "For what good it does."

"Yes, that's right! The *good* it does!" Lunata said. "Do something good with that!" She sat down next to him and placed her hand on his thigh. "I will be chieftain of Parchensis someday. We can unite!"

"I don't think there will be anyone left to be chieftain of after Saul takes Vertex," Lherzo said darkly.

"What are we going to do, Max?" Mindre asked.

"First, we find out what to do with the abacus and with Samuel," Max said. "Then we figure out how to stop him or we get away from here, far away from here. He's lying about everything. I don't trust a thing he says. Don't mention anything about my reckoning, it may be a surprise we need."

"Can we outreckon him?" Lunata asked. "He is only one and we are four."

"Maybe," Max said. "He doesn't have his army in here."

"That is no ordinary man," Lherzo said. "He is an army all by himself. Find out everything you can about him."

"Saul thinks very highly of himself," Mindre added. "Use that if you can."

Max nodded. There was much to learn and it could all go downhill very quickly.

They stood on the wall in the courtyard, far from the dead Darklings lying on the other end of the yellowed lawn. Looking at the terrace below they watched hundreds of Darklings milling about the steps and the streets below. A heavy gate separated the courtyard from the mindless mass of creatures, monsters that could spring to life under Saul's control at his will. Max felt a growing sense of hopelessness.

"We should have left with Sam when we had the chance," he whispered.

"Find out what he wants. Find out how we can stop it," Mindre whispered back.

"Here you are!" Saul called cheerfully from the doorway. "I do hope you are comfortable. I am going to use my nephew now. Are you ready, Maxwell?"

Max glanced at his friends. "Yeah, sure," he said.

Saul led him up the stairs to the second level, down the tapestried hallway and to his study.

"This is my laboratory, Max, where the greatest discoveries of the planet have been made."

"You made all this? It's amazing," Max said, looking around at the collection of devices. Saul had a huge ego and Max was ready to feed it. "What is the greatest thing you have built?"

"Oh, that would be my portal. I am the only living person ever to have bridged worlds. That has made it possible for you and Samuel to bring me gifts more powerful than anything on Abacabax."

"Is your portal here? Can I see it?" Max asked hopefully. The idea of using the portal to reach his mother and grandmother flickered through his mind.

"In time. Help me and I'll show you how it works." Saul regarded Max knowingly. "And yes, we can open the portal to find your mother if you wish."

"It is mechanical?"

"It is. Twenty-four gears, one for each of the different letters in the full name of Abacabax. There are over eight *million* letters in the full name. Anyone who can say the entire name can open a pathway to other worlds, but that feat is impossible. The word is far too long for any human to say, and even far too long to write in any book. My machine, however, tirelessly spells out the entire name and can open the bridge. It takes quite a bit of time to complete the full cycle, as you can imagine."

Saul grinned, pleased with himself. "Maxwell," he continued, "I'd like to show you my most important project. There is someone I want you to meet. In here."

He entered the bedroom. Max already knew what was within but pretended he did not.

Kneeling by the cage, Saul said, "This is Lydala. She is my wife."

Max did not expect that. "Your ... wife?"

"Yes," he said sadly. "She was one of the first to change during the plague. In fact, everyone in Tangram fell to its power, except for me. I protected myself with a mantra, a chant. The others were not as strong as me. Not even Lydala, I'm afraid.

"I've protected her all these years. Even when the Calculists assaulted Tangram and drove us to the upper shelves, I've kept her with me. I have tried every day to reach her mind."

Max looked at the creature in the cage, trying to picture it as a woman. He failed. "Is that how you figured out how to go into their minds?" Max asked.

"Yes, I suppose she's responsible for my other accomplishments. I can now reach into any mind, if it is weak enough or willing enough. This gave me the power to take back my laboratory and the portal, which let me bring both you and your brother here. There is a satisfying balance to all things, something lost becomes something gained, on every level and on every scale. The Calculists' obsession with becoming the New Origin leads to an Abacist becoming the New Origin. Calculists gaining Tangram leads to an Abacist taking Vertex. Losing Lydala and the rest of the Abacists leads to bringing Lydala back and birthing a new family of Scribists with me as the king." ⠆

"You're incredible. You can build a portal to another world, you can control minds! What else can you do?"

"Oh, Max, I've invented so many techniques. I can see through others' eyes over great distances. I can make a son murder his own his father. Even someone with a strong mind I can make lose control of their own muscles and put them at my mercy," Saul said, growing more excited. "I'm learning more every day, at an exponential rate! With scribing I can accomplish more than I dreamed."

"Scribing?" Max said, still playing dumb. "Is that like using your abacus?"

"It's using these written symbols. Normally only Primes can use a second form of reckoning, but I have defeated the curse of the line of inheritance. I can reach into minds and take any power I desire. I could have the greatest powers of all of the greatest reckoners from any of the families!"

That was it. Saul could scribe and Samuel lay comatose. Saul could enter minds and take abilities. It was a very simple equation with a very ugly result. Saul had taken Samuel's mind. Max had to keep Saul talking.

"Do you think you could teach me something? Maybe I could be your apprentice?" Ouch! Max thought. That was the hardest thing he ever had to say in his life. His mind kept turning. Saul could take the powers of the greatest reckoners from any of the families. The greatest reckoners Max knew were all standing outside in the courtyard. Would he try to take them all?

Saul smiled. "Oh, Max, I would love to have someone to share my accomplishments with. You can help me, tonight. You see, my sister did the unthinkable. She invoked the Exception, which breaks the power of the Abacist line. This has made Samuel very weak. You saw him, the state that he is in. It is because of her curse. I have used as much of him as I can, but it is not enough. His power has been split with you. You have within you the final piece I need to be able to reach Lydala's mind. Together, we can bring her back. We can save all of the Changed and we can even save your brother. Will you help me?"

"What do we have to do?" Max asked.

Saul smiled. "I have a flower, it's in the study. It will help us connect our powers. I'll get it and we can begin right away."

A flower? Max thought. He remembered the book in the study, "Dijin Herbology." The flower was surely salvendia, the same flower Mindre and he had taken during the Ritual of the Quintessence. Saul must have used the same thing with Samuel to steal his mind.

"I'll go down and let my friends know we're going to be busy for a while," Max said.

"That's a good idea, let's go."

Saul stood and hurried for the door. Max's mind was spinning. If Saul got that flower into Max's mouth, Max would end up like Samuel. And if he refused? Saul said he could immobilize even a strong mind. He could simply force Max to eat the drug. Max had learned more than enough. They would need to make their stand. Now.

Saul headed to the study and Max split off to the courtyard, hoping his friends were still outside. They were. Their silhouettes stood on the wall in the fading light. He ran to them.

"Saul doesn't just control minds, he can *take* minds," Max said quickly. "He doesn't know I know, but he's getting salvendia right now and wants to join minds with me."

Mindre sucked in her breath. "Max, don't do that!"

"I know, he'll take my mind and I'll end up like Samuel. And then I think he's planning to take your minds, too. All of yours."

Lherzo took out his abax. "This ends now," he said.

Mindre turned to Max, worried. She reached out, touched her fingers against his chest and held them there a moment. "Together," she whispered. She turned and strode past the doorway, taking up a position to the side of the door.

Max readied his abacus, mentally rehearsing his most powerful moves. Lunata crouched on the walkway, spreading twelve bones in a line and turning them into a ready position.

They could see Saul in the study through the window, lifting a jar half-filled with dried flowers to the light and examining the contents. Lherzo grinned, determinedly touching his fingers through the holes of his abax on both sides. Saul shook his head. Then he shook the jar. He looked around on the floor and held up the jar again to the light. It was empty.

Max looked to Lherzo, who flashed back a grim smile as he swapped abaxes. He took out his traditional abax and spilled small stones across its surface, shuffling them onto the lines.

Saul stormed towards the courtyard, whipping his long black abacus from his jacket. He stepped through the door. "What is this?!" he screamed.

Mindre's arms flew in a flash, Lherzo tapped his stone abax, Lunata spun her bones and Max let fly a flurry of beads.

Saul's eyes shot wide open, his hand rushing to his forehead instead of his abacus. He blinked rapidly under the assault of four simultaneous reckonings. His head stretched to the side, a grimace on his face, and then he snapped his head forward again. "You traitors ..." he growled. His fingers flew to his abacus, dancing in precise patterns shaped by decades of dedicated practice.

Max set another number. Their combined attack had done nothing! He clicked beads as fast as he could as Mindre wove another pattern in the air with fingers and arms.

Lherzo was Saul's first choice. He flew backwards off his feet, smashed into a column and slumped to the ground. Saul flicked up and down on the rods of his abacus and the stone column behind Lherzo pulled loose. Several tons of stone wobbled once, tipped forward and began falling slowly towards Lherzo below.

Lunata, partway through her calculation looked up and instantly changed her target, throwing her reckoning into the falling column. It cracked into pieces, burying Lherzo under a thousand chunks of stone instead of crushing him as one solid block.

Mindre struck with a rapid series of quick jabs which Saul simply threw off. He barely winced as Max's multiplication flowed right through him, making no contact.

Lunata was Saul's next target. With a few vicious clicks of his beads, Lunata spun violently, her head scraping in a sweeping arc against the stone pathway. She was lifted in the air and tossed like a doll out onto the grass. Saul flicked a few a beads on his abacus and the row of bones on the pathway scattered to the wind.

Mindre danced another calculation, her face slick with sweat, spinning as she completed her moves. One of Saul's legs jerked from under him and he stumbled.

Saul's expression shifted from surprise to anger as he glared at Mindre. "What are you?" he howled, focusing his rage on her hands.

Mindre gasped. Finger after finger bent backwards with a series of gruesome snapping noises. She sunk to her knees, her face screwed up in pain as she stared at the horrible sight of all ten of her digits twisting backwards.

Max reeled, a sick feeling in his stomach as fear washed over him. He fought through it and pulled up a division. It was the most digits he could handle without using the laced column. He clicked through the final steps of the calculation and ripped at Saul with his quotient, picturing Saul tearing in two with the force of the greatest division Max had ever tried.

Saul merely grunted. Regarding Max coldly, he began another calculation.

Max cleared his abacus. Nothing was working, his friends had gone down as quickly as one, two, three. He felt Saul's reckoning building in his body. He set up a random number to start his own attack as he tried to follow Saul's. Saul was sending a division in return, it was the same dividend Max had just tried to rip Saul with, an unimaginative choice, but the divisor was different. Max visualized it, feeling the warm rush of the reckoning passing through him as he followed it.

Max clicked up a product and threw the multiplication like a punch to Saul's head. The strike passed through him like a ghost.

A product flew back at him. Max struggled to find the numbers – they were so big! The pressure grew in his ears, he took a deep breath willing himself to relax and feel the calculation as they had done in practice. He caught the first digit and the rest of the digits seemed to flow automatically, rushing through him without harm.

Saul was clicking again. Distracted by the previous attack, Max had not even started his own attack. But what use was it? Saul was immune to everything Max had thrown. He was untouchable. Even worse, Saul had six more rods on his abacus than Max. Even if Max could use all fourteen rods on his abacus, it would make no difference.

Fourteen rods ... the fourteenth rod! Max could end the world right now. Saul himself said he did not believe the abacus could literally end the world, but maybe it could do enough damage to end Saul's world!

Max grabbed the leather lacing and yanked it as hard as he could. It jerked, slicing into his finger. He yanked again, feeling the pressure of Saul's next assault. Max needed to get to those beads immediately! He bit the end of the lace in his teeth and ripped with all his might, ignoring the growing force of Saul's reckoning.

Max was hit in the gut with a force like a block of cement, pain spraying through his body in spasms so powerful he saw streaks of light across eyes. He was knocked backwards, falling on his back as his teeth yanked the lace hard. The fourteenth rod on his abacus snapped in two.

Max saw the beads spin off into the air as if in slow motion. The ground began to shake. Saul looked about, alarmed. This is it, Max thought. The end of the world. *Third shake, the stone to break.*

"You stupid fool!" Saul yelled. He shoved his own abacus into his jacket and slid out a tablet and a charcoal stick. He began scribbling methodically as the rumbling spread. Windows cracked on the palace as tiles tumbled from the roof and the ground undulated with a deep vibration.

Max felt a sudden powerful ache in his hand holding the abacus. He released it, watching with horror as the frame buckled and cracked. The abacus imploded as if a monstrous invisible hand were crushing it into tiny bits and packing them together like a snowball.

The shaking subsided. The palace walls rattled and then were still. The quake was over before it had really begun.

Max stared in disbelief at the splintered pieces of his abacus on the grass. Saul stood motionless before him, grinning like a snake.

"That's it? That was your best? Did you think you and your friends could defeat me, the most powerful reckoner in all of history? The END OF THE WORLD cannot defeat me!" he screamed.

Max rolled over, his gut wracked with pain. He stomach heaved and he threw up in the grass.

Saul took a deep breath. He exhaled, the possessed expression on his face suddenly gone. "Stand up, Maxwell. C'mon, stand up," he said, speaking gently now. "Really, you did well. Samuel couldn't fight at all, I'm not sure how you managed it."

Max pushed himself to a crouch and wiped his mouth. He looked at his friends. Mindre knelt in the grass, elbows pulled tight to her sides, her fingers horribly poking in all directions. Lunata lay next to the two Darkling corpses, blood running through hands pressed against her head. Lherzo lay partially buried under a ton of loose stone, struggling to breathe.

None of them had weapons, not even Mindre who relied on nothing more than her body.

They had failed. Max had brought them here to die. He was the Hand of Death and this was the end of their world.

Chapter 14: Beyond the end of the world

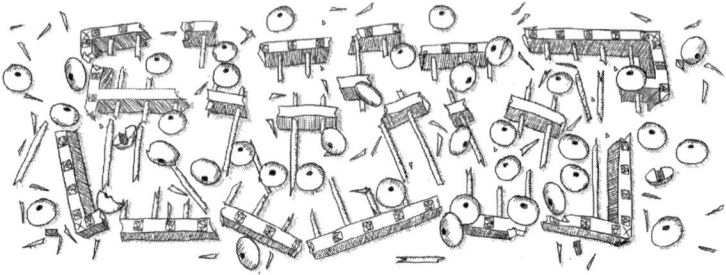

Darklings howled on the terrace below. Max turned his head towards his approaching adversary. Saul Teller had just faced the full force of simultaneous reckonings from all four tribes and thrown it back at them like it was nothing. They were left crushed and broken on the ground.

"You cannot stop me, Maxwell," Saul said matter-of-factly. "I am a god. I could cancel you all out right now with just a few strokes on this paper. But ... I am fair, so I will offer you a deal."

Max lifted one leg beneath him, setting himself in a crouch. He could barely breath.

"You took my salvendia, but it doesn't matter. I can still enter your mind if you allow it. You will open your mind and welcome me in. You will join me, here," he said, pointing to his head. "You, me and Samuel, together. The Exception overruled, our power consolidated. Oh, the things we will do together! You will like it, I promise you. It is why I brought you to Abacabax, it is what you were born to do, Maxwell."

Max shook his head. "You're a liar," he spat.

Saul laughed dismissively. "You haven't heard my deal. Here it is. You join me in greatness and become everything you were destined to become, or you will watch while I kill every one of your friends. I'll start with the Finger-Reckoner. Such a shame, she had potential. No one has scored a hit on me in twenty years until now, not even you with the Hands of Kael. I will twist off her arms and legs, I think. The Bone-Thrower is next. I'll pull her spine right out through her back. The Calculist I'll save for last, crushing him slowly under that pile of stones would be appropriate, don't you agree?"

Max went cold. Would he do that? Yes, of course he would. He felt terror rolling up his back, raising the hairs on his scalp.

"It is your choice, Max," Saul said. "Come now, don't be afraid."

My choice, Max thought. What choice was it, really? And then, that word resonated in his ears ... a *choice*. He had heard that before, *a choice to make* ... It was an eternity ago, in Quincunx. He could almost see Lady Carpus. She had told him there would come a time when he would need to make a choice. A choice between lives, she had said. A choice between what he knows and what he fears. And that he must choose what he knows.

Both choices were terrifying. Lose his own mind, or lose his friends? But Lady Carpus said not to choose what he *fears* but what he *knows*. So what did he know?

He looked over to Mindre. She was watching him, her eyes wet with tears of pain but also burning with love and courage. She had chosen to stand by him, not just now but every step of the way. If there was one thing he knew, it was that he would choose Mindre, and that Mindre would choose to die fighting.

He pushed himself to stand. He breathed in, looking at Saul through narrowed eyes. He did not need to choose either of Saul's options. He would make his own choice. "I choose my friends," he said.

His abacus was destroyed, but Max didn't even care. He thought of Mindre's fingers locked to his, four sets of five fingers. He multiplied all their power together. *Five times five, times five and times five again* ... an easy one, *six-hundred twenty-five!* He pulled up *five to the fourth power* in his own mind and launched it, picturing all four hands striking at Saul's face.

Saul's head snapped back and he stumbled. He turned to Max, a look of absolute surprise on his face.

Max reached for another calculation, something he knew. Ah yes, *thirteen squared* is *one hundred sixty-nine*, reverse all the digits and *thirty-one squared* becomes *nine hundred sixty-one*. He threw it out with a spin thinking of how the digits were spun around, and Saul spun backwards, dropping to one knee.

"How on the faces ... ?" he muttered, his hand flying to his tablet, scratching furiously.

Max knew other tricks with squares. How about *sixty-five squared?* Two-digit numbers ending with five can be squared just by taking the first digit, in this one it's a *six*, multiplying it by the number that is one more, *seven*, and then tossing a *twenty-five* on the end. *Six times seven* is *forty-two*, so *sixty-five squared* is *forty-two hundred twenty-five*.

Max was so caught up in throwing out mental calculations that he forgot to follow Saul's reckoning until it was too late. He caught the brunt of a sideways blow knocking him flat to the earth. His whole body ached, but he had no abacus he needed to hold onto, just his mind. He pulled up another number ...

-:- | -:-

Lherzo struggled to breathe. Caught under stones, *again?* Lunata couldn't rescue him this time. He strained to lift his head. He was lying face down, only his head and one arm were free, his abax nowhere to be seen. Max and Saul were now having it out, and somehow Max was now landing blows! Max was also getting hit himself and getting hit hard. Lherzo knew he had to help.

He looked to Mindre and winced. Every single one of her fingers were broken, pointing in different directions. He twisted his head in the other direction. Lunata was nearby, weakly crawling to her knees besides the dead Darklings, her bones nowhere to be seen.

He flexed his fingers on his buried arm, pinned beneath him under his chest. He felt the holes of his custom abax, still in his jacket. He breathed out to make a little space beneath him and slipped his hand sideways under the cloth against the surface of his abax. Could he reckon with one hand? Create a rock and drop it on Saul's head? No, not with one hand, he needed two anti-numbers for that. He could make only one.

He craned his neck, looking for something he could do. Mindre was disarmed with broken fingers. Lunata was disarmed with no bones. Dead Darklings reached their lifeless hands towards Lunata. And then ... an idea! He couldn't do much to aid the attack by himself, but maybe he could arm someone else.

He slid his fingers over the holes of his abax tight against his body, visualizing their locations. It was awkward, he was used to seeing their positions through the top side of the board. He closed his eyes and willed the picture into his mind, straining to make the calculation. He opened his eyes again, staring hard at the dead gray Darkling hands lying on the yellowed grass.

It was working. Layer after layer of skin and muscle vanished from the dead heads, sinew and cartilage shriveling away. Both of the Darkling's hands were stripped bare, the pieces dropping from the ends of the dead gray arms into a neatly arranged pile of white bones on the yellowed grass. Lunata turned her face, drawn to the motion in the corner of her eye. She stared at the bones, confused, then looked to Lherzo, her eyes wide with surprise. Lherzo's heart filled with joy as her mouth pulled into a toothy grin.

-:- | -:-

Lunata squinted at the bones. Her face stung, she could feel blood rolling down her cheek, her vision blurred from the swelling around her eye. A moment ago there had been fully-fleshed hands stretched out on the grass and now there were two beautiful sets of clean white bones, just waiting for her. Lherzo had managed to reckon from under the pile of stone. Highly unlikely, yet there it was. Yes, there were only ten bones, not twelve like she had grown accustomed to and not her chosen bones eithers, but they were bones. It would be like the reckoning she did as a young girl with her starter set. It would work.

Max was fighting back. Saul, who had defended every one of their blows, was now getting battered by Max who was fighting with *nothing* in his hands. Extremely unlikely! Now she could help him, but what could she throw at Saul that would do anything? Every one of her calculations had passed right through him. The only one of their group who had been quick enough to land any blows was Mindre and her fingers were of no use, broken.

Broken ... but Lunata knew algebra! Without hesitating, she divided the bones in two groups. These would need to be the fastest ten equations she'd ever thrown together.

-:- | -:-

Mindre sat with shaking hands. She was ruined but Max was not. He, who had surprised her time after time, was now giving her the biggest surprise of all: reckoning with no tools at all. It was impossible, simply impossible.

She cringed as Max got thrown again. Down he would go, then roll over and launch an unthinkably motionless attack. Down he would go again, only to prop himself up and try again. How could he withstand so much? He needed help, now. Mindre stood uneasily. She would kick the life out of that monster if she had to!

Pain shot through her thumb. The movement from standing up must have jarred it. She winced in pain again and then gasped. Incredibly, her thumb was moving on its own, straightening out! Burning pulsed deep within her bone and her thumb stood whole. Sudden sharp pain shot through her forefinger as it, too, moved of its own accord, straightening and burning within.

Through clenched teeth she looked to Lunata. The Bone-Thrower sat on the grass, furiously turning and moving about a line of small bones. Lunata had found a way to continue reckoning! Ouch! Mindre's middle finger snapped into position.

Mindre closed her eyes, breathing deep to calm the pain as finger after finger straightened and set into place. When the final bone set, she clenched her fists, saying a silent thank you to her clever friend. Her fingers worked! They ached badly, but not nearly as badly as Saul was about to ache.

-:- | -:-

Max's head spun, it had become so hard to think. Max's calculations were fast, but Saul's calculations were huge. Max could not mentally calculate on the scale of Saul's pencil and paper algorithms, but Max could move at the speed of thought. Max was scoring with every attack and taking hits with every one of Saul's attacks.

As Max searched for the next calculation, Saul jerked and stumbled. That was not Max's doing! Mindre stepped forward, fingers flitting in patterns as she touched herself up and down her body. She floated like a dream figure in his foggy vision, somehow whole again, fighting by his side. Hope surged.

He could feel her calculations in his own body, the pattern of touches in his temples, chest, belly and thighs. She was not reckoning on Max and yet he could still feel her touch, feel her connection. She was building up a simple sum, *one plus two plus three plus four*, and onwards, moving with lightning speed.

Triangular numbers, Max thought. So simple, so beautiful and so powerful. Inspired, he reached for the one-hundredth triangular number, the sum of all the counting numbers from one to one-hundred, like a trilliberry cluster with one hundred rows of fruit. Saul would never be able to follow that, not with the speed of the shortcut Max knew. *One plus two plus three plus four* all the way up to *one hundred?* That's just *one hundred times one hundred one, divided by two.*

Max finished the entire calculation in a split second. Saul took the full force of one hundred small hits, tied together with a speed and efficiency he could not follow. The blows hammered him relentlessly, driving him back, and back again. He bumped into the low wall, dropping his paper tablet in surprise. Quickly regaining his composure, he whipped out his black abacus. His eyes narrowed as he smiled wickedly at Max.

Max could feel Mindre still working her sum. Her numbers built up in a crescendo, finishing with a bang! Saul, fingers still moving over his abacus, tumbled backwards over the wall, a look of resignation on his face as he disappeared from view.

Max took a deep breath. Was he gone? Was he really gone? He looked at Mindre, standing deep in a stance with her fingers outstretched.

He dared not believe it was over. He crawled to the wall. Mindre walked forward apprehensively. They both peered over the edge. Far below them, Saul's body lay on the stone. Two of his Darklings sat upon him tearing at his shirt, while others, attracted by the unexpected offering, ambled forward.

Max watched in horror and fascination as they tore off the remainder of his clothing. They dragged his lifeless body across the stone towards the shadowy edge of the plaza. Saul's skin seemed to grow darker, draining of color as the writhing mass of creatures pulled him into the darkness. The last Max saw of him was the haunted image of his twisted face with eyes like hollow, soulless sockets in the slanted light. The remaining Darklings below receded into the shadows and disappeared.

Max watched and waited. There was nothing more. "Is he gone?" Max whispered. "We have to go see ..." He tried to push himself up but hadn't the strength. He was entirely spent.

"No, it's over," Mindre said. She turned to Max, her eyes wide. "We did it!"

Max rolled over onto the grass, head pounding. Mindre called out the news across the courtyard, where Lunata was pulling stones from the pile above Lherzo. He was yelling something sarcastically, Lunata answering him with laughter.

Max wanted to help, but he could hardly move. Instead he closed his eyes shut and breathed deeply. Was it really over?

He felt Mindre sink down onto the grass beside him. She rolled over onto his chest. He opened one eye, peering at her with a smile. Her hair hung down around his face. She smiled down at him, looking into his eyes and glancing down to his mouth. She placed her lips against his, and they were one.

Max opened his eyes. He remembered the others helping him inside, but he didn't remember falling asleep. He stretched his neck.

"He's awake," Lunata said.

Mindre was by his side, holding his hand. "Rest easy," she said as he tried to sit up.

Max sat up anyway, every muscle aching. His body must be covered with bruises, he thought. Or maybe just one big bruise over his whole body. Mindre stroked his cheek.

"You did it, you did it, Max," she said.

"We did it." Max smiled, looking around the room. Lunata's head was wrapped with white cloth, covering one of her eyes. Lherzo sat beside her with a bottle of cloudy wine, his clothing torn and dirty. Samuel lay on the couch. They must have carried him in from the service entrance. He was unconscious, but color had returned to his cheeks and he was breathing peacefully.

Lherzo poured some of the wine into a goblet and stood with effort. He put the goblet in Max's hand. "This will take the edge off your pain," he said.

Max took a sip. It tasted horrible.

"You'll get used to it," Lherzo said.

"Max, you reckoned with *nothing*. How did you do that?" Mindre asked gently.

"I ... I just didn't think of the abacus at all, just the pictures and the calculations. I guess I've always thought about numbers like pictures."

"Mentalism," Lunata called out, "highly unlikely."

"Maybe we can all try it later," Max offered.

"The third quake was a bit of an anti-climax, don't you think?" Lherzo asked.

"What would you rather?!" Mindre asked with a laugh.

"In our stories," Lunata said, "'death' and 'the end of the world' are not meant to be taken literally. Instead, they represent a great change. I think it quite likely we will be seeing some great changes soon."

"Maybe," Max said, "but not tonight."

They stretched out in silence, everyone too tired to talk more. Max fell asleep with his head in Mindre's lap.

The next day, they set the house and upper plazas in order the best they could. Max and Mindre ventured out on the lower plaza to the place where Saul had fallen. There in the shreds of torn clothing lay Saul's abacus, its black frame sitting lifeless yet still ominous in the morning light. Max picked it up carefully and showed it to Mindre.

"What if he's still alive?" he asked.

"Max, there's no way. That wall is over a hundred steps tall. And you saw him, he was … gone."

Yes, Max thought, he had seen him. He worried he would never be free of that ghastly vision. Saul's sunken eyes, mouth hanging open like a hole, his flesh as gray as the Darklings. "But don't Darklings take people? Turn them into Darklings? What if … ?"

"If they did take him," Mindre cut in, "that would only be just. Either way, he's dead."

Max frowned. No, he supposed it didn't matter, but he would have liked to know, either way. Had Saul become a meal for his beloved Darklings, or he had become one of their own? He pocketed Saul's abacus, deciding he would need to find a place to lock it away forever.

Back in the palace, they all worked together to drag the cage from Saul's room down to the front door. They released Saul's widowed Darkling, who crawled away hissing. Later they planned to begin herding the Darklings out of the city. There were hundreds of them within the walls and it would be a formidable job, but they could work together and perhaps it would take only a day or two.

Samuel awoke in the afternoon, weak and confused but cognizant. Max was greatly relieved. Saul had died with Samuel's mind inside his own and Max had feared Samuel might be lost. Yet Samuel had fully returned, physically weak but seemingly in full possession of his mind. Samuel stayed on the couch throughout the evening, sipping water and eating flatbread. They shared stories and filled in details of their experiences.

No one was sure what they wanted to do next. With the destruction of the Fourteen Hands of Kael, the voyage to Apex was no longer needed. Lherzo could, and probably would, return shortly to Vertex where he could claim leadership of the council. He could find Mindre's father and direct him to Tangram, if Mindre did not want to come to Vertex herself. Lunata would need to return to Parchensis at some point. She offered the others to come live with her in Parchensis, they could even study at the university if they so desired. The idea of a Bone-Thrower university came as a shock to the others. Bone-Thrower society was far more advanced than any of them had imagined.

Max said they should all wait a few days until Samuel was fully recovered. Tangram was safe, fully stocked with food and every luxury, filled with rooms and secrets that would be a delight to discover. Perhaps they could find this machine Saul had spoken of and use it to find his mother and grandmother. In any case, he and Sam would stay in Tangram, he thought. It was, after all, the Abacists' home and Max felt a strong connection to the gardens, art and architecture.

The unspoken question on everyone's mind was what would happen with the Great Divide, just days away. Scribing was undisputedly the strongest craft, but Samuel had not connected to the source of power and was too weak to try. Max thought that any of the others had a good chance of being selected.

That all changed the next morning. Lherzo and Samuel burst into the kitchen where Max and the others were eating breakfast. Samuel held a paper tablet and one of Saul's home-made pencils, "scribing sticks" as Samuel called them. He was smiling with his whole face.

"Look what Sam can do," Lherzo said.

Sam grinned at Max and started writing on the tablet. Max felt a familiar pressure and an image of two strong hands pushing him flashed through his mind. Max was almost too surprised to follow, but he instinctively recognized a sum and the push passed right through him.

"You can reckon!" Max exclaimed.

"Lherzo showed me how! I could never do that before!" Sam said excitedly. "I kind of gave up."

Lherzo shrugged. "Call me a crusader for the downtrodden. It's like I always say, you just have to keep picking those stones back up until you don't drop them anymore."

"Sam, that's wonderful!" Mindre chimed in. "Your connection to Saul – that must have been what did it. You've awakened, Sam, just like Max."

"And he picked it up so quickly," Lherzo said. "He's a natural! I think we should all practice together after breakfast. It will be interesting to see what he can do with scribing."

"Yes, let's do that!" Lunata said. "All four Primes! And you, of course, Max, who is in a class of your own!" She grinned at Max with her wide smile, and this time Max did not feel the least bit disappointed that he was the odd-man out in the company of Primes.

Their moment of excitement was interrupted by something else quite unexpected. A woman's voice called out from the entrance hall. "Hello?"

They looked at each in surprise. "Is that Grandma?!" said Max.

Sam sprang for the doorway, the others close behind. They ran through the house. Wendi and Rita stood in the entrance hall, dark bags under their eyes and smiles of joy and disbelief.

"Samuel! Maxwell!" Rita shouted.

"You found us! You made it back!" Max exclaimed. They embraced.

"I can't believe it!" Rita said. "You're both all right! We've been so worried!" She threw her arms around both boys and clutched them tightly.

"Saul?" Wendi asked, looking around nervously.

"I'm sorry," Max said, stepping back from his mother and turning to Wendi. "It's a long story. Saul is dead."

Wendi nodded. "I see," she said, thoughtfully, her eyes wet and mouth in a tight line.

"Come in," Max said. "I'll make tea and we'll tell you everything."

Back in the study, Wendi and Rita sat with cups of tea, astonished with each revelation as the young reckoners retold their tales.

"So you've both gained full reckoning ability," Wendi said. "That's simply astonishing! Max, you've done something unprecedented, we will need to explore this. Mentalism?

Incredible! And Samuel, you've only just gained your ability this morning. You can scribe, just as Saul believed. There is a very good chance you will be named New Origin, first of a new line, and there will be so much for all of us to learn. Although you won't be able to teach your abilities to others until you are fourth phase, that will happen before you know it. We may all be part of a new family shortly."

Wendi turned to her daughter. "And Rita, your son shared the Ritual of Quintessence with Mindre," she smiled. "Do you know what this means?"

Rita shook her head quizzically.

"Congratulations," she said, "your son has gotten married."

Max's eyes flew open wide. "We're ... married? What?" he asked, looking at Mindre incredulously.

Mindre smiled and shrugged. "Well, that's not what we call it, but I suppose you could say that," she said. "I mean, if you want it."

"Oh, I do! I mean, *I do*," Max said, putting his arm around her and smiling in wonder.

Rita sat looking back and forth between her sons and Mindre. "This is too much all at once. Both of you with unheard of abilities. Sam might be New Origin. And Max and Mindre, married?"

Rita shook her head in disbelief. "All right ..." she said slowly. "Samuel, you are under the strict guidance of your grandmother. I don't want you trying anything without her with you, all right? And Max, I think you're a little young, but what's done is done. I do want another wedding, however, a proper Abacist wedding with beads and paper cranes and polyhedra! We've got some planning to do, Mindre!"

"The moons are almost aligned," Wendi said. "It will only be ten days until the Great Divide. Our attendance is not required, but I think we should all be at the temple for the conjunction, which means we'll need to quickly find out how we can ascend in such a short time. There is a Calculist stair-climbing chariot in storage beside the stables. Since the other longwalker in the family can move a buggy, perhaps together we can move something larger." She smiled at Max.

"I've always wanted to see Apex!" Mindre said, squeezing Max's hand.

Wendi surveyed the young reckoners. "Though Samuel will likely be named our New Origin, I see before me five very strong candidates. I think each one of you have created powerful new forms of reckoning and have demonstrated true strength of character. We should start training as soon as possible, there is so much to do."

Wendi set her teacup down carefully and breathed out tiredly, her shoulders falling.

Rita reached over and placed her hand on her mother's back. "For now we need to get some rest," Rita said. "We've traveled very far, on very little sleep, and we're going to be busy these next days. This is something we never counted on."

Chapter 15: Apex

The Temple of Abacabax at the very top of the planet was a sight to behold. The top steps were carved into arches embellished with elaborate stone work that reminded Max of the finest ancient Greek architecture. Doors and circular windows hinted of secret spaces within where the temple guardians lived and performed tasks of a mysterious nature. The guardians were known as the Order of the Whole, a group of fourteen mystics who had access to guarded knowledge and the inner workings of Abacabax itself.

They arrived together in the abandoned Calculist chariot, a breathtakingly rapid trip that Max found terrifying. Mindre's father Roggolo, by invitation of Wendi, joined them on the voyage. Like all the others in the party except for Wendi, it was his first journey to the top of the world. All were excited, perhaps none more so than Samuel. His reckoning abilities with scribing were astonishingly strong, as if he had known how to reckon his entire life. He would certainly be named New Origin this night.

The evening was frosty and the doors were closed, the mystics locked inside until the time of the conjunction. While they waited, Wendi gave them a tour of the grounds. A thin layer of icy snow crunched beneath their feet as they walked carefully along the upper levels. Three levels of plazas, each a quarter of the size of the previous, ringed the top of the planet. Walking carefully up the icy steps, they gathered around the block at the very top. The world fell away in all directions giving Max an uncomfortable feeling of vertigo. He had grown used to seeing the steps always continuing upwards. Witnessing the place where they abruptly ended at a single point in space was disconcerting, to say the least.

Each of them took turns standing on the highest block. It was supposed to be a mystical experience, although apart from the queasiness in his stomach Max wasn't sure he felt anything supernatural.

"This block," Wendi announced when it was her turn to stand on the top, "marks the first letter in the full name of Abacabax. From here, any and all paths downwards spell the entire name."

Max considered this. Wendi had told them about the name and how it could be used to bridge worlds, but not that the full name described the structure of the entire planet itself. That, Max felt, was mystical in itself.

"The steps go all the way to X?" he asked.

"Most certainly," Wendi said, "though no one has ever been there. The steps disappear into the ocean halfway down at the Water Mesa. It is said that the corners of the X-block rise from the sea to the north, south, east and west."

Max tried and failed to imagine how large that final block must be. "Does it just end there?" he asked.

"No one knows what lays beyond the sea," Wendi said. "Some believe the pattern continues not only in all four directions, but underneath as well. Abacabax could well point to the six corners of space."

As astounding as Apex appeared, nothing could have prepared them for the spectacle that was to come. As midnight approached, the red sun faded like a dying ember through the unearthly mist of the atmosphere far below. The sky blackened and stars pierced the night sphere both overhead and downwards in all directions, giving Max an unsettling feeling of floating in space. Lights across the sky shimmered in fractal waves, an aurora something like the Northern lights back on Earth but in finer detail with fascinating swirls like ephemeral galaxies. It was the most astounding sky Max had ever witnessed.

Wendi led them to the double doors of the main entrance. "It starts soon," she whispered. As if on cue, one by one the circular windows opened in the wall spilling firelight onto the plaza. A bell rang, a hollow sound that hung in the air. All stood silent, watching and waiting.

As the tone faded, the heavy double doors swung open. Music starting playing, a series of single notes in a gradually ascending pattern. Figures dressed in white filed through the doorway, each holding a brass tube and a long mallet with a round ball on the end. They struck the tubes in sequence, creating an even-paced melody that rang out into the open air at the edge of space.

"Listen carefully," Wendi whispered to Max. "This is the music of Abacabax itself."

Max closed his eyes. There was something very familiar and comforting in the pattern. Max found it easy to ignore the steady rhythm of the lowest notes and listen to the slower melody of the higher notes. He was surprised to hear the same pattern in these higher notes as the lower notes, as if the song were simultaneously playing copies of itself at different tones and rates. He tried to think of what the notes could be, perhaps he could learn the pattern and try to play it himself on one of the stringed instruments back at Tangram. If the lowest note were A, it played A, B, A, C, A …

His eyes sprang open. He turned to Wendi. "They are playing the name of Abacabax!" he whispered in surprise.

"Indeed." She smiled at him. "That was quick, Maxwell."

"It's so … beautiful." Max was surprised that music structured so rigidly could sound so natural and mysterious. Perhaps music could be used to reckon, he thought.

The pattern of the song reached the note one octave above the starting note then wound down again through the pattern of the scale. Max waited, anticipating the sequence, listening as it reached what he expected would be the final note. The remaining mystics who had not played any notes in the song so far all struck their tubes simultaneously, creating a glorious spread of octave notes from very low to very high.

Max felt a shiver run down his spine as the final note sounded. He lifted his hands to clap and looked around uncertainly. The others were not moving to applaud, so he reluctantly relaxed his hands by his sides.

"Welcome to Apex," announced one of the mystics through his bushy gray moustache. "We are the Order of the Whole and we are pleased that you have joined us tonight. We invite you turn your attention to the heavens." He rolled his head back to gaze directly above.

Max took Mindre's hand as they stared into the sky. The moons grew closer, each of their two moons disappearing in front and behind of their parents. The grouping grew tighter and tighter, the individual forms merging into an oblong shape that narrowed to a single perfect circle. The sky seemed to grow darker as the singular form of the moons brightened. The brightening accelerated and then flashed, filling the night with a burst of intense light that stung Max's eyes, blinding him for a moment.

As the blindness faded and the details of the night sky returned, Max breathed in. He realized he had been holding his breath and felt dizzy. He turned to smile to Mindre. She returned his gaze with a look of astonishment, her eyes wide and pupils large.

They watched a few minutes longer, the moons slowly separating as they started their three-hundred-year journey once again.

"Please join us in the Great Hall," said the man Max presumed was their leader. The group of white-clad mystics turned and filed through the double doors. The rest of the visitors followed.

The Great Hall was a magnificent space, square in form and lined with columns. A fire burned in the hearth, lighting the intricate patterns on the white marble walls with a wavering glow. Max stood between Mindre and his brother, proud of both and eager for the ceremony and announcement to follow.

The elder mystic stepped on a low stone platform, his thin form framed by the geometric patterns carved into the wall behind him. He looked around at the guests, all were silent and attentive.

"My name is Panelles," the mystic announced. "It is my honor to address you this evening. Welcome to you, Lady Teller, Protectress of Abacabax. Welcome to the Primes of all four families. It is remarkable that all of you are present. Welcome to all our other guests, as well. Tonight, as should happen every three hundred years, is the time of the Great Divide. As the cycle begins anew, we are honored to address the candidates for the New Origin. Never before have all of the Primes gathered at Apex for the conjunction, an exceptional occurrence for this exceptional occasion."

He turned to Mindre and bowed. She nodded back at him. "Mindre of the first family," he said, "you have extended finger reckoning to all of your body, increasing the power of your reckoning one hundred times. Combined with your unmatched speed, you have risen to be amongst the most powerful of all reckoners on Abacabax, an astonishing accomplishment. You are to be commended."

Turning to Lunata, he again bowed. "Lunata of the second family, you have created algebra, the complement of muqabala, and are able to rejoin what was once broken. Your insights open a new realm of possibilities for the power of your line and the good of all inhabitants of Abacabax. You, also, are to be commended." Lunata smiled.

"Lherzo of the third family," he said, bowing, "you have discovered anti-numbers, an entirely new kind of number with the power not only to destroy but also to create. We will be thrilled to see this power come to its fruition. For this astonishing accomplishment you are to be commended." Lherzo nodded curtly.

"And Samuel Teller of the fourth family," he continued, "you bring us scribing, a form of reckoning with power far beyond all other reckoning. Its versatility can grant you nearly endless abilities, the likes of which we have never before seen. You, as well, are to be commended."

Sam grinned. Max looked over at his brother proudly, eager to hear the official decision that would surely follow.

"At every Great Divide," Panelles continued, "there has been one candidate from each of the families. As I said, these are exceptional times and there has been an unprecedented exception. You know the exception of which I speak, Lady Teller?" He turned his gaze to Wendi, eyebrows raised. Wendi said nothing.

"The Abacist line has been divided," Panelles said, "and with it the line of ascension." He turned to Max.

Max froze. What did this mean?

"Maxwell Teller, also of the fourth family, you are that exception. You have managed to turn inwards and unlock the power of Mentalism, with abilities limited only by your imagination. You are to receive more than our commendations. Tonight we hereby recognize you as the fifth Prime."

All eyes turned to Max. He looked about in stunned disbelief. He was now a Prime? He was not sure he wanted that. He met Mindre's gaze, she smiled in wonder. Turning to look at Sam, he was surprised to see Sam glaring at him accusingly. "Why are you being named?" Sam whispered angrily.

Max suddenly felt uncomfortable, not just for being named as a Prime but also by his brother's unexpected reaction. He had supported Sam in everything, why wasn't Sam pleased that he got some recognition as well? As Max turned to look back at Panelles, Sam's question rolled around in his head. Why had he been named as a Prime? If Sam were to be chosen, why bother to name another Prime just before the announcement?

Panelles did not return Max's gaze and continued addressing the gathering. "In recent years," he said, "Abacabax has been scarred by a plague, by war, by distrust between the families and a by a sickness of malaise among the populace. As Primes and leaders amongst your people, you are all tasked with devoting your efforts towards healing the planet. We trust you will enter this new age with a dedication to restoring balance to Abacabax and its people." Panelles nodded to each of the Primes.

"And now," he said, "we are pleased to acknowledge the next New Origin. We have been listening intently to the will of Abacabax. Tonight, Abacabax has made it clear that the New Origin and the start of the fifth family shall arise from the Teller line."

Panelles paused. Max held his breath.

"Samuel Teller," Panelles announced, "you have been chosen to become the next New Origin."

Sam burst into a wide smile, looking about at the others. Max breathed a sigh of relief and began clapping, not caring this time if applause was socially acceptable or not. The others joined in. All seemed pleased and proud to be a part of the moment.

When the applause died down, Panelles continued. "Upon reaching the fourth phase of life, you, Samuel Teller, shall gain the rare and exceptional ability to pass the power of your craft on to whomever you choose. You and your disciples and all of their descendants shall become the Fifth Family."

Panelles and all of the mystics bowed to Samuel, who nodded his head in return. Panelles then directed his gaze to Wendi.

"Lady Teller, Protectress of Abacabax," Panelles began. "In dividing the Teller line by invoking the Exception, you have further protected the rise of a New Origin. Because of the nature of the dual Primes within the Teller line, should Samuel Teller fail to assume the role of New Origin, we are fortunate in that the opportunity shall not be lost. In that case, the power and the responsibility of the New Origin shall pass to the second Prime of the Abacist line."

Panelles turned his gaze and peered intently at Max. "That is you, Maxwell Teller," he said, eyebrows raising.

Quiet murmurs spread through the room. Max was stunned. He would become New Origin if Sam should *fail to assume the role*? Sam would never let that happen. Unless … oh. There were other ways Sam could fail to claim the title, he realized, but those were ideas Max did not want to even think about!

Max looked at Sam. Sam was studying him, an unreadable expression on his face.

Max shook his head in disbelief. "I'm happy with second place," he whispered nervously with a smile. Sam's expression relaxed and he grinned once again.

Panelles nodded to Max and turned back to the younger Teller. "And so, Samuel, during the remainder of your third phase as you prepare for this great responsibility, you will have time to reflect on the nature of your role and what you wish to accomplish. May you use your abilities to the betterment of *all* of Abacabax," he concluded.

Panelles stretched his hands outwards. "Welcome to the fifth age!"

-:- | -:-

The weeks that followed were filled with excitement and joy. Samuel was beside himself. He began to study immediately upon their return to Tangram. He was certain the key to restoring balance lay in transforming the Changed back to who they were. Until he could assume his full role as New Origin, he planned to continue Saul's research. Perhaps, he thought, with his scribing and Wendi's herbology he could complete the work his great-uncle had begun. Wendi tried to dissuade him from what she said was an unachievable goal, but Sam was determined and claimed the work was the will of the Order of the Whole.

Lherzo and Lunata departed for their own lands within a few days of their return to Tangram. Upon his arrival in Vertex, Lherzo was officially recognized as general and new leader of the Calculists. Dirigo, who had not been allowed to join the march on Tangram, joined Lherzo on the council as his right hand. With the great losses suffered under the march to Tangram, they began the formidable task of reorganizing the military and reassuring a frightened populace that the threatening times had come to an end. Old foes were now new allies.

Lunata joined Lherzo in Vertex a short time later, bringing her favorite lizard with her. As the first Bone-Thrower seen in a generation, she was quite a curiosity at first but quickly earned respect and admiration from nearly all. She set up a practice as a healer and was in high demand for her unique and exceptional abilities. She and Lherzo were engaged to be married. They began immediately arguing about wedding arrangements, Lherzo wanting a grand military affair in Vertex while Lunata insisted on a wedding in the bone caverns beneath Parchensis.

Max and his family, including Mindre's father Roggolo, made themselves a home in Tangram. As word spread of the new opportunities, many Calculists and Dijins flocked to the city. The remaining Abacists who had been living in exile in the far upper shelves finally returned. Within months Tangram's population swelled and the city came to life with a bustle of activity. Many joined in the work of rebuilding the city to its former beauty. Wendi declined the role of governess, instead passing the responsibility to Rita. The elder Teller instead took on the role of master gardener, herbologist and teacher, while Rita tended to the civic affairs and oversaw the various councils she assembled. She was most interested in beautification, restoring the artworks lost in the last decades of neglect.

When she was not mitigating business disputes, designing art installations or planning for Max and Mindre's second wedding, Rita spent her free time with Roggolo, generating rumors of a relationship that neither would confirm nor deny. She grew very fond of her new daughter-in-law and continued to ask Mindre how long she would need to wait to become a grandmother. Max and Mindre both insisted they weren't quite ready for that yet.

In the midst of all of these changes, none of the Primes had forgotten about the task they had been challenged with by the Order of the Whole. While Sam worked on a solution to the Darkling problem, Lherzo and Lunata turned their attention to rebuilding the structure of the planet that had been damaged by the three quakes. With Lherzo's power to destroy and create matter and Lunata's abilities to separate and join material, they felt it was fate that had brought them together to solve this problem.

Mindre easily convinced Max that their role should be to build stronger ties between the families and inspire creativity in reckoning. Mindre had years of experience traveling as an ambassador, and Max had managed to unite the four families as had never been done before. Mindre also believed that Max's unusual imagination could serve as an inspiration to strengthen the populace's waning power of reckoning.

There were plenty of issues that required their attention. Rumors were spreading of others to the east with a strange new form of reckoning using circles and lines. Unrest was growing in the south among those who were not pleased with the new alliances. Most troubling were the reports of unusual and disturbing behavior among the Darklings beyond the Western Ascension.

Max and Mindre agreed that in order to solve the problem of restoring balance to Abacabax, they must first understand the problem. There was no better way to do that than to explore and learn as much as possible. The only problem now was deciding where to start.

Appendices

Denizens

Abacists. The fourth family, created at the time of the Third Great Divide, approximately 300 years ago. Powerful reckoners, few in number, most Abacists were transformed into "the Changed" or were killed during the War of the Plague. The capital city of the Abacists is Tangram, the northernmost city at 260,000 steps above Verdant Mesa. The line of ascension in the Abacist family passes through the second-born child in each generation, each of whom is known as the "second of all seconds."

Saul Teller. Eldest Teller, first of all seconds. Master reckoner and inventor. Responsible for the Great Plague sixteen years ago.

Lydala Napnaus. Wife of Saul Teller. Affected by the plague and transformed into one of the Changed.

Wendi Teller. Elder Teller, second of all seconds. Named Protectress of Abacabax by the Order of the Whole. Known as "The Longwalker" for her ability to travel incredible distances.

Samuel Naboros. Husband of Wendi Teller, father of Rita and Melani. Died during the War of the Plague.

Melani Teller. Daughter of Wendi Teller, first of all seconds. Died during the War of the Plague.

Rita Teller. Daughter of Wendi Teller, second of all seconds. Hidden on Earth during the War of the Plague.

Carfin Mefot. Husband of Rita Teller. Died during the War of the Plague

Maxwell Teller. Son of Rita Teller, first of all seconds. Born on Earth during the War of the Plague. Master of mentalism.

Samuel Teller. Son of Rita Teller, second of all seconds and the Abacist Prime. Candidate to be the next New Origin. Master of scribing.

Calculists. The third family, created at the time of the Second Great Divide approximately 600 years ago. Powerful militaristic family, large in number with many cities. The capital city is Vertex located at the center of the Western Ascension. The line of ascension in the Calculist family passes through the third-born child in each generation, each of whom is known as the "third of all thirds."

General Biggens. Leader of the Calculists, third of all thirds, the Calculist Prime (disputed) and presumed to be the next New Origin. Inventor of Tricalculus.

Kalkar Biggens. Oldest son of General Biggens and military commander.

Gerard Biggens. Second son of General Biggens and military liaison.

Lherzo Biggens. Third of all thirds, legitimate Calculist Prime and candidate to be the New Origin. Inventor of anti-numbers.

Dirigo Sling. Lherzo Biggens' comrade and right hand.

Gordon Clay. Commander and Reconnaissance Chief.

Basal Feldspar. Senior commander.

Bacchius Mancala. Eldest member of the High Council.

The Triad, or the Triangulators. Three Calculist women who can determine the past, present and future locations of anything, for a price. The house of the Triad is located in Vertex.

Bone-Throwers. The second family, created at the time of the First Great Divide approximately 900 years ago. Desert dwellers of unknown number and unknown power, believed to live in or around Parchensis Desert on lower Abacabax. Like the Abacist family, the line of ascension in the Bone-Thrower family passes through the second-born child in each generation.

Chieftain Tarsa. Leader of the Bone-Throwers, second of all seconds.

Zarza. Right hand to Tarsa.

Hamata. Son of Tarsa, first of all seconds.

Lunata. Daughter of Tarsa, second of all seconds and Bone-Thrower Prime. Inventor of algebra.

Dijins. The first family and original people of Abacabax, origins unknown. Forest dwellers and simple reckoners. Their most prominent settlement is Quincunx located deep in lower Abacabax. The line of ascension in the Dijin family passes through the first-born child in each generation.

Roggolo. Dijin ambassador and first of all firsts. Exiled from the Dijin capital. Very well-traveled.

Mindre. Daughter of Roggolo. First of all firsts and the Dijin Prime (or "Thumb"). Inventor of body reckoning.

Lady Carpus. Elder Dijin seer.

Iagollo. Assistant to Lady Carpus, childhood friend of Mindre.

Chieftain Oolong. Leader of the Dijins.

The Order of the Whole. Fourteen mystics who tend the Temple of Abacabax at Apex on the top of the world.

Panelles. Acting leader of the Order of the Whole.

Notes from the first family:
A short guide to finger reckoning

Dijin finger reckoning is very quick and easy for adding and subtracting numbers from 0-99. The system is built on connections between 5s and 10s, and two different ways to add or subtract digits depending on the digits' relationships to 5s and 10s.

Basic principles

The right hand is used for *ones*, from 0-9, and the left hand is used for *tens*, from 0-90. Zero is an open, empty hand. The numbers 1-4 are made by touching the thumb flatly against the pad of a finger.

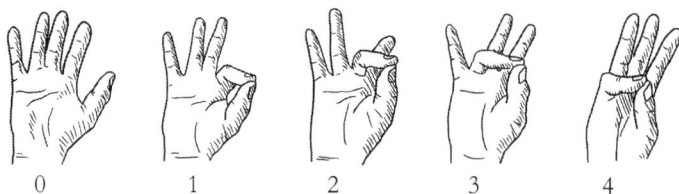

| 0 | 1 | 2 | 3 | 4 |

Five is a closed fist. The numbers 6-9 are made by touching the thumb against the fingernail of a bent finger.

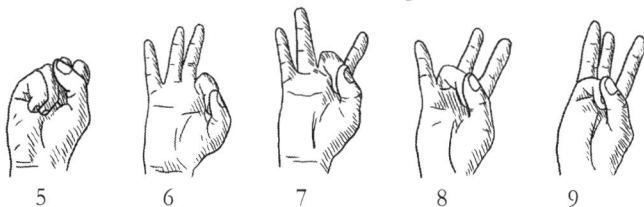

| 5 | 6 | 7 | 8 | 9 |

The left hand uses these same positions to count tens.

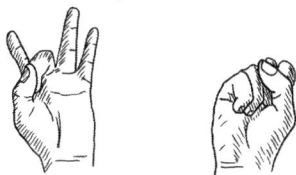

75 = 7 on the left hand (70) and 5 on the right hand

Adding and subtracting digits

If the thumb is already touching a finger, changing the position of the thumb from one finger to another changes the value on the hand by the number of positions moved. Moving the thumb two positions for example adds or subtracts 2 to the value in the reckoning.

Bending or straightening a finger so that the thumb moves from one side of that finger to the other changes the value by 5. For example, to add 2+5, the thumb starts against the pad of the middle finger to show 2. Bending that middle finger so the thumb slides to the fingernail side of the finger adds 5 to make 7.

This movement from one side of a finger to another is an anchoring movement for adding or subtracting numbers other than 5. To add 6, for example, the thumb is moved to the other side of the finger it is touching and then its position is incremented one position. When learning, it is helpful to do these two moves separately as shown below, but with practice these two moves blend into one. This move may or may not be accompanied by a change on the left hand depending on whether or not the addition or subtraction affects the number of tens. This will be discussed shortly.

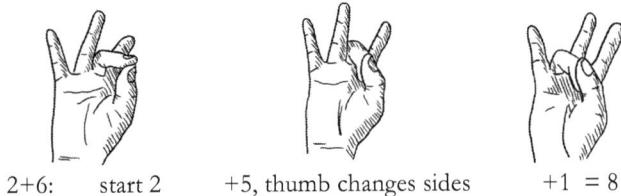

2+6:   start 2   +5, thumb changes sides   +1 = 8

Adding 4 can be accomplished by first adding 5 and then moving one position upwards to subtract 1.

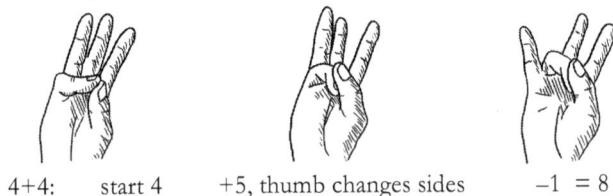

4+4:   start 4   +5, thumb changes sides   −1 = 8

330

Adding 7 or 3 can involve adding 5 and then incrementing 2 positions downwards (for +7) or upwards (for +3). Other numbers can be anchored in such a manner to 5, although for some operations it is easier to anchor the movements to 10 instead.

Two ways to add

There are two different ways to add a new number to the number currently on the fingers. Which of the two methods is used depends on what number is showing. We will use +8 as an example.

If the right hand is showing 1, to add 8 the right thumb moves +5 and then moves 3 positions downwards for a combined 5+3 as shown here:

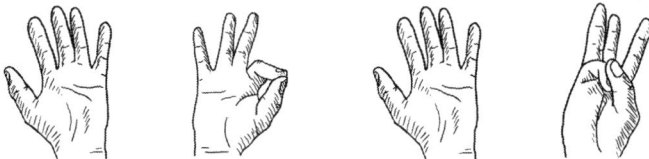

Right and left hands with 1   +8 =   Right +5 and +3, result 9

However, if 2 can be easily subtracted from the right hand, adding 8 is done as –2 on the right hand and +10 on the left hand. For example when the right hand show 3, adding 8 is accomplished as +10 –2 as shown here.

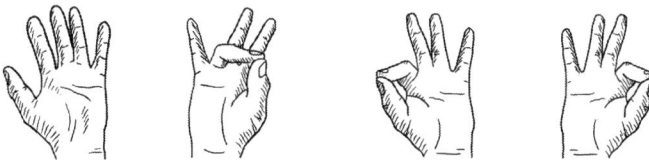

3   +8 =   Left +10,   right –2, result 11

Likewise, adding 7 can be accomplished with –3 and +10. Adding 6's are most often done as +5 and +1, and adding 9's are most often done as –1 and +10.

Incrementing 10s when adding

Any time during an addition when the thumb travels from the back (fingernail) side of the fingers to the front (pad) side of the fingers the left hand adds +10. This will become automatic with practice.

For example, here are two hands showing 26. When 5 is added, the thumb moves from the back of the first finger to the front of the first finger, so the left hand increments from 20 to 30. The result is 31.

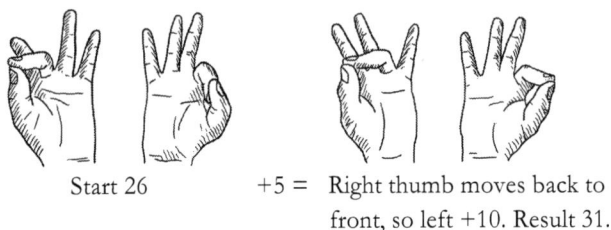

Start 26   +5 =   Right thumb moves back to front, so left +10. Result 31.

If 5 is then added again, this time the thumb moves from the front to the back so the left hand is not incremented.

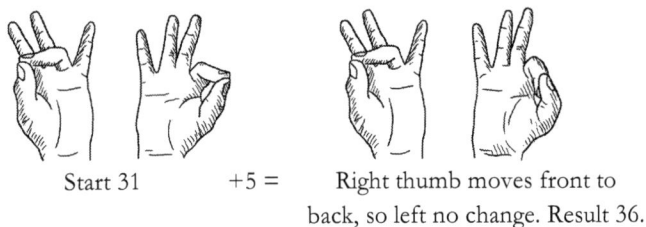

Start 31   +5 =   Right thumb moves front to back, so left no change. Result 36.

Multi-digit addition

With two-digit numbers, the digits are added separately to the appropriate hands. With 38 + 29, the hands start with 38. Add 20 on the left hand, then add 8 on the right hand, as a −2 on the right and +10 on the left. The result is 67.

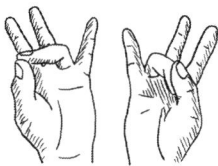 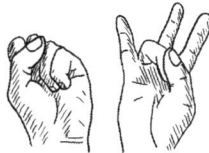 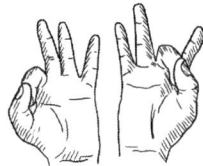

Start 38   Left hand +20   Left hand +10, right −1

Subtraction

All movements for subtraction are the opposite of addition. Adding 4, for example, is done with a +5 and −1, while subtracting 4 is −5 and +1. Adding 8 is usually done with +10 and −2, while subtracting 8 is usually −10 and +2.

When performing addition, when the thumb moves from the back to the front the 10s are incremented on the left hand. When subtracting, the opposite is done: when the thumb moves from the *front* to the *back* and the left hand moves to *subtract* 10. For example, with 22 − 5, the right thumb moves from the front to the back of the middle finger (a change of 5), which the left thumb moves from the 20 position to the 10 position. The result is 17.

These movements will become natural with practice.

Other operations

Finger reckoning is very quick but weak compared to other reckoning methods due to the limited number of digits and general use of only addition and subtraction. Some Finger Reckoners have been able to extended the art to include other operations and to increase the number of digits by using other parts of the hands or body. Details are unavailable due to Finger Reckoners' aversion to sharing techniques, even amongst themselves.

Notes from the second family:
A short guide to bone throwing

Bone-Throwers use numbers represented as powers of two. This makes operations quick and simple, though the unfamiliarity of the number system can make setting up the numbers more challenging. Bone-Throwers calculate with ten metacarpal bones from a pair of human hands. If hand bones are not readily available, small twigs or toothpicks may be used instead for practice.

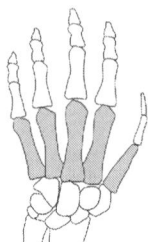

Basic principles

Bones are placed in a line. The line may be as long as the number of bones available for use, usually ten. Bones can be placed "fallen down" in a horizontal position or "standing up" in a vertical position. (Bones that are "standing up" are not literally standing and balancing on one end, they are simply turned so they are in a different direction.) Any bone lying down has a value of zero. The basic starting position is with all bones lying down and showing values of zero.

When a bone is turned so it is standing (in a vertical position), it has a value according to its position. The bone furthest to the right has a value of 1 when turned to the vertical position. The second bone from the right assumes a value of 2, the third bone a value of 4, the fourth a value of 8, and so on. The values double from one position to the next.

The following illustration shows the number 21 with six bones. The standing bones have values 16, 4 and 1. Together their sum is 21.

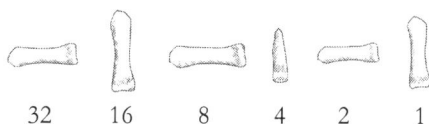

With these six bones, all numbers from 0 to 63 may be formed, each in a unique arrangement. With ten bones, the limit is much higher – numbers can be created up to 1023.

A second way to represent a number

Instead of standing or fallen bones, numbers are also representing by raising or lowering bones. Here, for example, the number 38 is made by raising the bones in the 32, 4 and 2 positions (32 + 4 + 2 = 38):

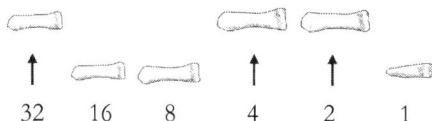

Both methods of representing numbers can be used at the same time to show different numbers on one set of bones. This is useful for operations where the two numbers to be operated on can be set up simultaneously. In the following illustration, the standing bones represent 21, and the raised bones represent 38.

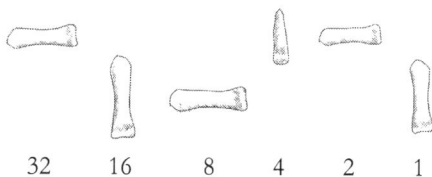

Addition

Adding numbers is accomplished by setting up both numbers to be added (as shown above) and then sliding down the raised bones, turning them as they are moved. This move may or may not be followed by some additional turns of bones, depending on whether the raised bone stands up or falls down when lowered. Here are two simple examples.

Example with 8 + 3

First set up the bones to show 8 by standing the bone in position 8.

Now set up the second number. Raise the bones in positions 2 and 1 to show 3.

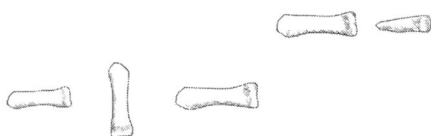

Slide down the raised bones one at a time, turning each from a fallen to a standing position. Because the bones are stood up as they are lowered, no extra move is required for each step.

The bones now show the result of 8 + 3: 11.

Falling bones

If a raised bone is standing up, it will fall to a horizontal position when it is lowered. Bone-Throwers say that addition is a process of building and no one falls without another standing up. Thus, when a raised bone falls down as it is lowered back into the line of bones, the bone to the *left* is turned. If this bone stands, the step is complete. If this bone also falls down, the next bone is turned and so on, until a bone stands. Each step of the calculation is not complete until exactly one bone is turned to a standing position.

Example with 11 + 3

The following bones are set up to calculate 11 + 3. The standing bones are in positions 8, 2 and 1 (8 + 2 + 1 = 11), and the raised bones are in positions 2 and 1 (2 + 1 = 3).

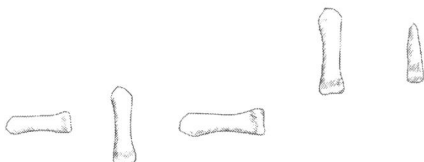

Step 1: Working from the left, lower the first raised bone and turn it. The bone has now fallen down and so the bone to the left is turned, causing it to stand and completing the step.

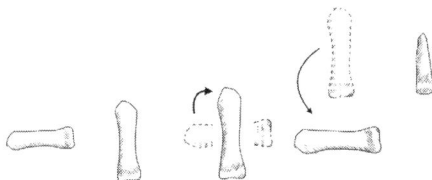

Step 2: The second raised bone is lowered and turned to a fallen position, so the bone to the left is turned. This bone is now standing, so the step is complete.

All bones are now back in the line, and the result of the addition, 14 (8 + 4 + 2) is revealed.

Chain reactions

When a bone is turned so that it falls over it may start a chain reaction if there are several bones in a row that are standing, each falling bone causing the next to fall in a domino-like effect. (If a chain reaction extends beyond the left end of the row of bones during addition, the result has exceeded the limit of the number of bones and will not work without introducing an additional bone.)

Example with 23 + 1

Here's a simple example with 23 + 1. The standing bones are 16, 4, 2 and 1 which represents 23. The bone in position 1 is raised, representing the number to be added (which is simply 1 in this example).

Sliding the raised bone down starts a chain reaction. Since the bone is turned so that it falls over, the bone to the left must be turned. This causes that bone also to fall over, so the next bone to the left must also be turned. That bone falls over as well, so the chain reaction continues to the next bone. Finally the bone is position 8 is turned to a standing position the step is completed.

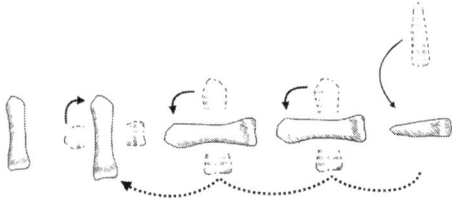

The result of the operation is 24 (16 + 8).

These examples have all used small numbers. Traditional bone throwing uses 10 bones, and so finding sums such as 683 + 259 is nearly as quick as finding these smaller sums. A challenge for those not raised as Bone-Throwers is the ability to quickly recognize and create numbers using powers of 2. This is a skill that develops quickly with practice.

Subtraction

One of the greatest mysteries in Bone Thrower reckoning is that subtraction uses the exact same moves as addition. The first number in the operation is set up on the bones using standing and fallen bones as usual. When entering the second number, however, instead of raising the bones to create the number, these bones are *lowered* instead.

The bones are now operated on just like while doing addition: lowering and turning the bones in the higher position. There is one small difference: when a chain reaction extends past the left end of the line of bones, the chain reaction "wraps around" and continues on the right side of the line of bones, proceeding as usual until a bone is turned to a standing position and the reaction ends. Surprisingly, this wrap-around will always happen *exactly once* during every subtraction, a phenomenon no outsiders have been able to explain.

Example with 34 − 9

The standing bones show the greater number (34 = 32 + 2). The bones representing 9 (9 = 8 + 1), are lowered *downwards*.

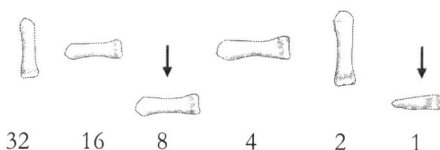

| 32 | 16 | 8 | 4 | 2 | 1 |

Step 1: The first bone is lowered and turned to a fallen position. This should cause the bone to the left to be turned, but there are no bones to the left. The maneuver wraps around to the right side of the line of bones and continues. The rightmost bone stands, completing the step.

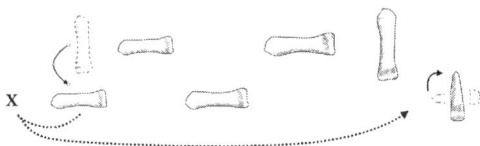

In steps 2 and 3, the next two raised bones are lowered and turned to standing positions. This does not affect any other bones.

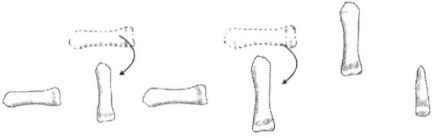

In step 4, the final raised bone turns to a fallen position as it lowered, starting a short chain reaction.

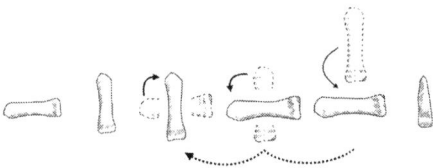

The bones now show the result: 34 − 9 = 25 (16 + 8 + 1).

Example with 51 − 45

Here is one more example to show a lengthy chain reaction that wraps around and affects both raised and lowered bones.

51 is set up by standing up bones 32, 16, 2 and 1 (51 = 32 + 16 + 2 +1). To make 45, bones are lowered in positions 32, 8, 4 and 1 (45 = 32 + 8 + 4 + 1).

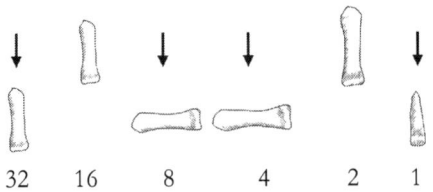

| 32 | 16 | 8 | 4 | 2 | 1 |

The first step sets off a long chain reaction. The first raised bone is lowered and falls down. The bone to its left also falls over, so the reaction continues, wrapping around to the right side where the rightmost bone is turned. This bone, too, falls over, as does the bone in the 2 position. Finally the bone in the 4 position stands up, ending the reaction.

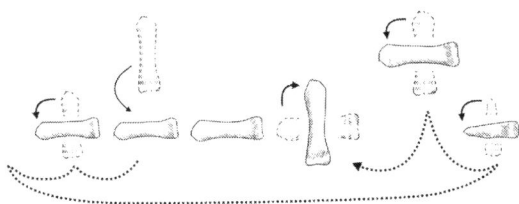

Note that during the reaction the bone in position 2, which is raised, is *not* lowered – a chain reaction only affects whether bones are standing up or fallen and does not affect their raised or lowered positions.

In step 2, the final raised bone is lowered and stood up, completing the step.

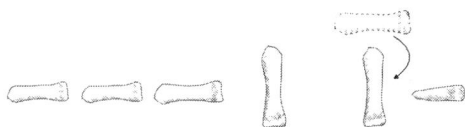

The result of the operation is now revealed: 51 − 45 = 6.

It is perhaps surprising that addition and subtraction use the same method (apart from the wrap-around chain reaction). When adding, the number to be added is raised and when subtracting the number to be subtracted is lowered, and then the same algorithm is applied. Little is known of the Bone-Throwers and why these complementary methods function is another of these mysteries.

Multiplication

Conceptually, Bone-Thrower multiplication is easy, but the process can be confusing with traditional bones. Bone-Throwers mark their bones on one side with burn marks to make multiplication much simpler. These marks allow a *third* way to encode a number on the set of bones, a practice called "double two-ness."

To multiply, a number is added one or more times to the line of bones *in different positions*. These positions are determined by the marks on the bones in the initial set up.

Example with 19 × 3

We will demonstrate with 19 × 3. Start with the bones in a line showing 19 with the markings in the 16, 2 and 1 positions.

| 32 | 16 | 8 | 4 | 2 | 1 |

Working from left to right, the first mark will temporarily be considered as the 1 position. Raise bones to represent the number 3, using the mark as a new reference point for the temporary 1.

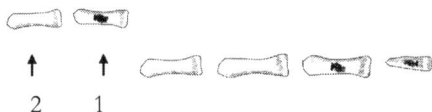

| 2 | 1 |

This number is now added in the usual manner. The marked bone may now be flipped over so the mark is hidden.

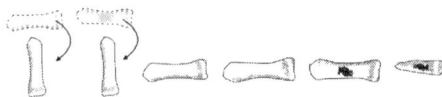

The next marked bone is now considered the new 1 position. Raise bones to again represent 3 with the new position for 1.

This number is added and the marked bone can be flipped.

There is one marked bone remaining. Use this as a reference for 1 and raise bones to represent 3.

Complete the addition. In this example, there is one two-step chain reaction.

The marked bone can be flipped. The final result is revealed. Bones 32, 16, 8 and 1 are standing, so 19 × 3 = 57.

| 32 | 16 | 8 | 4 | 2 | 1 |

Notes from the third family:
A short guide to calculating on the abax

To "calculate" literally means to reckon with stones. Calculists use small rounded stones called "abac" on stone tablets called "abaxes" to organize calculations efficiently.

Abaxes are sized to fit comfortably on the left forearm, held with the left hand gripping the right edge and abax cradled securely against the user's elbow and body. Calculists have pockets with large openings sewn over the left breast of their shirts to hold abac, making it easy to take out or return stones as needed.

A standard abax has four lines carved horizontally and a double line carved vertically dividing the board in two. Numbers are created by placing stones on or between the horizontal lines. Stones on the lowest line have a value of 1. Lines above increase in value 10 times per line, so the other lines have values 10, 100 and 1000. Stones are also placed above the lines to have values 5 times that of the line below, or 5, 50, 500 and 5000 at the very top.

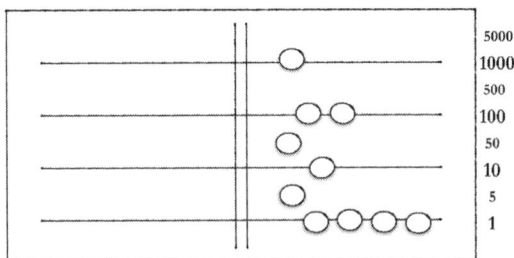

In the picture above, the number on the right side of the board is $1269 = 1000 + 2 \times 100 + 50 + 10 + 5 + 4 \times 1$. (Note: abaxes are usually not marked with numbers. Line values are included in these illustrations for clarity.)

Lines (or spaces between lines) may contain as many stones as there is space for, and where a stone is placed on a line is not important for addition or subtraction. Groups of stones are traded throughout calculations and at the end of the calculation, so that 5 stones on the 10 line for example can be traded for 1 stone on the 50 line, 2 stones on the 500 line can be traded for 1 stone on the 1000 line, and so on.

Addition

Nothing could be easier than Calculist addition. Simply place stones on the board to represent the first number, place additional stones on the same lines to represent the second number, and then make appropriate exchanges to minimize the number of stones needed to represent the result. (Beginners sometimes build each number on the two sides of the board and then slide them together, but this extra step is generally not needed.)

Example with 37 + 81

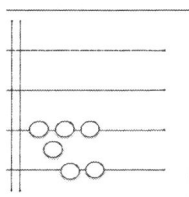
Set up 37

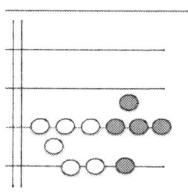
Add 81

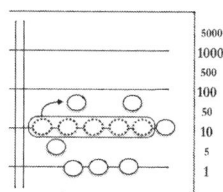
Regroup
five 10s = one 50

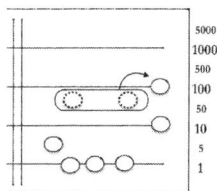
Regroup, two 50s for one 100

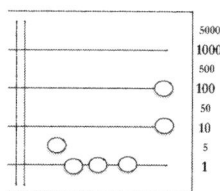
Final result: 118

Subtraction

To subtract, the two numbers to be operated on are placed on either side of the board. The larger number is placed on the right, and the number to be subtracted is placed on the left. During the operation, equal numbers of stones are removed from both sides of each line (including spaces between lines) until the left side is empty.

If there are not enough stones on the left side of a line to match the stones on the right side, it is necessary to exchange groups of stones on the right side. For example if a 100 stone is to be removed but the 100 line is empty on the right side, an exchange of a 500 for five 100s or some other exchange is made to bring enough stones to at least match the number on the right.

Subtraction is very flexible. All exchanges may be made at the start or during the process, and equal groups of stones may be removed from both sides of a line at any time and in any order.

Example with 826 − 152

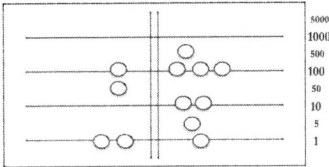

152 is on the right, 826 on the left.

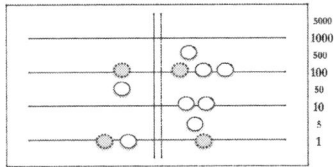

A pair of 100s and a pair of 1s can be removed immediately.

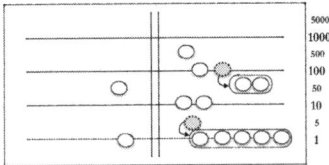

There is no match for the 50 or the 1 on the right. Exchanges must be made on the left.

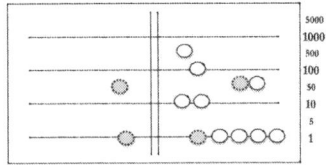

The 50 and the 1 on the left can now be paired with matching stones on the right and removed.

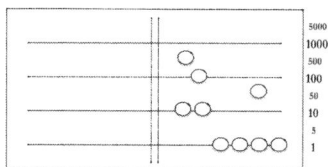

The left side is empty, the right side
holds the result. 826 − 152 = 674.

Multiplication

To multiply, values on lines (the digits) are multiplied together several
times until every combination of a digit on the right and a digit on the
left has been performed. Single digit multiplication is done mentally,
so a Calculist must have previously memorized multiplication facts up
to 9 × 9. The results of each mental calculation are placed in
appropriate places on the abax, which holds these partial results as
they are combined to find the result of an operation with much larger
numbers.

Determining these positions where the partial results are placed is
important and while the principle is not difficult, it requires a little
experience and practice to master.

Examples of different placements

All of the calculations in these next four examples are simple enough
that an abax is not needed, but they will demonstrate principles used
in more complex computations, namely that the location of partial
results depends on the locations of the two digits being multiplied.

2 × 7. The numbers are set up on each side of the board, close to the
center line. The product, computed mentally, is placed on the far right
of the board. Both the 2 and 7 are on the bottom line, so the result is
also on the bottom line.

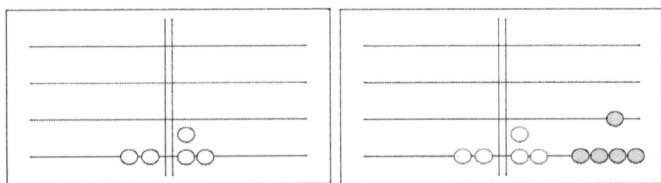

2 × 70. The same digits, 2 and 7, are multiplied to get 14. Since the 7 is raised one line (= 70), the result of 14 is also raised to the same line (= 140).

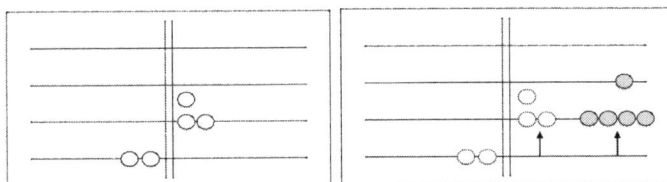

20 × 7. Because the 2 is raised one line, the 14 is also raised one line. It is helpful to think that results are placed on the line that is the same level as the digit on the right, and then raised by the same amount the number on the left is raised.

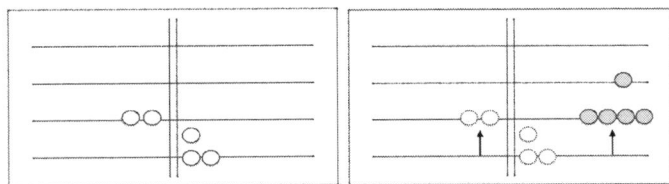

20 × 70. The 2 and the 7 are multiplied to get 14. To find the line where the 14 is placed, start on the line where the 7 is placed. The digit on the left is raised one, so the 14 is raised one line from that starting position. The result is 1400.

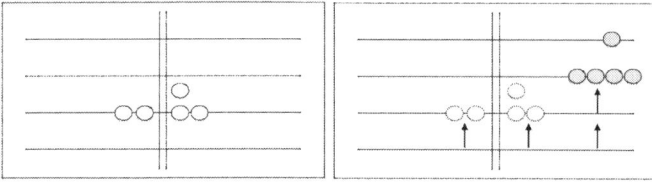

Multi-digit multiplication

In order to multiply larger numbers, place the two numbers to be multiplied on the two sides of the abax, near the center line. The top digit on the right (from 1-9) is multiplied with each digit on the left from the top down. Each result is placed on the right side in accordance the placement rules above.

When the top right digit has been multiplied by all digits on the left, the top right digit is now longer needed and these stones are removed. The next digit down on the right is now used for multiplying the digits on the left. This digit on the right will then be removed. The process continues until the original number on the right is completely removed and only the result of the multiplication remains on the right side of the abax.

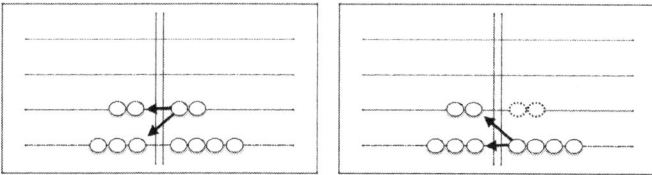

Stones should be regrouped whenever possible to keep the number of stones on the abax to a minimum.

Example with 32 × 70

The numbers are set up on different sides of the abax close to the center line. The top two digits, 3 and 7 are multiplied. The result is 21 (shown in gray on the figure below). Since the 3 is raised one line on the abax, the 21 is placed one line *above where the 7 is located* on the right. This "21" has a value of 2100.

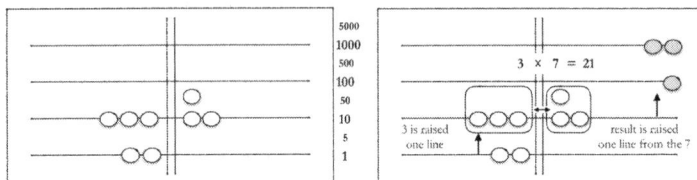

The next digit down on the left, 2, is multiplied by the 7. The result of 14 is shown in gray. Because the 2 is not raised above the bottom line, the 14 is placed on the same line as the 7 and is not raised any further. Its value in the calculation is 140.

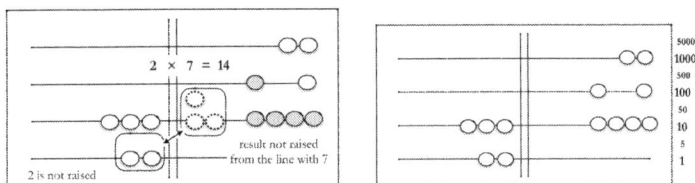

The 7 has now been multiplied by all digits on the left. The 7 is removed. There are no more digits on the right to multiply so the operation is complete. The result is shown on the right: 32 × 70 = 2240.

Example with 53 × 48

Caution! In this calculation, multiplication by the 5 produces partial results that end in a 0. This requires extra care when placing the result.

(a) 53 and 48 are placed on the abax, close to the center line.

(b) The top digits are multiplied, 5 × 4 = 20. The 20 is placed one line up from the 4 on the left. Notice that the 20 takes up two lines with 0 on the lower line and 2 on the upper line, so the bottom line of the 20 is *empty*. It is easy to make the mistake of placing a *2* one line up instead of placing a *20* one line up, so care must be taken. The partial result, 2000, is the product of 50 and 40.

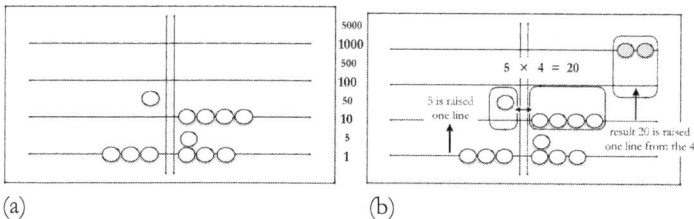

(a)

(b)

(c) The next digit down on the left is multiplied by the top digit on the right. 3 × 4 = 12. Since the 3 is not raised, this 12 is placed on the same line as the 4 and not raised again as in the previous step.

(d) The top digit on the right (4) has now been multiplied by all digits on the left and is removed, leaving more space for the next steps.

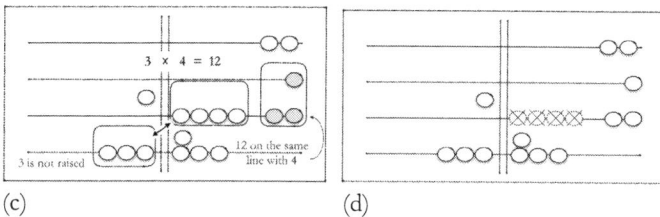

(c)

(d)

(e) The top digits are multiplied, $5 \times 8 = 40$. Again, be careful with the placement, one line above the line with 8 is the start of the 40 – a 40 has 0 stones on the lower line.

(f) There are now 5 stones on the 100s line. These are traded for 1 fifty.

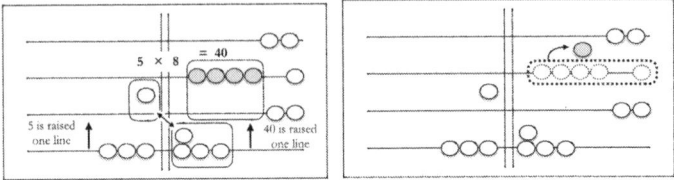

(e)   (f)

(g) The next digit down on the left is multiplied by the top digit on the right. $3 \times 8 = 24$. The 24 is placed on the bottom line.

(h) The top digit on the right can be removed. This is the final digit so the operation is complete. All stones can be removed from the left as well, if desired.

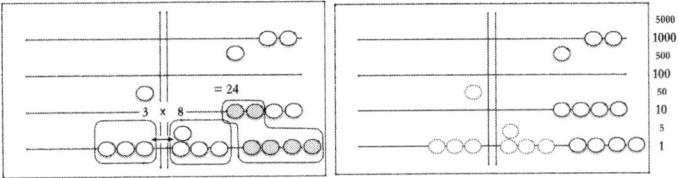

(g)   (h)

The final result is revealed on the abax: $53 \times 48 = 2544$.

A standard abax with four lines can handle all 2-digit by 2-digit multiplications, and some 3-digit by 2-digit multiplications (if the first digits are not too great).

Notes from the fourth family:
A short guide to the abacus

The abacus is an elegant and powerful tool. It developed directly from the abax and uses many of the same principles. Instead of placing and removing stones, an abacus uses columns of beads that slide up and down on rods, allowing for extremely quick calculations with very large numbers. Further, the abacus offers the convenience of a single device with moving parts all held together in a single frame that fits easily in a pocket.

An abacus has several rods with beads divided in two sections by a crossbeam. The top section has two beads that have a value of 5, and the bottom section has five beads with a value of 1. (Some abacuses have 1 and 4 beads, and some have 1 and 5).

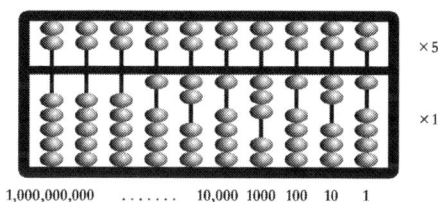

The rods represent increasing powers of 10 from the right, so numbers can be set up as we are accustomed to seeing. The number of rods can vary, in the examples here we will use a standard Abacist abacus with 10 rods.

The abacus is cleared by sliding all the beads on the top upwards, and all of the beads on the bottom downwards. Digits are formed by sliding beads towards the crossbeam. This is usually done with a pinching motion so that 1 beads and 5 beads are moved simultaneously.

The ten different digits are shown below, each on a separate rod.

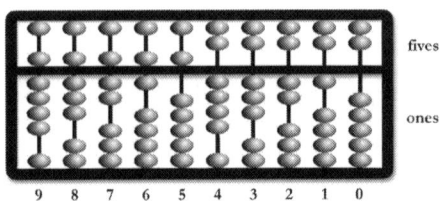

Addition on the abacus is very quick. It requires learning two different moves for placement of each digit. After practicing addition separately with each of these digits as described below, adding numbers of any size can be done very easily and almost automatically.

Adding 1s and trading 5
Begin with an empty abacus. 1 is added to the first rod (the rod on the right) by sliding 1 bead upwards with the right thumb. Continue adding one until all 5 one-beads are up.

When all 5 beads in the lower portion of the abacus are up, they are immediately traded for a five-bead. The trade is done in one movement, with the thumb sliding down all 5 one-beads while the index finger slides down 1 five-bead. Trades are always done by moving beads in the same direction.

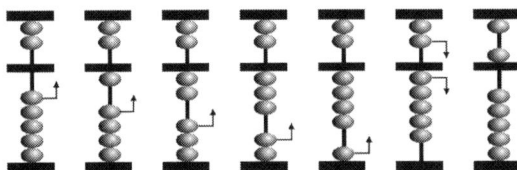

Counting 0 to 5, with a trade

Notice that when adding 1 to a rod that is showing 4 it is not necessary to raise 1 bead and then lower all 5. This extra motion can be eliminated by instead sliding the 4 beads back downwards and sliding down a five-bead at the same time, in effect performing a −4 and +5 at the same time to give the result +1.

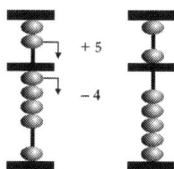

Adding one is done by (a) sliding up 1 one-bead, or (b) sliding down 4 one-beads on the bottom and 1 five-bead on the top if there are 4 beads available to slide downwards.

Likewise, every number added to a rod can be done in two different ways, determined by what number is already on the rod.

Adding 6s and trading 10

Starting with a cleared abacus, add 6 to the first rod. This is done with a pinching motion to bring down 1 five-bead and bring up 1 one-bead. Repeat this action to add another 6 to the same rod.

There are now 2 five-beads on the rod – these are to be immediately traded for 1 ten-bead. The 2 five-beads are raised with the index finger at the same time that 1 ten-bead is raised with the thumb. Notice that like the trade with 1s and 5s, all of the beads move in the same direction.

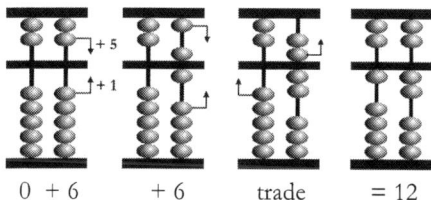

| 0 + 6 | + 6 | trade | = 12 |

Continue adding 6s with a pinching motion. After 2 more 6s are added, another trade is necessary, 2 five-beads for 1 ten-bead. The abacus now shows 24.

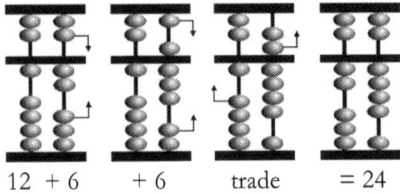

12 + 6   + 6   trade   = 24

Adding 6 and adding 1 have a common trait: when there are 4 beads available to be moved down, a different move is used to add these numbers. For +6, the 4 one-beads will moved down with the index finger while 1 ten-bead will moved up with the thumb with a twisting motion. Performing a –4 and a +10 gives a result of +6.

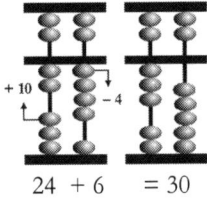

24 + 6   = 30

Adding 4s and 9s
To add 4 to an empty rod, 4 beads are raised at the same time with the right thumb. If the rod already has at least 1 one-bead that is already up, instead the move is +5 and –1, the index finger sliding down 1 five-bead while the thumb slides down 1 one-bead.

To add 9 to an empty rod, a pinching motion is used to bring 1 five-bead and 4 one-beads to the crossbeam. If there is at least 1 one-bead available to be moved down, adding 9 is done by lifting 1 ten-bead and lowering 1 one-bead at the same time with a twisting motion.

These two operations, with the two methods of adding each, are shown below.

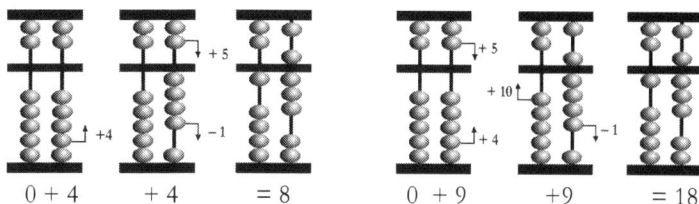

$$0 + 4 \qquad + 4 \qquad = 8 \qquad\qquad 0 + 9 \qquad +9 \qquad = 18$$

+4 and +9 are related in that if there is at least one bead available to be lowered, the second method of adding these numbers is used.

Adding 2s and 7s

Adding 2 involves either sliding 2 one-beads upwards, or if 3 or more one-beads can be lowered then +2 is done as a combination +5 and – 3. Both are shown here as we add 2 three times to make 6.

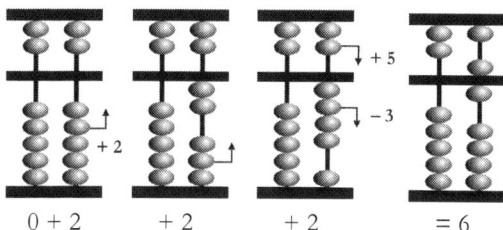

$$0 + 2 \qquad + 2 \qquad + 2 \qquad = 6$$

Adding 7 is related to 2. It is accomplished by pinching a five-bead with 2 one-beads if more than 2 beads are available to be lifted, otherwise +7 is a twisting motion to lower 3 one-beads and bring up 1 ten-bead. The series below illustrates both methods of adding 7.

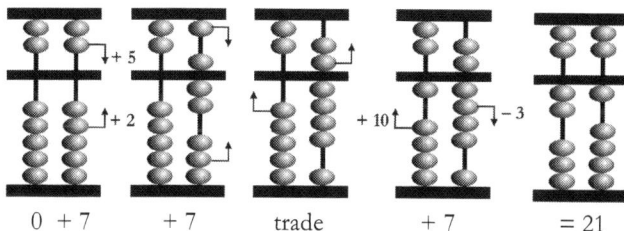

$$0 + 7 \qquad + 7 \qquad \text{trade} \qquad + 7 \qquad = 21$$

Adding 3s and 8

When adding 3 or 8, if 3 lower beads are available to move up they are lifted, either by themselves (for +3) or lifted while a five-bead is lowered (for +8). Otherwise, +3 is accomplished by +5 and −2 simultaneously, and +8 performed as +10 and −2 at the same time.

Practicing

Adding each of the digits repeatedly should be practiced many times. For example, add 6 repeatedly until a target number such as 300 is reached. By practicing in such a manner it becomes easy to add a digit to any rod regardless of what digit is already on that rod and perform exchanges quickly and naturally. These moves are essential for other operations.

Multi-digit addition

When the moves for adding each separate digit are mastered, multi-digit addition is very easy. The first number is entered on the abacus, then the digits of the number to be added separately on each of the appropriate rods.

Here is an example with 2845 + 946. One trade is required on the final step of the calculation.

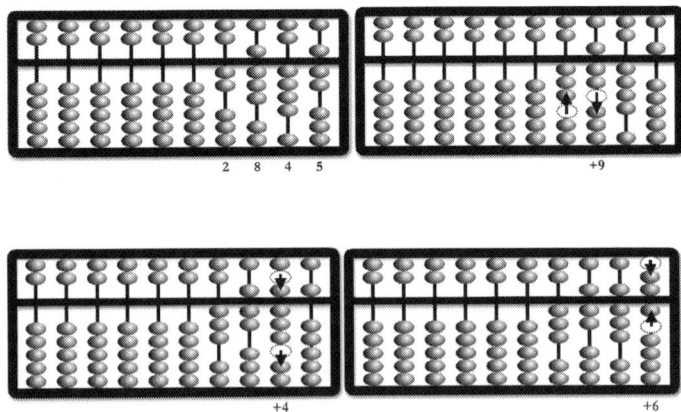

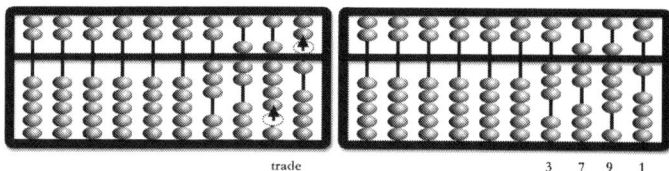

3 7 9 1

When completed, the abacus shows the result: 2845 + 946 = 3791.

Subtraction

Learning subtraction requires practice subtracting each of the digits as was done above with addition. Each of the moves for subtraction is the exact opposite of the moves in addition. For example, +9 is usually done as a twist with +10 and –1. Likewise, –9 is usually a twist in the opposite direction with –10 and +1.

Trading may need to be done before a digit is subtracted. If –3, for example, is to be performed on a rod with less than a value of 3 on that rod, first 1 ten-bead is traded on the next rod for 2 five-beads on the current rod so there are enough beads available to subtract from.

Here is an example with trading before subtracting. 3 is to be taken from 21 and the rod to be subtracted from has only 1 bead. First 1 ten-bead is traded for 2 five-beads. Now 3 can be subtracted as –5 and +2.

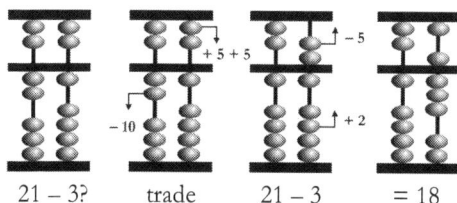

21 – 3?   trade   21 – 3   = 18

Advanced abacus users might instead perform –10 and +7 for the above operation and skip the additional step, but it is enough at the start to learn just different sets of moves to be able to use an abacus effectively.

Practice subtraction with each digit separately. Begin with 100 times the digit to be practiced and subtract that digit 100 times.

Multiplication

Multiplication is perhaps best understood with a demonstration of 2-digit by 2-digit multiplication. It will help to keep the following "mantra" in mind:

"Last 2, skip 2. First and last, skip 1. Clear the last."

This step sequence will be repeated until the operation is complete. We will demonstrate with 63 × 23. Set up 63 and 23 on the left side, with one empty rod between.

"Last 2, skip 2": Multiply the last two digits mentally (3 × 3 = 9), skip over <u>two</u> rods completely and enter the 9 as shown here.

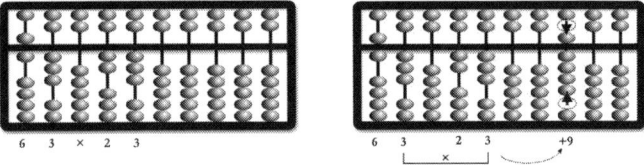

"First and last, skip 1": Multiply the first and last digits (6 × 3 = 18). Skip over <u>one</u> rod and enter the 18 starting on this rod.

"Clear the last": The last digit (the 3 in 23) is now cleared.

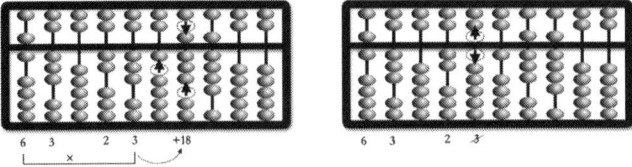

Repeat these same steps. "Last 2, skip 2." Multiply 3 ×2, skip two rods and enter 6. "First and last, skip 1." Skip one rod and enter 6 × 3.

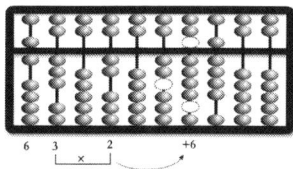

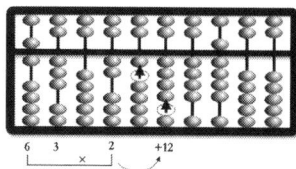

"Clear the last." We are done with the 2 and its rod is cleared. The calculation is complete and original number can also be cleared.

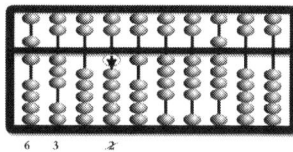

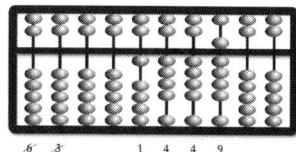

The result is shown: 63 × 23 = 1449.

Multiplying with other digit lengths

The sequence of steps, "Last 2, skip 2. First and last, skip 1. Clear the last," works for multiplying a two-digit number by a number of *any* length, as long as the two-digit number is placed to the left. Each time the sequence is completed, one digit is erased from the second number, so the sequence will be done a number of times equal to the number of digits in the second number.

If the first number has a different number of digits than two, the sequence is modified so that the starting "skip" number is equal to the first number's number of digits. This will ensure there is enough space for the partial results. Multiply each digit of the first number by the last digit of the second number, starting with the last digit of the first number and working through the digits to the left. The skip number decreases with each digit multiplication.

For example, if the first number to be multiplied has three digits, the steps are modified to: "Last 2, skip 3. Middle and last, skip 2. First and last, skip 1. Clear the last." This same sequence is executed until the second number to multiplied is cleared, regardless of the length of the second number.

The number of rods needed for multiplication depends more heavily on the number of digits in the first number than in the second, because the number of rods to be skipped at the start in each sequence is equal to the number of digits in the first number. With a 10-rod abacus, 2-digit by 5-digit multiplication is possible, but 5-digit by 2-digit is not possible with the above method. Thus, the shorter number should be placed on the left to maximize computing power.

Acknowledgements

Thank you to my wife Gerd Åsta Bones, without whom this book would not have been completed. I extend my heartfelt thanks to my friends and family for their suggestions and encouragement: Steve S., Mark K., Daniel M., Allan K., Peter N., Maggie N., Mike Sr., Marc K., Irene H., Alice M., Jordan P., Rachel P.Z., Dave F. and Tom P. In addition, I'd like to recognize Martin Gardner for sharing the Abacaba pattern with me so many years ago.

mikeNaylor

More

Explore the world of Abacabax further at: **abacabax.com**.
Free stuff, music, projects, activities, art, newsletter and more.

A kind request

Did you enjoy Abacabax? Please consider sharing your experience by giving it a rating or a review on GoodReads.com or Amazon.com. Thank you!

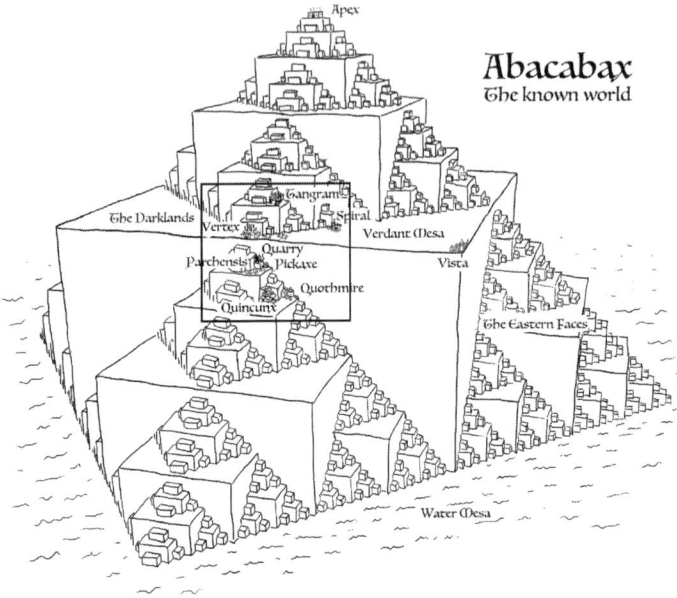

Abacabax
The known world

Apex

The Darklands

Tangram

Vertex

Spiral

Verdant Mesa

Quarry

Pickaxe

Parchensis

Quothmire

Vista

Quincunx

The Eastern Faces

Water Mesa

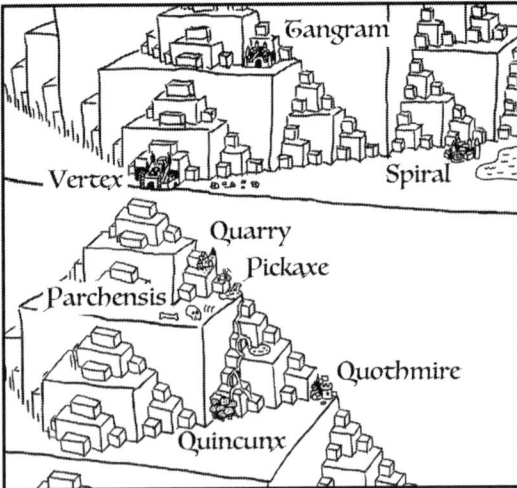

Tangram

Vertex

Spiral

Quarry

Pickaxe

Parchensis

Quothmire

Quincunx

Printed in Great Britain
by Amazon